A FISH STORY

by
Rev. Ruth Romeyn, Nurse and Pastor

*This book is dedicated to my
Creative Writing Friends
at Breton Woods
who cheered me on.*

***

*Thanks to all who have given encouraging words,
for saying you enjoyed the story
and related to it on a personal level.
Thanks also to those who have suggested
corrections for this revised, second printing.
Your comments have been heard with appreciation,*

*Thanks to my daughter Robin Romeyn Street
who helped prepare this manuscript for printing.*

*And thanks to my daughter Kim Romeyn Galloway
whose cover artwork captured the heart of the story.*

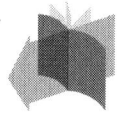

Chapbook Press

Schuler Books
2660 28th Street SE
Grand Rapids, MI 49512
(616) 942-7330
www.schulerbooks.com

ISBN 13: 9781943359448

Library of Congress Control Number: 2016949292

Copyright © 2016, Ruth Romeyn

All rights reserved.

No part of this book may be reproduced in any form without express permission of the copyright holder.

Printed in the United States by Chapbook Press.

TABLE OF CONTENTS

PART 1 The Early Years 1871-1873
C1   Getting Acquainted
C2   Getting to Know Each Other
C3   West Comes East
C4   East Goes West
C5   Dakota Territory— Settling In
C6   Summer Begins
C7   Summer Continues
C8   Separate Ways, Mutual Concerns
C9   Chipps Celebrates
C10 September 22—Christmas Day
C11 Meanwhile Back East

PART 2 One Year Follows Another 1874-1880
C12 Mira Sees the Sky
C13 One Season Follows Another
C14 Graduation
C15 Relocation Times Two
C16 Holidays, New Year and an Unexpected Arrival
C17 Unexpected Changes
C18 Confessions
C19 Chipps Booms

PART 3 One Decade Follows Another 1881-1886
C 20 Life and Death Moves Chipps Forward
C21 The Big Picture vs. The Big Puzzle
C22 A Dream Come True
C23 The Busy-ness of Being Alive

PART 4 One Century Follows Another 1887-1918
C 24 Jems Grows Up
C25 A Frontier Team All Over Again

Epilogue

Prologue

This story is about a team—a frontier team.

The American Frontier knew many teams—teams of horses, oxen, donkeys, mules, to be sure, but this story is not about those kinds of teams. If they are referenced at all it is only incidentally as part of the greater story.

This story is about a human team who brought hope, support, love, and healing to the people they were dedicated to serve. Without giving the story away, it is even about how one member of a team can still serve, when the other moves on.

But more than all that, it developed into a story of relationships within an extended family, and the healing and blessing that takes place when two or three people unconditionally love and accept someone who has experienced less loving relationships.

It is also a story about pushing the boundaries of *personal frontiers*.

PART 1

THE EARLY YEARS
1871-1873

Chapter 1 *Getting Acquainted*

She had come West years ago—ten to be exact—with her husband. They were a young couple, eager to minister to the needs of the folk on the American Frontier. They had never been there before. They had researched and heard and read stories, most of them heart rending, but also filled with adventure. The adventure had an allure, but the needs were what really drew them. Would they be up to it? Well, they would soon find out, for shortly after their wedding they boarded a train that took them West until the track ran out. There they were met by three wagons and drivers sent by their calling church to drive them to Chipps, a small town in a farming community in Dakota Territory. The wagons were pulled by teams of oxen, with a couple milk cows tethered behind the lead wagon. They hoped to acquire riding horses soon. Work horses were not needed as they were not farmers. But saddle horses would be essential for their work of pastoring and healing. There would be preaching, pastoral care, weddings, baptisms, sitting alongside of inconsolable grief, as men, women, children, babies, born and unborn were laid to rest. FUNERALS. No end of funerals, and now, her own husband's. Death and grief respected no boundaries.

She had often preached farewell messages at gravesides, and everyone knew that of the two—she and her husband—she was the best for this function. They told her privately. She often was called on when her husband was on circuit visiting settlements that had no pastor of their own.

But she was not ordained . . .

It seemed that the whole community had gathered. The earth had been washed clean by the storm and rain. The same storm that now brought them to this graveside. The air had a pristine quality to it. So clean; so fresh. The hole had been dug earlier in the day and the soil was piled nearby. She drew in a deep breath and resolutely walked from her house to the group and the grave. She was grateful for the thin veil which shaded her red, swollen eyes.

"Friends, thank you for coming. You know how much Franco enjoyed gatherings, the bigger the better. So I say on his behalf, thank you for coming; it is good to see each of you. *And after saying that he would always tell us of the*

abundance of food that we would enjoy as part of our gathering. And then he would give thanks. Let's do that right now—

*Heavenly Father, we have gathered for a final farewell, as we have done so often in the past. This time it is for our beloved Pastor, friend and husband. (*Her voice cracked slightly).

As we speak and remember, we acknowledge that everything that Franco did flowed out of a heart of love—love for you and all his fellow humans.

We know that lightning was the cause of his death. It seems strange, Lord, that of all the things on the frontier that might have scared Franco, nothing really did, except lightning. He often cautioned us not to be out in lightning storms, and he himself tried to avoid them.

Yet Lord, for reasons known to only you, Franco was out in a severe storm. Lightning struck him, and you used it as a dazzling occasion to welcome him into glory.

We respect and accept your choices. But our hearts and lives will long remember and miss this servant of yours who humbly and gently led, and wisely guided.

In Jesus' Name, AMEN"

At the AMEN the crowd began singing, giving her a few moments to collect herself.

She read from John 14, reminding them all that Jesus is preparing a place and would come again, and that meanwhile he would not leave them comfortless.

And she spoke of The Resurrection. Her voice was strong and clear and full of conviction.

She paused briefly and then continued,

"*Friends, Franco would also want us to remember God's faithfulness, goodness, and love. How he is always a shelter in the time of storm—that was the topic of Franco's first sermon in Chipps—and that we have a responsibility to seek that shelter. Yet ironically, God took Franco in a storm. We might want to ask, 'Franco, why didn't you seek shelter?' But he would help us see that God has taken him to the greatest shelter of all—heaven. And he would remind us of countless times when we have been sheltered by God as we have experienced life and death in our community.*

"*He would also encourage us to express our grief. He often said to me, 'Have a good cry, Mira. Allow yourself to feel; you need to feel before you can heal.'*

"*I could tell you many stories of our life and work together—but you know them because you have been a part of them for ten years. Rather let's share stories."*

And so they did for the next hour. But before anyone spoke she continued: "I have one story to tell you that I think you have never heard—the story of our names—Franco and Mira. Those are not our actual names."

Heads nodded. *Yes, folks wanted to know—but had been too polite to ask. They knew her as* Dr. Mira *and him as* Pastor Franco, *or* Rev. Franco.

"Franco's name is Franklin Welken. Somehow, as I got to know him in our courting days Franklin just didn't fit! It was good for seminary, but for the rest of life? NO! It was too formal for a man with such a sensitive and caring nature.

Frank? No, that was too abrupt. It needed a second syllable to complete it.

Frankie? Oh no, he would not hear of it; he had been called that as a child.

One day without realizing what I said, I called him Franco *and it stuck.*

"It sounded regal to me. Franco seemed regal. Franco was a king; a very down to earth king, but he had a certain quality about him that I know many of you saw too (heads nodded in agreement) that invited people to both follow him and work alongside of him. But most of all, as was apparent to us, he lived his life as a child of the King, here on the frontier that has few trappings of royalty.

"My name, Mira, *is a shortened form of* Miranda, *thanks to my father and the people I served with him back East. I'll save that story for another occasion. I'll just say here that Franco loved it, and knew the real reason for it, though he often kidded me that it was short for* mirage*—now you see me, but look again and I'm gone."*

When she finished speaking there were smiles on many faces, and the stories began.

Finally a song broke out again, a closing prayer, and the lowering of the casket.

She took a handful of dirt and gently sprinkled it over the casket, believing with all her heart that death had already been conquered for her beloved Franco. It was the portal to heaven for him, where he would spend eternity with his King, and Lord and Savior. Still, one must say the words, "Dust . . . to dust . . ." Her voice broke. Someone gently led her away and the crowd broke, heading towards the rustling cottonwood trees near the church where the women of the community would serve a huge repast in Pastor Franco's honor.

For Mira the public words were not her real farewell. She would return later and say her final goodbyes in private. She would place small rocks on the mounded sod and intersperse them with flowers—marigolds, and whatever else was seasonally available.

And there would be wild roses.

Mira would gently and carefully tend the grave for as many years God gave her breath, and water the flowers with her tears. She would think of her future, and as she did, sorrow would churn within her, remembering that they had no child to carry on Franco's name and family line.

Their legacy would be the work they accomplished on the American Frontier.

. . . but Miranda was not ordained. She had taken theology classes—not altogether unusual for a young woman in the 1800s, as some mission societies did send out single women. Miranda was considering becoming a foreign missionary, knowing she had gifts that could be used overseas even without ordination.

It was while studying theology that she met Franklin Welken. Goal-wise, he was totally oriented to "going west." Without ever having been there, he felt the West in his blood. But first education and ordination.

By the end of Franklin's first academic year other thoughts entered his mind as well—serious thoughts about wife and children. In the all-male environment of seminary what opportunity did he have to meet a young woman? Furthermore, he could think of no one from his growing up years that even slightly interested him, let alone someone with enough fiber and fervor for life on the frontier. *Maybe there will be someone among the pioneer women*, he mused. But he quickly dismissed that as an idea laden with potential problems. A man should go to his first charge—unless committed to celibacy—married. It was a topic often discussed among his peers and with the professors. According to his peers, women of marriageable age—and perhaps their pushy mothers—would be a distraction. According to the professors, *pursuing courtship within the flock that one is called to pastor is a "conflict of interest" and a seedbed for trouble. It is to be avoided.* Franklin conceded their point. *But,* he wondered, *do I have it in* me *to go single, and remain single?*

This, and another equally troubling question: *were I to meet someone here in the east, would she have it in her heart to love me enough to head west, and believe that it was truly the call of the Lord for both our lives?*

So it was with interest that Franklin noticed Miranda at the beginning of the Fall semester of his second year in seminary. She didn't appear timid, but maybe a bit unsure of herself in a classroom of men; she wasn't exactly pretty, but her auburn hair would stand out in any crowd; he noticed that her hands were delicate and smooth; *not much physical labor there*, he assumed. *Perhaps she was of the scholarly bent and a* privileged *life*. He tucked away these little pieces of information, and determined that he would observe her for some time before even trying to say *hello*. He wanted to be fair and reserve judgment.

She said nothing in class; the professors were too intimidating, with an obvious distaste for a woman in their classrooms—the first ever in their all male school. The male students had a similar attitude. As Franklin watched Miranda that Fall he saw that after class she would immediately head for the library or depart campus. He felt an urge to follow her in hopes of getting a glimpse of her life outside of campus. But he squelched the temptation—it might be counter-productive for him, and frightening to

Miranda, should she become aware. He would look for better ways of getting to know her.

Unknown to Franklin and the other students and professors, Miranda *did* have another life. A life that was as unsuited to a woman of that day as was the study of theology.

Miranda's father was a doctor and a progressive thinker, pragmatic. He would as easily set aside the rules of convention as abide by them. His bottom line was *that which accomplishes the greater good, and promotes health, well-being and safety.*

He had noticed that even as a child, Miranda had an uncanny aptitude for healing, whether emotional or spiritual, or truly medical. He often took her on his rounds as he made house calls. As she grew and matured she became as adept at delivering babies as he—perhaps better. By the time she was sixteen, many a night, when he was making a call in one home, she was out delivering a baby elsewhere. Following deep losses she was usually the one who provided comfort, words of hope, and a shoulder to cry on.

But Dr. Phillips would never compromise the safety of his daughter, even as he allowed and encouraged her to do many things that would have shocked their community—except that what she did greatly benefitted the community. He knew he must prepare her for life in a changing country and world.

What he allowed and encouraged her to do sometimes pushed the boundaries of propriety. She rode horse astride instead of side-saddle. Astride riding was considered common and vulgar for a well-bred young woman, but Dr. Phillips believed it was much safer. To protect Miranda's legs from chaffing he had below-the-knee soft leather pants and jodhpurs made for her to wear under her skirts.

There were times she was late to class, or didn't make it at all. A sign to some that a woman was too temperamental for theological training and pastoral work. Yet, her papers and test results showed quite the opposite.

By the second semester of his second year (her first year) Franklin knew he had to talk to this young woman. With great trepidation he approached her after class one day as she hurried towards the library.

"Ah, excuse me, Miss Phillips. Could you spare me a moment of your time?"

She paused. He was the first student to take the initiative to speak to her on campus. As her surprise registered, one of the many books she carried dropped. He quickly bent to pick it up and hand it to her. A slight smile spread over her lips as she took the book from him and thanked him.

"I'm—I'm heading to the library. I really must hurry, because I want to get home before dark. It is quite a distance to walk—especially on dark, snowy streets."

"I'm going to the library myself. May I walk with you?"

She nodded and they fell into step, both at loss for words. But he seemed safe enough; she had seen him almost daily for several months. And she knew how to size up men, and defend herself, should the need arise. After all, her father had taught her well before she ever made house calls on her own. At the age of sixteen she started to pack a pistol on night calls.

They found a table, and both pulled out their books, but before she could find her page, Franklin asked, "Miss Phillips, I have to know—why are you studying theology? And why do you hurry away so quickly after class?"

He was blunt and to the point. So would she be.

"I study theology because I feel a call of God upon my life to serve Him. I hurry away after class because women are not welcome here."

To the point, yes, but he thought he saw a small twinkle in her eye—like, *how can anybody be so absurd as to think that only men can study theology and be called by God to serve?*

They studied side by side for the next hour or two, but as the skies darkened she excused herself to walk home. He took note of her direction. But more than that, he had taken note of what he had heard from her lips, and had seen in the faintest twinkle of her eye. In those brief seconds she gave him something to grasp that had only been fleeting before. *She gave him hope.* Hope for a life, the good Lord willing, with a young woman to share the West with.

Yet as time passed she gave him little encouragement and he felt his hope begin to wane. He walked with her daily to the library and side by side they studied, she wondering why he said so little. And he watching the late afternoon skies darken, wishing he had the courage to walk her home, but not daring to ask. Perhaps she lived in an area of town that would embarrass her to have him see. Perhaps she came from a broken family. The list of *perhaps* went on and on, and he could not ask her, fearing that the worst might be true. And then occasionally he told himself *no, none of that can be true. Look at her hands, look at her dress, consider her intelligence, surely she comes from wealth, a class far above me. I would only be rejected.* So he said nothing. Just absorbed her presence. And prayed, indeed, wrestled with God.

As those thoughts rankled Franklin, Miranda's thoughts were equally troubling. *Why does he steal those sideways glances at me when he thinks I am absorbed in my books? What is going on in his mind? He can talk, I know he can, and from his comments in class, I know he is intelligent, and the professors like him. What are his goals, his heart's desires? He is handsome, with a good physique. His occasional smile on an otherwise very sober face is most engaging. But he seems far off.*

The situation was becoming awkward. The impasse had to be broken. Like her father, she would set aside convention if it doing so helped accomplish a worthy end. Exams were beckoning. She had missed classes because of her work. What better excuse than to ask that they review notes *together* rather than side by side?

"Mr. Welken—uhmm—Franklin, I missed three lectures, and have no one to get notes from, would you be willing . . .?" He was taken aback by the use of his first name. But recovered quickly. (However he *had been wondering why* she had missed the lectures. Everybody knew that was unacceptable for a committed student.)

"You would like to borrow my notes? Yes, yes, of course. Which ones?"

"No, that is not exactly what I had in mind. Just copying someone's notes leaves out so much. Would you—would you *review* yours with me, so we could discuss them?"

"Here?" Strict no talking rules were enforced in the library, and even this brief and soft interchange brought *a look* from the librarian.

Miranda took a piece of paper, dipped the nib of her pearl-handled pen into an inkwell and wrote, *No, not here. We'd be thrown out in no time.* A smile crossed her lips at the absurdity of some rules. She paused. She had gone this far. She would go for broke. *How about my house, Saturday afternoon? I live only six blocks from here—I'll give you the address. We've known each other about a half year now. And my parents will be home. They have been wondering what (or who) has been keeping me so attached to the library.*

There! She did it, and watched his face as he read the note. First a look of utter disbelief, and then a huge smile broke out on his face. He agreed, and moments later Miranda was convinced she heard him whoop as he headed to his boarding-house.

Saturday dawned clear and bright. Franklin brushed his suit; polished his shoes. At 1:30 PM he gathered his books, put on his overcoat and hat, and headed towards the address Miranda had given him.

He surveyed the neighborhood. Yes, somewhat upscale, but not ostentatious. He paced himself, and exactly 2:00 PM he rang the doorbell.

To his relief there was no maid or butler. Only Miranda opening the door and graciously welcoming him in.

"Just put your books on the hall table. I'll take your coat and hat." Turning toward the door at the end of the hall, Miranda called, excitement in her voice, "Father! Mother! Franklin has come. I would like to introduce you."

It was as simple as that. Not formal—Miranda did not use the doctor's title in the introduction. They welcomed him to their house, and thanked him for coming to study with their daughter.

Her father made a comment, however, that Franklin realized would need clarification, even before they began to study. He had said, *Miranda, as you know, occasionally misses class because of night time deliveries, but keeping up with her studies is also a priority for her.*

No, he didn't know. Not the "delivery" comment.

Miranda saw his look as she ushered him into the library, and stifled a little giggle. "I'm sorry, Franklin." *(There it was again, 'Franklin'.)* "That comment from my Father must have completely taken you off guard. I realize now, for the first time, that you do not know what I *do*."

"What do you *do*, Miss Phillips? I thought you were a student studying theology. And frankly, even that puzzles me." His voice had a bit of an edge to it.

Suddenly Miranda realized that this might be even harder than she had anticipated. She would choose her words carefully, but be forthright as well. Much was at stake, for both of them.

"Yes, I am a student, and I love my study of theology, but that is only part of my life. My father is a physician and I assist him with his work, including delivering babies. Many a night, he is off in one direction and I in another. We both go by horseback. Buggies are too slow and cumbersome."

If Franklin was shocked by her father's statement, he was nearly dumbfounded now. He didn't like what he heard. Delivering babies; horseback, alone at night. *What respectable woman . . . ?* But Miranda was respectable, he was sure.

To Franklin's credit he recovered himself with as much grace as possible and responded, "I would like to hear about your work sometime soon. For now, shall we review the notes that you need?" He almost added *notes that your work kept you from getting yourself.* But Franklin cut himself short of that comment.

At the end of two hours they had completed their work, and felt that the afternoon was a success, academically anyway.

But Franklin had a lot of thinking to do. The image of a young woman on horseback, delivering babies in the night imprinted itself on his brain. Intuitively *knew* that she did not ride side saddle. How *could* her father allow it, even encourage it? To say nothing of her being out alone at night. It was something he must not dismiss easily. Yet, he tried to keep judgmental thoughts from his mind. But one thing was sure—he did not want this to become common knowledge on campus, both for his sake and hers.

But pleasant thoughts entered his mind as well—*here is a woman who has the spunk that would be needed for life on the frontier.* She has the necessary fiber and fervor. And she was fascinating and intriguing with an allure about her that was drawing him in. Could this—might she—be God's answer to his prayers? Maybe even over and above what he was expecting?

Miranda and her parents were Christians, he was quite confident of that. Why else would she be attending seminary? But they were not practicing their faith exactly as he did. That, too, he was confident of. He longed to better know them and how they thought and believed. *Perhaps God's answer to his dilemma was in learning to look at life in a new and more open way.* In fact, that might be just what would be needed for life in the West on the American Frontier.

But keeping one's mind open and hope alive when personal beliefs—even a way of life is challenged—is a threatening experience. Franklin was on the brink of finding out how painful and complicated the journey of discerning God's will can be. Yet—he asked himself—isn't an open mind what is needed to be truly educated?

The daily library time continued through the school year, as did the Saturday afternoon study time at her house. Gradually the hours lengthened into dinner with her parents. The conversations were a mix of theology politics and farming/gardening.

Franklin found himself more and more taken in by Miranda, and her forward thinking father. He was like a breath of fresh air after listening to professors all week. *Eventually* Franklin would look back on these times recognizing that it was really Dr. Phillips who had prepared him for life on the frontier, where little was like one intended it to be. There were always surprises; the unexpected; and a leader must know how to act and respond. *But for the immediate*, Franklin's thoughts were as much, if not more, on Miranda as they were on theology and his longing for the West. He longed to ratchet the relationship up a notch or two. Yet seeing where she lived, and how she lived, and realizing that she truly had "another life," courage failed him.

Dr. Phillips often spoke of Miranda's gift for healing, referring to her affectionately as *Mira*.

"Mira?" Franklin questioned. "Why shorten a lovely name like Miranda to Mira?"

Miranda flushed at the question, as did Franklin, realizing how forward and personal it sounded.

But the question gave Dr. Phillips no pause. Instead, it gave him the opportunity to exercise his bragging rights.

"Miranda was only 13 or 14 when she insisted that we bring home with us a tiny newborn that we had just delivered. (Franklin's face turned scarlet at such an open and frank conversation.) We were not able to save the mother; in my opinion, the baby did not stand a chance. The father, with several other children and now no wife was only too ready to relinquish the care of the baby. It was the dead of winter; fortunately we had come by buggy rather than our usual horseback. The father found a small box; we wrapped the baby and placed him in it, surrounded him with well wrapped heated stones and drove home in a winter storm. Miranda would not give up on him, and with the help of her mother—who seemed to look on this child as the little son she never had—(Mrs. Phillips drew in her breath in a sudden involuntary gasp, as if to say *wherever did you come up with such an idea?* But Dr. Phillips continued smoothly)—and an occasional word of advice from me, we returned the baby to his father, six months later. A healthy, happy little fellow."

"As for the name *Mira*—well, following this amazing success in saving and nursing a baby, word got around that Miranda could *almost* perform miracles, and she has become known in the community as *Mira, the healer*. It's not that we do not know where healing comes from—we do, and everything we do is undergirded with fervent prayer. But we do not close our eyes to the fact that God blesses some people with abilities that almost appear to be miraculous. Miranda is one of those, and I couldn't be prouder, or more thankful. In the years that Miranda has worked by my side, I have taught her almost everything I know; in addition to her technical and diagnostic skills, she has compassion and insights into a person's soul."

The conversation stopped. Mira, embarrassed by the focus on her, felt she must say something. "Did I ever mention to you, Franklin, that I have considered going into overseas missions?" (She knew very well that she had not.) "That would likely give me the best opportunity for using my gifts—healing, and teaching the Bible." (The implication being that apart from working with her father she would not have *opportunity to use her medical skills; and as for her theological training, there would not be use for that either; certainly nothing that would parallel the opportunities that men enjoyed.)*

Her parents said nothing; they had not heard her mention overseas mission work for months and hoped that any thought of it was a thing of the past.

As for Franklin, the expression on his face, other than total surprise, was unreadable, although *dumbfounded and deflated* came close to what he was feeling. What he was learning about Miranda was too much, too fast, and too unconventional. Almost, well, *almost improper*. No, not *almost. It was improper*. But as that thought entered his mind, he knew it was unfair. *Unconventional, yes. Improper? No! Never, not Miranda.*

In their recent conversations—usually in the presence of her parents—Franklin often talked about his interest in the West and did so with passion. His desire was to serve as a pastor on the American Frontier. Growing up on a farm in Pennsylvania, he had lived a simple, austere life. While he knew that life on the prairie as a pastor would not be the same as life on a Pennsylvania farm, he believed that the subsistent living while growing up and the work ethic he had learned prepared him well for the frontier. As he gradually became aware of Miranda's skill with medical things, he began to think about a life with Miranda, as a team on the America Frontier. Perhaps his hope could be realized. But for all the times he had mentioned *the West* Miranda had given no indication of any long term plans of her own. Her comment caught him totally off guard.

Dr. Phillips watched Franklin closely now as he foundered, trying to think of something appropriate to say.

"Missions! Why, that's wonderful! A very noble cause! But don't you think for a young woman it might be . . .?"

"What about a *young woman*?" Miranda immediately countered, with a sharpness that she was not normally given too. Bluntness, yes. Sharpness, no. But she could be pushed too far, and he had touched a very sensitive nerve. This man, who she had secret, hopeful thoughts about, but who had kept himself at arms' length for so long, now expressed an attitude she found intolerable—and also unexpected. He had never expressed anything like this before. That is why—or at least one of the reasons why—she found herself attracted to him. And even dared dream a little. But *now* she might as well resume her thoughts of foreign missions, and put anything else out of her mind.

She had found herself drawn in by the passion that Franklin expressed for the American Frontier. But for fear of sounding forward or presumptive she had kept her thoughts to herself, praying that there might be a way. Now she realized he was no different from the other stuffy males who smirked at her presence in the classroom.

Dr. Phillips was quite sure that he knew what had just happened in the brief interchange between Miranda and Franklin. But it was not so much what had just been expressed that concerned Dr. Phillips. Rather, it was the conversations between the two *that obviously had not yet taken place*. Conversations about two dreams that could mesh, but only if they were openly and freely discussed.

Smells of dinner wafted through the sitting room; in a moment or two they would be called to enjoy a fine meal, but Franklin began to excuse himself, saying he could not stay this evening.

Dr. Phillips, ever gracious, accepted his regrets, and walked with him to the door. Without any further comments, he shook Franklin's hand and said, "There will be a way, young man."

Franklin had no idea what this meant. Dr. Phillips wasn't sure himself. He just knew that some fatherly intervention was in order. And perhaps the sooner the better.

Mira went to her room; what seemed like hours later she heard a soft knock and a tray being gently set on the small table outside her door.

Still hours later—about midnight—Mira heard a banging on the front door, and knew only too well what it meant. *No! Please God, not tonight! Not a delivery.* She covered her head, but only a few short moments later she heard a firm knock on her door. "Mira, we are needed—a difficult delivery. The buggy will be ready in 10 minutes." Her father gave her no choice, and she was ready. Soon they were moving down the street, neither saying anything. They worked together in silence, and by joint effort and combined skill they delivered a healthy, large baby, but Mira hardly smiled even at the baby's first cry. Tonight, despite the difficulty of the birth, it all felt routine, almost methodical. Yet she knew that alone, her father would have struggled greatly at great discomfort to the mother. But her small hands were able to guide the baby through a safe birth.

They rode home in silence. Only one comment was made—that of Dr. Phillips. "It begins with an apology."

Mira thought *never*. But she knew he was right. Ever so slightly she nodded her head in agreement. Dr. Phillips saw it and smiled in the darkness. He reached out and clasped her hand the rest of the way home. She could feel his strength.

There would be no church for Miranda that Sunday—the night was far too long and hard. More the emotional pain that she was dealing with than the physical labor of delivery. She thought she could deliver babies in her sleep if she had to. But delivering herself from the emotional pain of what had happened the night before was far different. She had been rude and ungracious, she knew. And more than that, *the first real glimmers of hope that in Franklin she had found a man who considered her his equal were dashed by his comment; a comment, she now realized, she hadn't even allowed him to finish.* She was glad that her parents did not insist that she accompany them to church this morning. There would be members of the Mission Society present, and Miranda wanted to avoid then almost as much as she hoped to avoid Franklin on Monday. Her life felt unsettled, and she had to think. Particularly about the *apology* that she had silently agreed to. But she also needed to examine carefully what she had at one time labeled *a call from God to foreign service.* Lately—since Franklin had entered her life in what she was hoping was becoming a significant relationship—she had been wondering if the *call* might have been her own way of justifying getting a theological education. But once she had her education, what next? The logical answer was foreign missions. It would be a way of using both gifts. But in real moments of honesty, she considered the risks and wondered if she would really be up to the challenge.

That Sunday morning Miranda engaged in soul searching, realizing that she was at a crossroads. She had made no commitment to the Mission Society. She had made no commitment to Franklin. So she spent several hours on her knees imploring God to help her to be open to His will and guidance. She placed before him her reservations about foreign missions, including *that her expressed interest in being a foreign missionary was not completely honest.* Honesty now compelled her to admit that it was a means of accessing a theological education. She placed before God her love of medical work. And most of all she placed before God her feelings for Franklin that were moving beyond friendship to a deeper attraction. After all this brutal honesty she felt she had cleared her mind enough to *hear* God and she began to listen and what she heard was, *it begins with an apology.* Beyond that, directions were not forthcoming.

It didn't seem like much, or particularly helpful, for that matter; not after all she had poured out to God. Her father had said the same, *it begins with an apology.* Well, at least she had a starting point; something that might possibly get a conversation going. Finally, with no further instructions, and with a determination to do *right*, Miranda gave in to the utter weariness that was overtaking her. She arose from her knees, washed her face, and ate a small breakfast. Feeling a sense of peace beginning to steal over her, she went to bed and slept for several hours.

Upon awaking, she had some new thoughts. Thoughts of what *apology* entails began to trouble her. She dropped to her knees at the side of her bed.

Heavenly Father, you and my earthly father gave me the same direction. You both said, 'It begins with an apology.' I can understand why my father said this, but from you, Lord, I expected something more 'spiritual'—like 'forgive,' 'submit,' 'humble yourself.'

What do you mean by 'it'? And by 'begins'? And what is involved in 'apology?'

Lord, I implore you—if I apologize, and I will—help me to get it right. I need to know what I am doing, why I am doing it, what to say, and how to say it.

Miranda paused, placed her head on her arms and waited. No additional directions came. Eventually some logical thoughts seemed to arise from her own mind and from her good theological training. It wasn't until she had it all worked out that she realized that these thoughts had been given to her by the Lord, himself:

<u>*It*</u>—*the healing process, and the moving forward from this point; the regaining of hopes and dreams.*

<u>*Begins*</u>—*starting an open honest conversation about feelings, dreams, hopes, desires, plans.*

<u>*Apology*</u>—*the starting point of <u>how</u> 'it' 'begins'. Apology breaks down defenses because it assumes responsibility for one's own behavior rather than blaming the other person; it invites further communication; it requires a spirit of humility, honesty, willingness to forgive; submitting in love to the desire of the other; openness to receiving love and forgiveness; eventual sharing of hopes and dreams.*

Then Miranda continued in prayer:

Lord, in my own strength I cannot do this, but I know I must—for my own sake, for Franklin's sake, for my parents' sake (I dishonored them, too) and most of all for your honor and glory.

Lord, Franklin and I are both young people who wish to serve you with our lives. I was beginning to hope that we might serve you together.

May your will be done in all of this. As you have clarified my understanding of what I must do, and how and why I must do it, please be at work in Franklin also, so at the very least, he will be gracious enough to hear me out.

Thank you! In Jesus' Name I submit this prayer. AMEN

Miranda got up and bathed, changed her clothes, and joined her family for dinner. Nothing was said about what had happened yesterday, or what would happen tomorrow, but both parents could see that Miranda—

their Mira—had fought a difficult battle, and matured and aged in the past 24 hours and was more prepared to face her own future.

Monday came. The apology would not be easy. What if Franklin ignored her, refusing even to listen? Well, she would find a way. She could not ignore God's directions. She knew her life would be on hold until this was resolved. She was convinced that Franklin's response, whatever it would be, would make the difference for the rest of her life, and his too. She was very grieved with herself for having cut him off midsentence. Perhaps what she thought he was going to say was not at all what he intended to say. Or, perhaps she was overly sensitive to the conventions regarding women. They both deserved to know.

They avoided eye contact in class, but Franklin fell into step with her as she walked to the library, however, he said nothing. She bided her time knowing that she had to handle this well. *Apology breaks down defenses* had rung through Miranda's mind all day.

As they walked Miranda gave Franklin the briefest of a sideways glance. Did he look defensive? She couldn't tell. He had reason to be. Still, he was walking with her, even though less than 48 hours earlier she had directed some very sharp words towards him. Not only that—on the possibility that he might have amorous thoughts towards her, her words would have cut deeply, and possibly shattered his hopes. *But if he does love me, why has he been so slow to express himself?* In answer to that, her thoughts rushed on. *A man has feelings too, and often has to put himself out on a limb, taking big risks as he expresses them. A man risks rejection when he is the first one to make feelings, hopes, desires known in a potential relationship. No doubt, he attempts to be quite sure of the likely response, before doing this. Perhaps I have given him no real indication of my feelings. That may be what has been holding him back. The time has come for me to take a risk that will work towards determining our future—together or separate.*

They reached the library steps. Not a word had been spoken as they walked. Now, instead of going up the steps, Miranda sat down. Franklin followed suit, still saying nothing. Miranda took a deep breath. It was now or never.

"Franklin, I was rude. Ruder than I have ever been in my whole life." Franklin said nothing. A silence that Miranda interpreted *as he has no intention of making this easy.* Miranda forged on, "I knew it the moment the words left my mouth—and even then I didn't apologize. But I do now." Her head was averted as she spoke, but she could feel his eyes on her. Now she turned and looked directly into his eyes. *An apology without eye contact would be no apology at all. They had to look into the soul of each other if this were to work*. "I am so sorry. I shocked and hurt you with my sudden sharpness and the assumptions I made. I didn't even give you a chance to finish your comment. I will also say that you touched a sensitive nerve—still I am without excuse and ask you to forgive me. Will you forgive me, Franklin?"

Miranda paused. Their eyes were locked now. "Miss Phillips, uuhm, *Miranda*, if I may?" She nodded, with a very slight smile which he took as encouragement. "Miranda, I was wrong, too. You were correct in what you heard, and even in hearing what I left unsaid. I too, made assumptions—about you, about women, about *young* women, based on beliefs that now I realize are deep in my soul, and I can't give a good reason or excuse. I have grown up watching my parents and grandparents honor and love each other for whom they are, *male and female*, both equally created in the image of God. I have seen and heard opinions to the contrary here at seminary, even taught as dogma. But I thought I was different from the men here. Now I realize that *I have acquired some of those very opinions myself*, and until I made the effort to hear myself through your ears, which I have been doing since I left your house, I had no idea how painful those assumptions come across when spoken or when demonstrated in other ways. So I too, apologize. *I apologize for hurting you, and for my prejudiced and uncharitable attitude towards women and their role*. I think you spoke out of pain that you try to repress. I spoke out of ignorant ideas that I thought I had rid myself of. In the past 36 hours I have come to realize that I still have much theological reflection to do on the teachings of Scripture which place great and equal value on all who are created in God's image. I have much theological reflections to do on the gifts and abilities that God disperses at his volition to his children."

The sincerity of his apology and the baring of his soul melted her heart. He had made himself *vulnerable* to her. She could hear her father advise *Miranda, that is a great gift; handle with care.*

Franklin continued, "Miranda, I realize even as I apologize, those ways of thinking may resurface when least expected—as they did Saturday night. When they do, please call it to my attention."

He reached out and squeezed her hand gently and briefly. It was their first physical touch, and was electrifying for both of them. And beyond the physical, it was a clasp that held within it the hope of a future together.

Franklin resolved that he would never again dishonor her for being a woman, but it was a resolve that would be difficult to keep. Not because she was woman or because he was man, but because they were both human, and had a lot to learn about communication. Even a casual comment, or something said in jest could easily be misconstrued. Franklin also realized that should they go together to the Frontier as a team, or anywhere else, he would likely walk just a little in her shadow. Miranda was a leader, and he would have to learn to have no problem with that.

Miranda had her thoughts as well. *I am the one who apologized first, but Franklin joined me in my walk to the library. If he hadn't, how long would it have taken for me to seek him out to apologize?* It was the beginning realization of the strength of character and commitment that Franklin had.

They went in to study and all week spoke little. Just enjoyed companionable silence as they studied and constructed their individual dreams which included each other, and the American Frontier.

Chapter 2 *Getting to Know Each Other*

Saturday came. The two o'clock study time. The suppertime with Mira's parents. No mention was made of the previous Saturday. There was no need.

There was an unspoken understanding that the time had come to begin working on a new level in their relationship. Mira's parents recognized this also, and after dinner excused themselves while Mira and Franklin returned to the parlor. There were games for two to play, and they did, but mainly they talked. Franklin told Mira of his growing up years on a small farm in the woods of Pennsylvania, caring for animals, working the fields, in the summer evenings helping his mother with the gardening. There were no siblings to share in the work responsibilities. It truly had been a hand to mouth existence and excellent preparation for life on the frontier. A preacher would have to provide for his family beyond the meager salary he would be fortunate to get. He was educated in a one room school house, learning the 3 Rs, but little beyond that. His parents, devout Christians, taught him well in the home, and when they noticed a deep interest in spiritual matters, arranged with their pastor for private tutoring, preparing him for Seminary.

Mira, in turn told Franklin her story. Also, an only child, but not living at the same poverty level as Franklin. Mira's mother came from a wealthy family, and was given a modest, but beautiful house, along with household help and a gardener at the time of her marriage. Dr. Phillips had pulled himself up by his own bootstraps, and by the time of meeting Mira's mother, he had established himself in a medical practice. He did not exact high fees and did as much charity work as work for pay. But he was a good business man, and was able to provide well for his family. That, plus the yearly royalties that his wife received from her family's business, enabled them to live very comfortably.

Mira told Franklin of her love for learning, and how at a young age she would accompany her father on calls, or be with him in the office. Her father made a point of teaching her all that was age appropriate, and by the time of her 18th birthday, she had a good grasp on what to do in almost any medical situation that they faced. She had few little friends to play with, and seemed to much prefer the adult world. Her summers, when not working with her father, were largely spent with their cook and gardener, gleaning from them what would later prove to be invaluable frontier skills. At the time, it satisfied her desire to learn, as well as gave her something to occupy her time.

It was in those years that Dr. Phillips insisted that if his daughter were to be involved in a life that was very much a *man's world* she would be safe. Thus, riding horse astraddle, and wearing functional and protective leather clothing under her skirt were necessities. She also learned what food and supplies to carry with her for emergencies. And unbeknown to anyone but Dr. Phillips and Mira herself, at the age of sixteen 16, when she started to make calls by herself—even night calls—he taught how to safely carry a pistol, and how to use it for her own protection. He also allowed her to carry it with her as she walked the six blocks to and from Seminary. *No one else knew until she told Franklin.* He both breathed a sigh of relief for her safety and shuddered as he contemplated the woman he was falling in love with. Her mother held herself aloof of the many activities that father and daughter enjoyed together.

Mira's formal education was at the local city school where she learned the basics, and acquired a great love for reading. Sundays were spent quietly, joining their congregation for worship, an occasional visit with friends, and time to read. The only work allowed was medical emergencies. At an early age Mira was fascinated by stories of missionaries, and began to wonder if the Lord was pulling her in that direction. As she was acquiring medical expertise working with her father she felt a longing to study theology as well. But was there a seminary that would be willing to take her, a female? Nationally, women's suffrage was gaining some momentum. But women in theological training—not too likely. There was only one way to find out . . .

Mira inquired at an all-male seminary near her home, was interviewed, and accepted. She never knew, but often wondered if her father had influenced that decision. By this time he was a well-known and influential man in the community, and was not known for taking *no* for an answer.

Mira and Franklin discussed all these things—the events in their lives that molded them into who they were, preparing them for each other, and for the work that the Lord had for them. They delighted in sharing each other's life-stories. It was a way of getting to know each other at a deep level.

Often Mira's parents joined them for parlor games, and then over a cup of coffee, the conversations continued. Dr. Phillips was an endless source of information, now taking it upon himself to gather information about the American West—as it was in the past, as it was currently, and what it might be like in years to come. All this he shared with Franklin and Mira, and it fueled their eagerness to be pioneers. Mira's mother listened and wondered how and why young people *would throw their life away* on such a foolish quest. *If they go,* she told herself, *I give them two years. By that time something will happen to make life too difficult to stay. Then they will come back home.* She was also resentful that her husband was so caught up in it. *Does he have plans of his own?* she wondered. *If so, it will be without me.* But she did not express her thoughts. She knew her husband and daughter too well. If they had their minds set on something, there was no holding them back.

But Dr. Phillips never mentioned even the possibility of him and his wife going West. He believed that in marriage the desires of the other person must be carefully considered and honored. He would not ask her to do something so completely against her nature. Dr. Phillips adored his wife.

Franklin and Mira began their final year at seminary as close friends, but this did not gain them respectability with their peers. *What God-fearing woman would try to establish herself in a man's world? And what self-respecting man would walk side-by-side with a woman, even deferring to her insights at times?* Such were the judgmental attitudes of the students, and they did not even *know* about her "other life"—her healing ministry, making night calls by herself, carrying a gun, etc. That information would have fueled the flame.

Franklin tried not to let the negative attitudes bother him. He was of the opinion that anyone but a *complete narcissist* would recognize that a capable member of a team enhanced, not detracted from the other. And a narcissist Franklin was not. If anything, his self-esteem needed building up. Mira did this for him. He felt complete when he was with her.

This was the year they would both complete their education. Franklin would graduate and then be ordained, but not Mira. She was not allowed to take preaching courses, and one could not graduate without preaching. Nevertheless, she entered this year with enthusiasm and determination. Her theological conversations with Franklin and her father—often taking the form of debate—proved to her that she could hold her own in any discussion. And her exegetical papers were second to none—one of her professors told her so privately. So this year she would speak up in class, even if it meant talking over someone else to be heard! Yet Mira knew that she must not be rude, or ever deliberately embarrass Franklin.

While Franklin and Mira were enjoying their time together and their developing relationship, something was missing in their conversation, and thus also in their relationship. *Franklin did not propose, and to not to do so kept their relationship at arms' length.* Talk, yes, but no touching or other expressions of endearment. Mira began to feel that she was being taking for granted, and did not like the feeling.

Ever intuitive, Dr. Phillips sensed that something was bothering Mira, and asked about it. "Mira, you and Franklin talk of going West as a team; of serving the Lord by serving people there. But I never hear the word *marriage* or plans for a wedding, or any plans for your *personal* future, for that matter. In less than six months the school year will be over. For both of you, your studies will be completed, and Franklin will graduate, and be ordained in our church, prepared for ministry. But *then* what? *How* will you go? You can't just both board the train . . ."

Mira's face flamed with embarrassment. But she needed to talk. Better to her father, who always understood and supported her, than to her mother. Mira opened her heart. "You are absolutely right, Father. And I don't know what to do. Franklin and I talk about working together in the West. I *know* he intends to marry me, but he just doesn't say the words. He doesn't talk about living together, having a family, a home. He doesn't even tell me he loves me. There is nothing *personal* in our conversations. They are academic and practical. And I am beginning to feel taken for granted. Yet, I believe that he really does love me. I just don't know what to do or say anymore. I love our time together, and the time we spend with you and mother, but it is all very *arms' length*. I don't want to be forward or improper. Is there anything I can do?" On the verge of tears, Mira pressed her hands against her eyes and swallowed several times.

Dr. Phillips watched her closely as he heard her out. He then slowly and deliberately chose his words. "Mira, you are my pride and joy. The day I fully entrust you to another man will be the hardest and the best day of my life. I truly believe Franklin is that man. I believe his intentions are the best—but Mira, he has never done this before, either. Perhaps, just perhaps, he needs a little more *help and encouragement* than what you are giving him. Like maybe your unspoken or spoken permission to come just a bit closer; to express himself personally."

Mira looked at her father wide-eyed and speechless for a moment as she was comprehending what he had just said. When it registered, she jumped up and gave him a big smile. He responded in turn with a smile and a wink. Mira waltzed out of the room glancing at the clock. In another three hours Franklin would be at the door to study, have dinner, and spend the evening.

But once in her own room, she realized that she didn't have the slightest idea what *help and encouragement* might look and sound like. She had learned nothing from her mother, and wasn't about to ask. Following her own intuition would probably be best. But she checked that idea, realizing she must seek the Lord out on this. So she dropped to her knees at her bedside.

Lord, my father told me to do something about how Franklin and I relate. He is right. I know he is. But how, Lord? How can I do this in the right way? I don't even know how to begin. Help me to understand that this is all new for Franklin, too.
She implored the Lord for wisdom, direction and ideas. Then, as happened so often when Mira prayed, there was silence, as though God had not heard her. But Mira, having been through this routine with God before, remembered that the answers usually came when she got up and started to do something. When she used the brains and intuition God had given her.

She got up and stretched her arms above her head several times. She rotated her head, then her arms. She pulled her knees, one at a time toward her chest, for twenty times. She glanced in the mirror while doing this, and burst out laughing at how ridiculous she looked, petticoats, hooped skirts and all. *These are going to have to go. They'll never work on the prairie.* And she laughed the harder, thinking of her mother's horror, if she were to shed them. The laughter felt so good; she had not laughed in a long time. She and Franklin were too serious.

Oh, thank you God! That's it! That's your answer: Try a little humor . . .

Two o'clock came. The doorbell rang, and Mira met Franklin with a burst of energy. "Franklin, I'm all studied out. I think you are, too. There are no tests next week—let's have some fun. She took his arm. "Come to the parlor. Mabel will be serving tea and crumpets, and then let's go out and walk. We shouldn't waste a beautiful, crispy winter day."

Franklin went with her to the parlor. "This *is* a surprise, but I couldn't agree more. The day is heaven sent, and sometimes I wonder if my brain can absorb any more facts, especially on a day like this. I think *country* still flows through my veins."

"My father says that physical activity increases the flow of blood to the brain, and increases our ability to learn."

Franklin agreed with Dr. Phillips' words of wisdom, but he also sensed that there was more going on than just the need for more blood to the brain.

Mabel brought in the goodies, and Mira ate heartily—she had skipped lunch. And Franklin was *always* hungry. He still missed his mother's cooking, and how she could make poverty seem like riches when she prepared meals.

After polishing off the plate of crumpets and two cups of tea a piece they dressed for the out-of-doors. There was a January thaw. Though the day had started out crispy it was now slushy underfoot and the snow on the lawns perfect for packing.

This was the first time they walked together with no books in their hands, and Franklin, rather hesitantly took her arm, and Mira in turn slightly leaned in against him. They felt each other's warmth, even through their woolen coats as they walked. Suddenly Mira broke away. She grabbed a handful of snow, made a soft snowball and threw it at Franklin, hitting him squarely in the chest. Not to be outdone, Franklin nailed her good with an onslaught of well-aimed balls. The *fight* ended only when stern neighbors walked by with disapproving looks.

They brushed each other off and resumed their walk, this time with Mira leaning in closer, but her muscles were tense. She knew now was the time, yet she could hardly force the words. Franklin sensed the tension.

"What is it, Mira? I didn't hurt you, did I?"

"Oh, no! I can't remember ever having so much fun!"

"So . . .?"

I have to keep this light hearted. Lord, give me the words.

She looked up at him with what she hoped was a playful smile. "Franco," (this was the name she always used when she thought of him, but she had never said it before; now it just slipped out). "Franco, aren't you *forgetting* something?"

"Forgetting? What do you mean?" He was completely serious, but she was determined to keep it light.

"Franco," (*there*, she said it again, and it sounded so right. *Franco. Franco and Mira*). She looked him straight in the eyes, maintaining her smile. "Franco isn't there a question you should ask me?"

He returned her look, but there was no smile. And then suddenly her meaning was clear, and his face broke out in a broad grin. He grabbed her hands and moved her towards the bench that was at the intersection. "Mira, *honey*, no, I have not forgotten. But maybe I have not fully realized how important *the question* is. May I explain?"

Mira, nodded, speechless after hearing him call her *honey*. Terms of endearment were rarely spoken in the Phillips' household. This would take getting used to.

"Mira, honey, I've gone over this a hundred times in my mind, but have hesitated for two reasons—I haven't known if you were ready— marriage proposal does bump up the relationship, you know—AND, *I don't have anything suitable to give you right now to seal the promise.*"

Mira looked at him with wide, non-comprehending eyes. "Not *ready*? Oh, Franco, how can you think that? I am *so ready*. And *to give me, to seal the promise?*"

Relief flooded over him, hearing that she was ready. But that still left *the gift*, obviously more important to him than to her. "Well, actually I do have something. It's just that I can't give it to you now. It is my mother's, given to her the night before her own wedding by my father. Something that has been handed down for so many generations, that no one anymore knows the exact origin."

"Oh, Franco! That's so romantic. I'll treasure it, whatever it is."

"Wait a minute," he teased. "I thought you were waiting for *the question.*"

"Oh, I am, I am."

"I'll keep this simple." He took both her gloved hands in his and knelt before her in the snow. "Mira, I love you with all my heart, and want to spend my life with you, serving the Lord on the American Frontier. If you feel the same way, will you marry me?"

Smiling, and with tears of joy in her eyes, she responded, "Oh, I will. I will."

Right there, on a street bench for anyone who might be passing by to see, he took her in his arms and kissed her tenderly, withholding the passion he felt welling up within him.

Catching his breath, Franco said, "As for the gift, my parents will bring it when they come for our wedding—that would be much safer than to mail it, and it will be yours the night before. Giving it to you the night before the wedding would be in keeping with family tradition. Until that time my mother will wear it."

"Franco, your mother—how can she possibly give it up? To ME? She doesn't even know me."

"Mira, honey, my mother has always told me that the next totally happy day in her life will be the day that this treasure is passed on to her own daughter-in-law."

Mira drew in her breath sharply. She could not comprehend such mother-love. And this from a woman she had not even met. But then a troubling thought entered her mind. "Franco, you have obviously communicated more to your parents than what you have told me. You have even said that they would be coming for our wedding. Don't you think that we should now go and talk to *my* parents?" There was a slight edge to her voice, and Franco caught it.

"Honey, they do not *know*. I've just told them about this amazing woman I met, and the deep feelings and growing admiration I have for her. And of course, they know about my plans for frontier ministry. I'm sure they have put 2 and 2 together, just as your parents have. Your parents will be the first to *know*. That's how it should be. Now that I think about it, I suppose I should have asked your father's permission."

"Oh, no, Franco. He would not expect that. Right now he is waiting for us to come back to the house with an announcement. "

At Franco's look of surprise, she continued. "Well, you know my father, and how perceptive he is. He more or less put me up to *pushing* you a little—I would never have dared without his backing."

Franklin replied good-naturedly, "So long as I know that this is what you want, I'm willing to thank your father for the push. I think I needed it."

The same neighbors walked by, going the opposite direction, their look even more disapproving. But Franco and Mira only laughed. As they were getting up to walk home Franklin asked, "Where did you come up with *Franco*?"

"Oh, I don't know. That is how I always think of you. *Franklin* is so formal. *Frankie*—well you told me that you were called that as a child, and did not like it. *Frank* is too abrupt—it needs another syllable. But *Franco*, well that's how I always think of you—Franco. It is regal sounding, and you are regal, Franco. A child of the King."

He pulled her to him for another kiss, and they walked back quickly arm in arm.

What a difference a little fun and humor and an open honest conversation makes.

Mira was right. Her parents were in the parlor having tea. Her father greeted them with, "Well . . . ?"

Mira felt like bounding into the room but remembering that her mother *always* expected ladylike behavior, she simply said, "We have an announcement," and Franco took over from there.

Rejoicing in their good news, Dr. Phillips took Franklin's hand, giving it a hearty shake. "Congratulations, Franklin, we are absolutely delighted." Then turning to his wife he said, "Aren't we, Priscilla?"

"Congratulations, and welcome to the Phillips family, Franklin." Then turning to Miranda and glancing at her left hand, she raised an eyebrow and said, "Is it time to start making plans? When is the date?"

Not missing the glance, Mira said, "Date, Mother? Franklin just proposed, and now you are asking me about the date so we can *plan?*" She paused, took a deep breath and went on, "You are right, we must set a date." But she wanted to say, *can't you just enjoy the moment with me?*

Franklin jumped in to save them from the awkward moment. "I agree, setting a date will help us all. My parents will need some time to make plans as well."

"Do you think they will come?" Dr. Phillips asked hopefully.

"I think there is a good chance. They haven't had a break in all the years that they have been farming. While they live frugally, I know they will make every effort to come."

"Great, and of course, they must stay with us. That is, if you agree, Priscilla."

"Of course, I agree."

They spent the time until dinner discussing plans, finally all agreeing that the Sunday after graduation would be for Franklin's ordination, Franklin's parents to arrive earlier that week. The wedding would be the Saturday afternoon following ordination. The days between completion of school and the wedding would be spent on purchasing supplies, packing, and last minute wedding plans.

But for now Franklin would be in touch with his parents, continue his correspondence with his calling church in Chipps in Dakota Territory, and work with the local church to arrange his ordination. And their studies! Both were determined to complete school with the same achievements that marked their academic efforts this far.

The evening of his engagement to Mira, Franco walked back to his boarding-house, thanking God for the heaven-sent day and for the heaven-sent young woman who he knew now was truly his. He was regretful that he could not give her his mother's treasure at this time; still, it had to be done in keeping with family tradition. Meanwhile, they had sealed their commitment to each other with a kiss. Many kisses.

As the winter wore on and spring was in the air, Saturdays were no longer for studying but for fun, conversation and planning, and many long walks; snowball fights when possible, and sleigh rides. Franco handled a team with great skill. Over dinner, and in the early evening Franklin told them about his growing up years.

"My parents left Boston nearly penniless in 1845 in a covered wagon pulled by a team of horses. Their supplies were meager, their determination admirable, but their plans were not well thought out.

They hoped to get as far as St. Louis and there join a wagon train, and possibly go as far as Oregon. Or, if that did not work, maybe head north to Dakota Territory. They readily admit now how poorly prepared they were, and lacking in understanding of the distance, the weather, and a multitude of hardships that pioneers endure—or die—along the way. On the other hand, life in Boston no longer held much hope for them either."

At this comment Mira's mother looked at him sharply, as if to say *Why not?* But all she said was, "What is your family name or names?"

"Well, as you know, my father's name is Welken—Hiram Welken; my mother's was Kroft—Nina Kroft."

"Kroft—is that with a C or K?"

"Mother! What are you . . .?"

"Actually, Mira, that's a good question with a rather complex answer. I'll just be brief. My mother's family name was actually Undercroft, with a *C*. Then about 30 years ago my grandfather had it legally shortened and changed to *Kroft*, with a *K*."

Mira could see that his response left her mother with more questions than answers, but Franco picked up the story of their move. "About halfway through Pennsylvania as they crossed a stream a wheel came off their wagon and the back axle broke. They had hit a rock. The wagon tipped, and the few supplies they had sank to the bottom of the stream. They managed to get their team and themselves to the nearest bank—the bank opposite of where they had begun the crossing. They were totally drenched, shaken up, but otherwise unhurt. They assessed the seriousness of their situation. They could not even build a fire to warm themselves and dry their clothes. And they had no food."

Franco paused, turning to Mira. "Just think Mira—only 25 or 30 years later, we get to take a train—travel in comfort—almost to our final destination." Mira nodded, still digesting the story Franco was telling them.

But Mrs. Phillips had a comment. "They must have felt desperate and hopeless, with no place to turn." Her voice had a softer than usual quality, almost as if she had some understanding of their situation, or at least of their feelings.

Franco responded gently, "Desperate they were, but not without hope. Both remembered a farmhouse with a few buildings several miles back. They discussed their options—crossing the stream on foot, and trying to get their team to cross as well, or walk on, hoping they might find something ahead, nearby. At this point in their journey going back to what they had seen made more sense than moving forward to the unseen and unknown.

"It was near evening and they could waste no time. Fortunately with no wagon behind them, the horses cooperated with going into the stream once again, and after a couple hours' trek they found the farm. There they were greeted by a middle-aged, childless couple, living on the edge of poverty. But more positive people my parents had never met. My parents were invited to spend the night, and were given dry clothing and a warm meal, with the promise that the next morning Mr. Pierson would take my father back to the stream in hopes of retrieving whatever they could find. They managed to pull out some pieces of the wagon that loosened as it tipped and my mother's trunk with their clothing and books. Unfortunately the trunk was not waterproof, so the books were totally ruined, but the clothes were salvageable. Mother used to love to tell how Mrs. Pierson chuckled over her hoops and petticoats, advising my mother that such things would be totally impractical in the West." Suddenly Franco blushed, realizing what he had just said in front of two women.

But Dr. Phillips laughed and said, "Tell us what she did with them."

Franco recovered himself quickly and said, "Well, I'm not sure about the hoops, but all the clothing and blankets were laundered, and the petticoats were carefully stored, and a few years later were used to make baby clothes for me!"

Ever practical, Dr. Phillips responded, "Sounds sensible. Too bad about the books, though. But tell us more about your parents. Obviously they stayed with or near the Piersons without moving further west. How did that come about?"

Franklin nodded. "Well, the short answer is, they had no wagon or supplies now, and no more money than what my father carried in his pocket in a small pouch—a few coins.

"As they were eating the evening meal of their first full day with the Piersons, Mr. Pierson made them an amazing offer. He said that as he and his wife had prayed the night before, asking God how they could help this stranded young couple, the answer came to both of them at the same time. *Invite them to stay. Take them in.* It was the obvious solution for the situation that both couples found themselves in. Mr. Pierson was in fragile health due to scarlet fever he had had in his younger years, and was finding that he could do less and less strenuous work. But he was a good teacher and supervisor. My father knew nothing about making a living from the soil, or caring for farm animals but was a quick and able learner. And my mother—well, she always says that Mrs. Pierson taught her everything of value that she knows. However you look at these desperate situations, the outcome for both the Welkens and the Piersons could have been planned only in heaven. But it also took hard work and commitment on the part of both couples to make it work. I was born about three years later, and no child could have had better *grandparents* than what I was privileged to have in the Piersons."

When Franklin paused Mrs. Phillips rang for dessert and coffee, and said, "Franklin, your story is amazing. And the story of your parents—I would like to hear more."

Mira was surprised at her mother's interest, almost warmth, and wondered what was going on in her mind.

Dr. Phillips was fully intrigued and said enthusiastically, "I'm eager to hear about those growing-up years on the farm, and how your parents and the Piersons worked out a partnership. But I understand if you wish to tell us in *installments.*"

"Thanks for listening," Franklin responded. "I look forward to telling more. Actually, it means a lot to me to visit the memories with you."

Later that evening Franco told Mira more.

"Mira, there is more about my parents leaving Boston than what I told your parents, and I do want you to know. The reason I'm not telling them now is because I want your parents—especially your mother— to get to know and accept my parents for who they *are, not for who they were and where they came from.*"

Mira looked at him, "Please go on."

"My parents were born and raised in Boston to wealthy families; the families had related businesses and both lost their money in businesses gone badly. As a young man, my father was involved in the family business, and he and my mother were married shortly before the financial ruin of both families. They saw their only hope for the future in going west. The year was 1845. But like I said when talking with your parents, they never got farther than the forests and farmlands of Pennsylvania. Mira, my mother may have lost some style, but in her poverty she never lost her class. She worked in the gardens and lived in a small house—at first not much more than a little shack—with as much grace and dignity as a queen in a palace. Your mother will probably think her clothes a bit out of style, but they will be in good taste. I want your mother to see my mother without **knowing** that *she came from money and the upper class of Boston.* Do you understand that, Mira?"

"Yes, I understand very well. I just hope . . ."

"I think I know what you were about to say, Mira. But I think it will go well. I picked up on a softer side to your mother than what I have ever seen before—it was when I talked about the desperate situation that my parents found themselves in. Do you remember what she said?"

"She said something about them feeling desperate and *hopeless.*"

"Yes, and the tone of her voice softened when she said that. Almost as though she could feel something of what they felt. Do you think your mother ever felt desperate and hopeless?"

"My *mother? Desperate and hopeless?* She has never had a *want or care* in her life. She is always completely in control of herself."

"Maybe. Maybe not, but perhaps in time we will learn more of her story."

They dropped the topic for the evening.

From this point on their Saturday afternoons were spent in fun, and the evenings in talking and making wedding plans with Mira's parents—Mira and Franklin wanting to keep it simple, her parents coming up with lavish ideas for their only daughter. Arriving at acceptable and reasonable compromise took some of the fun out of it. It was Mira who finally came up with a solution that appealed to both parents. "Mother, I would like a ceremony with limited guests, but you can decide the place, and make it as fancy as you wish. Father, the reception—you choose the place and invite whoever you wish, but please include all of our regular patients. What to serve? You and mother choose."

Even if this were not quite the wedding they had envisioned for their daughter, both parents were delighted at having so much freedom of choice and more than enough to be responsible for. As for Mira and Franco, they virtually let go of wedding planning— except to respond to an occasional question from her parents—and spent their time studying, talking about what they thought life on the frontier might be like and just enjoying each other's company. *And that was the greatest fun of all.*

Before many Saturdays passed Dr. Phillips reminded Franco that there was still much of his story that they wanted to hear, particularly growing up on a farm in the forests of Pennsylvania.

"I was born in 1848. By that time my father had built a modest two room log cabin only about 15 feet from the Pierson's house which by this time was in poor repair. My earliest memories go back to when I was 4 or 5 years old, so some of what I'm telling you is what I remember from my own experience; some is what my parents and the Piersons told me. My parents' house had a fireplace, and also a cook stove. My father tells me that in those first two or three years he developed muscles he never knew he had and that his smooth *city hands* became calloused as he cleared land for farming—mother even got into the act, helping him saw logs. He also remodeled the Pierson's house, making it more snug and warm than it ever had been. I was equally at home in both houses, wearing a little track between the two as I freely went back and forth.

"You probably wonder *how could a city boy have done all my father did?* Well, he always gave credit to Mr. Pierson who, as I told you was frail by this time, but still an excellent teacher, supervisor—and more than anything, an *encourager*. Mr. Pierson—and by the way as I talk about both Mr. and Mrs. Pierson from this point on, I'm going to refer to them as *Grandpa and Grandma* for that is what they were to me—Grandpa was reluctant to take any credit, always saying *that if my father had not had it in him, he (Grandpa) could not have brought it out.* The relationship that Mother had with Grandma was much the same.

Franco paused momentarily, and Dr. Phillips jumped in with a comment, "Your grandparents obviously had many fine qualities, including great wisdom."

Franco nodded his head, and picked up the story. "Both my grandparents and parents. By the time I was five, mother was already teaching me numbers—I have to smile now at how *primitive* it was. As I told you, all her books, and I presume this included pens, ink and paper were ruined in the river, so we really started from scratch, using small woodchips, dried beans and peas, and kernels of corn to form numbers and letters. To learn counting, adding, subtracting, multiplying and dividing we made small piles with the items. I was able to see what numbers meant, rather than dealing with abstract figures on paper. On rare occasions, when we went to the stream we would pick up small pebbles, and use them for the same purpose. Stones did not attract mice like the corn, beans and peas did so my mother preferred them! On even rarer occasions—maybe once or twice a year—Mother and I would go with Father to the small nearby town to buy supplies. One year she bought a small slate and some chalk for me. To this day, I don't think I have ever felt richer or more empowered, for even as a small child, I realized that this was the key that would unlock a future of education for me. My mother continued to teach me at home until I was about 10 when a small one room school opened about a mile distance from our farm. It is open only six months a year so that students and teachers can help in the family farming and gardening. Initially we had less than 10 students—but there were books, and a big blackboard in front to the room. What more did a teacher and students need?

"But the first two teachers did not work out well. They knew little about teaching, and had no care or concern for children. When I was 12 my mother, though she had no formal training as a teacher, became the school's teacher. Because of mother's teaching at home I was far ahead of the others. As you might guess, I did have a few lessons in *humility* to learn. Supplies continued to be meager, but each year, from her small salary, she purchased a few books. She still teaches there, and by this time she has built up a respectable library, and has maps, and furnishes some of the very impoverished children with slates. Mother works hard in her garden and puts away food that she shares with children during the school year. Children, who otherwise would be too hungry to study. She has devised a way for baking potatoes and other edible roots on the school stove. On other days she puts on a big pan of beans seasoned with bacon. Probably doesn't sound like much, or good to you, but for a child who comes with an empty stomach, even a daily potato or a cup of cooked beans makes a difference in how the child will get through the winter."

Dr. Phillips interjected a supportive, "*Indeed!*"

"My mother's example has encouraged families who have fared relatively well to occasionally share of their food stores as well. I honestly believe that this is why the school has become popular in the area. Now the "school board" is looking into building a larger two-room structure, and getting a second teacher. Fortunately, Mother's salary has increased slightly year by year. That, plus the increasing income from the farm would have finally moved my parents beyond a hand to mouth existence, except for one thing—the War."

Franco paused, realizing that he had now introduced another topic. Were they ready to hear more? But Mira was still focused on how his parents were so totally giving of their limited resources.

"Oh, Franco. It's a life that I can hardly imagine . . ."

"Mira, honey, it's the life we will have, and maybe we will have even less, in Dakota Territory. Do you think you will be able to adjust?"

Before Mira could reply, her mother responded. "Miranda, it's not too late . . ."

"Mother, Franco's question was to me. I would like to answer him."

She turned toward Franco and said, "What I mean is that *I had no good mental picture of what your life was like before coming east to school. As I see it now, though you were poor in the things of the world, you had wonderful parents and grandparents, and your schooling—though those early years, to use your word was* primitive, *you learned well*. And, if I remember correctly, you have already told me that your local pastor taught you theology."

"That's right. When my mother taught me all she thought she possibly could—she told me that any additional books would *be beyond her*—she suggested that we ask Pastor Brewer if he would teach me. And since I was interested in Bible knowledge and theology, that became our focus. By this time we had a good saddle horse, so going in to town once a week for lessons was doable. As it turned out, I often stayed with the Brewers from Friday until Monday. My assistance to Brewers, doing odd jobs, and assisting with the Sunday service became my 'keep'. As I look back on this now, I think my parents preferred that I spend some time away from the influence of the ever increasing number of soldiers seeking shelter, food, and medical assistance. Since roads and travel were improving my parents were able to come to church regularly as well, rather than just attend an occasional Sunday service in the summer. They often brought with them two or three soldiers who were well enough to travel."

"Franco, it's getting late, but I definitely hear the beginning of another story. Will, it keep until next week?"

"It will keep."

"Then if you will excuse Priscilla and me, we will leave the two of you to your dreams and plans."

After the Phillips left the room, Mira told Franco, that although she was much less prepared for pioneer life than he, with his help she was confident that she could do it. Franco assured her that he had confidence in her ability and added, "Mira, anytime you might doubt your own ability, just remember my parents, and how totally unprepared they were for life on a farm in the forests of Pennsylvania, and how they not only survived, but flourished, if not financially, certainly in other ways."

"Franco, I know it will be difficult, but I believe we can do it together *as a team*, God helping us."

Dinner was hardly finished the following Saturday evening when Dr. Phillips said, "And now Franco, the war stories. I've been looking forward all week to hearing them."

"Please understand that my role in any of what my parents and grandparents did was quite minimal, and I spent much time with the Brewers during these years. So the real stories will be best told by my parents. But I can prepare you for their stories by giving you some of my memories."

"Good plan. Let's go to the parlor." Dr. Phillips led the way, stoked the fire, while Priscilla rang for tea. Franco and Mira settled comfortably on the sofa.

"I don't remember which year it was, but I know it was winter when the first wounded soldier knocked on my grandparents' door. Grandmother opened the door, only to have him fall at her feet. Neither grandparents were strong enough to pull him inside, so grandma came over to get my parents, and I followed on their heels. This was the first soldier I had ever seen and a severely wounded and starving one at that. Grandma and mother quickly fixed a pallet for him near the fireplace; father and I, as gently as possible picked him up—although I'm sure that father could have done it by himself—and placed him on the pallet. Grandma was ladling broth from the ever present soup pot that hung from the tripod in the fireplace, while mother positioned herself at his head. Father got down on the floor, gently raised his head and shoulders and allowed him to recline against him while mother slowly spooned broth into his mouth, at first as much ran down his chin as down his throat. But it revived him. Before long he drifted off to sleep. As he slept Father and I undressed him. He was filthy, and his clothes full of fleas. We searched his pockets for identification but found none. Father threw his clothes into the fire. Grandma had already provided a blanket from her chest, and Grandpa was heating a large pan of water. Mother and Grandma stood ready to bathe him, but Father sent them to our house. *This was no job for ladies.*"

Dr. Phillips caught Miranda's eye at this comment, both remembering how she had often begged her father to go along to the hospital when he had been caring for troops, but he—perhaps at his wife insistence— told her that *this was no job for ladies.*

"Well, we got him scrubbed alright, and he slept on for several more hours. When he stirred Father and Mother got him to swallow more broth. The next morning when he awakened he was able to talk, but unable, or seemed unable, to remember anything. This was of great concern—for all we knew, we were quartering a deserter. Physically he improved a great deal that first day, no doubt thanks to Grandma's broth, beans and bread. We gave him a set of my clothes and a rather worn pair of Grandpa's shoes, and sent him on his way the next day, with a satchel of food. He never did tell us his name—but we sensed he knew that he was endangering us. As we talked about it after he left, we realized that though he had no *war wounds* he was a *war casualty* no less, a frightened young fellow, starving to death. Where he went from our place or what happened to him, probably best not to know."

Everyone sat silently for a few moments, and then Franco spoke again, "Several weeks later two men came, more alert, less starved, but both with infected wounds. My parents and grandparents had already talked about what to do when—not if—this happened, and continued to happen. Grandpa and Grandma would move in with us, and when the weather warmed a little Father would build a lean-to onto our cabin for Grandpa and Grandma. Until then, well, we would be crowded. Father and Mother took my loft room, and Grandpa and Grandma used their bedroom. I didn't mind at all hunkering down by the stove. But even before these two soldiers came Father and I constructed a *dogtrot* between our two cabins. Built exactly over the path I had worn smooth as a child. This enclosure enabled Grandpa and Grandma to go back and forth between the two buildings safely in the cold.

"These two men also did not tell us their real names and we did not ask. None of us knew anything about caring for wounds, let alone infected ones. But our goal was to get them up and out as soon as possible."

Franco paused, deep in thought, and then went on, "You know, after awhile we quit worrying about quartering possible deserters. We just saw them as hurting young men who needed care, and we would do our best to provide that for them. But back to these two. Their uniforms were not so tattered that they couldn't be worn, however, Grandpa insisted on boiling them, and lost no time in setting large pans of water on the stove and over the open fire, while the men enjoyed the warmth of fire, wrapped in blankets. Meanwhile Grandma prepared them food and insisted that I serve them. When I saw how much she gave them, I knew I would have to do with less. And Father and Mother, well, they planned their attack on the wounds—one infected lower arm, and one infected thigh, both from bullet wounds. The logical thing was to clean them, and allow them to drain. The arm wound was relatively easy—the soldier insisted that the bullet had only grazed him and was not lodged in the flesh or bone. Even though it was cold outdoors, for several days Father took the soldier outside while he slowly poured large amounts of warm water over the wound; then he would take the soldier back inside and set the arm to soaking in a large pan of warm water. This they did several times a day. In about a week's time the wound was nearly healed, and the soldier was on his way. But the thigh wound was more difficult. As far as we could tell, the bullet was lodged in the bone. Although we tried cleansing the wound, and having him sit in a tub of water, he developed a high fever, and died several days later. My first experience with death."

Again everyone was silent. Mira took Franco's hand and held it tightly, remembering her experiences with dying and death. And Dr. Phillips' mind was on all those he had ushered from time to eternity in the difficult days of the war.

"With thoughts of spring and summer in our minds when Father and I would be working in the fields and Mother in our garden, we really wondered how we would manage. Oh, there were times when we had no 'guests'—as we decided to call them—but at other times we had up to six. Grandma emphatically said she had no problem with keeping up with the cooking, provided she had beans, flour, cornmeal, potatoes and milk. Grandpa said he could 'boil the laundry' and dress the wounds. But it was mother who came up with the most ingenious plan—*the less sick and wounded do what they can to care for those who were sicker.*"

Franco paused, and then added with a grin, "Once they knew that they would have responsibilities, it was amazing how soon many were better after a night of rest and a couple of meals. And many were also ready to ship out on Saturday, once they heard that they would be expected to attend church on Sunday."

Dr. Phillips chuckled, "There are many ways to motivate people. Sounds like you folks found some good ones."

"Yes, it's true. My mother with her cunning insights, and Grandpa, though a mild man, knew exactly how to handle soldiers. I would hear him talking to them in the evening and each man knew from the get-go the rules of our dwelling. Every morning before breakfast he read to them the Ten Commandments and the Golden Rule. I think for the days they were with us they were the most respectful and disciplined soldiers of the army. Sadly we lost many to death, and that was hard on Grandpa. Even at my young age, seeing him at the graveyard in our backyard, I realized that in their deaths he was mourning not only the young men of our nation, but also the children he never had."

Mira noticed a slight nod of her mother's head. The look on her face was sympathetic.

Franco went on, "The soldiers saw this side of him, too. And frankly, I think that is why they respected him, and obeyed his rules."

A very quiet *no doubt* escaped Priscilla's lips.

Franco paused. The memories were taking an emotional toll on him. Mira moved in more closely as if to comfort him. Dr. and Mrs. Phillips were respectfully quiet. All were deep in thought with their own memories of life and death.

After a few minutes Franco continued, "There are many more stories from this time in our lives, but frankly, they are quite blended in my memory, so if you don't mind, it would be better if my parents shared them with you. But I think you should know that these men and the way my folks cared for them left a big impression on me. Even for about a year after the end of the war, soldiers would come as they were trying to make their way home. Often they stayed only a night or two, just to get some food and rest. By this time, financially we were very strapped, all our money and garden produce going for food for the soldiers and mother's school children. And Grandpa and Grandma were becoming spent. They never did move back to their cabin.

"Father and Mother were becoming weary also. I once heard Mother comment to Father as she was trying to figure out where to get more rags for bandages—they had already torn up all their curtains and sheets, and begged at church for more—that she wished that she still had her old petticoats to use. Father cut her short. The first and only time I have heard him reprimand her. *Don't ever think or say that again. They were used for Franklin, and that was the right thing to do. And as for all our blankets that are worn and boiled to shreds, well, I believe that God will provide. But little Franklin in your remade petticoats is something that must never be regretted. It's a memory that I hold almost sacred.* Mother bowed her head in embarrassment at having displeased my father. But she knew he was right. *God would provide.* Yes, my parents were spent also. The war affected, and would continue to affect everyone for a long time."

Dr. Phillips nodded his agreement.

"One evening they took me aside and told me that if Grandpa and Grandma didn't slow down, they would not be with us much longer. I immediately knew the unspoken request: *would I put my education on hold for awhile, giving up my weekends at the Brewers so that I could almost totally relieve Grandpa of his work.* Of course I would! What my parents did not know was that now the war being over I had begun to inquire at seminaries, and was accepted at the very seminary where Mira and I are now studying. What I foolishly had not taken into account was that there wouldn't have been any money for tuition even if I had been free to go."

Franco paused, and then went on, looking at Mira, "It was a huge disappointment at that time, although I did not tell my parents, and certainly not my grandparents—who by the way lived until 1870, and then died within a few days of each other the first year I was at seminary. But just think, Mira, if I had not stayed home to help, but instead come to school, I would have missed meeting you, and we would not be making plans to go together to Dakota Territory."

Mira said nothing, but snuggled up against him more closely. They still had so much to learn about each other.

"When soldiers stopped coming I moved into Grandpa and Grandma's cabin. We also began to use it as a lodge for weary travelers who stopped by. It was a potential source of income, but my parents being who they are, would receive a gift if offered, but they never charged a fee. How many times I heard them tell the story of how they were taken in, penniless, by the Piersons."

Priscilla shook her head, only slightly, but Mira knew she could not understand such altruism.

Franco continued, "Penniless then; almost penniless now, except that they did inherit Grandpa and Grandma's farm. So while there is little cash flow, at least they have an investment. Crops have improved in the last few years; that, plus my mother's salary from teaching have made it possible for me to study here. And they have assured me that they will come for my graduation, ordination, and our wedding. A neighbor will gladly watch over the property and do the chores. They even hinted at wanting to help us get 'outfitted' for the West, but I assured them that the church people from there have already told me to send little, as the previous pastor, in his hasty departure, left his goods behind. And supplies are readily available in Yankton. What we will find there will probably be more suitable for our needs than what we might purchase here."

Mira noticed the disappointed look on her father's face, for she knew he was hoping to send with them at least a boxcar full of supplies. "Father, I think we must listen to the advice from the people there. But anything you can do to help me with medical supplies will be most appreciated. And books—all kinds of them—of course."

Dr. Phillips smiled at her and said, "Then that is exactly what we will do." Mira could see him begin to compile a mental list. She figured it would probably fill a boxcar and any extra room could be used for all the trunks of clothes that Priscilla would insist on!

This turn in the conversation would propel them towards talking about the future rather than the past, however Dr. Phillips had one more thing to ask Franco about—his amazing grandfather, but the question would keep. The rest of the evening they would talk about wedding plans.

The following Saturday night Dr. Phillips once again opened the conversation, "Time is running short. If I know the two of you, the month of May will be spent studying, but for tonight Franco, I want to hear more about your grandfather. I'm sure he knew much about life that would benefit all of us. Can you think of any words of wisdom he might wish you to take to Dakota Territory?"

Franco paused as a flood of memories passed through his mind.

"Oh! Where shall I start? What he and Grandma and my parents taught me is so ingrained into who I am that to isolate any one thing is difficult." Franco paused again, and then began very soberly, "Grandpa's favorite Psalm was Psalm 46. He quoted it like this: *God is our refuge and strength, a shelter in the time of storm.* I heard him discuss this often with the soldiers. But my memory goes back much further than that. I was very frightened by thunder and lightning storms when I was a child. And I think that Grandpa had a healthy respect for storms, if not fear. I remember him often telling my father and mother that if they were out working and a storm came up *they must seek shelter* and not stay out in it, no matter what they were doing. *Seeking shelter in the storms of life—physical or spiritual*, was a guiding principle in my grandparents' life, and I am trying very much to make it a guiding principle for me, too."

Mira took his hand and held it tightly and whispered, "For us, Franco. For us."

Dr. Phillips fell into a deep meditation, and everyone was respectfully silent. After a long moment he said, "It would serve us all well."

Chapter 3 *West Comes East*

Pennsylvania was hardly *the West* and Hiram and Nina Welken were hardly *typical* western pioneers, given their roots in the high society of Boston. But it had been so many years—25 plus—that they had been **living** as pioneers. *What will it be like in the East once again?*

Franco was pensive as May began. His parents would be coming soon; there were mountains of studying, plans for ordination, final plans with their calling church in Dakota Territory, preparation for the move, and his desire to spend more and more time with Mira. Just to be near her; to get to know her better.

The Friday after final classes, and just before exams Franco and Mira received a wonderful and freeing surprise. Because both had maintained excellent academic standards throughout their years at seminary the school was not requiring them to take final written exams. Franklin would have to sit for one comprehensive oral exam on Wednesday of the following week, shortly before graduation.

The Sunday night before his parents were to arrive would be Franco's last night at the boarding-house. The Phillips had invited him to stay with them the remaining nights before going West, Dr. Phillips commenting with a chuckle, "Surely your school will not object, what with having two sets of parents to chaperon!"

This Sunday evening would be the only time remaining for Franklin and Mira to have an in-depth discussion until after heading west, and there was something that Franklin hoped could be resolved before they left. If it were not, it could erupt into negative consequences at a later date. He might not be able to solve the problem, but he could not in good conscience take Mira from her family without discussing it with her. He wished he had not waited this long.

Franklin liked Priscilla, but he knew that Mira harbored negative feelings towards her. Dr. Phillips always treated Priscilla with deepest respect. But why the coldness between mother and daughter? Franklin did not think that Priscilla was really a cold and hard woman. He had seen occasional moments of softness and warmth when certain feelings were expressed or comments were made. Perhaps his mother would be able to get through to Priscilla but he would not ask her to try. If that were to happen it would have to be as the ladies developed a friendship.

Before returning to his boarding-house for one last night Franco and Mira sat quietly discussing what ever came to mind, certainly his parents' arrival the next day. Franco wondering how his parents would react to the finer side of life once again, and Mira wondering how her mother would relate to house guests that she did not see as her social peers.

"Mira, let's just let our parents work it out; in many ways our parents are as different as the east is from the west, but they do have something wonderful in common—a daughter and son deeply in love, about to be married. *But I do wonder if I was wrong in not telling your parents more about my parents' life in Boston.*"

"No, Franco, I think you were exactly right, it is important that my mother accepts your parents for who they are—not for family lines or where they came from."

"I hope you are right. And speaking of your mother, Mira, I have been watching you and your mother, and there is something I must ask you."

Mira sat up straight and stiffened her back. "That's sounds serious."

"Yes, it might be—not that it will change anything between you and me . . ."

Mira let out a sigh of relief.

". . . but it is important."

"Franco, what is it?" she asked moving closer once again.

"Be prepared, Mira, my mother will shower you with love. You will be the daughter she never had, and I do not want *that* to be cause of further strain between you and your mother."

"Further strain?"

"Mira, honey, you **know** what I am talking about—the coolness, sometimes even sharpness between you and your mother."

Mira was slow to answer, her head bowed. Franco gently raised her chin so she would look directly at him. Her eyes were filled with tears, and her voice trembled as she responded, "Oh, Franco, I don't know. Your mother never had a daughter—that's one thing. But *my mother has no son.* I've often wondered if that might be behind her coolness toward me; her disappointment in me."

Franco said nothing, giving Mira opportunity to further explore her thoughts. "I just know I have never lived up to her expectations for me. As I examine my life and choices I have made, I wonder if I subconsciously chose medicine and theology *because if I were male that would make a mother proud.* But Franco, when I closely examine that thought, I know I chose to follow those lines of study because that's where my interests lie, and I believe that is where God has led me. So where does that leave me in relation to my mother?"

Mira paused. Franco remained silent, waiting for her to go on.

"She seems frustrated that I have so little interest in social life with other young people; the world of parties, and fine clothing. She abhors the thought of me riding horse astraddle. She thinks it crude and vulgar. I don't think she knows that I carry a gun. And as a matter of fact Franco, I have even been carrying it, concealed, when walking to and from classes. Which means I have had it with me on campus, including classrooms and the library. And by the way, I will be taking my pistol west with me. Father insists."

"I understand, Mira. I'll be taking a rifle. I hear hunting is good, even necessary for food. But we digress."

"I know. So, getting back to mother. She seems distant much of the time, *almost as if her mind is on something else, or somewhere else*, rather than on our own family. Yet she never goes anywhere or does anything except to church and a few social activities with Father. I wonder if, since I am a girl, she is disappointed that she and Father have not been able to have more children. Father told me she had a very difficult time while pregnant with me, and with my delivery, and should never have another child. The only time I felt close to my mother was when together we took care of a baby boy for six months whose mother died following childbirth. After we returned him to his father, Mother was silent and melancholic for months. Gradually she improved. But Franco, *it's your visits that have brought some joy to her once again*. Even if she doesn't much show it, Franco, she loves you, and I fear that she will become despondent again after we leave."

"Mira, I'm sorry, *but please do not carry your mother's inability to have another baby, or your being female instead of male, as your own personal burden of guilt*, even as I will not feel guilty for leaving and taking you with me. Her feelings and difficulty in dealing with reality are not our fault. But it is something that your parents have to deal with in an adult and godly manner."

"I know, Franco, but it's hard not to think about it, especially when I have memories of going to my grandparents' house—Mother's parents—when I was a small child. Mother would play with their little orphan boy and ignore me."

"*Orphan boy?*"

"Yes. He was a few years older than I—not very well behaved, but my mother seemed to be intrigued by him."

"How in the world . . . ?"

"I know what you are going to ask. Years ago when Mother was 16 or 18 she and her mother took a long trip to Europe to tour and visit relatives. There they heard about a distant cousin who had recently been orphaned. Both mother and grandmother *fell in love* with the adorable little boy with auburn hair, so the story goes." (Franklin glanced at Mira's auburn hair.) "They took him home. My grandparents raised him as their own; they had no son. The label, *distant cousin Pete* stuck; that is how we always referred to him, and still do."

"And your mother—what is her relationship with your grandparents and cousin now?"

"We don't see much of her parents—my grandparents. Maybe once or twice a year. Distant cousin Pete, as I said, is older than I and left home a few years ago. He was a Union soldier in the War, and survived with a leg wound that my father treated when he returned home. But he was restless. Word has it that he headed for Oregon, and as far as I know, no one has heard from him."

"Your mother—does she ever talk about him?"

"No." There was a note of finality in Mira's response and she and Franco discussed her mother, cousin, or grandparents no further that evening. But Franco remained concerned about Mira's attitude toward her mother. Both of them were capable of deep and loving expressions, he was sure. *So what was keeping them apart? And what would the mother-daughter relationship between Mira and his own mother that was sure to develop do to the tenuous relationship between Mira and her mother?*

He considered consulting Dr. Phillips, but realizing that since this was a personal matter rather than professional, it would perhaps be uncomfortable for the otherwise objective doctor.

The Phillips' carriage stopped by Franklin's boarding-house Monday morning at 8:00 AM to pick him up and then head to the train station. He had his one suitcase of clothes with him. All, but the few books he still needed, was boxed and would be delivered to the train station early on the day of departure. Franklin was nervous—he had not seen his parents for the three years he was at school. *What would they be like? How had time and hard work affected them? How would they be dressed?* Mira was excited, and a little nervous too. She tried to pin the reason for her nerves on the meeting of the two mothers. Priscilla sat primly, what she was thinking no one knew. Only Dr. Phillips seemed completely at ease. He saw no reason to worry and fret. His only concern—but he would not express it—was that this same train would soon be going the opposite direction with his daughter on it. *Would he ever see her again?* That gave him pause. Even the forward looking doctor did not envision the improvement in travel and communication that would be happening in coming years.

Franklin spotted them the moment they descended from the train car, his father giving his mother a hand. Franklin ran to them and gave his mother a warm embrace, and then turning to his father did the same. Mira and her parents slowly made their way towards the Welkens, giving them a moment or two to reunite. But Franklin was eager to get to the introductions. "Mother, Father, please meet Dr. and Mrs. Phillips and Miranda." Dr. Phillips shook their hands and quickly said "Welcome, and to you we are Charles and Priscilla." Nina was eager to enfold Mira in an embrace, but her good manners restrained her as she was greeted by and returned the greeting from Priscilla. Then turning to Mira she opened her arms and as Mira moved towards her she wrapped her in a warm embrace and whispered, "I am so pleased to meet you, Mira-honey. I can't tell you how much I and Franklin's father have been looking forward to this day. What a happy time for us all." Mira was so choked with emotion that all she could do was return the hug and nod her head in agreement.

"Now it's my turn to meet this young lady," Hiram said as Nina passed Mira off to him for a warm embrace and words of greeting. Priscilla watched carefully, taking in their clothing. Hiram wore a conservative, but not dated, dark suit. Nina, a lovely dark green dress with a gathered skirt, but no hoops (and by Priscilla's judgment, no petticoats); a fitted bodice revealing a lovely slim figure, high neckline with a collar of white lace, and fitted, long sleeves. Her hat, or rather bonnet, was of the same fabric, complementing her dress, however, by Priscilla's standards, terribly dated; not what was worn in the east by ladies. But Priscilla did concede to herself that Nina was lovely, and her graciousness in her greetings impeccable. And Hiram? Well, it took only a moment or two of observing and interacting with him to know from where Franklin got his fine qualities and manners. Priscilla took it all in, and determined that she would get to know them in this visit, and find out about their background.

Mira had yet to speak. She had been prepared for a hug from Franco's mother, but not quite his father. Even Franco's face registered surprise. He had only ever seen his father interact with young men—himself, and the many young soldiers who had passed through their home.

Franco came to Mira's side and took her hand while Dr. Phillips invited them to the carriage, saying, "We can take your luggage now, or have it delivered. What is your choice?"

Hiram responded, "We are traveling light, only the one suitcase that we have with us. Let's take it now."

Priscilla noted the suitcase, and wondered how they could possibly have enough clothing for two weeks, including what they would wear to the wedding. Then the thought struck her *maybe they plan to wear what they are wearing now. It's not bad, but it's not* wedding attire, *either.*

As if she could perceive Priscilla's thoughts, Nina said, "Oh Priscilla, I hope you will come shopping with me—and perhaps Charles with Hiram. It has been so many years since we have been in a fancy store, I'm not sure we know how to do that kind of shopping anymore."

Priscilla came through with grace (more grace than Mira, who was still speechless as she took this all in) saying with enthusiasm, "We can do that as early as tomorrow—or if you like we can hire my dressmaker. My dress is finished, as is most of Miranda's new clothing, so if you'd like, I can contact her today, giving her more than a week to get it done. Perhaps you would like to see our dresses as soon as we get home, to see if you like her sewing. As for as Hiram and Charles shopping together, may I rather suggest Charles' tailor?"

Nina took her up on her offer, and Franklin would take his father to the tailor as Dr. Phillips had his practice to attend to. Mira was no longer helping him.

Mira marveled at her mother's graciousness towards the Welkens, and at the same time was a bit suspicious. Was her mother up to something? As for Priscilla, she was wondering *what did Nina mean when she said she was not sure they knew* how to do that kind of shopping any more. *There must have been a time when their life was very different from what it is now. What is the story of their going west?* She would find out, but very carefully.

The Welkens settled in with surprising ease at the Phillips' house. Their manners were perfect. They were conversational, not overbearing with their own stories of eking out a living on a farm during hard times. They spoke freely of their life with the Piersons, and the years of feeding and caring for soldiers. But one thing they did not talk about was their early years in Boston. The one thing that Priscilla wanted to know more than anything else, but her own good manners restrained her. She bided her time.

Tuesday, while Franco took his father to the tailor the three women went to the dressmaker. The day before Priscilla had a private conversation with the dressmaker, insisting that she scale down the price of all her fabrics and her charge for making the dress. Priscilla would make it up to her later, and Nina would never know, as she was not familiar with current prices for fine fabrics. Dr. Phillips did the same with the tailor and suggested that he talk Franklin into a new suit as well.

Nina was a dressmaker's dream. Tall, slender, perfectly proportioned; black hair that was just beginning to silver at the temples. If she had a distracting feature, it was slightly stooped shoulders coming from years of hard work. But that was easily remedied with a graceful waist length cape of silver fabric which tapered towards the back from the hook which fastened it just below the high fitted bodice of her dress. The silver of the cape accentuated the silver embossing of the satin burgundy dress and picked up on the silver in her hair. The neckline was high, and sleeves long, slightly gathered at the shoulder. The skirt fell in gentle gathers from an inverted "V" that reached up to just below the bodice. Her gloves were a matching burgundy, and her hat was made of black felt, with a small band of silver and a dainty feather.

At the reasonable price the dressmaker offered, Nina selected fabric for two other dresses, the dressmaker assuring her that these two dresses would be ready by the weekend so she could wear them to Franklin's graduation and ordination, and the other in time for the wedding. Nina was excited and Priscilla very pleased. Mira wondered if she should tell Franco about the *deceit*, but decided against it, at least for the time being. Maybe their mutual joy and enthusiasm was the bridge that would open conversation and genuine friendship between the women.

Franklin and Hiram came home from their first fitting, both pleased with the reasonable price of the tailor. Franklin had resigned himself to wear his worn suit. This new suit would serve him well for "Sunday preaching" in the West for many years to come. Hiram knew that he too would wear his suit until it was threadbare, and he would wear it with pride and joy.

The week passed swiftly, Mira drilling and grilling Franco every spare moment in final preparation for his oral exam. Following the exam, the professors held a brief conference, and then congratulated Franklin for doing well. He returned to the Phillips' house thoroughly relieved, and was greeted by words of congratulations and a dinner to celebrate not only his, but also Mira's outstanding success in seminary. They would always look at their academic achievement as a mutual accomplishment.

Nina had several fittings that week. Miranda and her mother were busy packing, unpacking, and repacking trunks—Priscilla had ordered several new large trunks, insisting on voluminous petticoats, corsets, hoops and hats, with the promise to send more later if needed. Nina took Miranda aside and told her, "Mira-honey, no disrespect to your mother, but you will not want to wear those things in the west. They will be far too cumbersome for the work you will do; special occasions, maybe, but believe me, once you rid yourself of them, you'll never want them back. But take them anyway; they will make wonderful curtains and baby clothes!" So Miranda thanked her mother for her thoughtfulness, and then in a private moment added her jodhpurs, leather drawers, boots, and locked that trunk. (Her pistol she would carry in her handbag.) When Priscilla wanted to make changes—that is more repacking—Mira held her ground. "Thanks, Mother, but this trunk is perfect just as it is. It cannot hold one more petticoat, dress or hat; not even anything small. The other three trunks can still use some readjustment, and as each is completed we will lock them, too. Not to be opened until Franco and I are in our new home in Dakota Territory." Though her words were firm, she said them with a smile, thinking of curtains, baby clothes, and riding gear. Priscilla was pleased with Mira's smile, and pushed Mira no more on packing her clothing. Next week would be spent on household items. They would use Priscilla's old steamer trunks for that.

    The graduation ceremony was Friday afternoon in the church that the Phillips attended. Miranda and both sets of parents sat near the front, Dr. Phillips insisting that Miranda sit near the aisle, and he sat next to her. Following the handing out of diplomas to the graduates and giving other awards and recognitions, both the President and Dean approached the podium.
    The President began, "We have one more award that is a first for this seminary. When we announce the person's name we ask you to withhold your applause and comments. *Will Miss Miranda Phillips please come forward?*"
    A hush fell over the audience, but Miranda did not move, unsure of what she had heard. As she paused the Dean said, "Miss Phillips, if you are here, please come forward." Still she sat, but Dr. Phillips, ready for the moment, rose and gently helped her up, whispering, "Mira, you are being called, let me give you a hand." As he walked her to the stage and up the steps, Franklin stepped forward from his seat on the stage and walked with Mira to the podium. She relaxed, feeling his strength and support, even when he stepped back to his seat.
    "Miss Phillips, you have finished a two year course with straight "A"s in every subject. And you are the first and only woman to have attended this all male seminary. You reached our high standards for excellence without much recognition or support from the faculty—for this

we apologize, and the best excuse we can give is: this is *new territory* for us, too, and has required some readjustment in our thinking.

"We cannot give you a diploma, because your course of study—as it now stands—leads to neither graduation nor diploma. But it is an honor for us to recognize what you have accomplished by giving you this *certificate of achievement.*"

Miranda received it with the grace she had learned from her parents—a smile and slight nod of her head.

The President continued, asking Miranda to remain near the podium, "Change will be coming soon to our Seminary. At a recent Board meeting it was decided that beginning next Fall, we will open the doors to all women who qualify, to take a two year Biblical and Theological curriculum—much like what you took, Miss Phillips. It is a change that was not easy for many of us to agree to because we are an old school, steeped in tradition. You have shown an amazing example, and we recognize that times are changing. Successful completion of this new course of study will lead to graduation and a diploma.

"Miss Phillips, we want you to know that the first diploma will be yours, and I am now personally inviting you to participate in that future graduation ceremony to receive your well-deserved diploma. If you live far from here—as we hear you will—we invite you to come back for the occasion; if that is not possible, we will send you your diploma. Either way, the first diploma offered by this new course of study—very similar to what you have done—will be yours. Now, we invite you to comment."

Miranda felt dazed, but she regained her composure as she took a deep breath (something her father had taught her to do in stressful situations). She looked at the President and Dean and then her father, mother, and Franklin's parents, and the audience. Miranda who had never spoken publicly found her voice. (Franco told her later her was praying for her.) She turned again to the President and Dean, and her words flowed smoothly. "Thank you. To receive that diploma will be a great honor, even as hearing your kind and gracious words, and receiving this *certificate of achievement* is an honor. As many of you know, Franklin Welken and I will soon be married and then plan to move to Dakota Territory to serve the Lord, by serving the pioneers there. I know that what we have learned here will benefit us well. So on behalf of Franklin, our parents, and myself, I thank the Seminary." She smiled, and in a gesture of respect, slightly inclined her head, and shook hands with the President and Dean. Despite the President's request to withhold applause, there was scattered response in the audience and among the graduates. Franklin came forward again and walked Mira to her seat to rejoin their parents. She could feel their pride radiate. Even her mother smiled, and whispered to Miranda, "You have done us proud."

No matter the position one held on the very tenuous subject, no one found fault with the graciousness of the President, the Dean and Miranda. That would go a long way toward future progress.

Friday evening and Saturday were spent quietly in the Phillips household. Franklin's ordination was part of the Sunday morning worship service, and he would be preaching. Mira insisted that he wear his wedding suit—after all he would soon regularly wear it for preaching. Charles and Hiram wore their new suits as well.

After the service a dinner was held in honor of Franklin and Miranda's accomplishments; it also served as a "send-off" dinner, since the following weekend would be filled with wedding activities. As Miranda listened to the many well-deserved words of praise that Franklin received for his preaching, a thought stirred within her: *I never knew that I could speak publicly, but I did just briefly on Friday. It came so naturally; I wonder . . .*

Well, she could not think about it at the moment but later that afternoon when she and Franco had a few moments alone together she told him about what had entered her mind. "Franco, I never have spoken publicly until my brief comments Friday afternoon. I was totally non-prepared for the moment. Yet the words just came . . ."

"I know, Mira, I was praying for you, and the Lord gave you the words."

"Yes, I believe that, and I thank you for your prayer and your unwavering support. But it was more than your support, and more than words from the Lord. *I loved the **feeling** of talking to an audience. Even as I believe you love it, Franco.*"

"Mira-honey, what are you telling me? What are you asking? What are you suggesting?"

"That's the problem, Franco. I don't know. But I do know that speaking publicly felt right and natural."

"I don't know what it means, either. Let's wait and see what unfolds. I have a feeling that there will be opportunities for both of us in Dakota that neither of us have yet imagined. Step by step God has opened amazing doors for us. Let's wait and see what happens, and then go through the doors as God opens the way. *I'll probably be delivering babies while you are delivering sermons!*" Franco said with a grin.

Mira smiled in response, grateful that he was open minded.

"Oh, I know you are right, Franco. And I am not trying to rush anything. But I did want you to know what I experienced. I am so excited. I feel like a big unknown is opening up in front of us, and beckoning us to come and serve."

Mira paused, and when Franco said nothing, she went on, "Franco, do you think that when the time comes for the Seminary to give me the diploma, we might be able to come East to receive it?"

"Mira, that's certainly something we would not want to miss. But remember, a new plan such as the President was talking about, could take years to accomplish. It is one thing to open a program to women. It is another thing for them to come, and to complete the course. This is a very new, and quite a radical undertaking. Let's hope and pray that there will be success, but let's not be disappointed if it does not happen in two years' time."

Mira knew he was right. Her father had already, in a private moment on Saturday given her the same advice. He had also told her that he would do everything in his power to make it happen. He had spoken with such passion that she suspected that he was already at work.

The next several days passed in frenzied activity. Dr. Phillips, while continuing to attend his medical practice found time to work with Franco and Hiram in packing medical supplies—carbolic acid, chloroform, laudanum, and various homeopathic remedies; instruments and office equipment for examination of patients; books on anatomy of the human body; medical books and journals, particularly those that would help Miranda prepare remedies from plants that grew, or could be grown in Dakota. He included seeds for many such plants, although Hiram cautioned Franco that by the time they arrived, it would be too late in the growing season to plant for the current year. Franco reiterated what he had been told earlier—to not ship tools and implements for gardening, as the previous pastor had left his behind and such supplies were also available in Yankton. The packed supplies were stored at the depot with the instructions that they be loaded on a railway car that would take them all the way to Yankton.

Though Priscilla had never spent a day in her life doing housework or cooking she was insistent that Miranda be well supplied. Tensions began to rise, Miranda wanting to severely limit what was sent, even reminding her mother that supplies were available in Yankton. Furthermore, it was not likely that she would do formal entertaining. Nina had several dress fittings, but sensing the tensions, offered her help. She was about to suggest taking *bare essentials*, but when she saw the lovely silver and China that Priscilla had already purchased, her eyes filled with the tears of a painful memory. And not only that, she intuitively knew that what she would say now would impact the future relationship she would have with Priscilla and Mira, as well as the mother-daughter relationship of Priscilla and Mira. "Mira-honey, your mother is wise in suggesting that you take these beautiful dishes and silver. Although I have not told her my experience, she understands how important beautiful things are. I remember so clearly how in the first years of living in poverty in Pennsylvania I longed *just to see, just to hold*, something beautiful. But we had nothing beautiful, nothing lovely. Nothing from our past, except the small gift Hiram gave me on the night before our marriage. Take these gifts from your mother and let them be a link to your life here in the East." Then turning to Priscilla she said, "Thank you, Priscilla, for your understanding and thoughtfulness."

Priscilla looked a little blank, not *really* understanding the significance of Nina's words. Mira, in respect for Nina and her obvious deep feeling, turned to her mother and thanked her for the lovely gifts and assured her that she and Franco would use them with fond memories of the many wonderful evenings, including dinners that the four of them had enjoyed in the past couple years.

The tensions were eased and the rest of the packing went well, filling three steamer trunks. These trunks, along with Mira's trunks of clothing were sent to the depot for shipping to Yankton. When Franco saw it all—to say nothing of what remained to be purchased in Yankton— he shuddered, thinking to himself that there would have to be at least two, maybe three, wagon trips between Yankton and Chipps.

The days were busy, but the evenings were spent in family time. Nina's dress was delivered Thursday afternoon while Franco and Mira were finalizing wedding ceremony plans with the pastor, and Priscilla and Charles were reviewing the reception list and plans. The reception would follow the private church ceremony and would be held at the Phillips' house, open to friends from church, and longtime patients from Dr. Phillip's practice—especially those who knew Mira well.

Nina used this time to model her dress for Hiram. While appreciating her beauty, he bowed his head in sorrow. "Hiram, whatever is the matter. I thought you would . . ."

"Please, don't misunderstand. I've never seen you look more lovely. And that's just the problem. I am reminded of all you have given up and how you have lived in poverty all these years, and never a word of complaint."

"Oh Hiram, I haven't given up a thing, and neither have you. It all was *taken* from us, but we are by far the richer for it. I would not change a thing about our lives. I would not exchange the *riches* we have in Pennsylvania with the *wealth* we had in Boston. Never, ever."

"Do you really mean that, Nina?"

"Yes, I do, with all my heart. But I am also happy to enjoy these couple weeks with the Phillips. They are most generous people. And just think of how our lives have been enriched by their daughter, Franklin's lovely bride."

"If you are happy, Nina, then I am content. And she is lovely, isn't she? Franklin has done well, in many ways."

"Indeed he has. I wish that the Phillips might visit us some day. I truly do love Priscilla. She is kind-of the sister I never had. I just wish that she and Mira were closer. And not only that, there is something about her that is so sad; so *missing*. With more time, I might be able to break through. There is a mystery about her."

"Have you noticed, Nina, how Charles adores her?"

"Oh, yes. Have you asked him about her?"

"No. It doesn't seem appropriate to do so. I did ask Franklin. He too is concerned, especially about the relationship between Mira and Priscilla. Franklin sees the sadness in Priscilla, and has asked Mira about it. He mentioned three things that seem significant. An intrigue that Priscilla had years ago with an orphan boy that her parents raised as their own son; her difficult pregnancy with Mira, and not being able to safely have another child; and a baby boy that Mira delivered whose mother died. Priscilla and Mira took care of this baby for six months in the Phillips' home, and were finally able to return him to his father. Priscilla went into a deep, lengthy melancholia after this. Mira told Franklin that it was not until he started to visit with regularity that Priscilla finally fully recovered."

"Well, it seems quite clear to me—Priscilla is bitter because she does not have a son, and Mira had to bear the brunt of it. Now with Franklin leaving, I fear for Priscilla's mental health."

"And that, my dear, we can do nothing about, except pray."

"That we will."

They sat together in deep thought. Finally Hiram broke the silence, "Nina, this changes the subject, but I think you will like what I have to say. When we were at the railroad station Franklin and I inquired about the possibility of him and Mira getting off with us—it is right on the way—and spending a few days. It would be good for Franklin to be home, and to share it with Mira. Guess what! There is no extra fare; all they need to do is be back at the depot when a west bound train comes through, and get on. Isn't it marvelous, *the day we live in*!? Remember us 25 years ago with worn out horses and a dilapidated wagon. Franklin was able to send a telegraph to Yankton and have the message carried to the people in Chipps to let them know of a four day delay in their arrival."

"Oh, Hiram! What a marvelous idea! Does Mira know? And yes I can remember us 25 years ago—kind of like what Mira and Franklin will have once they leave the train at Yankton. And they won't have the Piersons. But I'm not worried. They will get along just fine, with many wonderful people to help and support them."

"Would you like me to answer your question?"

"What question?"

"*Does Mira know*? No, she doesn't know. Franklin wants to wait until Sunday to tell her. She has enough on her mind right now. They will be carrying traveling necessities with them."

"This is so wonderful, I don't know if I will be able to not tell her." She paused, but Hiram said nothing until she added, "But I won't."

"If you have a hard time, think of Franklin. I don't know if *he* will be able to keep it to himself that long."

"I think our home will be a good place for Mira to shed her first set of petticoats. We do need some new curtains."

"Curtains, or baby clothes?" Hiram asked in fun, remembering the baby clothes Nina and Mrs. Pierson had made from Nina's petticoats.

"How about *both*?"

Now it was Hiram's time to be surprised. "What are you saying, Nina?" he asked with alarm in his voice. While Nina had a good sense of humor, she never joked about anything serious. This sounded serious.

"I was going to wait to tell you until we are back home—but I can't wait; I'm going to have a baby, Hiram!"

"You are *what*? . . . You are going to have a baby, Nina?"

"Yes, I didn't know for sure, but the dressmaker suspected. She promised not to tell. Didn't you notice the high and flaring waistline of the two new dresses I wore this past weekend, and now this dress for the wedding?"

"But Nina, you can't go on the basis of what your dressmaker suspects. Maybe she just wanted an excuse for making dresses this style. I will say that the style is absolutely stunning on you. What you have been hiding you are hiding very well. No one, other than a dressmaker, would guess."

"Oh, Hiram, I wanted to be sure before I told you. And I am not going on the basis of my dressmaker's suspicion. I hope you don't mind, but when I was out for one of my fittings, I stopped by Charles' office. He agrees—I'm pregnant. But not only that, he finds me in perfect health, and very strong from years of hard work. He says that while it is rather uncommon for a woman in her middle forties to be pregnant, it certainly can and does happen. He feels that with taking good care of myself—eating well and keeping physically active—I should be able to go full term and have a healthy baby. Hiram, isn't it a most amazing thing? I've never felt better than what I feel right now."

"It truly is amazing and I rejoice with you. And I don't mind at all that you spoke with Charles. In fact, I am glad you did."

"Don't forget—you had a part in it too! And will continue to have a part, even as you have been with me through other pregnancies."

Again they were silent, thinking of a couple small graves on their property. Franklin wasn't their only child. Nina had two other pregnancies that she was not able to carry to term.

But this was not a time to dwell on sadness. Nina jumped up with an idea. "Hiram, if I can get Priscilla and Mira to agree, how about if all three of us model our dresses for you and Charles and Franklin tonight after dinner? I know that it's not a traditional thing to do, but so what? I think I can get Priscilla and Mira to agree. After modeling our dresses, Franklin could give Mira *my cross*. I know that also would be breaking with tradition, as it has always been given the night before the wedding, but this just seems like the right time. Wouldn't it be wonderful to see Mira wear it for a whole day before the wedding? And I can't wait to see Priscilla's face when she sees it!"

"Great ideas, Nina, both of them. Franklin will agree to giving the cross tonight, I'm sure. And if they are who I think they are, they will like the idea of a fashion show—if it is the three of you modeling." Hiram paused a moment, and then went on with a chuckle, "Franklin has already asked if we brought the cross. He was expecting to see you wearing it. You should have seen his face when I told him we forgot it."

"Hiram, you didn't tell him *that*, did you?"

"He believed it only for a moment. His relief was so great when I told him I was joking, I felt sorry for him. I think he aged ten years in one moment."

"Just one more thing . . ."

"No more surprises, please Nina, I've had about all I can handle for the day."

"No more surprises. Just remember, *I still have to convince Priscilla and Mira to don their dresses for the three of you. They are both strong-willed women. They might not think it proper.*"

"I'm not worried. You are very persuasive."

Nina went off to find Mira and Priscilla. To her delight they were as excited as she. All agreed, however, that none would wear their complete ensemble for this "showing." No hats, no gloves, Nina no cape, Mira no bustle, train, or veil. That all would wait until *the day*.

Hiram found Charles and Franklin in the library. Franklin asked, "Did you have a good rest?"

"No rest, just lots of talk."

"After all these years you still have that much to talk about?"

"More than a young man like you might think possible." Hiram glanced at Charles, who gave him a sly grin and a wink.

"Anything I can help you with?"

"Thanks, not at the moment. There are plans for tonight, however— Franklin, your mother and I would like you to give Mira her gift tonight. That way we can all see her wear it for one day before the wedding." Franklin expressed his joy and approval. Then Hiram continued, "Also, we are invited to a *fashion show* after dinner."

Franklin and Charles both groaned. As if they had ever *been* to a fashion show!

"Oh, don't worry. You will enjoy this one. It will be held in this house, in the parlor I presume, and the three models will be Priscilla, Nina, and Mira—that is, if Nina can convince the other two."

"She will, I'm sure of it." Franklin knew his mother well. When it came to fun and innovation, no one could say *no* to her ideas.

"Charles, our time is getting short. Only a few more days before we leave. In all this frenzy of activity we have hardly had a chance to talk. Do you have any free time tomorrow, now that we have all the goods packed and at the depot."

"We'll find time. How about stopping by my office tomorrow afternoon? It's in walking distance from our house."

As the men retired to the parlor after dinner the women helped each other dress—so many unreachable buttons. Nina and Mira insisted that Priscilla lead the way to the parlor. The men stood as Priscilla entered first, elegant as always. Her dress was a silk, dusty rose. The tightly fitted bodice was overlaid with lace, which formed a high neckline and collar. The long sleeves were of the same lace. The bodice dipped into a low "V" at the waist, accentuating her trimness. Yards of silk, supported by many petticoats and a below-the-knee hoop, cascaded from the waist.

After she was sure that Priscilla had heard many well deserved words of praise, Nina entered. Hiram kept his comments in check as Charles and Franklin exclaimed over her loveliness. For the first time in her life Priscilla acknowledged to herself that she was not the most beautiful woman in the room, and surprisingly did not feel threatened. For the first time in life she realized that the truest beauty—Nina's—came from within and had little to do with style, figure or face. Although Nina lacked none of those. This dress certainly had style, and her flashing blue eyes, heart-shaped face with high cheekbones and full lips that held an almost perpetual smile, engaged anyone who looked her way. After receiving the words of praise with a slight nod of her head, Nina stepped aside to join Priscilla, taking her hand. Both women knew that the evening was not theirs. It was Mira's.

Mira entered to the acclaim of everyone. Franklin was overwhelmed. He had never seen Mira wear such a lovely dress. Her choice of clothing was usually very plain. Even though her attire was incomplete without train, bustle and veil she looked lovely, her dress similar in style to Nina's with the high inverted "V" waist and skirt cascading in gathers from the bodice; her skirt however, was made of three tiers of light green silk; and as with Priscilla's dress, the bodice was overlaid with lace, forming a high neckline with collar; the sleeves, of the same lace were tailored to the wrist, with a small puff of gathers at the shoulder. On their wedding day the dress would be completed with a train of lace that would attach with small buttons to the high waist. A small bustle would be worn under the top tier. For her veil Mira had chosen a sheer, very light green silk that shimmered with a silver sheen. The veil was gathered by an ornate silver clasp that was studded with several red cut-glass stones, to rest atop her hair. The front of the veil would fall just below her chin, and the back would cascade to reach her train.

Mira, unaccustomed to words of praise about her appearance was glad to hear Hiram say, "And now one more surprise before the evening is over." With that he handed Franco a small box. Mira, thinking that the attention would now turn to Franco, started to walk towards Nina and Priscilla who were already moving towards the men.

"Mira-honey, come here. I can finally give you what I promised you long ago when I asked you to marry me."

Nina took Mira's hand, keeping Priscilla's in her other and they joined Franco in as he opened the box. He reverently withdrew a silver filigree cross. The crossbeams were encircled by a delicate crown, inset with tiny rubies. After the initial exclamations over its beauty a hush fell over everyone as Franco hung it around Mira's neck and firmly secured the clasp.

"Franco, thank you. I've never seen anything so beautiful. Please tell us the story that goes with it."

"This cross has been in the Welken family longer than anyone can remember. Legend has it that it goes back to the crusades—purchased in Jerusalem. We have not been able to verify that. But it has long been the Welkens' dearest treasure. That it was not *lost* in the financial crash is a story I do not yet know. Maybe someday you will tell us, Father? Mother? It is always to be given by the eldest son to his bride the *night before* the marriage. To say this always was done, we cannot verify either, and tonight we break just slightly with the tradition. We are giving it *two nights* before our marriage—my parents wanting to see Mira wear it, as our remaining time together is growing very short."

"Nina, this cross also obviously survived your accident in Pennsylvania. What have you done with it all these years?" Priscilla asked.

"It is the only thing that survived the accident, besides ourselves, our horses and a few drenched pieces of clothing. I was wearing it at the time, and have worn it every day since. And Mira-honey that is what we want you to do. Wear it every day, until you pass it on to the next generation. It has little value in a box."

Mira nodded and gently touched it. "I will. How can I ever thank you all?"

It was Hiram who responded, "Mira-honey, Nina has said many times that the day she received this cross was the happiest day of her life, and the next happiest day will be the day Franklin gives it to his bride. That day has come. It is a happy day for us all." With that they all, the Phillips and Welkens, gathered in a group embrace, and Franco offered a brief prayer of thanksgiving.

Charles stepped back from the group and rang for a bottle of wine, stating, "We are not drinking families, but an occasion such as this calls for a toast."

As they relaxed with their small glasses of wine, Priscilla could not take her eyes off the cross. Suddenly she more fully remembered the story she had heard years ago of a young couple leaving Boston after the loss of their family wealth, with nothing but a priceless family heirloom. She had heard of the accident along the way—that they had perished in a river after their buggy overturned.

That was the last Priscilla had heard of the story, and had dismissed it from her mind. Now she remembered the story in sharper detail and realized that Hiram and Nina were the young people who had "perished." Suddenly the mystery of Nina and Hiram was solved for Priscilla. Their families had been far wealthier than the family Priscilla had come from, and had held more social class than hers. Priscilla also realized that for all the treasures she could shower on Miranda, nothing could compare to the cross, or the class that was inherent in both Hiram and Nina. It was another first for Priscilla —the first time in her life, or at least the first time in many years—that she felt *almost* content, for she felt accepted by people who came from higher social standing than herself. Nina and Hiram had that rare quality of helping others feel comfortable with who they are and what they have, because they completely accepted each person as they are. They had no airs about themselves. If asked, the Welkens would have said that the true lessons of life had come from the years of living the pioneer life with the Piersons, not from Boston high society.

During the night Mira heard a knock on the front door. Out of habit she got up, dressed quickly, and reached for her medical bag. Only when she did not find it in its usual place did she remember that she did not *have* to go out! But why not accompany her father one last time? She joined him at the door as he was reassuring a distraught man that he would be out shortly.

One last night of work with her father! What a privilege, to say nothing of time for talking in the buggy as they returned home, Dr. Phillips holding back the horse from barnstorming. The delivery had gone smoothly, and they were home in time for an 8:00 AM breakfast. Mira then went to bed and slept until 2:00 PM, while Dr. Phillips went to his office.

The Phillips' household was amazingly calm Friday afternoon and evening. Charles and Hiram returned from the office at four thirty, in time for tea, followed by a late dinner. Charles excused himself to go to bed, as he had little rest the night before. The others enjoyed coffee and dessert in the parlor, Franco and Mira talking together, and Priscilla, still curious, asked Nina and Hiram about life in Boston. They told her that they had never been back, and both sets of parents had died in poverty only a few years after the financial collapse. Other than that, they turned the conversations to life in Pennsylvania. And attempted to draw Priscilla out on her own life, but she showed no willingness to talk about it.

The wedding ceremony, with only a few people in attendance went smoothly, just as Franco and Mira had it planned. The reception, also well planned, was a wonderful time of celebration. Mira wore her full wedding ensemble, to the delight of her patients who had only ever seen her dressed very plainly, often in her riding habit. Amid expressions of congratulations and well wishes many words of appreciation were given to both Mira and Dr. Phillips for their dedication to promoting health in the community. Some brought their "babies," now in various stages of growth; even the baby who Priscilla and Mira had taken care of for six months. Now four or five years old, he won the heart of everyone present, but Priscilla kept her distance, perhaps to protect her own heart. Saying good-bye to all these people who had done so much to grow and mature her as she served them was difficult for Mira. Franco, Hiram, and Nina watched with growing admiration. Dr. Phillips graciously walked each guest to the door with a word of thanks. Priscilla smiled her appreciation, perhaps with even a small amount of pride in her daughter.

Sundays were quiet days at the Phillips' house, including morning church, meals requiring only minimal preparation and clean-up, and time for rest, reading, and conversation. The day after the wedding was no exception. Franco and Mira took one last walk through the Seminary campus. Hiram asked Priscilla to accompany him on a walk through the neighborhood, giving Charles an opportunity to engage Nina in a private conversation.

"Nina, I have already told Hiram and he has agreed to me telling you—Priscilla and I will come out to Pennsylvania for your delivery."

At the surprised look on her face Charles responded, "No, I haven't told Priscilla about your baby yet; nor have I told Franklin and Mira. I'm sure you and Hiram want to tell them yourselves. With your permission I will tell Priscilla after you leave."

Nina nodded, "You are free to tell Priscilla; but I am very surprised that you and Priscilla would come all the way to Pennsylvania for my delivery! You don't expect that something is wrong, do you? Or did Hiram twist your arm?"

"*No!* to both questions. You are fine, and it was my idea. Hiram did not twist my arm! It is something I want for you and Hiram, and the baby. With your permission, of course."

"Thank you! Our appreciation is deep. But we must talk about Priscilla. How do you think she will handle . . .?"

"Then you know about her sorrow about not having another child?"

"I don't really *know*. I've just sensed it."

"Well, facts are facts—you are expecting, Nina, and Priscilla must know sooner or later. So in the next week or two I will tell her."

"*Facts are facts*, Charles, but our sensitivity to Priscilla's feelings is also important. How will she feel about you knowing, and not her?"

"I didn't mean to sound calloused. Priscilla's feelings are extremely important to me, and I am glad they are to you also. She will handle my knowing before her well. She has always respected that as a doctor people confide in me, and that I respect their privacy. That will be no problem. But it is possible that some of her lifelong sorrow over not having another child will surface. I hope it will not result in melancholia, or jealousy."

They were both silent for some time, feeling deeply pain that Priscilla had lived with for many years.

Charles broke the silence, "You know, Nina, other than me, she has few friends; few people she trusts. I don't know how you, and Hiram, too—even Franklin—broke through to her."

Nina smiled, "Charles, you, I, Hiram, and Franklin accept her just as she is, and love her unconditionally. Our big concern is that Mira isn't there yet. Hiram and I will be praying that someday the relationship will be healed. Maybe actual physical distance between them will be good. And eventually, when they meet again things will be better."

"That would be my heart's desire. And thank you for your wisdom and prayers. I do fear that once Franco and Mira, and you and Hiram leave, she will revert to her withdrawn self. It has been years since I have seen her as outgoing as she has been in these past two weeks—except for the Saturday evenings that Franklin has been spending with us."

"Then you must come to Pennsylvania as soon as possible and stay as long as you can."

"Ohhhh! Not so fast. I must first tell Priscilla about the baby and be prepared to deal with negative emotions. Then convince her to travel with me to Pennsylvania. Furthermore, I should not leave my practice for longer than a month, unless I can find really reliable replacement. Franco told me that you occasionally have hard winters! Let's hope that once we are there we won't get snowed in."

"Forgive me! I didn't mean to be pushy. Hiram tells me that that is my one fault, when I get excited. But I am so grateful that you are coming—as I am sure Hiram is. We do have a doctor, but most deliveries are done by midwives. We have the extra cabin on our property, or the

Pierson's lean-to that they used when we cared for soldiers, or you and Priscilla could use Franklin's loft. . ."

To Charles' amusement Nina kept up her excited chatter until the others returned from their walks.

Franklin and Mira used the time to leisurely relive two years of seminary memories—how first they met and quietly studied side by side, and chuckling over recollections of students and professors. Franco directed their walk to the library steps, a place that held so many memories. After sitting Franklin asked, "Mira-honey, do you think you can handle one more surprise?"

"Right now I feel that I am bursting with so many good things, and I feel I could live on the surprise of this beautiful cross forever, but *yes*, if you actually think that you can surprise me with anything else, I'm sure I can handle it."

He took her hand and said gently, "Mira-honey, it looks like we will be arriving in Yankton four days late."

Mira jumped up, her heart pounding. "Four days late? You mean we won't be leaving here tomorrow? What about your parents? When did this all change? Why didn't you tell me?"

Now Franco was the surprised one. He hadn't expected such a reaction, and in that brief moment he realized that there were appropriate and inappropriate ways to spring a surprise. This, at least for Mira, was an inappropriate way to surprise her. She liked to be involved in the planning of events.

Franco looked up at her, "Mira-honey, I'm sorry. It's not like that at all. I'm only trying to tell you—and now I see that I chose the wrong way—I'm trying to tell you that my parents invited us to spend a few days. My father and I checked out the railroad routes. They actually live right along the way. With no extra fare, we can get off the train, spend time at my parents and re-board a west bound train a few days later when it passes through. I even telegraphed ahead to Yankton to have a message relayed to the people of Chipps that we will be late; they telegraphed back that they can make the necessary adjustments on their end. They were not expecting me to preach the first Sunday, anyway. I was only trying to spare you disappointment if it did not work out; and to not bother you with any extra things to think about on the days just before our wedding. But I should have consulted you. I'm sorry."

Mira sat back down and took his hand, "Franco, I over reacted. And I am delighted. But yes, it would have been nice to have discussed it.

We have so much to learn about *being a team*. I'm hoping that we will be able to do a lot of talking on the train, but I know we will want to spend as much time as possible talking with your parents. I feel I could never get done learning from them."

They sat quietly for a few moments, but suddenly Mira felt a moment of panic. "Franco, that means four more days without my medical bag. What if something should happen along the way, and I need it to help someone. I should have thought about that before, but I gave it to my father to pack with the other medical supplies—now sitting at the depot, or perhaps already in a railroad car. I can't believe my father agreed to pack it rather than have me carry it. He *never* goes anywhere without his."

"I wondered about that as we were crating all the supplies. In fact, I even asked him, but he said that you needed a break, and to go ahead and pack it. So we did."

"Do you think . . . ?"

"I don't know Mira. I suppose if the crates are still in the depot, *maybe*, but if they are in the car, *no.*"

Mira jumped to her feet, and pulled Franco with her. "Let's hurry home and talk to Father. If anybody can retrieve it, he can."

They hurried home. Seeing Mira's stricken look Dr. Phillips was glad to hear that it was *only* the medical bag that had Mira upset, and agreed to try to retrieve it early in the morning. The baggage department at the depot was closed on Sunday.

Priscilla used their neighborhood walk for one last opportunity to ferret out any information that she could from Hiram about their life in Boston. She seemed to think that her own personal happiness was in some way tied up to the way of life that was above what she ever had, even in her *good life*. She could not let it go yet. It seemed mysterious to her, so she tried again, taking a little more subtle approach. "Hiram, you and Nina seem so suited to each other, how did you meet? Do you still have friends in Boston? I know you said your parents both died, but there must still be some connection to your life there. Train travel . . ."

Though he did not show it, Hiram was irritated now. Nevertheless, his graciousness came through; that, and his compassion for this troubled woman walking with him. "Priscilla, once our parents' wealth was lost, so was their spark for living. You might think that people—my parents, that is—who had in their possession a cross so beautiful and full of meaning would have other spiritual treasures, but they had none. Neither did Nina's parents—who by the way were our relatives—a couple cousins removed.

Both families *went down* together. Both sets of parents died a few years after we left Boston. As we told you before, they died in poverty. They died in bitterness. As for Nina and me—our parents arranged our marriage."

Hiram gave a mirthless chuckle at the memory. Priscilla looked up at him. "Don't get me wrong Priscilla, there is nothing funny about it. Only irony. Nina and I loved each other, and the families' financial collapse gave us an opportunity we would not have had otherwise. We were young and knew nothing about anything, but had heard of *the west* and managed to get a wagon and horses, but little else, and headed out, with only a vague idea of a destination. The accident was a *god-send* and everything from that point on, hard as life has been, has been blessing."

Priscilla gently shook her head. Hiram noticed and thought he knew what she was thinking, and went on with his story. "It has been healing for Nina and me to come here, Priscilla. To be in your home, to visit you and Charles, to get to know Miranda, to see how warmly you have welcomed our son. It has been good for us to taste the "good life" once again. But what we have now, our life in Pennsylvania, and our welcome here in your home, and our hope for the future, whatever it might be—we feel that we have the best of what God gives his children. We would not change a thing, but we would like to help you find *peace*, dear Priscilla. You will not find peace, or answers to life's problems by probing into what life in the fine society of Boston was like—the life that Nina and I grew up with. That is not who we are anymore, though perhaps we still have some of the manners and bearings. And there is one more thing—"

Again Priscilla looked up at him. "I fear that Miranda will be leaving tomorrow with unfinished business."

"Unfinished business?"

"You know what I am talking about, Priscilla, and it is related to your lack of personal peace. I'm talking about *the unresolved tension between you and Miranda.*"

Priscilla was shocked at the frankness of his words; shocked that anyone could read her so well. *Peace*! She tried to release herself from his firm hold on her arm, but he held it more tightly, and continued to talk. "Yes, peace, Priscilla. Nina and I found peace only when we learned from the old couple who took us in that peace can be found even in great loss. And peace can never be found without confronting what needs to be confronted. Nina and I do not know what your loss has been—only that it was devastating, and still influences you; we believe that it is *your loss that has come between you and your daughter.*"

Priscilla was too proud to cry. She just blinked hard and pressed her lips together. Hiram fell silent, thinking that he might have pushed her too hard, but gradually he felt the tension leave her arm. "I think we should return now. Thank you, Hiram. You have given me something to think about."

By the time they reached the house Priscilla seemed to be herself.

The rest of the afternoon and evening was spent in conversation and games. But Priscilla and Mira made no effort to spend mother-daughter time together.

Chapter 4 *East Goes West*

Dr. Phillips left before daybreak to retrieve Mira's medical bag, and to add another crate to the already mountain of supplies. To their surprise, many people had brought wedding gifts to the reception. They had opened them with deep appreciation, but the real thrill of having received would come later when they began to use them in their own home.

By the time the others arrived at the depot Dr. Phillips was waiting for them on the platform, the train ready to board departing passengers. Even amid promises of possible future visits, farewells were difficult, Priscilla having the hardest time of all, especially saying good-bye to Nina. As Nina kissed her cheek Priscilla held her hand and would not let go until Nina said, "Until we meet again."

"Then you believe we will meet again?"

"With all my heart!" Nina replied. "You know our husbands—they have a way of making things happen."

Priscilla could then kiss Mira and Franco, and gave her hand to Hiram, who drew her into a gentle embrace and said, "Priscilla, you are the sister that Nina and I never had." With that he kissed her cheek and handed her to Charles who was watching his wife closely, always concerned about her emotional well-being.

Priscilla filed Hiram's words away in her mind, thinking they were among the most beautiful and meaningful words she had ever heard expressed to her.

The excited four boarded the train, leaving Charles and Priscilla to wave until the train disappeared from sight.

Other than two nights spent together in privacy at the Phillips' home Franco and Mira felt like they were living the first days of their new life together publicly. They were thankful that the noisy wheels on the track allowed them private conversation. Proper or improper, Franco put his arm around Mira's shoulders as she snuggled against him, and smiled down on her. Mira, his mirage, his miracle. She was wearing her new green velvet dress, which would soon prove to be much too warm.

As if sensing his thoughts, Mira smiled up at him and said, "Franco, your mother—oops, I can call her mother, now too! *Mother* advises that I leave these petticoats and corset at their home, AND change into something far more comfortable and suitable for traveling farther west. Fortunately, I have a couple of dresses in our bag."

"Mira, you look absolutely lovely in this dress, but for comfort's sake, the sooner you can change, the better. And your hair, Mira, it is so beautiful please don't ever . . ."

For traveling Mira had braided her long, lovely auburn hair, and pinned the braids in a coronet atop her head, wearing only a small hat. Errant tendrils escaped the braids, gently softening her otherwise rather plain face. To see Mira was to see her lovely hair. She thought of the beautiful snoods that women of the church had crocheted for her—they would help control the lengthy mass when not braided. But still, long hair was so much work, and hot. And Mira had heard that some women actually were . . .

"Franco, about my hair," she began half teasing, half serious, "do you have any idea, how much care long hair takes—and I will have no one to help me . . ."

"Don't even think it, Miranda," Franco said, using her given name, and sounding unusually stern. "I will draw water for you. I will warm water for you. I will brush your hair every night. But as I was trying to say *don't ever cut it.*"

Mira, who could hold her own when differences in opinions were expressed, replied "I don't promise *never to cut it*. But I can promise you that it won't be soon, *if* ever." She paused briefly, and then added with a smile "and I can't wait to hold you to your promise to help me care for it."

That problem solved, their conversation moved on.

Hiram and Nina, seated across the aisle, were engaged in their own conversation, looking as much a newly married couple as Franco and Mira. Hiram was carefully telling Nina exactly Dr. Phillip's instructions for her pregnancy. "When I told Charles of the poverty, hardships, hard work, and barely enough food during those early years, he said *that* is most likely the reason you did not carry our two babies full term."

"Oh, Hiram, that makes me feel . . ."

"Not a word of it. He did not say that to make us feel guilty. He understands that there was nothing we could have done differently. He told me this to encourage us to believe that with our situation in life being improved now, with good care, there is no reason for problems with this pregnancy. Of course, you are—we are—to follow his instructions very carefully."

"Oh, I know, I know. He already told me," Nina said with animation, attracting Mira and Franco's attention.

"What's got the two of you so excited?" Franco shouted across the aisle.

"We'll tell you later. At home."

While Franco turned his attention back to Mira, Hiram picked up the conversation with Nina. "Charles stressed to me three major things—good nutrition, eight to ten hours of rest every night, if not more, and no *back breaking work outdoors or heavy lifting.*"

Nina nodded. Hiram went on, "that also means no more school teaching."

"Did Charles say that?'

"No, *I'm* saying that. I'm giving meaning to the words of wisdom he spoke."

"But the children; they need me. If nothing else, they need the food we supply them from our garden."

"Nina, I know this is a lot coming at you fast. We will work it out. But I know you know that now this baby is our priority. We'll even discuss it with Franco and Mira when we break the news to them in a few days."

Again Nina nodded her head, somewhat subdued, thinking about changes a baby would bring to a couple in their forties with a grown son and wife. They reminded each other of Charles' promise to come in the fall for the delivery. That would serve as an incentive to follow his instructions very carefully.

Once again Franco interrupted, "Are the two of you hungry yet? We are ravenous. That basket of food is waiting to be dug into." Food had been packed by the Phillips' cook—enough to take them to the Welken homestead, where they would restock for the rest of the trip.

The four disembarked with their handbags and Mira's medical bag at the small depot in the town near the Welken homestead. Their trunks and crates would go on to Yankton.

Franklin had mixed emotions as the homestead came into view. Excitement at being able to show Mira where he had grown up, but he also thought of the small graveyard not far from his parents' house—two small siblings and the elderly couple, the only people he had known as grandparents. But Franklin, like his parents was not one to dwell on the past, or what might have been. He clasped Mira's hand as his father guided horse and buggy onto the path leading into the farmyard.

Sensing his excitement Mira looked up at him. "Franco . . .?"

"I'm okay, Mira-honey. It's just that it is overwhelming—I haven't been home for three years. Seeing the old landmarks and places where I used to work and play brings back many memories. Changes have occurred, and that's not necessarily bad—but I can't show you just exactly *how it was.*"

Mira sat silently, holding Franco's hand. She was amazed at how intensely he communicated his feelings just through his hand.

As they pulled up near the house Nina exclaimed, "Look Hiram! Look at how well our neighbors kept up everything while we were gone."

As Hiram and Franco helped the ladies from the buggy the Welken's dog barked his greeting, and then recognizing Franco, went into a frenzied welcome. After playing with him briefly Franco introduced Mira to him. Mira was not a *dog-person* but seeing Franco's excitement, realized that a dog would likely be a member of their household in Dakota. Perhaps a wise idea, she admitted to herself.

Nina grabbed Mira's hand and took her into the house. It was small and plain, given what she was used to, and the curtains could use re-doing. But Nina was obviously proud of her little home and Mira wanted to affirm this. What could she truthfully say?

"Oh, Mother it is so comfortable and cozy—and there's the loft. Franco told me we could sleep there."

"Yes, you can. Or in the lean-to, or the old cabin. We keep all three ready for use. It's not unusual for passers-by to stop for lodging for a night. And we are *so* excited to have you here."

As the women talked the men carried in their bags, and then went to look at animals. Nina and Mira joined them a few moments later. Mira tried to take it all in and then began to mentally transpose what she saw here to their future home in Dakota Territory. *What will be the same? What will we have to do differently? We'll have a lot to talk about once we re-board the train.*

Nina brought a basket and scissors with her outdoors, hoping the lettuce would be ready. It was, along with a few small radishes. Back at the house Nina brought up jars of canned food from her cellar—vegetables, fruit and jam. Their potatoes were gone, so there would be no potatoes with meals until July.

"Mira-honey, tomorrow we'll go to town to buy a few supplies. I let flour, etc. run low before we left. We need to bake bread and begin a new sour dough starter. You could take some of that with you on the train. Franco loves sour dough bread. I'll show you how to make it, and how to keep your starter going."

Mira nodded her head, but questioned herself. *Will I really be up to life on the frontier? Even with Franco? Well, it's too late to worry about that now! I'm committed.*

That evening as they relaxed on the porch Hiram opened the topic. "On the train you asked what we were talking about with such excitement. Well, now we will tell you." Hiram paused and took a deep breath, and as he did so Nina began.

"Oh Franklin! Mira-honey! We have such great news. We are going to have a baby! The two of you will have a brother or sister."

"*Mother*! Are you sure? How can . . . ?"

"Yes, we are sure. Mira's father confirmed it by a physical examination."

"But at your age . . ."

"Franklin," Hiram replied sounding stern, yet humor came through in his voice, "when one is in the mid-twenties, mid-forties sounds ancient, but believe me, it's not. But, in our joy we do take it seriously. Mira's father instructed us well, and he sees no problem, so long as his instructions are followed carefully."

"But you have already lost two babies with early delivery. How will this be any different?"

Mira sat quietly thinking the same thing. Hiram continued the conversation, "This is a different time under different circumstances. We live comfortably now, with plenty of food, and your mother *will* take very good care of herself—no more hard outdoor work, and no more teaching school."

Hiram's words left no room for any comment other than encouragement and support.

"Oh, how I wish I could be here for your delivery and to help you in the days that follow. Do you have a doctor or midwife nearby?"

"We do—both. But I can't tell you how much we wish the two of you could be here. However, we know that that is out of the question. So hear this, Mira-honey, your father and mother are coming for the event."

Mira's jaw dropped, as did Franco's. Mira was the first to respond, "What?! My parents are coming? That is *beyond* likely! My father, maybe. But mother, *never*!"

"Mira . . ." Franco did not like her tone.

Hiram interrupted him. "That's what I would have thought had someone other than your father told me. But I went to his office shortly after Nina broke the news to me—which, by the way, was only two days before the wedding, so this is still new to us, too. Your father was encouraging and affirming about the whole thing. He *volunteered* to come, and to bring your mother with him, Mira. He is quite confident that she will agree. And frankly, now we are too. We know that it'll not be easy for her, for many reasons. But we also think she will agree. It might even be a time of healing for her. We certainly are praying along those lines."

"Mother doesn't yet know?"

"We did not tell her, and your father decided to wait with telling her until after the wedding, giving her a few days to get her life back to normal. They are probably talking, even as we are speaking."

"I really wonder . . ."

"Mira-honey," Nina interrupted her, "in your excitement these past couple weeks, you probably missed something significant that was happening within your mother. She really took to Hiram and me. We connected on a deep level. She was inquisitive about our life in Boston. We told her briefly about growing up in wealth, and losing it all. Gradually she came to realize that we are who we are in part because of that background, and even more because of our life with the Piersons in Pennsylvania. But more important than any of that—*and I don't know how*—but somehow we convinced her that we accept her for who she is, just as she is, and that wealth, class, and prestige, hers or ours, have nothing to do with our love for her. It took the full two weeks for this to happen, but when we said good-bye at the depot she clung to me, and would not let me go until I said *until we meet again*. She will come, Mira-honey. She will come. Do not sell your mother short."

Feeling the sting of mild rebuke in Nina's words Mira said nothing more. It would take a long time for her to let go of the hurt she harbored at feeling rejection from her mother.

The women spent much of the next couple days cooking and baking, Mira learning whatever she could from Nina. The sour dough starter would be a huge help. It was so easy. To feel confident about bread making was a good boost for the ego of someone who felt unsure in the kitchen. The men worked outside, Franklin strengthening muscles that had become flaccid in the past three years. But their evenings were spent talking. Franklin could not help but express concern for his mother. "Mother, you are going to give up teaching aren't you? And that huge garden that you use to feed all your students—you can't do that anymore. And all the canning."

"Franklin, I'm not an invalid, and your father and I have already agreed that I will not be teaching. One of the first things I will do after you and Mira leave will be to turn in my resignation. Can't you just imagine the talk in the community?" she said with a giggle. "As far as the garden goes, what do you think of this? Your father and I would like to invite the school children to come this summer and help with it. We would teach them gardening skills, and promise them that if the garden produces well, we will continue to furnish the school with potatoes—one each day for each child as long as the supply lasts. The new teacher will have to be willing to bake them each day. As far as canning goes—I'll be able to manage that. Remember, the baby is not due until late November or early December. And the canned food will be a tremendous help after the baby comes."

Franco admitted that they were preparing wisely. Yet he had misgivings! Having a baby at 40 plus, especially when two pregnancies had gone wrong just didn't seem wise. But there was nothing that could be done now, except his mother taking the very best care possible of herself. But he determined to have a word with his father. After all, he was a married man now, too. This could not happen again.

Charles watched Priscilla closely for signs of melancholia in the days following the departure of the Welkens but saw none. One evening, the very evening the Welkens were telling Franco and Mira about the coming of Mira's parents, Priscilla opened the conversation Charles was hoping to have by stating, "Charles, I think that Nina and Hiram would like for us to come to visit. What with train travel these days, do you think it might be possible? I know life there is far different and more difficult than what we have here, but . . ."

"Oh Priss," (that is what he called her in private) "I have been waiting for just the right moment to discuss this with you. I think a trip to see them just might be possible, even fairly soon, say, in six or seven months, or so. For you see, there is a bit of news Hiram and Nina want me to share with you, along with an invitation. I waited this long, for I was sworn to secrecy. They wanted to get home before telling Franklin and Miranda. Well, I think they have had sufficient time, and I can't wait any longer to tell you!"

Priscilla was sufficiently curious now—she who never showed much emotion or animation now jumped up. "Charles! Out with it. The way you are sounding, it could be only one thing! Nina is pregnant, isn't she?"

"How did you know?"

"I don't really *know*. But I noticed the last few days of her visit here she occasionally seemed to be off in a world by herself. I didn't think much of it then, but what she said to me at the depot, *our husbands have ways of making things happen, don't they?* And now, what you are saying—it just adds up."

"Well, you are very perceptive. Hiram and Nina would like us to come for about a month, middle November and into December. The best we can calculate, that's about when the baby is due. If I can get my practice well enough organized—hopefully find some eager young doctors to cover for me—I would like to go as soon as late October or early November. Snowstorms can impede train travel by late November and December. And for Nina's sake I would like to be early. Plus, time away from the practice would be good for us. Except for the couple weeks when the Welkens were visiting, I have rarely taken time for family."

"You are not anticipating that Nina will have problems, are you Charles?"

"No, and she is strong and healthy. Still . . ."

"I know, and I agree."

"Then you are willing to go, even if it means being away from home for a couple months, and living, well, rather primitively?"

"I am willing. Oh, I can't tell you, Charles, what a difference knowing Nina and Hiram has made in my life. It is as though we have family now, and I have friends."

The rest of the evening was spent in talking about how to prepare for being away from home that long, and trying to imagine how primitive it might be. Hiram and Nina had spoken freely about how they had roughed it in the early years. They said less about their present living conditions.

"Nina did ask me to suggest to you not to bring all your fine clothes, but rather just plain, very warm clothing."

"I can't wait to get some new frocks made. My dressmaker will wonder what has come over me! Maybe I should write to Hiram and Nina to accept their invitation, and ask Nina to reply with some specifics. Maybe even ask her if there is anything that she thinks she might need."

"Writing them to accept the invitation would be a gracious thing to do. I know they will be delighted to hear directly from you that we are coming. And speaking of *dressmaker*—your dressmaker will get a chuckle from this. She guessed that Nina was pregnant. It was after one of her fittings that Nina came to see me in my office!"

"And speaking of sewing—remember all the baby clothes I made when I was expecting Miranda?"

Charles nodded, remembering Priscilla's happiness when she first learned she was pregnant.

Priscilla continued, "And poor Franklin! Nina told me that she made his first clothes out of the petticoats she was wearing when their wagon tipped. Mrs. Pierson told her that there was no place for voluminous petticoats in country living. What she didn't use for his clothes she made into curtains. Well, no petticoat clothes for this baby. I'll get out my needle and thread and purchase fabric. I'll put together the finest layette any baby ever had."

The next day Priscilla bought fabric, patterns, and miscellaneous sewing notions. Sewing was a skill she had, perhaps because of her love for beautiful clothing, but it was a talent she had let slide in her years of melancholia.

This baby would have enough clothes, diapers, blankets and stuffed toys to take him or her well into the second year of life.

It had been long since Charles had seen Priscilla so happy and industrious. He thanked God from the bottom of his heart and wrote a letter of his own to Hiram and Nina, advising them to buy or make nothing for the baby for at least two years!

Charles circulated word at the local hospital of his need, and soon had more than enough applicants eager to cover for him, several obviously hoping for the beginning of a long term work relationship.

Franklin and Miranda boarded the train after sad good-byes, especially for Miranda. She felt she was leaving her true mother, even though she had known Nina for only about three weeks. Everyone had carefully avoided promises to visit, although all hoped that visits would take place in years to come.

But back on the train it didn't take Mira long to ask, "Franco, when do you think it will be possible to see them again. Especially now that there will be a new baby?"

"Mira-honey, as much as we love them all, my parents and yours, and the baby-to-come, life in the West is what we must focus on now. Remember how we have often talked about being a Frontier Team? Now it's becoming reality. I believe, Mira-honey, it will take everything we can give. We must not let even family get in the way of our goals."

Seeing her stunned look Franco realized that speaking more gently and thoughtfully was something he would have to work on. He remembered that early in their relationship he had committed himself to always honor her. *But it doesn't necessarily come naturally, no matter how good my intentions. I wish I would have discussed this with my father.* After silently reproving himself he said aloud, more gently, "but we will go back for your graduation."

After a pause, where both had mentally reviewed this short exchange Mira responded, "You're right Franco. I just didn't realize how difficult it would be to leave your parents. This is the first time in my life that I feel like I have family—except for my father. This is even the first time in my life that I feel like I have friends, except for you."

Franco pulled her close and Mira went on, "And I promise you, Franco, that I will do my part in Dakota. Tell me how you expect a day, or maybe even a week will go."

"First I expect you to get up, and get the fire going, and while breakfast is cooking you will go out and milk the cow and gather eggs. Then you will serve me breakfast, clean the house, work in the garden . . ."

Mira's face blanched as she gasped, "Franklin . . ." She thought he was serious.

Franklin was about to kick himself. Two blunders right in succession. He released his hold of her and said, "I'm sorry, Mira-honey. I was joking. Obviously, we have to learn a lot about how to communicate with each other; how to hear each other."

"Apology accepted." She took his hand. "You see, Franco? This is one of the reasons I regret not having stayed longer with your family. I do not know how to live in family. I can take a joke, at least I hope I can. But you just got done saying *that we will have to give it all we got, and not let family get in the way*. And then when I ask you what a day will be like, you begin by *telling* me what you will expect of me—well, it didn't sound like a joke to me, and it did not honor what *I'm going to Dakota to do.*"

Taking a deep breath, Franco tried again, "In all honesty, Mira, those are things that will have to be done, but I was wrong in dumping it all on you, even as a joke. We both have a lot to learn about teamwork. As far as that list goes, I would say that taking care of the fire will usually be my work. Finding kindling and firewood is difficult, from what I understand. Some coal is available. It comes by train, and probably expensive. But people do pick up buffalo chips—hence the name of our town, Chipps—for a quick, easy burn."

"No more jokes now, remember Franco?"

"That wasn't a joke. But don't worry, I won't expect you to go out *picking*. As far as cows and chickens and garden, we'll have to work out a plan. Remember I will be riding circuit, and you will be making medical calls so there will often be times when one or both of us are gone."

"We'll probably have to hire someone to be available to do outside work when we are gone."

"I think you are right. And even when we are home let's not be too busy for each other."

Mira rested her head on Franklin's shoulder, content that they had begun talking about what she thought was a reasonable approach to their new life and work. She slept until it was time to dig into the food basket.

As they ate Franco sat, thinking deeply about what he knew they must discuss before their arrival—their house. He had a general idea of what it would be like since he was the one who had made the arrangements with the church leaders in Chipps. How would he tell Mira that it would not be like his parents' cozy log cabin in the woods? Having spent time with his parents was good—but it might also have given Mira a false idea of what life in Dakota Territory would be like.

"Mira when you first started seriously considering going west how did you imagine us living? What did you see in your mind as you thought about a house?"

"Mmmm, let me think. I saw a one room dwelling. A simple kitchen on one end with a few cupboards and cook stove. A table with a couple chairs. A couple more chairs for relaxing in the evening. A bed and dressing area on the other end, separated from the kitchen by cloth hanging from a wire or rope that stretched across the room. Outdoor privy, and water to be drawn from a well."

"Pretty close, I would say . . ."

"But now that I see how your parents live—their cozy cabin in the woods, sturdy and no doubt fairly easy to keep warm in the winter. And several well-built outdoor buildings . . ."

"Mira-honey, your first description more closely fits what we will have. We need to prepare ourselves mentally. It will be primitive. The house will be livable, but might need considerable work to make it comfortable. The pastor who lived there was single, and not home much. Life in Dakota Territory is very different from life in Pennsylvania. But I understand that with supplies being brought to Yankton by train, many people, if they can afford it, are improving their property. However, in the area where we will be, and probably much of the Territory, trees are sparse, and there is very little logging or lumber mills."

Mira was silent, thinking before she replied. Franco watched her face closely for expression of emotion. Before long, she broke out into a smile and said, "Then it won't be different from my original thoughts. That is what I have prepared myself for. But I don't know what I will do with all the stuff my mother insisted on sending. And believe it or not, your mother supported her, and said I take the beautiful china, etc."

"I'm glad we will have that, Mira. We don't have to use it immediately. Maybe just when we celebrate special days, like anniversaries and Christmas. But I do eventually plan to build you a house, much nicer than the little shack that we will call our first home. Remember, I learned a lot about building from my father, and Grandpa Pierson."

"Franco, one thing comes to mind right now, that in all the excitement of the last few weeks—and I don't think even my father thought about—and I haven't heard you say anything—"

"Oh-oh, what is it Mira?"

"Well, I'm trying to tell you. We have in the train car crates and crates of medical supplies, to say nothing of the trunks of clothes and supplies my mother insisted on. I know that you have made arrangements for an extra wagon or two for transportation from Yankton—but where will we store it all once we arrive in Chipps?"

"Frankly, I don't know. I didn't think about storage—just getting the supplies there. Perhaps someone on that end did, when they heard our need for extra wagons. Maybe the general store will have some storage room. Or there might be a small empty shed that we could rent."

"I will need to organize my medical supplies and medicine, for easy retrieval when I need them."

"I agree. How could I not have thought of that before?"

"I didn't think of it either—we just had too much on our minds, what with finishing school and getting married."

"It will be a matter we can take up with the church leaders very soon. When they realize what a blessing your work will be to the community, I'm sure that they will agree to help us find something workable."

"In the next few days let's make that a prayer priority. Oh, and prayer for your parents and the baby."

"And prayer for your parents as well. Especially that your mother will agree to the trip to Pennsylvania."

Mira said nothing more about that trip. Just thought to herself *that I have to see to believe.*

The rest of the trip to Yankton was spent in trying to imagine and plan how they would spend their first few days settling in. They agreed that getting to know the people they had come to serve was a priority. This might mean not getting the kitchen organized, a meal on the table, or books on shelves. In fact until there was a designated storage area little unpacking of the crates and trunks could be done. Fortunately, everything was well labeled so they would be able to find the essentials.

They added to their prayers a request *that God would give them the grace to always put people first, even at their own inconvenience.*

Chapter 5 *Dakota Territory—Settling In*

Their train pulled into Yankton Station. The year was 1873. For Franklin and Miranda there would be no turning back. A needy community awaited them, and they were eager and committed.

A school/church had been built some years earlier, but the pastor had moved farther West—to Oregon it was rumored, although no one knew for sure. He had taught school children and performed the pastoral functions. Since his departure the community had hired one of the local women to teach. A woman who knew the 3-Rs, but was looking forward to assistance from the new pastor and his wife in the new school year.

In the absence of a pastor the building was used on Sundays for lay-led worship services. Weather permitting, Sundays were also times for social gatherings. People came as far as 10 miles by buggy or horseback bringing picnic lunches to share.

It would still be some years before train tracks would reach Chipps, but there was talk of the telegraph coming as soon as the summer of 1873.

In the correspondence that Franklin had with community leaders he was advised that they prepare themselves for a "rugged time," especially in the first years. Mira and Franklin discussed this often in their train conversations, but neither felt intimidated. Rather, their hearts pumped with hope and excitement. The work would be a team ministry; a mission. And they had each other and the strength and love of the Lord to sustain them.

Franco was the first to notice wagons with teams of harnessed oxen. "Look, Mira! Three wagons, all pulled by oxen! Let's hope that at least one is for us!"

"I see them—one has two cows tethered behind. I wonder what is in the barrel and crate latched to the sides?"

"I dare say that one is for us. I asked for two cows, and a crate of chickens. Let's go see!" Franco made a dash for the door before remembering his manners to assist Mira with the train steps. But she had no trouble—how freeing it was to be dressed to fit the west. She grabbed his arm and together they half-ran to the first wagon. It was for them, as were the other two, already loaded to the hilt. Their goods had arrived several days earlier.

They were greeted by three drivers from Chipps, who told them that they had pulled into town the previous night, and had gotten up early this morning to load the wagons. From the looks of them they had spent the night sleeping under the wagons.

"If the weather holds, I think it will," the leader of the trio said with an eye to the sky, "we can make it to Chipps by dark. It might storm, but shouldn't be a bad one."

"What time is *dark*?" Franco asked. Mira heard the concern in his voice and held his arm a little tighter.

"If you go by a clock, this time of the year, about 9:30."

"So you are saying that from here to there takes about 12 hours?" Mira asked, thinking of how far they could travel by train in that time.

"Loaded like we are, Mrs. Welken, at least that long. By horseback, less. For loads like this we use oxen. Slower going, but surer than a team of horses."

"Speaking of horses," Franco began, but was cut off by one of the drivers who seemed less confident that the weather would hold.

"We gotta get movin' . . ."

He in turn was cut short by the third driver, ". . . unless they be needin' more supplies . . ."

Now the lead driver spoke again, ". . . which they don't. We can't carry more. The church folks will donate. They're not gonna need nothin' for a year."

"But we were told . . ."

"Mrs. Welken, if the early pioneers had a fraction of what you have they woulda thought they were in a king's palace."

Embarrassed, Mira said nothing more, but she *felt like* defending herself by telling him that they were told they could get last minute things, like cooking supplies in Yankton. Franco, remembering their need for horses, put his concern about the weather aside for a moment and with more boldness than was his wont, started to say, "We *both* need a riding horse for our work. Where . . . ?"

The three gave Mira an apprising look, but said only, "A rancher to the north of you has riding horses," and with that driver number one got up on his wagon. "One of you on the bench of the second wagon, the other on the third."

Franco helped Mira onto the second wagon. He took the third. Both taken aback by the curt communication. But Mira smiled. *Perhaps Dakotans don't use two words when they can get by with one.* Still, she felt chafed. They weren't even given opportunity to ask questions, like *what about eating along the way?*—they had finished their last food that morning on the train. *And what about* necessary *stops? And where would we find shelter if the storm hit?* The prairie looked barren, hostile. *And a rancher to the north of us? What does that mean?*

As it was, the journey to Chipps went without mishap, though rough enough to make Miranda think her teeth had shaken loose. She had hoped to sight women along the way to observe their dress. In the twenty miles she saw few, coming to realize that homesteads were far apart and the buildings often a good distance from the road. One woman, however, was brought to her attention by her driver. Though he spoke little he was quick to point out a woman working in the field wearing man's breeches. "Her husband died last year. Now she runs the farm, and takes care of 5 children." Miranda couldn't tell if he said this with admiration or scorn, and he offered no further information. So she dropped it, but muttered under her breath *Looks like a sensible woman to me*!

Rest stops were made under an occasional tree—cottonwood, they were told. The day had almost no wind, but the leaves rustled a welcome. Mira had never seen a tree so large and could not resist putting her arms around it. But it would have taken three Mirandas to completely encircle it. When the sun was high in the sky they stopped at a murky stream to water the animals. The barrel latched to the wagon had water for the travelers and chickens. The lead driver distributed jerky and dried fruit to eat as they traveled, with the advice to not eat it all immediately. It would have to do them until they reached Chipps. Mira's driver's mouth had been in constant motion all morning. It was more than jerky that he was chewing. She knew no one who used tobacco, but from his frequent spitting over the side of the wagon, she figured it must have been. They pulled up in front of their house about 9:30 PM. The storm had stayed to the southwest, and they were home.

"Neighbors will come tomorrow morning to unload. You'll find everything you need for tonight and tomorrow morning in the house. John and I will put the cows in the barn. Sid, you put the chickens in the coop."

The trio—that is how Mira would think of these three men—untied the cows, removed the chicken crate from the wagon, and walked to the nearby buildings before Mira and Franco could thank them. They went into the unlocked house. Enough light came through the small south window for them to find a lantern. Franco used a smoldering ember from the cook-stove to light it. Remembering that keeping a fire going, no matter how small, was of utmost importance even in hot weather, Franklin added a couple pieces of wood to the embers. A moment or two later they heard the trio unharness the oxen and walk away with their teams, leaving the wagons.

For a moment Miranda felt desolate. Couldn't they have been friendlier? Her driver barely spoke the full 20 miles, and when he did, it was usually in brief answers to her occasional question. Franco had fared little better with his driver. And the leader—he was so rude Miranda didn't care if she never saw him again!

They briefly looked over their living quarters. It seemed clean enough, and the bed was made. The kitchen cupboards had some basics—cornmeal, salt, a small amount of flour (enough to make a batch of sourdough bread, she hoped), a small can of coffee, and several jars of canned food. "Enough to keep us going for a few days. We could use eggs and milk."

"Eggs! Don't count on them right away—not after the hot dusty, ride our chickens had crammed in that crate. And speaking of milk—I totally forgot—those cows will be bursting by now, unless they are completely dry. I'll go out and check right now." He took the lantern and went out.

Miranda continued her surveillance of the house, more by touch than sight. It was getting dark rapidly. A wooden floor with a couple rag rugs. One window with a faded cloth pulled to the side and secured with a string. Two straight chairs next to a small table. Exposed rafters. And a door on the west wall directly across from the east door through which they had entered. Perhaps it was a backdoor, used when coming in from outdoor work. But strangely, there was a rocking chair in front of it, suggesting that the door was little used. She would ask Franklin to check it out with her in daylight; she wasn't about to open a door in a strange house at night. With a sigh she sat down. There was so much to take in—she could sense that even in the darkness. This was totally not the Welkens' cabin. It was more like she had originally expected and she would make the one room dwelling into their first home.

Her thoughts were interrupted with Franklin coming through the door. "Dry, totally dry, both of them."

"Does that mean no milk? What good is a cow that doesn't give milk?"

"Well, it might not be bad news. I think it means that they both will be having calves, and probably soon. But don't worry Mira-honey, until then I will find someone to buy milk from."

The lantern was flickering—probably low on kerosene. They blew it out and in the light of the moon coming through the window found their night clothes.

"Franco?"

"I know, Mira-honey, I will light the lantern again, and go out with you. There's got to be a privy somewhere on the premises. I think I saw one near the barn."

For tonight bathing was totally out of the question. And much against Mira's good training, they draped their clothes on the back of a chair for tomorrow's use, and fell into bed, too tired to talk. They just offered a brief prayer, thanking God for safe arrival.

It seemed they had only just fallen asleep when a knocking awakened them. "Doctor, Doctor, we need you. My wife . . . "

Before the man finished stating his request, Franco was up, going to the door, while Mira reached for her clothes.

Through the open door (Franklin did not invite him in) Mira heard that the man's wife was in labor, actively for two or three hours. Could the doctor come? "She'll have to ride with you. We have no buggy or horses yet." Franklin calmed him with a few questions, while Mira quickly pulled on her clothing and grabbed her bag.

Stepping inside, Franklin asked, "Are you sure you want to go, Mira? I can't go as we have no horses, and he brought only the one he is riding. You will have to ride double with him."

"I have to Franco. This is what we are here for." With a quick kiss, Mira stepped outside, and greeted their caller who was back in his saddle.

Mira went off with a total stranger sitting astraddle behind his saddle, one arm around his waist. With the other she clasped her medical bag that Franco had wedged between her and her companion. For more reason than one she thanked God that her father had retrieved it from their packed crates. It gave her a little distance from the stranger who emanated many smells of the earth. They flew like the wind. The only word from her companion was, "Don't worry, Old Grey here knows the way and every stone and hole in the road. He could do it blindfolded." Nevertheless, Mira was thankful for the bright moonlight. She made note of objects along the way, and pressed her medical bag more tightly to her body. In it she carried her loaded gun, and smiled at the thought of her wise father who had taught her well. Wouldn't he love this!

The distance was short, taking only about 10 minutes. Mira slid off the horse by herself, not comfortable with being helped by a man she did not know. Inside, one lantern gave a soft, but inadequate light. In the dimness Miranda heard a moan and saw a young woman on a bed. With a strong contraction her moan changed to a cry of pain. The young man went to her, and took her hand, saying, "It's okay, Maggie, the doctor is here now, and Mrs. McPherson will be coming."

Mira stepped to the bed and took her other hand. Immediately she felt like she was in familiar territory. How often she had done this. "Maggie, you can call me 'Mira'. I'm here to help you. I have helped many, many women give birth. It's hard, I know, but keep thinking of that wonderful little bundle you will soon be holding in your arms. Slowly Maggie's body relaxed and she gave Mira a smile. Mira noted a small frame with a very large belly. With the strong contraction she had just observed Mira would have to do an assessment for dilation soon. Maggie's husband volunteered that labor had begun about 9:00 PM. "We saw your wagon train pass by, and I promised Maggie I would get the doctor for her. She will be the first in our area to have a real doctor."

This didn't seem to be the right time to tell him that she was not a *real* doctor. Her father always told her that in this work gaining your patient's confidence was half the job. When another contraction passed Mira realized that enlisting the husband's help could be beneficial.

"Excuse me, but I don't know your name."

"Call me 'Jed'—Jed McAlister," and with that he removed his hat, and executed a little bow.

"Jed, I need your help. First, we each need a pan of warm water to wash our hands, and clean towels. We also need a basin of cool water and a clean cloth, to wipe Maggie' brow."

"I'll have that for you in a second, the water is already warm in the reservoir."

Miranda didn't know what a reservoir was, but she was grateful for the instant warm water. They both washed thoroughly up to the elbows with soap, Jed removing his shirt.

After one more contraction Mira said, 'I have to examine Maggie now from below to see how far she has come along. Jed, I need you to stand by her head and gently wipe her forehead with the damp, cool cloth.

The examination revealed that dilation was advanced. "Maggie, if you continue doing as well as you are doing, I think you will have a baby in another hour or two!!"

She helped Maggie through another more painful and longer contraction. When it was over and Jed had relaxed Mira asked him to gather a supply of towels and clean sheets, and to boil a scissors.

"Oh, we have that all ready here on this table. We even have a little crib for the baby—everything the little guy will need. But I'll set the water with scissors on right now, and stoke the stove."

"You've done a great job in getting ready, I can see."

"Our neighbor lady was here today and helped Maggie. She wants to come to help. Do I have time to call for her now? She said anytime, day or night."

"How far must you go?"

"Only a couple minutes up the road by horse. Hers will be standing ready."

"You have time," answered Mira, relieved to have him out of the house for awhile. Now perhaps she could get a little better history between contractions.

Jed grabbed his shirt, and put his hat on to leave. "Oh, Jed, one more thing. Could you get a brighter lantern, and put it at the foot of the bed?"

"This is the only one we have, but I'll bring another from the McPhersons. It won't take long." At the door he paused, turned, and came to the bed and kissed his wife, and then was on his way.

Another contraction was heavy upon Maggie, but when it passed she relaxed, and said, "He is a good man."

"I can tell. And soon I want you to meet my husband, too."

"Our new pastor," Maggie said with a smile.

Mira's thought turned briefly to Franco, no doubt beside himself with worry. Well, it couldn't be helped. They had no time to prepare for this night, other than having covenanted with each other to make serving God by serving people their priority.

As for Franco, he spent the night on his knees in prayer for his wife and patient, and mentally kicking himself for not insisting on getting horses yesterday. Then they could have gone out together, safely, and he would not have had to entrust his wife to a strange man on horseback, heading towards *who knew what* kind of situation. He did not even know where they went—just the direction.

The night sounds of the prairie were different from the woods of Pennsylvania. He heard coyotes in the distance, but worried they were wolves. He wasn't sure, but thought that the rustling in the rafters were bats, or perhaps mice. The rafters would have to be enclosed, and soon if Mira were to sleep in this room. Mice scurried over his feet as he prayed. *What shall we get, Lord? Traps or a cat? Mira doesn't like cats.*

And so the night went, one sound, one thought after another, Franco bringing them all to the Lord in prayer, asking for wisdom and safety. Finally he fell into a deep sleep, content that he had cast his cares on the Lord, and there was nothing further he could do at this time.

Dawn came early on the prairie this time of the year, just as night fell late. Franco was awakened by a knocking, accompanied with a shout, "Pastor, Pastor, your wife sent me to get you." He stumbled to his feet trying to orient himself, wondering how long he had slept. Conflicting emotions stirred in his heart. *Your wife sent*—that meant she was alive! *Thank you, Lord.* But was she safe? Was the patient safe, and the baby? *Oh, dear Lord, no! Don't let there be a problem greater than what Mira can handle.*

All those thoughts in the second or two that it took him to go to the door.

"All is well, we have a son. The doctor asked me to get you. She wishes to spend some time with my wife and son. Our neighbor lady is with us now too, preparing breakfast. We want you to join us. I brought a horse for you to ride."

Seeing Franklin's look of surprise, the farmer asked rather doubtfully, "You can ride, can't you? I didn't know last night that you had no horse or buggy—else I would have brought one then, rather than have the lady ride double with me, a stranger. If I made you both uncomfortable, I'm sorry. But I wasn't thinking clearly, or acting quite normally last night."

"Apology accepted. Congratulations! And yes, I can ride. Give me a moment to pull on my clothes."

In the easy gallop to the McAlister's homestead Franco was overwhelmed with gratitude that Mira was safe, and that a baby had been brought into the world. Still, he had concerns for Mira's future safety. They would have to talk about how to handle these situations filled with so many unknowns.

And they would get their own horses. TODAY.

Mira greeted Franco at the door, while Jed took his horses to the corral. "Franco, come and see the baby. He is in his little crib, and Maggie is resting after an exhausting night. And, oh! Meet Mrs. McPherson. She was a great help with the baby. Said she had several of her own, and often helps with babies in the community—humans and animals!

Franco was greeted warmly by a slim, attractive middle-aged woman who was working over the cook-stove. The aroma of bacon, eggs, and pancakes was overpowering. Both Franco and Mira remembered the jerky of the day before. And the tobacco.

They ate their fill, with little comment, except for Mrs. McPherson urging everyone to take seconds. When the meal was finished she began the conversation.

"How was your trip?"

"We traveled many days by train, with a stop at my parents in Pennsylvania."

"Pennsylvania? I thought you were from Boston, or New York, or some such place."

"Actually, you're right, Jed, at least partly. Mira has lived in Philadelphia all her life. I grew up in the woods in Pennsylvania where my parents have a farm. I went east to go to Seminary, and there Miranda and I met."

"Then you are a farm boy—that is good for Dakota-living."

"The farm is still in my heart, but here my focus will be pastoring, and hopefully some gardening, and looking after our animals. We already have two cows and chickens. We must get riding horses."

"Pardon me for asking, but I didn't understand what you said about meeting Miranda. Did you mean you met Miranda *in the East, or at Seminary*?" Mrs. McPherson asked.

Franco looked at Mira. Obviously he wanted her to answer this one.

"I was interested in foreign missions, so I went to Seminary to prepare. As the Lord would have it, I met Franklin—or Franco—as I call him. When he began telling me of his dream of "going west" I was immediately intrigued. With much conversation and searching out the Lord's plan for both of us, we decided to come to Chipps as a team." Mrs. McPherson eyes grew wide in admiration, as she smiled her approval.

Jed jumped in with another question, "But you are a doctor . . . ?"

"Well, not quite. My father is a doctor, and I trained under him, but have no formal education as a doctor. I am, however, very experienced in deliveries, and many illnesses. I can stitch wounds, set bones, but I cannot do internal surgery."

"That's doctor enough for me. I'm going to call you *Doctor*."

And so, Mira became known as *Doctor* in the community.

"And the rest of your trip?" asked Mrs. McPherson.

Franco picked it up, "After many days on the train, we were very glad to pull into Yankton, and especially glad to find three wagons waiting for us, already loaded with our supplies."

"And the ride from Yankton?"

Both Franco and Mira hesitated to answer, but Jed came to their rescue, "The three men who picked you up are the best men we have here. Don't speak much, and hate to be asked questions. But anybody has a need—they'll take care of it before asked. One thing you will soon learn is that word gets around quickly here. Yet no one gossips."

As Jed was speaking, they heard horses draw up to the house. It was their lead driver with two saddled horses in tow. *What brings him here to McAlisters with two saddle horses?* Mira and Franco wondered.

"There's Jake right now. Let's go out to see what's up, Pastor," Jed said with a wink towards Mrs. McPherson.

With brief negotiations Franco and Mira became owners of two excellent riding horses. And Franco also learned that *Jake* was *Mr. McPherson,* the rancher, and husband of the lady inside. Sid and John were two of his ranch hands. Mira and Franco would come to depend on this trio of men.

It was time to leave. Mira was exhausted, but she took one more moment to admire the baby, and then another moment to observe Maggie, checking her pulse, respirations, and noting the amount of bleeding. Everything seemed normal, and Maggie slept through the gentle assessment.

"Mrs. McPherson, thank you for helping with the baby and the wonderful breakfast. I hope we will have opportunity to work together in the future."

"I'm sure we will, and thank you for what you did. You were amazing."

Miranda blushed with pleasure at the praise. Only later did she learn that Mrs. McPherson was THE midwife in Chipps and surrounding area. She had graciously stepped aside, giving the new young woman a chance.

The men were still talking, waiting for Miranda. As she stepped into the bright sunshine eager to get home, Jed approached her, "Doctor, most Dakota farmers do not have much cash this time of the year . . ."

Miranda was caught off guard, having given fee for services no thought at this time. But that was not the way of honest hard working Dakotans. Before she could say anything, Jed continued, ". . . so I was wondering if for now you would accept a dozen eggs and a jug of milk."

A dozen eggs and milk! A gift from heaven! As Miranda thanked him, Jed went on, "Your husband told me that last night there were mice in the house. We happen to have kittens, just weaned. I've already given Pastor Franklin one . . ." Mira glanced at Franco who was holding a kitten, gently petting it. ". . . and I got to thinking, maybe you would like one . . . ."

"Thank you, Jed. You are most generous. I'm sure that one will do for now—it's a small house." *How many mice could there be?*

"As you wish, but remember . . . "

"I will, Jed. And it was a pleasure to help you, your wife, and new baby. I'll be out tomorrow to see them. Meanwhile, let me know if I can help in anyway."

Mira walked over to Franco, giving Jake a quick greeting.

"Mira-honey, look at these beauties. They're ours! Even a western saddle for you."

Mira then realized that Jake had sized her up well the day before, or else Jed had given advance notice that she was not a side-saddle lady! After all, without protest she had ridden with him double, her legs spanning the wide rear end of a horse.

She turned to thank Jake for all he and the others had done for them in the past 24 hours, but he was already heading towards the road on his own horse.

Franco helped Mira up on hers. Tired as they were, they kept their horses at an easy pace so they could enjoy the morning before the day got hot."

"These are beauties—perfectly matched. Let's call them *Dapple* and *Grey*."

"Great idea. It's going to be hard to know which is which. But speaking of names, Mira, did you catch it that *Jake is Mrs. McPherson's husband?*"

"What??! Why didn't they tell us? We could have said . . . "

"You're right, we could have, and we have Jed to thank for saving us from that blunder. We will have to be very careful about saying anything to anybody about anybody. In a small community like this, as Jed says, *word gets around fast*. Besides, I think they might enjoy playing *no-harm-intended* little games at the expense of newcomers. All in good fun. But nevertheless, we must be very careful in what we say, and to whom we say it."

"Well, thank the Lord, we were spared this time."

"Indeed."

After a few moments of quiet, peaceful riding Franco broke the silence. "Mira-honey, there is so much to talk about. What an initiation we've had! And you did great. I have a feeling that your ability and fame will soon spread."

"Oh Franco, you don't know how scared I was last night—at least until I entered their house and actually saw a woman in labor. Then it all fell into place. But I was worried about you, too. I left in such a hurry, you couldn't possibly have known what was going on."

"We'll talk about my night later. For now, just let me say, I know you have to get some sleep. *The trio* is coming about mid-morning to unload our books. There's a small office with a desk and shelves built onto the school-church. Perfect for our books. The men know you have to sleep so we will keep the noise down. Perhaps after noon or tomorrow we can start working on the other crates."

Mira was nodding in the saddle when Franco helped her down, but a glimpse of the kitten peeking out from his shirt, awakened her enough to say, "Franco, about the cat . . ."

"I know, Mira-honey. We will work something out. But there *are* mice in the house." He didn't tell her that they scampered over his feet during the night. Nor did he tell her about rustling in the rafters.

Mira said no more, remembering the traps her mother's gardener insisted she take. Mouse traps and rat traps. Traps, and beans for planting, even late in the season. *Nobody should go west without these essentials.* Mira had wondered how he knew. But he was right. The cat, however, would not prowl the house, no matter how many mice. She would cage it before she let that happen.

Mira quickly fell asleep, taking just enough time for a trip to the privy and to wash her hands and face with the warm water from the reservoir.

Franco sat quietly at the table for a few moments watching her sleep. What a treasure she was. Often strong willed, but that would serve her well on the prairie. A strong will, tempered with gentleness. *That* would serve them both well, and everyone else.

As for the kitten—Franco would have preferred a dog. But perhaps a kitten was the best way to get started. A kitten, two riding horses, two cows, 12 chickens. He felt like a farmer, and it was past time to go out and do chores.

As he walked Dapple and Grey to the small fenced enclosure attached to the barn he wondered about food supply for the animals. *How long will our cash hold out if we have to purchase hay? And when will I receive my first pay from the church?*

The trio came at about 11 o'clock and easily carried the crates of books to the school/church office, and with crowbars opened each crate. Franco and Mira would shelve the books later—after the shelves were dusted. As Franco was doing chores earlier he had noticed a lean-to attached to the west side of the house. The wood looked much newer than the rest of the house. Now he asked the men about it.

Jake answered, "When we heard about all the supplies—especially medical things that we had to pick up in Yankton—we built it. Figured the doctor would need an-easy-to-get-to-place for her things."

"I am most grateful, and she will be, too." But Jake brushed him off, not one to make a big deal over something as simple as building a little room.

"I'll send some hands over tomorrow, to finish unloading. A few women will come this afternoon to clean the shelves and knockdown the cobwebs."

Franco thanked them as they mounted their horses. Even with the lean-to, he wondered where they would put everything, especially Miranda's trunks of clothes and household supplies. Franco would have liked to ask them if there was storage space somewhere in town but these were not easy men to ask questions of. Perhaps the women would know. Or perhaps the loft in the barn. Mira would need her clothes soon. But organizing the medical supplies would be her priority, and now she had a place to put them!

Meanwhile, Miranda was dreaming of cats and how not to acquire more, and what to do with the one they had. She awakened about noon, only to find the kitten snuggled at her feet, and Franco smiling down on them both.

"Franco, how could you?"

"I didn't. He jumped up by himself, and has been sleeping there for at least an hour. A cat is something you will have to accept Mira. This house has many mice, as you will see, once you look in the cupboards."

"But I brought traps. We must unpack them today. I think I know which trunk they are in."

"Mira-honey, traps are fine. They will catch some mice, but they will not keep others from coming. The presence of a cat will, hopefully even the presence of a small one. Nevertheless, we will look for your traps, and set them in places where the cat will not get caught. But we will keep the cat; it is a necessity, and was a gift. I've already named him—Mouser."

Mira knew Franco was right, and thus Mouser became a trusted family member. Part of the team. But he did not sleep on their bed.

"Breakfast seems hours ago. I'll fix something for dinner while you freshen up," Franco volunteered. "I put the eggs and milk in the springhouse. We could have boiled eggs and milk."

Mira did not know what the springhouse was, and right now didn't really care. She just needed to get to the outhouse, and what she wouldn't do for a complete bath, hair-wash, and clean clothes. Maybe tonight she could hold Franco to his promise to help wash her hair.

"Eggs and milk will be fine, and I'll do what I can to help as soon as I take care of myself. And I must get that sourdough to working."

Franco was sidetracked at the springhouse by a neighbor who had stopped by, giving Mira a few moments to explore the cupboards. The mice had paid their respects. Maybe even taken up residence. She hoped Franco had the stomach to take a close look.

She noticed that whoever had put basic supplies in the cupboard had put everything in tins or glass. *So mice must be a common pest to contend with. This must be how it is done. Good storage containers and cats.* But the dishes were uncovered. Finding her traps was a priority.

Looking more closely at the glass jars, she noted several jars of beans, some tomatoes, and three jars, the content of which she did not recognize. Dark, chunky, and totally lacking in visual appeal. She set them on the table to ask Franco as soon as he returned.

Franco's eyes fell on the jars as soon as he entered. "Mira-honey, where did you find those?"

"In the cupboard, along with mice droppings. Doesn't it look awful? What is it?"

"Oh, Mira-honey, that is the best food possible. Let's have it for lunch and keep the eggs for supper."

"But what is it? Canned mouse? Or perhaps rat! The chunks are big enough."

"Don't be ridiculous. It's canned beef. And I guarantee you—even your cook in Philadelphia cannot fix better beef than home canned beef. Grandma Pierson and my mother canned meat when we butchered. It saw us through winters when hunting couldn't sustain us."

"If you say so, and of course I will try it. Do we heat it, or eat it straight from the jar?"

"We heat it. I'll get the fire burning brighter. Can you find a couple pans? I would like some of those tomatoes, too."

"I've found some pans and a few dishes and eating utensils—I wouldn't call them *silverware*. But please get water to boiling. Everything we use for this meal must first of all be washed in very hot water."

They were a team, even if one member was feeling a bit balky at the moment, and soon the water was boiling, dishes and pans washed.

And Miranda agreed that the canned beef was delicious.

Remembering that women from the church were coming early afternoon to help with the dusting, Franklin washed the dishes while Mira mixed the sourdough starter with flour. There was just enough flour for one batch of bread. Having looked through the cupboards she made a mental list to take with her to the general store.

Four women came early afternoon, bringing their own brooms, buckets, and cleaning rags. After brief introductions they began to work, two in the office and two in the lean-to. But it was not dusting that they did. They did a scrub-down of the walls, shelves, and floors. They apologized for not having it done before Franco and Mira's arrival. "But you know how undependable travel is. We decided to wait until you got here so it wouldn't be dirty again before your arrival. These prairie winds can blow dirt through wood!"

Like clockwork, when the two women in the lean-to were finished scrubbing, Jake's hired hands showed up and began carrying in Mira's medical crates, and crowbarred them open. After talking with Franco, they divided the steamer trunks between the walk-way in the barn, the office and house, using most of the available floor space. The wagons needed to be empty and returned to Jake's ranch. Farmers and ranchers can get along without a lot, but not without their wagons. And Franco was spared having to try to find storage place in town.

Franco had suggested putting anything that did not fit in the office and lean-to into the hayloft, as there was no hay there, but he was told that that was not a good idea. With the first cutting of hay, he would have to get some—if his horses and cows were to survive the coming winter.

The women who cleaned the office continued their work with the seats and floor in the church. One of the two who worked in the lean-to joined them; the other began in the kitchen cupboards. Miranda offered to help, but the lady, who by now had introduced herself as *Jane,* declined, knowing Miranda was eager to begin her work in the lean-to. So, while Franco shelved books, Mira began with her medical supplies. Once out of the bulky crates and packaging that protected bottles the medical supplies seemed less, and quite easily fit on the shelves. She would organize them later. She stacked the crates just outside the door, thinking that she might eventually line them against the wall along the far side of their bed and use them for their clothing, as there was no chest of drawers or clothes closet. She took one of the smaller crates with an intact lid and put it on their bed with a decided purpose. There would be use for it tonight.

By four o'clock the workers were gone, and Mira and Franco were content that even though not organized for efficiency, books and medical supplies were out of crates and on shelves. Franco opened a small crate containing his clothes and personal items. It would serve as his personal storage area.

"Which trunk would you like to open, Mira-honey? I'll give you a hand."

She was eager for fresh clothing, soap, and etc. "Any one will do. I packed them all in the same way with personal affects in the top compartment and clothing in the bottom."

Mira let out a shriek of pleasure at her first glimpse of what seemed to be pure luxury items. The cat disappeared under the bed, not to be seen for several hours.

"Franco, my hair—do you suppose that *we* could wash it tonight?"

"Mira-honey, I know what I promised you, and I know how much it means to you. I have already looked around for a wash tub. All I could find was a rusted stock tank in the barn."

At Miranda's look of horror, he quickly went on, "Don't worry! Even I wouldn't use it. Tomorrow we will go to the general store. I'm sure they will have tubs. And we need a copper boiler to heat water for bathing and washing clothes. The reservoir isn't large enough for those needs. But tonight we will heat as much water as you need in smaller pans, and I will pour it over your head as you wash your hair. We'll make it work this one time, and you will be both drenched and refreshed. I just might ask the same of you."

"Thanks Franco, I knew I could depend on you to be innovative."

"You're welcome. Shall I start the water boiling for our supper of eggs and milk?"

"Not quite yet—I want to bake the bread. I hope you know how to regulate the fire so we can get the oven to bake bread.

"We'll have to guess. I'll start putting in some chips. I hear they burn fast and hot."

"Thanks, and by the way, one of the ladies brought soup. Let's have that, and we can boil the eggs and save them for breakfast."

Before long the bread was in the oven. To say it was a complete success, would be an overstatement. But learning to regulate temperature by feeding the stove with chips and guessing the temperature was something that would come only with experience.

"Franco, I am so eager to walk outside and see everything. Is there a garden?"

"Yes, there is, just getting off to a good start. We'll have to find out who planted it, and thank them. But it is already Wednesday night, and I have to preach Sunday and need time to prepare. Going to the garden will have to wait. Will you be up to discussing a few ideas for the sermon after we get our hair washed tonight?"

"Of course. I'd love too."

As Mira cleaned up the supper table, Franco put on water in the few available pans, and stoked the stove again. The water in the reservoir water had also warmed nicely with the heat from the oven. Before long Mira and Franco left the stifling heat of the house and were outdoors washing each other's hair. For any onlooker, had there been one, it would have appeared to be a good natured water fight.

They went inside drenched, but much revived and ready to begin preparation for what they had come to do—feeding the people with God's Word.

"Old student-sermons—somehow they don't quite fit here. The basic research will be helpful, but not the sermons. Since our drive from Yankton with threatening storm clouds in the southwest the Lord has laid Psalm 46 on my heart—*God shelters us; gives us strength and safety so that we have no need to fear in the storms of life.*"

"Great choice. Let's read the Psalm, pray about it, and then talk about it."

Mira began praying, and Franco joined in.

"And now what are your thoughts on Psalm 46?" Franco asked.

They began a conversation that wasn't entirely responsive to the other person's comments. Rather it was a way of together exploring for hidden treasures of the Word.

"It seems to me that this Psalm is about *fearless trust in God, whatever the circumstance his people find themselves in.*"

Franco nodded, "I wonder what the circumstances were for the first people reading this, and even for the writer himself."

"Notice how the writer refers often to what God has created—and how these things can stir up both fear and awe."

"How they can have both devastating affects, and how they can be used for safety."

"I love the *be still* verse. I wish I practiced *being still* more often, trusting God for safety."

"What kind of storms have you faced Mira? And how did God shelter and protect you?"

"And you, Franco?

As they talked Franco found himself distracted by Mira's hair. Try as he might, he could not keep his eyes off it. Finally he said, "Mira-honey, get your brush and comb. I'll brush out your hair while it dries and we talk."

As they talked Mira jotted down notes. And thus began what became a tradition. Every Wednesday night they washed hair, and while Franco brushed Mira's they talked, and without fail, God blessed them with ideas for powerful sermons. Even when Franco rode his monthly circuit he came home by suppertime on Wednesday and stayed until after breakfast on Thursday morning.

These hours built structure into their week, and became a sacred time that anchored them in the Lord and bound them firmly together as a Frontier Team.

That night Franco and Mira were startled out of a deep sleep. They heard a loud click—at least it sounded <u>loud</u> in the quietness of the prairie.

Thinking it might be the click of a pistol, Mira reached for her bag.

"No Mira-honey, it was not a pistol. That was a trap."

"But I did not set a trap."

"Just lie quietly for a moment."

She did, and then they heard it again.

This time Franco allowed her to get her pistol, but added a caution, "Mira-honey, we are here to help, not harm. And our door is latched on the inside"

"I know . . ."

"Let's think this through carefully. No intruder has come in. It couldn't be the kitty getting into anything. After all, you put him in a crate for the night. But he might be seeking revenge from inside the crate after what he went through with you dragging him out from under the bed."

Mira cringed at the memory.

Franco went on, "But there isn't anything metal inside the crate. Anyway, the sounds came from the cupboard area. It must be mice in the cupboard."

They got up, lit a candle, and with trepidation walked towards the cupboard.

Franco opened the doors very slowly—and there he found two sprung traps with a mouse a piece. Jane apparently had set them after cleaning the shelves.

"Go back to bed Mira-honey. I'll take care of them."

"Now?"

"Now."

Mira couldn't fall back to sleep. She heard sounds all night long. Franco knew that soon he would have to also tell her about possible bats in the rafters. But first he would talk to Jake about making a ceiling. She finally fell asleep after Franco promised to get the water warmed early so she could rewash the dishes and wipe down the cupboard shelves.

Their breakfast was cold boiled eggs, sourdough bread, and milk. Milk! Mira watched in dismay as Franco poured most of his in a saucer for the kitten. It was the last of their milk.

"Mira-honey, Mouser is still too small to catch mice."

"I know. But how will he learn without his mother to teach him?"

"Instinct."

Franco redirected the conversation. They had to talk about money and how to wisely spend the little they had. "Mira-honey, at the board meeting tonight, I'm thinking of asking for an advance on my salary—say one month. Your parents were most generous in how they outfitted us, but we've already identified some essentials to buy today. I used most of the money that my parents gave to buy Dapple and Grey. Even though Jake gave us a good deal, we are like the Dakota farmers—*not much cash this time of the year*! For now my biggest concern is food for each day."

"Including milk."

"Including milk, until the cows freshen."

"Freshen?"

"Yes, freshen—*come in.*"

"Come in?"

"Mira-honey, *give birth.*"

"Oh. Why didn't you say so?"

"Looking them over yesterday, I would say it will be soon. And, I found one egg, so the chickens will be co-operating, too. And, while living here, we have to speak the way the folks speak. Like *dinner* is the noon meal; *supper* is the evening meal, and *lunch* is the snack between meals."

"I know, Franco, I know. I guess I'm just a little cranky from two nights with little sleep."

"I understand, and tonight I will put Mouser in the office, with the door open to the school. He can't spend another night in the crate, and maybe his presence in that building will discourage mice, even if he can't catch them yet. We must reset the traps Jane left, and find the ones you brought—we can set them all over the house, so long as Mouser is in the school, and then when he is here, we can set traps in the school and office. But we must remember to remove them before people come for church on Sunday, or anytime Mouser is with me there."

And so a plan was worked out for cat and mouse and house.

Mira got up from the table, "I can be ready soon to go to town, now that that the water is hot."

"Great. I'll feed the animals and get our horses ready. Did you make a list?"

"Mental."

"In addition to the things we already talked about I need some writing supplies. I didn't bring much."

Miranda had, but where they were in her trunks she did not remember. It would be awhile before she would have all that unpacked.

It was a brief ride to town. They took their time, enjoying the refreshing morning air. From the talk of the farmers, they could soon expect very hot days.

The store owner helped them with their purchases and offered to give them credit if they needed it. When they realized that they had not planned ahead for carrying a copper boiler and tub home he said he would send them with someone by buggy or wagon going their direction. *Another lesson on how people on the prairie look out for one another.*

Mira refrained from asking "when" but her immediate thought was that she would have to wait even longer for a bath and to wash clothes. *Washing clothes* reminded her that she would have to find her washboard in the trunks.

Noting her expression, Franco promised her another "water fight" if needed. She envied how well he could take things in stride. *It must come from all his years of living on the poverty level doing without the things that I thought were necessities.*

They were home by mid-morning, Mira expecting to head right out for the promised visit to Maggie. She smiled in anticipation, only to find excitement awaiting them on their doorstep. It was a mother and child—a 5 or 6 year old, their buggy and horse parked nearby.

He told them his name and then, trying not to cry, showed Mira a cut on his thigh. His mother had carefully slit his pant leg to expose it and had applied pressure. It started to bleed again as they removed the pressure, but not profusely. The mother said that he had fallen in the house on a piece of glass from a broken jar. Mira breathed a prayer of relief; that would mean a relatively clean cut. Still, it needed cleaning and suturing. The cut was about one and a half inches long. Suturing would hurt, but it was not large enough or deep enough to warrant chloroform.

Mira asked Franco to get a pan of warm water from the reservoir and a clean cup. They would cleanse it outside. Franco gently poured cup after cup of water over the cut, talking to the little guy and gaining his confidence. Meanwhile Mira went inside and prepared her needle and sutures, even some clean, pressed "drapes" she had brought. She covered a trunk with one of her petticoats and quickly tore and rolled bandages from another, mentally noting that her work this afternoon would be to prepare for emergencies like this cut and worse. Her medical work definitely would not be limited to birthing.

Franco put Jimmy on a chair and propped his leg on the trunk. His mother placed a firm, reassuring hand on his shoulder. Jimmy began to whimper as Mira explained to him what she would do to fix his leg. "I can't do it without it hurting a bit, but I'll work fast, and before you know it we'll be finished and it will start to heal. You can count the stitches when we are done."

The first stitch brought more than a whimper, but Mira praised him for holding still. Meanwhile Franco found Mouser and placed him in Jimmy's lap. Mira alerted Jimmy to each poke of the needle just before he would feel it, but Mouser was such a wonderful distraction and comfort, that Jimmy made no further cry, and in five minutes the wound was sutured. Jimmy counted 8 stitches.

As Mira wrapped his leg she told the mother to keep it clean and dry, watch for bleeding, limit activity for a couple of days, and come back on Saturday morning. Jimmy handed Mouser back to Franco, looking up into his face. Ever perceptive, Franco asked, "Would you like me to carry you to the buggy?" Jimmy nodded *yes*.

"I'll be glad to, but I think at home you will be able to walk just a little. You are quite a load for your mother!" Later they learned that Jimmy's father had disappeared in a snowstorm 3 years earlier, and was never found or heard of again. Mrs. Samson was trying to make ends meet by keeping a few cows, chickens, and taking in sewing and washing. She rented out her land in exchange for hay and grain for her animals.

As Franklin helped her into her buggy she quickly retrieved a block of cheese from her bag and gave it to him, "At this time of the year we Dakotan's don't have much . . ."

Franklin thanked her warmly. Right now cheese was better than money!

It would be a phrase that they would hear often—any time of the year. And while initially Mira did not bring in much money from her work, over time their cupboard shelves and springhouse came to be well stocked.

"Franco, thanks for helping. You're a real natural, especially in your interaction with Jimmy. He gave you looks of adoration. How did you even think to distract him with Mouser?"

"Thanks Mira-honey. When I was a little boy my kitties absorbed many of my hurts. And he is sweet, isn't he? We need to find out a little more about them. They look rather poor to me."

"Just what I was thinking. Her dress is worn, but neatly patched. As soon as I'm finished cleaning my instruments and rinsing my bloody petticoat I'm going ride over to Maggie. I promised Jed that I would come today. I shouldn't be gone long. Would you warm up the jar of meat and the jar of stewed tomatoes for *dinner*? There's still some bread. Oh, and would you reset those two traps and put them back in the cupboard? I'll shelve our new supplies when I get back."

Moments later she was up on Dapple and off down the road, hoping she would recognize Maggie and Jed's place. *Was it only yesterday morning? So much had happened since.*

Mira was gone just a few moments when another buggy pulled up. Somebody driving their way, kindly stopping to deliver the tub and boiler. "And look, Pastor, the storekeeper added a 5 gallon bucket. Figured you didn't have one but certainly would need it to fill these." He was off down the road almost before Franco could thank him. Hopefully all these kind people would be in church on Sunday so he and Mira could express their deep appreciation.

Mira's trip was uneventful. Maggie's sister had come to stay for several weeks and would provide the help that Maggie and baby needed. Mira admired the baby and visited briefly with Maggie. "Jed insists that you take home another jug of milk. Says that your cows haven't *come-in* yet."

"Thank you. The milk is much appreciated. We'll use some of it for *dinner*. Franco thinks the cows will *come-in* soon. I can't wait for two little calves," Mira answered feeling quite prairie literate.

"Oh, and one more thing, Doctor. Jed and I have already talked about having little Marigold baptized. No rush, but we would like to talk to Pastor. Do you think he could stop by soon—and maybe you could come, too? You know, just to visit."

"We would like that. I'll talk to Franco and we'll let you know."

Franco brought in water from the cistern, wondering about the source of supply, and if they would have to conserve use, especially since they had animals to care for. But his immediate concern was to draw enough so Mira could enjoy a bath. And he blessed the storekeeper who thought to send so large a bucket.

The first thing Mira saw when she entered the house was the large tub in the middle of the floor. At her shriek of pleasure, the cat once again disappeared.

"Mira-honey, while you were gone, someone—I didn't even get his name—delivered our wash tub and boiler. As soon as we are finished with dinner, I'll fix you a tub of warm water. It's already heating on the stove. Then I'll disappear to my office for several hours. Latch the door from the inside, and cover the window with something, and you can soak for as long as you wish. Light a candle or lantern. Else it will be too dark."

"You are so good to me, Franco. I'll do as you say, after cleaning the dishes and making another batch of sourdough. Now that we have more supplies, I can double the recipe, and won't have to make a fresh loaf every day. Oh, and please take Mouser with you."

"I said I would." But the cat had completely disappeared from sight.

After a long bath Mira organized shelves of bottled medicine and tins of medicinal powders. Then she retrieved every petticoat that her mother had insisted that she pack. She would continue to use one she had used to drape her trunk while suturing Jimmy for that purpose. Another she cut into smaller squares to use as surgical drapes around wounds. Several others she tore and rolled into bandages. She made up several emergency kits and put one in her medical bag along with the other medical basics she already carried. Some of the many sheets her mother had packed could be hung over the shelves to keep out the dust.

She even toyed with the idea of writing a letter to her mother asking her to send more petticoats. Her mother would take pleasure in knowing that she had been right about the need for a large supply of petticoats. On the other hand, if Mira asked too soon, Priscilla might get suspicious about their use. After all, she had heard the story of what Nina Welken had done with hers!

But she should write to her parents, and also Franco's. Maybe tonight while Franco was at the board meeting.

Feeling refreshed by her bath and pleased with what she had accomplished Mira walked over to see Franco. Franco waved several neatly written papers in front of her face. "Look, Mira-honey. Thanks to your efforts of writing notes last night, the writing supplies I bought this morning, and a few quiet hours this afternoon I have made good progress in structuring our first worship service in Chipps, and writing the sermon."

"I'm eager for Sunday and I'll leave you to your work now. I just have to check in this trunk for a few supplies." Mira began to unpack the trunk that was stored in the office hoping to find her flatirons and washboard. She remembered packing them in the same trunk as the traps and pots and pans. Quickly finding what she wanted, she closed the lid and carried a heavy load to the house.

Mouser had come out from hiding and was standing near his empty saucer. "All right, I'll admit it. I saved some milk for you before taking the rest to the springhouse. You can have it now. But you will go with Franco to the school/church tonight. And you will stay there all night."

Mouser would agree to anything, so long as he had a saucer of milk in front of him. He expressed appreciation by rubbing against Mira's ankles while she pressed and folded the drapes. But the drapes had a problem—they needed hemming, and Mira did not like to sew. In fact, she didn't know how to sew. Her stitches were always uneven. Yet no one could suture a wound more meticulously than Mira.

After supper, Franco, carrying Mouser, returned to the school/church. He spent several hours that evening with board members discussing his duties and responsibilities as pastor to Chipps and the people in a radius of at least ten miles. Representatives of the small churches in the outlying areas were present. Franco jotted down notes, eager to share it all with Mira.

Meanwhile, Mira had every intention of enjoying a relaxing evening writing letters. Franco had given her some of his new paper, pen, and ink. She fixed a cup of tea and sat in the rocker, thinking of her first two nights on the prairie. Both had been interrupted. The first by the birth of a baby, and the second by death of mice.

Just as she nodded off, empty cup still in hand, she heard someone call, "Doctor, Doctor, my wife is having a difficult birthing. She needs you. I'll get your horse."

Before Mira could get to the door to see who it was, he was halfway to the barn. But glancing out, it looked like Jake. Surely his slender wife wasn't pregnant, ready to deliver. Maybe women of the community called on her *for* delivery, not just to help with babies!

Mira got her supplies and scribbled a note to Franco. *I'm going with Jake to a birthing; don't know where.*

Jake held her bag while she swung herself up on Dapple, muttering to herself, *drat these skirts, and Jake too. I didn't even have time to put on my leathers.*

Swallowing her frustrations, she called to Jake, "Do you know what the problem is?"

"Cora said *breech*."

Mira felt herself go pale. She had assisted her father with breeches, but had not delivered one by herself. In the short ride she remembered her father's words, full of wise instructions:

Never turn a breech. Women from the beginning of time have had breech births—some successful, some not, but the risk to the baby in turning it and the pain to the mother is greater than letting nature take its course. Attempts at turning the baby usually are not successful, or necessary. Instead, try to keep the mother from pushing too soon, coach her in breathing and relaxation until fully dilated.

Mira's examination concurred with Cora's evaluation—breech. The baby seemed small, but according to the mother's calculation, full term.

Cora told Mira that she had tried to turn the baby by pushing on the mother's abdomen. At that moment Mira realized that Cora *was the community midwife*. Still, she had asked for Mira's help. Recognizing a teachable moment, Mira carefully shared with Cora her father's instructions. Cora received them well, grateful to have the help and wisdom Mira provided.

They worked with Jennie through her contractions. Between contractions Mira got a bit of history. Jennie had already had several children, all live births without complication. The children all did well, even as babies. They were spending this night at a neighbor.

As they talked, Mira's eyes took in the room—everything in order for a new baby, just as it had been at Jed and Maggie. Mira saw the advantage of getting to know and teach patients before the time of birth.

Hearing voices on the porch Mira asked Cora who was out there.

"Oh, that's Jake and Ike. Jake takes care of the father while I help the mother and baby. He always comes along with me on night calls. And then works all day himself. The man seems to never tire, knows exactly what to do for whoever has a need."

Mira determined to soften her heart towards this brusque man.

After a night of hard labor, a small, healthy baby boy was delivered at 6 AM. As before, Cora took care of the baby and Mira the mother. Before long, the baby was placed in his mother's arms, and the men were called in to admire him.

Cora set about to make breakfast, and Jake left to get Franco. By 7 AM, while mother and baby slept the others sat down to a breakfast of bacon and eggs.

Jake left as soon as he had finished eating. While Ike and Franco talked on the porch the women chatted as they cleaned the breakfast dishes.

"Who will help Jennie in the house?"

"Their oldest daughter is a teenager. She will do just fine. We just didn't think the children should be in the house during labor and delivery."

"I agree."

"Oh, Doctor-dear, I hate to think what would have happened if you hadn't come. You spared me from doing something really foolish."

"And I appreciate your assistance—you knew just exactly what to do to get that little guy to take his first breath, and I could spend all my time with Jennie."

Perhaps soon she and Cora could devise a plan for working together on all obstetrical and childcare cases. Mira was sure she had as much to learn from Cora as vice versa. To use each other's skill would be advantageous for both, and most of all their patients.

Mira fell into bed with a warm, happy feeling. Franco and his parents called her *Mira-honey,* and now Cora called her *Doctor-dear.* Perhaps this name would stick, too. That for a young woman who had heard few terms of endearment while growing up . . . well, she slept the sleep of the contented and blessed.

While Mira slept—she didn't even awaken when Franco came in to fix a cheese sandwich—Franco worked on his sermon and reviewed his instructions from the night before, trying to organize his work for the following weeks. About 3 PM Ike stopped by with two freshly shot rabbits. "Hope you don't mind me coming to your office. I figured that your wife might still be sleeping. Sure appreciate what she did for us last night. Without her it could have gone bad for Jennie and baby. Cora isn't rattled often, but last night she was. That's when Jake said, *I'm going for the Pastor's wife.*"

"I'm thankful Mira could help."

They talked briefly and as soon as he was gone Franco went to the house, entering quietly. Mira, just beginning to stir, sat up abruptly when she saw Franco dangling the rabbits.

"Franco, what . . . ?"

"Our supper for tonight, Mira-honey. Ike shot them for us. Payment for a long and hard night of work. I can butcher them right now, and then we will roast them in the oven. Nothing better! There's not much meat on these, but it will be enough. Rabbit and sourdough bread. Mira-honey, this is the life. The leftovers we can keep cool in the springhouse until tomorrow."

"Rabbit! I never . . ."

"That's right, Mira-honey—rabbit. You'll love it. Rabbit will be a big part of our diet. I was thinking of going out myself to hunt some soon. I'll be tanning the pelts, too, later. I'll tell you more about that, but not now."

"Well, give me a few minutes to wash my face and get dressed. I might as well learn the butchering process today. Maybe I'll learn something helpful, in case I ever have to do surgery."

After supper they settled at the table with cups of coffee, eager to talk about Franco's meeting with the Board. They had previously agreed to not talk about "work" during family time or while engaged in tasks around the house.

"Mira-honey, I have my sermon written—again thanks to your good work of writing out notes as we talked Wednesday night. I even had time to organize all the instructions and advice the Board gave me."

He handed Mira a neatly written paper, and watched her face as she read.

EXPECT CHANGES IN SCHEDULE AS NEEDS ARISE:

<u>Work in Chipps & vicinity 3 weeks every month,</u>

    Morning Devotion and Bible Class with School Children.

    Preach Chipps 3 Sundays/mth.

    Visit Parishioners and Non-Church Members wkdays.

    Sat—"off" unless pastoral emergencies.

Salary as previously agreed upon—willing to give a month's advance.

<u>Circuit work in 4 outlying areas;</u> (likely modification of schd. during winter). each area has small School/Church; cot provided for pastor's use.

    Thurs AM 4th wk, travel to area church.

        Carry own dinner.

        Afternoon Bible class, school.

        Visit parents of school children.

        Supper with local Board Member; Meet with Board.

    Fri AM Dev at school.

        Visit Parishioners. Dinner with parishioner.

        Afternoon Bible class, school.

        Late afternoon—return to Chipps.

    4th Sun—arrive at circuit church for AM service.

        Din & Sup with parishioners.

    Mon AM Dev. & Bible class, school.

Visit non-churched in community.
Din & Sup with parishioners.
Tues AM Dev. & Bible class, school.
Visit newcomers in community.
Din & Sup parishioners.
Wed AM Dev. & Bible class, school.
Visit & Din with parishioners.
Afternoon—return to Chipps.

Visitation and meal schedule prepared by local Boards.
Some outlying parishioners, in good weather come to Chipps for church. Before school starts for the season, the time normally spent in class with children will be spent calling on families with children.

Food for horse provided.
Bring own breakfast food.
Compensation—10% of Sun. offering on circuit.
Likely gifts of food to take home.

"If anything, they are organized."

"Well, not quite—much of it was spoken in conversation; I organized it. But I think it's workable. Circuit week is only one week per month. I'll come home Friday nights and stay until Sunday morning, and then be back home again on Wednesday evening. We'll be able to do our sermon planning and hair-wash. On circuit weeks I'll be gone only three nights of seven. I'm really pleased. I was dreading being away from you as many as 5-7 nights."

"I was dreading it too."

Franco thought he heard a slight quiver in her voice.

"Mira-honey, are you . . .?"

"No Franco, not afraid. It's just that those days and nights when you are gone will be lonely."

"I know. Which reminds me—the Benson's who live a couple miles down the road have a litter of just weaned puppies! We can have the pick of the litter."

"A dawg?"

Franco raised his eyebrows.

"I said *dog*—well maybe I said *Dawg*, with a question mark."

"Mira-honey, life on the prairie is safer with a well-trained dog, plus it will provide good company."

"But in the house?"

"Indoor/outdoor. For starters I will fix a little bed for it right here, inside the door. Later he will be able to be outside as well, maybe leashed until he learns our boundaries."

"Franco, sorry if I sound like I am complaining or have regrets about coming. There's just so much that is different for me. I promise I will adjust."

"I'm not criticizing, Mira-honey. The changes for you are great. You're doing very well. You've already delivered two babies, and sutured one wound. More than I've done. I got two free breakfasts following your hard nights of work!"

Seeing her smile, Franco went on "Wait until you read the next page, Mira-honey." Franco handed Mira a paper with the following:

Mira to lead worship in Chipps on the Sunday that Franco is on circuit.

Will receive 10% of offering.

Mira and Franco to plan schedule for devotions and Bible class for Chipps' school.

"Franco! I'm delighted. How did you get them to agree to this?"

"I didn't. It was their idea. But I'm in favor of it. I'm so glad you are. Their reasoning is: *lay-people have been leading worship; surely with your seminary education you are more qualified.*"

"You mean *no one objected on the grounds that I'm a woman?*"

"A few raised the question—but it seems that on the prairie people are more open to the unconventional. *Doing what is expedient seems to matter most.*"

"Did you tell them that I have not had preaching classes, and technically did not even graduate?"

"No, I didn't say that. But I remember you saying how *natural* it felt to address a large group of people—*you loved the feeling of talking to an audience.* And you have great ideas for sermons. I have no doubt about your ability. We'll continue to prepare together. And we must continue to seek God's timing for graduation and ordination. *That may be a bigger concern for you personally* than for anybody else. Here you *are* and *will be* appreciated for who you are and will be encouraged to work according to the gifts God has given you."

Mira said nothing.

"Mira-honey, this changes the subject. But I want for us to talk about Saturdays—tomorrow and future Saturdays."

Mira nodded her head for him to go on.

"I learned many important things from my pastor in Pennsylvania about *being* a pastor. He said that it is important for pastors to observe Sabbath on Saturday—possibly even starting on Friday night. That is what I would like for us to do—especially the Saturday-Sabbath."

"Tell me more."

"Except for emergencies, let's try to relax, and NOT *do specific ministry activities*. Just things around here, like work in our garden, read, take care of our animals. Go for horseback rides. Have a few good meals—provided we have food to fix!"

"I like those ideas a lot. I think rest from pastoral work will prepare us for the week ahead. But there will be people who stop by—like tomorrow Mrs. Samson and Jimmy will be coming."

"It will be good to see them again. I wonder how little Jimmy is doing. I keep thinking of his big blue eyes looking up at me, pleading with me to carry him to their buggy."

"Hopefully Mrs. Samson will tell us more of their story. And we can talk to her about helping to care for our animals when you are on circuit. I'm even thinking of asking her to do some sewing for me when I start getting really busy—as I will with the Board wanting me to be involved in the pastoral work. I think I am as excited about working with the school children as I am about preaching. Maybe I can even start hygiene classes. Teaching children—especially here on the prairie—about good health care practices seems so important. Perhaps we can also hire Mrs. Samson for washing and cleaning. I wonder how much work she would do for us in exchange for the milk we do not need for ourselves and the calves. She could use the milk for churning and making cheese, and sell it. And when I get paid for preaching, I would be able to pay her something."

To Franco's amusement, Mira had a way of *running-on* when excited.

"Now you are really thinking like a prairie woman. I'm proud of you Mira-honey."

Mira and Franco fell asleep that night resting securely in the belief that they were doing God's will exactly where he wanted them—on the American Frontier, working as a Team.

And they had their first uninterrupted night of rest since arriving!

Over a breakfast of a fried egg a piece, sourdough bread, and coffee, Mira voiced her concern about low food supply. "We can have bread and cold rabbit for dinner, but other than that, except for a few staples in the cupboard, we have nothing to eat."

"Take heart Mira, I'll check for eggs. And I had a brief look at the garden yesterday—the lettuce looks ready, and some small radishes; possibly even peas. That, with a couple boiled eggs will be a fine supper. And we can ask Mrs. Samson if she has any milk and cheese for sale. I have enough change to pay for it. With milk and flour and an egg I can make pancakes for Sunday morning breakfast. And I suspect that tomorrow we will receive gifts of food from parishioners. If not, remember the storekeeper said we can buy supplies on credit. I would rather do that than ask for the advance that the Board said I could have."

Mrs. Samson, or *Bessie*, as she insisted being called, came about 9 AM. Jimmy was eager to show them his wound, but not until he had Mouser firmly in hand. The wound was healing well; no sign of infection. Bessie beamed as Mira complimented her on taking good care of it.

"Doctor-dear" (Mira smiled. Was her new name making the rounds in the community?), "that's what I do. I take good care of my Jimmy, my animals, and anybody else that I can help."

"I'm so glad to hear you say that, Bessie, because Mira is going to need your help, and Jimmy's too, when I ride circuit."

"Anything we can do, Pastor, we will do. Just tell me how we can help." Jimmy looked up at Franco as if to say *you can count on me, Pastor*.

And so they worked out a plan for when Franco would be gone: Bessie would milk the cows and check the other animals in exchange for milk. When Franco was home and did the milking himself they would give her the milk that they did not need for themselves and the calves; and Franco and Mira would receive some cheese, butter and buttermilk from Bessie. Even after supplying Franco and Mira, Bessie would be able to increase her sale of dairy products. Mira also told her that soon she might need help with washing, cleaning, and sewing. Bessie was pleased, knowing that once the calves were weaned the deal would be to her advantage, even with taking on some extra duties.

Jimmy felt two inches taller, just at being asked to take care of Mouser and gather the eggs.

The rest of the day Mira and Franco observed Sabbath, with a short but delightful visit from Jimmy in the afternoon, bringing them buttermilk and cheese. He was equally delighted with the few coins Franco gave him, promising to give them to his mother.

Chapter 6 *Summer Begins*

Franco awakened to the sounds of the prairie—the rustling cottonwood standing between house and school/church, the birds, lowing cattle on a nearby farm waiting to be milked, the occasional bark of a dog, the crow of a rooster, birds chirping. He propped himself on his elbow and in the dim light of dawn smiled at Mira. She looked peaceful, disarrayed hair framing her face. She could sleep longer but he would get up, wash his face in the cold cistern water, check the animals, and review his sermon notes. Their first Sunday on the prairie. He must not delay getting the day started.

By 8 AM he was stoking the stove and making pancakes. Mira began to stir, and then muttered something about wrinkled "Sunday dress." *Sunday dress*! What about *Sunday suit*? His wedding suit—it was still in their traveling bag. His mother had washed and ironed his shirt, but by now both shirt and suit would be very wrinkled.

"Mira-honey, we *both* have ironing to do. I'll put the irons on to heat right now. Glad you remembered to get them from your trunk. We'll give our clothes a quick touch up after breakfast. I don't think people will arrive before 9:30—if that early."

"I can't believe I forgot, Franco. And truthfully, I know nothing about taking care of men's clothes—or my own, for that matter. I've never had to."

"Well, how difficult can it be?"

They were soon to find out. Ironing on the table did not lend itself to sharp creases, sleeves or ruffles. But the end result was presentable. By 9:30 they were ready and put Mouser on mouse patrol in the house—they were continuing to have night visitors, cat and traps notwithstanding.

Mira and Franco greeted the first arrivals shortly after 9:30, but spoke with them only briefly. This couple, along with a half dozen children had arrived with a large farm wagon, transporting several tables, and began to set them up under the cottonwood. Before long other families arrived, all congregating under the tree. No food was set out—only baskets, sacks, tins, and crates were placed *under* a table that had been set to the side. While Mira wondered what it was all about, Franco smiled knowingly. The smell gave the contents away—gifts that would be more appreciated than food.

Bessie and Jimmy arrived shortly before 10 AM. Jimmy hurried to Franco. "Pastor, may I help you ring the bell?"

Ring the bell! Franco should have done it as early as 8 AM, then 9 AM, then *9:30*. Oh well, the people came anyway.

"Great idea, Jimmy! Let's do it right now." And thus a tradition was begun. Jimmy would be the bell ringer, a task he would take as seriously as anything else that Pastor Franco asked him to do.

The people found their seats. Many children sat on laps or floor.

Franco began informally by thanking the congregation for coming, and for the expressions of friendship already given by many of them during their first week—especially the help and gifts of food. He went on—

"Getting to know each other can be awkward. Especially, *what shall we call each other?* This past week many of you have already called me *Pastor*. I like it. Every time I hear *pastor* I am reminded of what I came to Chipps to do—*pastor the flock of Jesus*. Some of you may be more comfortable saying *Reverend*. I like that, too. *Rev. Franco*. My first name is actually Franklin, but a few years ago Miranda dubbed me *Franco*, and to those I am close to I have been *Franco* ever since. I hope you will be comfortable using this name. And now it is my privilege to introduce my wife, Miranda—*Mira-honey, please stand.*"

Mira stood, and as Franco held out his hand, she walked over to join him. "Friends, meet Mrs. Welken—already known to some of you as *Doctor*. Miranda and I were married just two days before starting our long journey to Dakota Territory. Mira, please take a moment to tell our new friends about yourself."

"This morning we have gathered for *worship*, so I will keep my comments brief—but I'm looking forward to meeting everyone at the picnic following our worship service. Franco is right—it is hard to know what to call each other. I love being called *Doctor*, but you should know—although I have much experience in doctoring, having learned from my father who is a physician, I am not formally educated in the medical profession. So if you call me *Doctor* please keep that in mind. I like, Franco, am here to serve you, and already have had the privilege of helping some of you." She looked at Jimmy and smiled, who in turn whispered loudly to his mother, *I think she means me.*

"As Franco said, my first name is Miranda, but I go by Mira, a name given me by my father's patients long ago. So here we are, *Franco and Mira*, and we think of ourselves as a Team who has come to the American Frontier to serve the Lord as we serve his people. And now let's worship our Lord."

As she returned to her seat the people clapped, and Franco raised his arms in greeting and blessing: *Grace, mercy and peace be yours in abundance from God our Father, the Lord Jesus Christ, and the blessed Presence of the Holy Spirit. AMEN.* The congregation responded "AMEN."

The Board had already told Franco that the singing in the worship services left much to be desired. The congregation seemed to have little musical talent, although it was rumored that a few people could fiddle, and others could play the harmonica. Fortunately, Franco had a good singing voice, and the congregation responded to his enthusiasm by singing along, surprising even themselves by how good they sounded. Old favorites that had not been sung for a long time were suggested, and they could have sung the whole morning, but Franco had to move the service on.

As he read the Law he sensed a restlessness—had it been a while since they had heard these words? He followed the Law with Jesus' command to love God above all, and neighbor as self. His congregational prayer was praise, thanksgiving, petition and confession. And then the sermon.

Friends, I hear that you have storms here on the prairie—all kinds of them, tornados, rainstorms, windstorms, thunder and lightning storms, hailstorms, snowstorms, blizzards . . .

(Bessie drew in an audible gasp. Jimmy clutched her hand tightly. The woman behind her gently placed her hand on Bessie's shoulder.)

. . . and then there are the storms of life. I want to assure you: God *is* our security and shelter in all these storms. *But we have a responsibility to seek shelter.*

Let's hear the Word of God from Psalm 46,
and then we'll identify some of the storms that overtake us, and the security we have when we seek shelter with our God.

I don't much like storms, especially lightning. My parents always told me to not stay out in a thunder and lightning storm. Father and Grandfather set good examples—
If they were working in the field, and a storm was brewing they would unhitch the team and walk them back to the barn as quickly as possible, and they would take shelter in the barn with the animals, or come to the house.
It's a lesson I've never forgotten—to seek shelter in the times of storm.
Psalm 46 isn't so much about seeking shelter from the storms of nature,
as it is about *finding shelter with our God when the problems of life* seem overpowering, threatening to devastate us.
It doesn't say there won't be storms; it says that God is our refuge in storms . . .

His sermon was short, but powerful. He concluded with these words:
So, friends, seek the shelter that he so freely offers—
Listen quietly; hear his voice tell you that he always is your security in all the trials and troubles of life.

The shelter that we receive may be the comforting promises of his Word.

Often his shelter takes the form of another person that he provides, to walk with us in the difficult times of life.

We are all on this journey of life together. Let's support and love and encourage each other in the storms of life. AMEN

After the closing song and benediction Franco reminded the congregation that all were invited to the social time under the cottonwood tree.

The tables were quickly set with picnic food to share. The table to the side was soon covered with jars of a variety of canned food, tins bearing handwritten labels, and other items wrapped in cloth. By an unspoken agreement no one took from this table. The picnickers sat on the ground—most had brought blankets. Mira and Franco had several invitations to join families, and were able to get acquainted with many people. Later that afternoon Franklin wrote down as many names as he could remember, beginning to assemble a visitation list.

As people packed their dishes Jake and Cora walked Mira and Franco to the untouched table. Cora was the first to speak, "Pastor Franco and Doctor-dear, the food on this table and the containers underneath are *welcome gifts* from the community. Not having enough food and kindling can be one of the biggest problems on the prairie. These gifts will help you get started."

Mira expressed her thanks for the food, while Franco examined the items below—a few bundles of wood, several baskets and sacks of corn cobs, some that looked (and smelled) as though they had been picked up from a hog yard, chips, kerosene, and coal. Franco recognized the value of these gifts and extended his hand in thank you to Jake, whose response was, "Let's get these to the barn. Looks like it might rain tonight. But don't worry pastor, *there won't be a storm.*" Cora helped Mira carry the jars, tins, and other items to the house.

They felt blessed as they went to bed. Later that night they heard a gentle rain refresh the earth—the kind that soaked in rather than washed off. And Jake was right—there was no storm.

Miranda and Franco had made plans with the McPhersons to have Monday dinner with them and stay the afternoon. Franco to meet ranch hands who had not been to church, and Mira to meet the wives of those who were married.

But before going to the ranch, there was work to be done.

Franco rose early to do routines that were becoming part of their prairie living—caring for the animals and bringing in water for the day. Some days would require more than others—Mondays the copper boiler needed filling for wash day; Wednesdays and Saturdays water for bathing. Another 5 gallon bucket would save on the number of trips back and forth to the cistern; and perhaps another tub for rinsing clothes would help Mira wash efficiently. Maybe she was right—they could ask Bessie, who would gladly take on more work, to do their washing and ironing sooner rather than later. On the other hand, perhaps Mira should learn the necessary skills for prairie living as soon as possible. So until he went on circuit he would encourage her in this part of the struggle. When the cows began producing more milk than what their calves would need he would feel more comfortable in asking Bessie for help beyond caring for the animals. It was only three more weeks until he got his monthly pay. With that, and the generous gifts of yesterday, their garden (they still didn't know who planted it) and the little that Mira would take in throughout the month, they would get by.

All these thoughts and considerations filled Franco's mind before breakfast.

Following an egg breakfast—thank Goodness, most of the chickens were now laying—Franco helped Mira with the hot, heavy wash water. He then went to his office carrying with him some bread soaked in the last little bit of milk they had on hand. *Mouser, here's hoping that you live up to your name soon.*

Franco settled at his desk writing out tentative plans for the week:

<u>Mon</u>—choose Scrp. for S. sermon,
 McPherson ranch, dinner there;
<u>Tues</u>—Jed & Maggie, morning lunch; *talk about baptism.*
 Ike & Jennie, dinner there; *talk about baptism.*
 Stop by Bessie & Jimmy (bring change for milk).
<u>Wed</u>—general store; pastoral call to Bensons;
 ???puppy; ???rabbit hunting;
 Evening, bath/wash hair; sermon discussion.
Thurs & Fri—sermon preparation, pastoral visits.

Mira had never spent much time on personal appearance, except for her hair. But there was something about being Franco's wife that made her want to look her very best. The wash water was much too hot so she had a few moments to spend on herself, wishing she could remember in which trunk she had packed her folding-leaf mirror. Perhaps tomorrow she would have time to look. There were also other items she was beginning to miss.

For now, she could mix up another batch of sourdough bread and do the breakfast dishes, before attacking the daunting pile of laundry. She had watched her parents' housekeeper do laundry often—

First the whites. That would be easy—with no petticoats there were few whites. *And then on through the rest, by color and amount of soil.*

Except for dust that infiltrated the fabric, the clothes were not terribly soiled. Common sense told her that shaking everything first would lessen the need for scrubbing against the washboard. But wringing large objects such as towels and sheets was difficult; how she wished she had a hand cranked wringer like her parents' housekeeper used. Maybe they could get one on a trip to Yankton someday. Or maybe she could soon turn the washing over to Bessie. *If the milk exchange we worked out with her is not enough to cover washing I could pay her out of the money I will get from preaching.*

Mira got through the washing, rinsing, and wringing. With aching arms she went out to the clothesline, only to realize that the clothespins were still in a trunk somewhere. *Think, Mira, think. Which trunk? It would make sense that we put them in the same trunk where I found the irons and washboard. I'll try that first. That'll give me a good reason to go over and see, Franco, too.*

"How's your morning going, Mira-honey?" He smiled, noticing the tendrils of hair that escaped her braids.

"I would deliver a baby any day before doing the washing. The morning is flying and we will soon have to leave for Jake and Cora. Would you help me hang the sheets, and get rid of the water?"

"Of course."

"But first we have to find clothespins. I think they might be in this trunk."

They found them near the bottom, and decided to carry other items to the house as well. Mira conceded that what her mother and cook insisted on sending would make her kitchen work a little easier—good knives, eating and serving utensils, and pots and pans with lids. Even a cast iron roasting pan that would do wonders for rabbit. But she was not yet ready to unpack china and crystal. It would seem to out of place in their little shack.

Franco helped Mira hang the sheets, and while she hung the smaller items Franco poured the cooled wash water on ground that had plants which would not be harmed by soap. He watered the garden with the rinse water, and took a moment to examine the growing plants. "Mira-honey, you should see this; the gentle rain of last night made the lettuce grow an inch, and the carrots, beans, and radishes look great, too."

Franco saddled the horses, while Mira put herself back together. Fortunately, her drenched clothes had already dried in the dry air. She took an extra moment to pull on her leather drawers. She would enjoy this ride to the ranch.

Franco put Mouser on house patrol, and they began an easy canter.

Cora welcomed them, inviting them in. Mira tried to mind her manners, but couldn't help but stare at the beautiful spacious kitchen-eating area. A large cook-stove; beautiful wooden furniture, including a large table and many chairs; several paintings on the wall, a bookshelf filled with books; a hutch filled with lovely dishes. *My china and crystal would look good here.* There were several closed doors that apparently led to other rooms. But this, without doubt, was the *living room,* even if there were a parlor behind one of those doors. Mira had no idea that such beautiful homes existed on the prairie.

"Cora, forgive my asking—I smell food, but your stove is not in use."

"Oh, Doctor-dear, in the hot weather we cook in the *summer kitchen* so we can keep this room as cool and comfortable as possible."

As she was speaking Jake came in, tossed his hat in a corner. His greeting was, "Good haying weather. It is dry enough, even after the soaker last night. Hope you are ready to spend the afternoon in the fields, Pastor." He gave Mira the briefest of nods.

"I am, if you are willing to have someone who hasn't been in fields for three years!"

"Thought that being out with the men would be a good way to get to know them. We'll take it easy on you first time around."

It truly was a *dinner*—fried chicken, potatoes and gravy, fresh green beans, lettuce and radishes, buns, and creamy pudding for desert.

Ranchers and farmers do not linger over dinner. Twenty minutes had hardly passed and Jake was on his feet. "If we don't hurry, Pastor, the men will be back at it before we reach the field."

With brief introductions, Franco was given a scythe and was told what area was his to cut. After a few swings, he realized that he hadn't forgotten how. A few more swings and he also realized that he was in for a good case of aching muscles. *Oh Mira-honey, am I going to need a liniment rub tonight!*

There was no chance for conversation while working, and after an hour and a half, sweating profusely, Franco went to the water jug. Jake joined him. "How you holding up? If you've had enough for today, no one will mind—but the way to get to know these men is to show them that you understand their kind of life; hard work; little talk." Franco nodded his head, surprised at the *lengthy* comment from Jake.

"I'm okay. Probably good for another hour."

"Good—the women will be coming about 3 o'clock bringing lunch. Working like this, a man needs fuel and plenty fluids every couple hours." With that, Jake returned to lay another swath. Franco rested a few moments longer, then feeling rehydrated returned to his work. He wasn't exactly keeping up, but given his years away from physical labor, he wasn't doing poorly, either.

Shortly before 3 o'clock Franco saw a small bevy of women approaching. The other men saw them too, put down their scythes, and walked towards the women. No greetings were exchanged, but the men quickly dropped to their knees around the table cloths that were laid out and spread with cheese sandwiches, cookies, and cups of coffee. The women fell back, each with a coffee cup and cookie in hand.

"Men, we ain't much for talking while eatin' or workin', but Pastor wants to say a few words."

Franco thought he heard an emphasis on the word *few*.

"Thanks for letting me work with you—as you can tell, what I did compared to what anyone of you did, doesn't stack up too well."

"You done good, Pastor."

"It don't make no difference *how* much you did; point is you *did* it."

"You know how to swing that scythe, man—anybody can see you're a farmer."

"Well, thank you for those words—I grew up on a farm, and it's still in my blood. But my real work now is to be a Pastor in Chipps and surrounding area. I hope you all, and your families will come to church; and come fall we'll be seeing your children in school—my wife and I will both be teaching some classes. And speaking of my wife, you see her there with the women. She delivers babies and does some doctoring—is willing to come out to your homes, or you can come to our place, where she has a large stock of supplies. She's talking with Jake's wife today, hoping to come up with a plan on how they can work together.

"I don't have much more to say right now—just feel free to stop in to see us, come to church, let us know if we can help you with illness, or anything else going on in your lives. We don't have all the answers, but will do what we can. I know you don't take long breaks, and the sandwiches are gone—looks like you didn't even save a cookie for me, so I'll be on my way. (He heard a few chuckles at the last comment.) Hope you don't mind if I come back another time."

"Anytime, Pastor, anytime. We can always use a strong set of arms and shoulders for this work."

Franco walked over to the women, feeling confident that he had made at least a foothold in the community. Mira introduced the women to him, and then they all scattered their individual ways. Cora, Mira, and Franco walked back to the house.

On the way home Franco was so quiet that Mira wondered how it went.

"Franco . . .?"

"Mira-honey, have you unpacked your bottle of liniment?"

"Yes. Why?"

"My mother always rubbed down my father after a hard day of work in the fields. I'll be needing that tonight."

"Consider it done—with pleasure."

"Thanks." He said no more, but his thoughts raced on. *I still haven't talked to Jake about the bats, and about buying hay. Strangely though, I haven't heard bats for several nights. Maybe they left, once people were in the house again, and a cat. Or maybe it was only mice. Still, we need a ceiling before winter, and our animals hay.*

That evening Franco brought Mouser to the school/church with nothing to eat but bread soaked in water. *I hope those cows calve soon.* Franco took a dead mouse from a trap and put it in front of Mouser. He only gave it a sniff and a look of disdain.

While kneading liniment into Franco's sore muscles Mira told him of her conversation with Cora. "I think Cora is as eager to work with me as I am to work with her. She has the names of at least six women in the community who will be delivering in the next several months—all within reasonable riding distance. We are going to visit them several times before their due dates. Some are experienced mothers; others first time. Especially with the first time mothers we want to teach them about self-care, baby care and child care. Cora will be so good at this—she already visits the mother a few days before birth to make final preparations; but she never thought about doing teaching earlier than that—good nutrition, and mothering skills for children of all ages, etc. She is excited about the possibility of me teaching hygiene in school, too. Would you believe that Cora and Jake have four sons? One in his early 20s and married. The other

3 teenagers. They didn't eat with us because in the summer they prefer to live in the bunkhouse with the unmarried ranch hands. Did you know that Jake is already a second generation rancher? That makes his sons third generation."

When Mira stopped to catch her breath Franco asked, "And what about the delivery itself? Who will the husband contact first? You or Cora?"

"We are thinking that whoever lives closest to the family should be the first to be called—to do assessment and be with her in the early stages; then when the time draws closer, the husband can come for the other. It really is nice to have two of us at the time of birth—one to take care of the baby and the other to attend to the mother. Cora thinks this will help save lives in certain situations. Cora prefers the baby work."

"What are the people going to think of this—two women doing the work that one person normally does? Does that mean they pay double?"

Mira was quiet for a moment. She and Cora had discussed this. "Cora doesn't have a fee. Never has received a penny. She says that when a Dakota farmer says *this time of the year we are short on cash* they mean *we barely have enough money to live on—anytime of the year*. But Cora is often given food. She uses it to cook meals for the unmarried ranch hands. I have never seen anyone as generous as the McPhersons. But Cora says *we've been blessed. How can we not give in turn?*"

"But that really doesn't answer my questions, Mira. If ever I learned anything from my parents it's this: *no matter how small the business, amount of money involved, or goods exchanged, work out how you will handle the finances.*"

"I understand what you are saying, Franco. Basically, my father would agree too, although he often worked benevolently. Cora would agree with what you just said. However, she is so aware of the poverty around her and that people here have to watch out for each other. She and Jake are doing well, but nobody here lives in the kind of financial climate that brought about your parents' financial ruin. This is an entirely different situation. Cora suggested that whoever is called first should receive the gift, if one is given. How does that sound to you?"

"That part sounds fair. And I suppose you are right about the situation that my parents came from as being very different from what the people on the prairie live through. I'll accept what you and Cora have decided about *pay* for deliveries. But have you considered the many hours you will spend teaching women? The many trips to their houses before the birth? No compensation for that does not sound fair to you and Cora."

"Oh, Franco. It will work out. I'm surprised to hear you express concern over this."

"I have been poor all my life, but I've tried to live up to my responsibilities. I have tried to not owe anyone anything. The prairie people have pride. *Being on the receiving end when you cannot do anything in return is hard for many people. They would rather do without.*"

"I think I understand that, Franco. But your implication seems to be *that I never have had a want or need.* Financially *that is true. But I have needs too; especially the need to be accepted—all my life. A different kind of need, but a need.* Perhaps that takes us into an area that we can't discuss right now. However, I will talk to Cora about the points you made—especially about the time we would spend traveling and teaching mothers. *But I know doing that will fill a need in me.*"

Franco tossed and turned all night. Even the liniment rub hadn't totally eased his muscle pain. And he was hoping and praying that Mira wasn't getting herself in too deep in an area where she had no experience—situations that had financial implications and obligations. He failed to realize that she and her father had constantly faced similar situations in their medical work. Though a good business man, her father always erred on the side of giving. Perhaps that was the genius of being a good business man. And Franco failed to bring to mind that his parents and the Piersons, during the war years and the years following, gave without ever expecting anything in return.

Miranda herself *wondered if putting people in a position of owing something* was really the reason Franco did not want her traveling in the community and teaching. *Why, it's akin to riding circuit! Might I be getting into his "area" without his supervision?* Cora, who seemed to read people well—including men—might have insight on this.

When they arrived at Jed and Maggie the following morning lunch was already on the table. Maggie's sister was still there helping with housework, meals, and the baby. Jed came to the house as soon as he saw the horses draw up to the house. After greeting them Mira walked to the crib to admire the baby. Was it only a week since this delivery? Mira felt like she had lived a life time in this new world.

Franco sensed an urgency in Jed—this would be a brief visit; farm work cannot be delayed. So as soon as they were seated Franco got right to the point. "I understand you want to have your baby baptized."

"Yes, Pastor, we do," they answered together.

They discussed the significance of baptism—*it means much more than giving a name to the child; it welcomes the child into the family of God; it is a sign and seal that the child belongs to God first of all, and also to the congregation of believers, including the parents.*

"Oh Pastor, we believe that with all our heart, and hope that the baptism can be soon. Perhaps Ike and Jennie would like to have their baby baptized on the same day."

"That's a great idea. Mira and I are heading over to their place. We'll talk to them about it."

Jed had managed to drink his coffee, eat his sandwich and a couple of cookies during the conversation. Now he stood up, "Want to come outside for a while, Pastor? I hear you had quite a workout at Jake's yesterday. I won't work you that hard."

Franco did not feel like using a muscle, but grinned and said, "Okay, let's see what I can do."

While the men pitched hay from a hayrack into the hayloft Mira fielded questions from Maggie, realizing that she knew less about caring for newborns in their first few months than she realized. She did, however, tell Maggie about how she and her mother had taken care of the baby whose mother had died, for six months. As she was telling the story to Maggie Mira saw that it was really her mother who had done the most for the baby. *I wonder how mother knew so much? I'll have to ask her someday.* She also remembered how very troubled her mother became after giving up the baby. *Oh, dear Lord, there is so much I don't know about life and living. Help me learn. I must learn if I am to be effective here. And help Franco and me to be supportive of each other, even when we do not totally understand each other's motives.*

Franco stopped at the cistern pump, took off his shirt, and gave himself a good wash down. Dust from dry hay fairly enters the pores, and there was no time to go home before traveling on to Ike and Jennie. Maggie gave Mira a towel to take out to him, but he needed it only for his hair. The air, almost totally lacking in humidity, dried the droplets on his skin immediately.

As they cantered along the path Franco commented, "As much as I like farming, I hope it doesn't become an expected part of pastoral calls." But word got out in the community that Franco was of farming stock, and more often than not that summer he was handed a pitch fork, shovel, or another tool. And he found that working side by side with the men was a natural time for pastoral care. It was private and the only time the men would talk. He got himself a good pair of farmyard boots from the general store and always carried them with him. Dress shoes could be washed off but they didn't easily give up absorbed odors.

They arrived at Ike and Jennie in time for dinner. Taking just a moment to admire the baby, they, minus Jennie, sat down to eat. Having had a difficult and exhausting delivery, she was still limiting activity, running her household from her bed or easy chair. But no one seemed the worse for it. The oldest daughter was doing a great job.

They had a brief discussion about baptism and Ike and Jenny were pleased at having a joint ceremony with Jed and Maggie. It would be the Sunday after Franco's first circuit.

"Well Pastor, are you ready for pitching a little hay—the boys and I have one cutting in the field ready for loadin'. This is the best hay we've had in years. Want to bring it in before we get more rain—although rain is always welcome in Dakota."

"I've got about an hour. Then we have to head home. Bessie and Jimmy will be there about 2 o'clock. Will probably be waiting for us. Jimmy cut his leg last week, and Mira stitched him up. She has to take the stitches out today."

While Franco spent an hour out in the heat pitching hay, Mira visited with Jennie and her daughter, learning about raising a family on the prairie. Learning much more than she taught. *But then again when I sit down with pen and paper and reflect on the many things I've learned from Father (even Mother,) about child care, and especially about preventing and treating illnesses, I know I will have a lot of practical information to develop into lesson plans on healthy living. Enough to teach mothers, and even boys and girls in school.*

As Franco had predicted, Bessie and Jimmy were waiting for them. Jimmy had retrieved Mouser from their unlocked house. Now, cat in arms, he sat with leg propped on the step, bandage off. One glance showed that it was well healed. He beamed at Mira's praise for taking such good care of it. She went in, got her scissors and tweezers, and in no time removed the stitches.

"Doctor-dear, we brought cookies and milk. Thought we could have afternoon lunch with you and Pastor."

"Great idea. I'll stoke the stove to make hot water for tea."

They went inside. It was Franco who stoked the stove and put on the kettle, while Mira got out the cups and saucers, very glad that she had taken them from her trunk the day before.

"Pastor, what does *stoke* mean?"

Franco looked at Jimmy and smiled, "Stoke—I bet you say *fire up*. You *fire up the stove* when you want it to burn hotter, right?"

"Right. So why do you say *stoke?*"

"Well, I guess *stoke* is city-talk, and *fire-up* is prairie-talk. I think I'll have to learn more prairie-talk. Will you teach me?"

"You bet! But first could I be excused and take Mouser out to play?"

"You're excused."

"What a fine boy you have," Mira said as Jimmy sat down on the front step, Mouser in hand. "I'm looking forward to having him help me with Mouser when Franco is on circuit."

"Thank you. He is such a comfort to me."

"Would you like to tell us about your husband?"

Bessie nodded, and began a sad story of her husband, presumably lost in a blizzard, but his body was never found.

"Does Jimmy know?"

"Only what's appropriate for a child to know."

"Perhaps you would like to tell us more, later."

"Perhaps. But the important thing is, Jimmy and I have good memories and are learning to carry on. We are looking forward to helping the two of you, especially when Pastor is on circuit."

"I can't tell you how much that means to us."

"It will be our pleasure. How are your cows doing?"

"Eating the hay, and drinking lots of water, but so far, no imminent signs of birth."

"Be sure to call me if you need help. Most women around here know as much about these things as the men. We have to. The men are too busy during the day. Anyway, animals usually don't need human help."

After they left, Franco put his arms around Mira, "Mira-honey, we have much to learn about life on the prairie, and life in general."

"So true. And can you believe how much everyone eats? Yet they are as thin as rails. Are you hungry for supper?"

"I can always eat, but I think a lettuce salad and boiled eggs will do again. I hope the beans soon blossom. I'll cut the lettuce, pull up some radishes, feed and water the animals. Oh, and I should rub down the horses and clean their hooves."

"I can help. How about I take care of the horses?"

"I welcome your help."

Later that evening Franco told Mira his idea for the Sunday sermon. Psalm 69:2, 73:2 and Ephesians 4:27—the importance of having a firm and secure foothold, and not giving the devil a foothold. "Let's not talk about it now—let's each mull it around for the next 24 hours; what it means, how it applies. I'll be thinking about *what in prairie living might give the devil a foothold.* And how can each of us get *a good foothold.* What do you think, Mira? Can we come up with a meaningful sermon on that topic?"

"God helping us, I'm sure of it. I'll think about it, maybe jot down a few thoughts."

"Thanks, I knew I could count on you. Your insights and understanding of Scripture are valuable to me."

"Thanks Franco. It works two ways."

"Now to change the subject, do you want to come with me to the general store tomorrow—or *John's General*, as I hear it is called? And the owner is affectionately known as *General John!* He was in the Civil War."

"Can't see much point in it since we don't have any money. The last little we have we must use for milk, cheese, and butter. I wish those cows would *come-in.*"

"We can charge, you know. Ike was telling me that most people do. General John is really good about working with people. Some folks he carries along for years, but apparently he eventually gets paid, because next to Jake, he is the richest man in the community. But my real reason for wanting to go is to talk to John. Get names from him of people in the community that don't come to church and add them to my pastoral list. My plan is to start by just paying some neighborly calls and inviting folks to church. Even if they are unsure about a new pastor, the picnic after the service might entice them! Also, the store might be a good place just to hang around a bit and meet people who come to buy. At least if the General doesn't mind."

"Thanks for inviting me to go, Franco, and I apologize for sounding a little bitter about not having money to spend. That gives me something to think about as far as *footholds* go. *Bitterness and disappointment* might be powerful examples of footholds the devil uses. But actually, I should stay home and do more unpacking and organizing in the lean-to."

"Whatever you think best. And thanks for that insight on footholds. I think those are two powerful suggestions that we can work on tomorrow night. Since you won't be going, I'll bring my rifle. I have to get bullets. Do you remember where we packed it? I think it was in one of your trunks."

"It most likely is in one of the trunks in the barn. We could look tomorrow morning. It is too dark now, and I'm bone tired."

Franco left for John's General about 9 AM. Daylight had found them rummaging through the barn trunks. Along with the rifle they took out several more household items that Mira would find helpful in the kitchen. With their meager food supply there was still cupboard-space. She hoped Franco would soon bag a rabbit.

Mira had made another breakfast of eggs—*bless the chickens*—scrambling them this time with a small amount of milk that Bessie brought the day before. She saved the rest for the cat. *Drat that cat for drinking milk and not killing mice. And drat those cows for not coming in.* She checked herself. *Oh-oh! Am I giving the devil a foothold? Sounds like a foothold called* bad attitude.

Mira had hardly begun her work in the lean-to when she heard a wagon rumble up to the front door, and a small child screaming. She quickly ran out, only to have a baby thrust into her arms. "Hot coffee burn on her leg."

Mira quickly took the mother, Agnes, into the house and then handed the child back to her. Collecting her thoughts she made preparations to treat the baby. She laid out several thick towels on the trunk top (*thank you God, that I took them out of storage this morning*) and covered them with the washed petticoat she had used for Jimmy. Grabbing a clean pan, she ran to the cistern for fresh, very cool water. Then she dropped several surgical drapes (still unhemmed) into the water and took the screaming baby from the frantic mother. No amount of comforting would help now. They had to get rid of the pain first. The anterior aspect of the lower leg was a brilliant red with a few small blisters. It was a burn that did not go deep, but was very painful. Mira covered it with a soaking, cool drape and almost immediately the screaming turned to whimpering. Mira instructed Agnes to rotate the cloths, leaving them dripping wet, and to do this for the next half hour—by that time the worst pain would be gone. Agnes quieted and began to gently talk to her baby as she soaked her leg.

Meanwhile Mira got a couple more pans of cool water and brought them to Agnes. Returning to her supplies she retrieved clean dry dressings and a roller bandage that she had made from her petticoats.

"I'm glad you did not try home remedies, Agnes. For this kind of burn clean cool soaks work best. I don't promise you that there will be no more discomfort, but I expect that after this ordeal she will be so tired that she will sleep for a long time. After that the worst should be over. Do you still nurse her?"

The mother nodded, watching in fascination as Mira quietly talked to the baby and gently patted the burn dry and dressed it with the clean bandages.

"Great! That will be all she needs. Do your best to keep the bandage clean and dry. I'll ride out to see her tomorrow and Friday, and on Saturday you can bring her here again. By that time, I expect she will need no further dressings. But keeping the bandage clean and dry is very important. It will relieve pain and prevent infection."

A figure appeared in the doorway holding a chicken upside down, legs tied together. "I'm Agnes' husband, Jeff. I bet you think we are terrible parents letting our baby get burned with coffee."

"The thought never entered my mind. Accidents happen. I'm so glad I could help."

"Sorry I didn't come in; I just couldn't take the screams. I feel so guilty. I was holding her. Her little hand and arm were so quick, she just bumped against the cup I was holding."

"Did some spill on you too?"

"Well, now that you ask, yes it did—probably most of it. Right here on my thigh." Mira gave one look and turned scarlet. There was a large wet spot over his left crotch.

"Not to worry Doctor, my old pants is so thick, it barely soaked through."

"All the same, let Agnes check it when you are home. The same treatment I used for the baby will work for you. Be sure your rags and water are clean."

I'll bet it was his own pain, not the baby's screams that had kept him from coming in immediately. Come to think of it, he may have been dousing himself with water in the barn—he was nowhere to be seen for the half hour we spent treating the baby. And probably used water from the stock tank. Oh well, it's doubtful there are any open areas.

All the same, Mira fervently wished Franco were home. He could have examined Jeff. And how he ever managed to catch a chicken before coming was beyond her. And then she realized *it was probably their dinner, already caught and awaiting its fate.*

Before leaving Agnes, offered to chop the head off the chicken. Mira declined, saying that Franco would be home by dinner time, and he would take care of it. Once they were gone, Mira picked up the chicken, cut the strings binding its legs and tossed it in the coop with the other chickens. Franco could deal with it when he wanted chicken soup. Agnes had told her that it was an old layer, and too tough for roasting, but it would make delicious soup.

For their noon meal (Mira still had a hard time thinking of it as *dinner*) Mira heated a jar of canned meat and a jar of vegetables, thanking

God for the gifts given on Sunday.

It was becoming increasingly difficult to not talk about their work at mealtime because their work was their life, so Mira told Franco about the baby, and about Jeff. Franco immediately agreed to ride out with Mira the next day. Their name was on the list of unchurched that General John had given him that morning. They were very poor. Franco was no stranger to burns having helped his parents treat many soldiers who had sustained burns in battle.

With excitement Franco told Mira about his morning at *John's General*. General John had gladly shared names of community people, and was delighted with Franco's suggestion of hanging around the store an hour or two every week. Not only that, he encouraged Franco to make a few necessary purchases on credit—*everybody does it*—and worked out a reasonable plan of payment.

"Mira-honey, I got another 5 gallon bucket, bullets, a pair of boots, and a most amazing thing. Something called *matches*. General John explained that these little sticks of wood will save tremendously on the amount of fuel we use in the summer, because we will not have to keep a fire banked day and night. *And* without a fire in the stove all the time our house will stay cooler in the summer. All we have to do is take one of these little *match sticks, scratch it over something rough, and a flame will appear. That flame we hold to the kindling and it will start to burn. Just that easily we will have a fire going*. Isn't that amazing?"

Mira agreed that it was, although she had heard of such magical sticks before. Her father had told her, but she had never seen them in use. They had to be used with great caution because of the poisonous phosphorous in them. He said they should be used outdoors to avoid inhaling the fumes which could cause *necrosis of the jaw*.

Franco was taken aback by this information, but Mira assured him that she saw their value—*when used with caution they <u>would</u> make life on the prairie easier*. If they became popular in the community, proper use would be a good teaching point. They decided that they would talk to General John and suggest that when he sold them he teach *safe use* right then and there. People listened to General John.

Mira changed the subject to the chicken Jeff brought. "I tossed it in with ours—Agnes said it was tough, but would make a good soup."

"Well, let's have soup for supper instead of rabbit that I was hoping to shoot this afternoon. I don't want a strange chicken in with our flock. They will probably peck it to death."

Mira's eyes went wide with horror. "I don't understand, Franco."

"Oh, it's just the way of nature. I'll need you to help me. As soon as we're done eating set on a large pan of water while I catch the chicken and chop its head off. When the water boils pour it in this new bucket, and bring it outside."

Mira looked at him with questions on her face.

"Trust me Mira I know what I'm doing. Butchering chickens is not the same as butchering rabbits."

Mira brought out the bucket of water, only to see a headless chicken jumping about. Franco was allowing it to bleed out. Suddenly she understood the phrase *acting like a chicken with its head cut off*. When the chicken did a last feeble flop, Franco picked it up by its legs and plunged it back and forth in the water. "Hot water loosens the feathers, making it easier to pick them off," was Franco's answer to her unspoken question.

Where was I when our cook did all this? Mira wondered. *We ate chicken often.*

Franco pulled the chicken out of the hot water and let it cool a bit. "I brought a knife, and the cast iron pan for the meat."

"Good thinking. Let's see if we can pull these feathers off."

The chicken plucked easily. Mira and Franco dropped the feathers in their other bucket. "Look closely, Mira. See all those little hairs, and pinfeathers? Since we do not skin chickens, we have to get them off, too. The way we do that is to singe them in a fire. I made a little pile of hog yard cobs—don't think you want to use them in the house—and poured a small amount of kerosene on them. Now with one of our new matches we will make a small fire."

For people who had never seen a match ignite, and then start a fire, it was a magical moment.

While the kerosene burned off, the cobs ignited, and soon they had a fire that burned high enough for Franco to pass the chicken through several times. He then handed the chicken to Mira, took the bucket of water and doused the fire. "In this dry weather we must be super careful. But look Mira, the cobs hardly burned at all. We will leave them right here to burn them again when needed. I'll have to look for some small rocks and make a circle around it."

By this time Mira was speechless. She offered a silent prayer of thanks to God for Franco's skills for living.

"Now, Mira-honey, this is when I really need you. You hold the two legs, about the height of your waist. I'll put the feather bucket under the chicken to catch the innards while I butcher. I'll have to bury this all, so it does not attract wild animals."

Franco pumped cool cistern water into the pan, placed it to his left as he squatted down in front of Mira and the chicken. In about five minutes the job was executed, and Mira was on her way to the house to try her hand at soup. "Mira-honey," he called after her, "please separate out the heart and liver." She didn't ask why. Inside, she stood in front of her labeled tins, wondering which of the dried vegetables to add to the pot of chicken.

Meanwhile Franco looked over the innards hoping to extract the lungs and any other soft, edible parts—those, along with the heart and liver would make a good meal for the little pup he hoped to get from the Bensons that afternoon. Maybe even Mouser would be willing to try a bite or two of the delicacy. Franco quickly slipped over to the school/church. No questions asked, Mouser ate, and licked her paws in a gesture of thanks. *Well, that shows she likes meat; just not dead mice.*

Before leaving, Franco set on the copper boiler to warm water for their evening routines. Nice thing about a cook-stove—the surface area was large enough for something as large as a steamer, and a pot of soup, even a kettle, should any one stop by for tea.

"Oh, Mira-honey, I learned something else from General John this morning. About once every two weeks he sends a wagon and driver to Yankton to pick up supplies. One will be going early next week. He said he would be willing to order supplies for us. But not only that, the driver carries letters and packages from our community, and mails them in Yankton (we pay General John for the postage) and he brings back mail from the Yankton post office."

Mira's expression brightened with this bit of information.

"So, if we have letters to send East, we can give them to the General on Sunday at church."

"That's good news, Franco. Maybe he will bring back letters for us! I was going to unpack this afternoon, but I think I'll write letters instead. And continue my thoughts for this evening."

Mira set the kettle on for tea, got her writing supplies from the lean-to, thankful they had come across them while rummaging in the barn trunk.

What would she say? Where would she start? How much detail? Should she tell of both hardships and blessings?

She started with a letter to her parents. Much of it she would copy for Franco's parents, and add some prairie life details that they would relate to better than her city-parents. Although her father would enjoy it all, and especially her medical experiences—the breech, the burn, the cut, the chips, hog yard cobs, matches, and butchering the chicken.

She wrote the entire two hours that Franco was gone, including an impassioned plea that both sets of parents ask their churches to roll bandages and make hemmed 12x12 squares for dressings. She signed off just as she heard Franco return and put his horse in the barn. She had not written anything specific about their pastoral ministry, thinking that Franco would want to write about that.

Writing is exhausting work. I might better jot down and compile daily notes and send them every time there is mail service. Thus the idea for <u>Mira's Journals</u> was conceived.

Before coming in Franco did the evening chores. Later he would make a quick trip to the garden to cut lettuce and pull up radishes. But now he wanted to introduce the puppy to Mira and find an empty crate for his bed.

Mira greeted him at the door.

"Look Mira-honey, this is Benny—named after the Bensons."

"He's cute," she responded, her voice lacking enthusiasm. *Cute, but I'm going to call him* Dawg.

"I'll get one of the empty crates for his bed. Do we have any old rags, or pillow that I could use for bedding."

"None at all—I don't even have cleaning rags. Only good towels. But there is the packing that was around my medical supplies. Would that work?"

"I think so. Here, do you want to hold him while I get the crate and packing?"

She didn't, but took him anyway as Franco handed him over. Holding the wiggly little guy, she had to admit that he was friendly, and his face had a certain charm.

Franco went to the lean-to and found packing that would work temporarily as bedding. He deftly made a soft little "nest" for Benny in a crate, and with one of the cords that had been used to hold supplies together, fashioned a little collar and leash which he attached to the crate. He put the collar around Benny's neck.

"Do you have the liver and heart? The Bensons said he is eating small table scraps. If we chop them and place them on a saucer by his bed I think he will quickly get the idea that this is his new home."

He ate with relish, but Franco could give him only water, not milk, for once again their milk was gone.

"How are we going to work out *living arrangements* between *him* and Mouser?"

"Well, eventually they will have to learn to get along with each other, but for now, we'll alternate them between the school/church and our house. Mouser to stay the night over there, and Benny leashed over here. But I do want Mouser to spend time here during the day—we are still trapping many mice. I think before long Mouser will start catching. I fed her a few pieces of the chicken—lungs and other soft parts that I was able to save from the innards. She loved them, so now she has the taste of meat. By alternating them between the two places they will get used to each other's smell, and then after a few weeks, under supervision, we can introduce them to each other."

The soup was surprisingly good, the well boiled-meat, tender. Franco carried the leftovers to the spring-house (enough for tomorrow's dinner and some for Benny and Mouser), and buried the bones.

The evening was spent much as the previous Wednesday evening. They enjoyed luxurious baths and hair washes, and discussed sermon ideas as Franco brushed Mira's hair, Mira jotting down notes.

They decided on DISCOURAGEMENT *as a powerful foothold that the devil uses to keep Christians from being joyful, fruitful, and flourishing. Christians must have their footholds firmly grounded in God and his Word, to be able to withstand the many and varied attempts the devil uses to get them to fall prey to discouragement and giving up.*

Franco would develop the ideas more fully on Thursday and Friday. Wednesday night they fell into bed exhausted, but content.

Unfortunately, Benny was not so content—his first night away from his mother and litter mates. Franco was up several times to comfort him, finally taking him to the barn so Mira could sleep.

The sunshine streaming through the barn window awakened Franco. He had fallen asleep on straw, Benny comfortably curled against him. He quietly got up and tied Benny's leash to a post. The puppy slept while Franco did the chores. He washed his hands and face at the pump and then went to the house and quietly opened the door. Mira was still sleeping. He slipped in, took his notes from the table, and went to his office, hoping to get in an hour and half of sermon writing before breakfast—if only Benny would sleep for awhile.

Mouser welcomed him as he took a moment to pet him. "Sorry kitty, no breakfast for you yet. We are out of milk. This morning your breakfast will be bread soaked in a beaten egg. That, I'm afraid, will be your new friend's breakfast, too."

Franco settled at his desk, his ear tuned to the barn and Mouser rubbing against his legs. Benefits Seminary had said nothing about.

Mira awakened about 7:30. Seeing that their notes were missing from the table she assumed that Franco was in his study. They had a busy day ahead, but she felt rested and up to it. Once Dawg settled down she had slept well. Apparently Franco had too. She looked over to the crate. *Dawg was gone, leash and all.* She almost called for Franco, but checked herself. He wanted this dog. He could worry about it. *I just hope that Jimmy will like taking care of Dawg as much as Mouser.*

She took several moments to dress and braid her long hair. One of these days she would look for her snoods. Franco liked her hair down at night. By packing her hair in a snood for the day she could save herself the morning braiding. Besides, it would look pretty.

Next she mixed up a double batch of sourdough—she hoped to give Agnes a loaf, and starter. They looked so poor. She wondered where their meals came from.

Franco came in at 8 o'clock, Mouser in hand. After greeting him, Mira said, "Looks like you've been hard at work already—you look a bit tired, and here I have been sleeping. And how did that straw get in your hair? I did get a batch of bread mixed up, and breakfast is almost ready. Since you have Mouser with you, did you bring Benny to the school/church? He really settled down nicely after that last time you got up with him—what time was that? About 2 AM? Oh, dear, here I rattle on and on. Let me finish getting breakfast on the table. Hope you are okay with poached eggs and bread. Isn't it amazing the many ways eggs can be served?"

Franco sat down, saying nothing until after they thanked God for a new day, and for bread and eggs.

"Speaking of eggs, Mira, I thought of a new use for them—pet food! Here's my idea—these little animals need more than milk. They're starting to need solids. So how about this? Since we have plenty eggs, we could beat several of them, add a little water to thin them, pour it over bread and give some to both Mouser and Benny. They'd love it, and it would be good for them. What do you think?"

"Sounds good. Using eggs for them would stretch our precious milk, and supply good nutrients."

"Thanks, I was hoping you would see it that way. And yes, in response to your earlier comment, I made good progress in writing. Thanks for all your insights last night."

"It's a pleasure working with you, Franco. I thank God every day for the times you and I spent discussing theological ideas and the truths of Scripture with my father."

"Indeed. I too give thanks for those hours. How much we learned from him—especially how to develop and defend the truths of Scripture. I think his ability to do that comes from his logical, scientific brain."

"Thanks for that comment. If ever we took the time to do it, we could write a book on *What We Have Learned from Our Parents—Christianity in Practice.*"

"I agree. But I have a feeling that the only book we will have time to *write* is the book that the people on the prairie will see us live out every day."

"You're probably right, but having our experiences in writing would be a tremendous legacy for future generations."

"True, but now we must get on with *a day in the life* of our book. I'd like to be at Jeff and Agnes about the time Jeff has his morning lunch. So how about if I help you clean up here, and then feed Mouser and Benny, and saddle the horses?"

"Thanks. Do you want me to whip up a couple eggs?"

"Yes, please. And add about a fourth cup of water."

They arrived at Jeff and Agnes Spencer at 9:15, recognizing the place from Agnes' description to Mira. Agnes held baby Iris while Mira unwrapped urine soaked dressings and laid them to the side—she would ask Agnes to wash them thoroughly and hang them in the sunshine to dry. To her great relief the wound was healing well, even the little blisters were smaller. Mira felt Agnes' eyes on her face. "It looks good, Agnes."

"Oh, Doctor, I was so frightened because I could not keep her from wetting herself."

"I understand. Do you happen to have warm water in your reservoir—we don't need cold today. We can go outside and gently pour water over her leg, just to rinse it off. I don't think it will hurt like it did yesterday."

Mira took Iris outside. Franco lingered behind a moment as Agnes got the water. "I was hoping to meet Jeff this morning. Mira told me about him."

"Oh Pastor, he wants to see you, too. Wants to talk to you privately. He's in the near field. Would you carry this jar of coffee to him, and his morning sandwich?"

"Of course. Just point me in the right direction."

They went out, Agnes directing Franco to the field.

Very gently Mira thoroughly rinsed the burned area, patted it dry, redressed it, and instructed Agnes on washing and drying the soiled bandages. "If her little leg needs rewrapping tomorrow we can use the same bandages once they are washed and dried in the sunshine."

Franco returned in about 15 minutes—all the time Jeff could spare for his lunch break. "Agnes, Jeff showed me his burn. It is not deep but needs better care than what he is giving it. His pants are too tight and rubbing it raw; the blisters have opened. If he is not careful he will get an infection. That would be very dangerous. Does he have pants that fit loosely?"

Agnes looked frightened. "He's a hard man, Pastor, and doesn't like me telling him what to do."

"*I've* already told him. Does he have another pants? If he doesn't, I'll bring him one of mine. We are about the same size."

"Yes, Pastor, he does. I will lay it out for him to put on when he comes in for dinner."

"Tomorrow when Mira comes to see the baby, she will ask about Jeff, too. If necessary, I will come back."

"Thank you, Pastor."

As Mira and Franco were cantering along, Mira said, "That was a side of you I've never seen before."

Franco smiled, "I've met men like him before, in the soldiers that came to our house. I learned a lot from my grandfather and father on how to deal with them. We'll have to keep a close eye on him. Not first of all because of the burns, but because of the nature of the man. I don't trust him."

Franco continued on as Mira turned on the path going to Bessie. She was greeted by Jimmy, "Doctor-dear, how is Mouser?"

"Mouser is just fine, and now she has another friend."

At Jimmy's look of concern she realized how Jimmy heard her comment. "Oh no, Jimmy, you are still Mouser's *first friend*, but now we have a puppy too, just waiting for you to come to play. His name is—Benny."

Without even thinking to hold her horse's reins for her, Jimmy ran to the house, "Mama, Mama, Pastor and Doctor-dear have another friend for me to play—I mean *help*—with. A puppy. His name is Benny. Oh Mama, can I go now?"

Bessie took Jimmy's hand and walked to Mira. "Remember, Jimmy, we always hold the reins of a lady's horse, and then tie them to the hitching rail."

"Yes, Mama, I know, but I forgot because I was so excited."

"I understand, and I think Doctor-dear does too."

By this time Mira was off her horse and gave the reins to Jimmy.

"I'm sorry, Doctor-dear."

"Not to worry, Bessie. I loved his greeting. His enthusiasm warms my heart. And I also have a deep appreciation for how wonderfully you are teaching him."

"Thank you, Doctor-dear. Can you come in for tea? Where is Pastor?"

"I can come in. Pastor went with me to the Spencers, but had to go home to work on his sermon."

"I'm so glad you are helping them. I worry about them. Not just about the burn—yes, I heard about it. News travels fast. Please don't think me a gossip, but Jeff is given to drinking, and can get rather violent. Even when sober, he can be—I think, *hard* is the word Agnes uses. Other times he is friendly, and a pleasant neighbor. I just never know what side we'll be seeing. I don't let Jimmy go there alone. And now I have probably said too much."

"Not at all—these are the kind of things Pastor and I must know if we are to work effectively in the community. And frankly, in just one meeting Franco has already picked up on some of what you are saying."

They changed the subject when Jimmy entered. "Doctor-dear, I hope you don't mind. I found our old curry comb, and I brushed Dapple down a bit."

"Thank you, Jimmy, you are going to make yourself indispensable to Pastor and me."

As Mira left, she heard Jimmy ask, "Mama, what does *indispensable* mean? I hope it is good."

"It means that you will be their valuable helper."

"Can I go this afternoon to play with Mouser and Benny?"

"Did she invite you to come today?"

"Well, not exactly to come *today*. But if I'm going to be *indispensable*, I think that means I should do something for them every day."

"You may go this afternoon with some cookies. And I think they could use more milk than what the doctor took. You could call it *welcome gift* for the puppy."

"Thank you, Mama. When will it be time to go?"

Mira heard only the very first part of the conversation, but it warmed her heart. Now she must hurry to Cora—fortunately Franco had agreed to warm the soup for their dinner. *Oh, thank you Lord for matches. They'll make our life easier. Help Franco to remember not to breathe the fumes.*

Cora met her at the door. "This is a nice surprise. Where is Pastor? Can you stay for dinner?"

"Thank you, Cora. Franco is working on his sermon. This will be just a brief visit, but I have a couple of things to talk to you about."

"Nothing serious, I hope."

"The first regards the Spencers."

"You've been treating their baby for a burn—word gets around, you know. How is it?"

"Little Iris's burn is superficial and healing nicely. I believe, however that Agnes would benefit from instruction on parenting."

Cora nodded.

"But that is not the real thing that is bothering me. Franco spent about 15 minutes with Jeff in the field, and he sensed that Jeff—oh how can I say this?—that Jeff might be an *unreasonable* man. And Agnes used the word *hard*. Then I stopped at Bessie—and you know Bessie is so kind—but she says that she won't let Jimmy go there alone."

"We know Jeff well. He used to work for Jake, but Jake had to get rid of him because of his drinking and violent behavior when drunk. We don't really know Agnes. When Jeff moved away he wandered around for awhile and came back a few years later and settled on that property east of Bessie. Did she tell you that he is renting from her?

"No, never said a word about that."

"Well fortunately, he is keeping his end in the renting agreement. You know, Doctor-dear, there are times when you would think Jeff is the nicest, most agreeable man you have ever met. But be careful. Poor Agnes."

"Do you think we can help her, especially with the baby?"

"Well, you could for the next week or two just stop in to check the baby's leg, but really to build a friendship. You don't have to worry about

134

Jeff yourself—it's just that if he thinks you are getting too close to Agnes, he might take it out on her."

"You don't think he would hurt the child, do you? The way he described how the burn happened totally sounds like an accident, and he felt terrible."

"Let's give him the benefit of the doubt, but keep our eyes and ears open. And now, Doctor-dear, what else?"

"It's about our teaching classes, remuneration, and what Franco thinks about it all. He has some concerns, and now I am wondering *if Franco is really leveling with me on why he is not in favor of it?*"

"And Doctor-dear, *you want to be home for dinner?* Sounds to me like we have a whole afternoon of talk. I will very gladly listen and discuss, but I suspect that you and he have more talking to do first, and if he doesn't want to talk more, take a pen and paper and write it all out as a prayer before the Lord. You will be amazed at the insight God will give you.

"That, and just give Franco more time to think it through too—like the week he is gone on circuit. He will then realize as never before what a fantastic team the two of you are and how you both complement each other in what you do. My guess is that in a month, maybe two, you will find that these problems are no longer so big."

"Do you really think so, Cora?"

"Yes. Remember you have been married less than a month, and have come here where life is so different for you. You can't take on and solve everything at once. Don't question his motives; give him time. Very often answers just happen in the normal course of events. I strongly suspect that will happen with the personal things you are concerned with. But I do share your concern about the Spencers. With your permission, I will discuss it with Jake. He might have some insights to share with Pastor."

The soup was simmering when Mira tied her horse to the hitching rail. Franco was at the table, intently chopping something. He looked up and smiled at her questioning face. "I'm chopping the chicken skin very finely for Benny and Mouser. I also skimmed the fat off the soup. They will love it."

"You never cease to amaze me with your innovations, Franco. You obviously know much more about prairie living than I. But Cora says *we complement each other.*"

"That is a compliment we both can be pleased about. Are you glad we came, Mira-honey?

"Franco, I can't think of a place where I'd rather be than here on the Frontier with you."

Other than a couple visits from Jimmy to *help* with the animals, Thursday afternoon, evening, and Friday were spent quietly, Franco working on his sermon, and Mira continuing her unpacking, organizing, and repacking her trunks with things not immediately needed. And she took up Cora's suggestion of writing out what was weighing on her heart—her fear that Franco might be seeing her plans for visiting in the community (for teaching) as *competition,* rather than *complement.*

***

Thus <u>Mira's Prayer Journals</u> were born—not to be confused with <u>Mira's Journals</u>, which she would soon undertake as well.

***

On Friday she paid a quick visit to Agnes to check on baby Iris. The dressings were soaked again, but other than a bit red, the burn was healed and needed no further dressing. Mira asked Agnes to wash and dry the bandage and dressings and return them the next day. She wanted to see the baby one more time. And Agnes assured Mira that Jeff was carefully following Franco's instructions to pour clean water on his burn and to wear loose fitting pants. But Jeff was nowhere in sight.

By bedtime Franco commented to Mira how ready he was for their Saturday-Sabbath.

The nights were getting shorter and shorter, the sun setting late and rising early. But since there was still no milking to do they would sleep in Saturday morning.

That was the plan, anyway, but at 7:00 AM they heard a team and wagon pull up to the barn. Franco got up and looked out the lean-to door. It was Jake with a load of hay, already pitching it up to the loft.

"Mira-honey, it's Jake, pitching hay into our loft. I have to go and help."

Mira groaned, but said nothing. *For all his good qualities, I still don't like the man. Couldn't he just ask us, or even tell us. But no, he just shows up and this is how it is going to be.*

They worked an hour unloading the hay. Mira got herself dressed for a day that was beginning differently from what they had planned. But the breakfast she was preparing was the same as usual—eggs. *How shall I fix them today? Boiled, fried, poached, scrambled? I know—we still have some cheese and a little milk—I'll make an omelet.*

She was still grumbling to herself when Franco entered the house, Jake right behind. "Mira-honey, could you fix a couple more eggs? I'll cut the bread and pour the coffee. Jake has something to discuss with us."

Jake tossed his hat in the corner, gave her a nod, and sat down.

"Pastor, you asked about paying for the hay. Here in the West we do a lot by trading rather than paying. You did give me money for the horses, but as you said at the time, you knew that you got the better end of the deal. And you did—I wanted to be sure that they were good horses for both of you, and after seeing you both ride, I see that they are. Here is the other part of the deal— if you agree to it anyway. I'll breed the horses and the foals will be mine. They're good mares—had foals before. As for the hay—you just keep letting me breed, and I'll keep you in hay—even for your cows. If there is ever a drought—which there often is in Dakota—we can renegotiate."

Franco and Mira looked at each other. Mira had no idea of the value of hay or mares, but she nodded and Franco extended his hand and said, "It's a deal."

"I thought you'd see it that way. As soon as we finish eating we'll go out and talk over the details of the breeding." Mira hid her smile behind her hand. *Men talk!*

***

Mira was never sure who got the best end of the deal. The horses produced many excellent foals over the years, and the Welkens always had enough hay for their animals, even grain for their chickens, and straw bedding for the stalls. *Ultimately,* she concluded, *with trading and bartering, as long as all are satisfied, and needs are met, all are winners.* Such was life on the frontier. Watching out for the others while taking care of self and family.

***

When Franco asked Jake about Jeff, his response was "Men like Jeff are no good to have in a group of cowhands." And at Franco's attempt to discuss the need for a ceiling, assuring him that he could do the work himself, Jake's only response was that lumber could be ordered through General John.

Jake turned the team and wagon, stopped at the front door, opened it and said, "Cora sent this chunk of dried beef for you—thought you might be needin' meat." Mira wasn't sure he heard her "thank you," he left so quickly.

And Mira had no idea what to do with a *chunk of dried beef*. Boil it? Bake it?

But Franco knew. "Mira-honey, it makes the most delicious sandwiches you can imagine. All we have to do us cut off thin slices. It is cured in brine and hung to dry, so it doesn't need cooking."

So once again they had enough to see them through several more meals. But Mira was feeling the strain of wondering *where* their next meals would come from. And what about the nutrition of many of the people they came to serve? It would be one thing to teach about nutrition, *but what to do if the means weren't available?* This would be an entry for her prayer journal.

Their day had gotten off to a different and earlier start than anticipated, but by 10 AM they felt like they were on track for Sabbath— just as Agnes pulled up, Jimmy with her. She had picked him up along the way.

Franco greeted Agnes and asked her about Jeff. She said that he was following the instructions and the burn was healing. Franco accepted her words, but made a mental note to ride out to see him on Monday. Franco took Jimmy to *work* with the animals, leaving the ladies to their own conversation.

Baby Iris' burn continued to look good, and Mira praised her for taking good care of her baby. She then tried to turn the conversation to good nutrition. "What about you Agnes? You are nursing your baby. Are you eating well yourself? You know nursing drains a lot from a mother."

"I know, Doctor. We manage. Our garden is producing now, so that helps, and when he has time, Jeff shoots rabbits. Come fall, if we have a good crop, we will be just fine. And in the winter Jeff will get a deer or two."

"That sounds like a good plan. Especially if your garden is producing. Beans, carrots, potatoes, tomatoes. All good for anybody, especially a nursing mother. Will you be able to put some up for winter?"

"There will be enough potatoes for storage, maybe some tomatoes for canning. But the other things we use as soon as I pick them—they make a rabbit or old chicken go much further. (Mira knew she was referring to soup.)

"I have an extra loaf of sourdough bread and a starter. Could you use them? I'm afraid they will spoil on me."

"Are you sure, Doctor? We could use them, and I do have flour and some sugar to keep the starter going. Bread and soup make a fine meal.

But . . . but don't tell Jeff. He don't want us beholden to anybody." Mira heard fear in her voice.

"I won't tell him. You wouldn't want this extra loaf of bread (she handed her the loaf) getting moldy on me, would you? And neighbors always share starters. I got mine from my mother-in-law in Pennsylvania. She made me promise that I would share it. So you are helping me keep my promise."

"Thanks Doctor. We'll be in church tomorrow. At least Baby and me."

They enjoyed a dinner of dried beef sandwiches—Mira agreed that they were delicious, even if the beef came from Jake.

"Mira-honey, we'll have to hang the rest of the dried beef from a rafter so the mice won't get it. Over the stove will be best—the heat from the stove will discourage flies. But we should loosely wrap it. Do you have cheese cloth?"

"No. But would couple of surgical drapes work?"

"Very well. You're a genius."

While Mira cleaned up after the meal, Franco hung the beef. And finally they went out to do what they had wanted to do for so long. Explore the garden together.

As they were cutting lettuce Franco cautioned, "Mira-honey this might be our last cutting. See those little white butterflies. They lay eggs on the lettuce leaves, and you know what comes out of butterfly eggs."

"*Caterpillars*. Maybe we shouldn't even eat this cutting, and spare me the joke about extra meat."

"This will be fine. Just wash them carefully, and look for caterpillars, but there won't be any. Today was the first I've seen the butterflies, and I check for them every day. "

Suddenly Mira's taste for fresh lettuce plummeted and she changed the subject. "Look Franco, the beans. They're blossoming. Fresh beans will be a welcome change from lettuce and radishes. And I have a packet of *bean seeds* for planting. Shall we do it now, so that when these are finished another crop will be on the way? Fresh beans all summer! Maybe even enough to can!"

Franco smiled at her enthusiasm, thankful that there were still enough hours in the day to enjoy their Sabbath.

Chapter 7 *Summer Continues*

Franco sat up in bed with a start. A clap of thunder had awakened him and also set Benny off to whimpering. *Better comfort him before Mira wakes. I wonder how Mouser is? But then cats seem to weather storms better than dogs—or man.*

On this second Sunday on the prairie Franco felt well prepared to deliver his sermon on *footholds*. Still, reviewing his notes one last time would be wise. He looked out hoping to dash over to his office, but the storm was too intense. *Perhaps the congregation will heed my advice of last week and seek shelter rather than come out for church.* He felt both relieved and chagrined at that possibility.

The thunder and lightning abated by 7 AM and Franco went out to do chores. Mira awakened as he came in, dripping wet, a half hour later. "Looks like an all-day rain. I'm just glad that the wind has died down and the thunder and lightning has moved to the east. But I doubt that anybody will come to church—the storm was too intense. The road looks fairly impassable and there will be trees branches down."

"And to think I slept through it! Was it really that bad?"

Franco nodded, and began to make breakfast as Mira readied herself for the day. *Wish I had taken that chamber pot from the trunk. I could store it in the lean-to for emergencies such as this.*

The rain continued and as 10 o'clock approached Franco did not bother to ring the bell. "Mira-honey, what do you think of this? *If* anybody comes we can have a devotional time, and save today's sermon for circuit preaching, and you can use it here—as is, or your own version of it on the Sunday that I am gone."

"Sounds like a good idea, but do you *really* think no one will come?"

"General John is the only one I know who has an enclosed buggy—more like a carriage than a buggy. He lives just a short drive from here, so he might come. Bessie has a buggy but it has only a canopy—no good in a downpour. And the road out her way will be too muddy."

"That means we won't see Agnes and Iris, either."

"I know. But I will go by horseback tomorrow to check on them—I feel uneasy about Jeff. And I'll stop in to see Bessie also. Jimmy will be disappointed about not ringing the bell today."

"Thanks Franco. What would I do without you?"

"You don't have to worry about that. We're a *team*, remember? A *frontier team.*"

"Franco, no church means no potluck, and no potluck means . . ."

". . . means dried beef sandwiches, and a jar of applesauce. I can't think of a better combination."

As they were talking, General John and his wife drove up. Franco and Mira met the General at the door. He was carrying a steaming cast iron pot and handed it to Franco. "Here, put this on the stove, while I hold the umbrella for my wife."

"Smell this, Mira-honey. This will beat even dried beef and applesauce, but why not get out the applesauce and bread anyway? And I will ask the General and his wife to stay for devotions and eat with us—I rather think they expect an invitation."

Franco was right. They readily accepted the invitation.

As a gracious host, Franco asked the General and Mable to share favorite Scriptures, and a meaningful hour of conversation and prayer followed.

Over the meal, conversation became more diverse, and the rain a little less intense. The General took their letters for their families, but told Franco and Mira that because of the severe storm it would be several days before his driver would go to Yankton.

As they left The General asked, "Will you be coming to the store on Wednesday, Pastor?"

"I'm planning on it."

Monday morning came fresh and clear. After helping Mira with the wash water Franco saddled Grey and headed out to Jeff and Agnes, carrying supplies for a dressing change if needed. The road was even worse than expected. No buggy or wagon would get through for a couple of days. If traveled too soon deep ruts would result.

Franco called his greeting from the porch and as Agnes opened the door he was assaulted with the smell of festering flesh.

"Agnes, what . . .?"

"Pastor, Jeff is deathly sick, burning up with fever. Can you help?"

Franco walked to the bedside with a determined step. "Jeff, what's going on here?"

Jeff looked at him with glassy eyes, "Git out of here, Preacher. You and your fancy wife ain't done me no good."

Franco ignored the rude comment. "Jeff you are deathly sick—we are getting you out of this room, to the porch." He turned to Agnes. "Agnes, fix a pallet out there while I get water. We have to get his temperature down, and his wound cleaned." But Franco doubted there was anything he could do to actually help.

Franco got the water, and then literally dragged a very weakened, but uncooperative Jeff to the porch. While Agnes applied cool compresses to Jeff's face and arms, Franco did what he could to cleanse the wound. It was clear to him that the infection extended far beyond the local site—likely to his blood stream. If so, Jeff probably would be gone by this time tomorrow.

"Agnes, I'm going home to get more supplies. I should be back within two hours. Meanwhile, every five to ten minutes change the cool compresses. *But, your top priority is your baby right now. First of all meet her needs.*" Then in a voice loud enough for Jeff to hear Franco added, "And if Jeff gives you a hard time, you have my permission to walk away. I'll take care of him when I get back. And Agnes, open all the windows and doors to air out the house, and drag all the soiled linen and towels outside—don't put Iris anywhere near the dirty stuff, and keep washing your hands thoroughly. And what about the animals—have you had a chance to take care of them?"

"Yes, while they both were sleeping I went out and did what I could."

Sleep! Agnes looked as though she had none herself.

Franco told Mira what he had found and then added his assessment. "Mira-honey, I've seen this before. We are going to lose him. But meanwhile I want to keep him comfortable, for Agnes' sake as much as for him. Do you have Epsom salts to soak the wound, and quinine for his temperature?"

Mira nodded and got the supplies. "Franco, I want to go with you."

"No, Mira-honey. The road is too bad, and believe me, other than keeping Jeff as comfortable as possible, there is nothing beneficial we can do. I've seen this too often."

Mira knew he was right, but her heart ached for Agnes and Iris, and for Jeff, too. She couldn't help but feel compassion for a man who was victim of his own bad choices. From what Cora had told her, he had set his life journey towards self-destruction years earlier, and now was reaping what he had sown. Her father would remind her *that bad life choices of an adult usually have their roots in a pain-filled childhood.*

When Franco returned he found that Agnes had done as he told her—the soiled linen, even the mattress was on a pile in a corner of the porch. The windows were open, and Agnes was inside nursing Iris. The cool compresses had done little for Jeff's fever so Franco gave him the dosage of quinine as prescribed by Mira, and then amid protests, set himself to applying an Epsom salt soak to the burn area, holding his breath to keep from gagging.

When he was finished he said, "Jeff, you are very, very sick. Are you prepared to meet your Maker?"

"Awe, Pastor, I know what's going on, and the best thing to prepare me is a few good swigs of whiskey. Can you get me some?"

"Jeff, whiskey might help you now, but it won't prepare you for eternity. We need to talk. Time is running out. I don't think you will be here tomorrow. You are dying."

"Talkin' won't help. Whiskey will."

Franco thought long and hard. And finally concluded that Jeff was probably right, but for all the wrong reasons. He consulted with Agnes before saying or doing anything more, first telling her that Jeff was not likely to live, as the infection had spread throughout his body. She nodded her head, as though she had come to the same conclusion. He then asked her about his history with alcohol.

Agnes told him that when moderately drunk Jeff was usually quite mellow. But as a drinking episode would progress he would become violent until he passed out.

"Agnes, I am going to talk to Jeff about turning his life over—whatever days or hours remain—to Jesus. If, after that conversation, he remains belligerent and unchanged, I give you permission to give him small amounts of alcohol ever 3-4 hours. Just enough to ease his discomfort and keep his behavior more manageable."

Surprise registered on Agnes' face, but she nodded in agreement, realizing that Franco really understood how difficult a man Jeff was, and how difficult these last hours could be without something to ease his mental and physical distress.

"Agnes, I want you to stay inside while I talk to him, but you are welcome to listen through the window—he is your husband and it is your right to know what happens."

Franco went out. "Jeff, here is how things stand. This is what we are going to do."

"Think you know it all *Pastor?* You and Agnes got it all planned out?"

"Your time is in God's hands, Jeff. But until you take your last conscious breath you have some choices. I am first going to tell you about the way of salvation, although I expect you have heard it before. Then you have a choice—to accept Christ as your Savior for all of eternity—or to reject him for all of eternity. After you make your decision, whatever it is, you can have small amounts of whiskey every 3-4 hours. I have told Agnes that she can give this to you *to keep you reasonably comfortable*. It will be your choice. You can also have quinine and the cool compresses."

Franco told him of the love of Jesus and the way of salvation. But Jeff refused. "That kind of love makes no sense to me. The only thing that has ever helped me is the bottle."

Franco felt drained but stood up, and said, "Have it your way, Jeff. And as I told you, Agnes will give you small amounts of alcohol, but not enough to make you drunk. Just to help you rest more comfortably. You will be able to think and make choices. In the quietness of your own soul you will be able to tell Jesus that you accept him."

"I need that drink, *now*."

Franco went in and asked Agnes where the whiskey was stashed.

"In the woodshed, Pastor."

Franco returned with one flask (there were several) and instructed Agnes on its use, with the promise to return in the morning. He also told her to expect Jeff to become increasingly weak, and not to give him any alcohol after he stopped asking for it. Before leaving he emptied the remaining flasks and buried them behind the woodshed.

Franco would often look back on these moments, and wonder if he made the right decisions. But when he remembered that Jeff had been completely lucid when he rejected the offer of salvation, and that the amount of alcohol that he recommended Agnes to give him would not seriously impair his thinking, he realized he would do it again in a similar situation. And down deep, he knew he had prescribed the alcohol as much to give Agnes a peaceful night as for Jeff's comfort—maybe more.

And he never did tell Mira. And hoped that Agnes never would.

Franco found that Bessie and Jimmy, except for the mud, had weathered the storm safely. Out of earshot of Jimmy, he told Bessie to expect a funeral in 2-3 days.

"Pastor, I did not realize that things were so bad. Is there anything I can do?"

"Not really, I think Agnes has things well in hand. I gave her instructions on keeping him comfortable to the end. I don't expect that he will give her any real trouble. He is not strong enough. It is after the funeral that she will need help."

"You are right, Pastor. I will be there for her and the baby. And since they rent from me, I will have to figure out what to do about the crops. Will you and Doctor please make that a matter of prayer?"

"Yes, we will and I will stop by tomorrow to update you. With these roads, getting out will be difficult for you."

Franco chatted with Jimmy for a few minutes updating him on Mouser and Benny, and assured him that they could manage without him for a couple days.

Franco briefed Mira on Jeff's condition and on Agnes and the baby.

"Mira-honey, I've got to go to talk to General John—perhaps he can get word to Jake. Someone has to dig a grave and make a coffin. I presume the burial can be right on the property. It would be too difficult with the impassable roads to bring his body to the graveyard here."

Mira nodded, but said nothing. This wasn't how she anticipated their first death and burial would be.

Veteran of life on the prairie, The General had helpful suggestions. He would send his driver by horseback to Jake, confident that Jake would see to the grave digging. And he gave Franco instructions on coffin making. "We can't get new lumber out there on horseback, so here's what I want you to do—Jeff has some tools and nails. I know because he got them from me. Just pull pieces of wood off the woodshed, the barn, or any other old building. They are all in pretty bad shape. Agnes will probably have an old quilt to line it."

Franco agreed, breathing a prayer of thanks once again, remembering his grandfather and father making coffins.

"Mira-honey, we will have to burn or bury the soiled linen and mattress. But if we use an old quilt to line the casket, I'm afraid Agnes won't have any left."

"Franco, remember how I protested all the supplies my mother insisted we take? One trunk is full of linen and quilts. We can give some to Agnes!"

"You're an angel, Mira-honey. I can't think of a better use."

"Well, it's the least I can do—I feel totally useless in this situation."

They spent the rest of the day quietly, Franco in his office thinking about what to say at the graveside, and Mira working with the laundry and making entries in her journals. *Was it only the beginning of their third week? It felt much longer. How she wished she could speak to her father and Franco's parents. And yes, even to thank her mother for all the supplies. Things that she thought would take a life time to use.*

Franco left by horseback shortly after breakfast on Tuesday. He was careful not to let his horse walk on the wagon wheel tracks, staying well to the side. The road had begun to dry on Monday, but he did not want to leave deep horse tracks where wagons would ride. Jimmy was waiting at the side of the road with a basket. Bessie had prepared some food for Agnes.

"Pastor, can I come with you? I really want to help."

"Not today, Jimmy, but soon. I know that Agnes will need you a little later."

"He is a bad man, isn't he? My mother won't let me go there alone."

"I know, Jimmy. Sometime soon I will tell you more about Jeff, but now I must see what I can do. Tell your mother *thank you* for the food. I know Agnes will appreciate it."

Agnes was sitting on the front step, baby in her arms. "He quit stirring and talking about 4 AM. But until then, he fought whatever I tried to do for him—except the alcohol. "

"Did you get any sleep, Agnes?"

"Only a few winks."

"I'll take over now, and stay as long as you need me. I want you and Iris to go inside and try to sleep. Here is a basket of food from Bessie. You must eat, also. The next couple days are going to be difficult."

Agnes put up no protest. That she was hungry and tired was evident.

Franco sat on the edge of the porch near Jeff's head. He didn't even bother with dressing change, but rather, in a soft voice read Scripture and prayed. He concluded his prayer,

"Lord, I don't know if Jeff heard or processed any of this, but please, Lord, whatever his level of consciousness, speak words of invitation to his heart and soul, and claim him as your own lost child.

In Jesus' Name, AMEN."

Franco stood up, feeling relieved of a heavy burden that he had been carrying for several days. He went to the barn and did the chores and scanned the walls, looking for boards that were large enough, and loose enough to remove. He tugged on a few. General John's idea would work! He also found tools in the woodshed, but would not start on the coffin until after Jeff took his final breath.

He didn't have long to wait. Back at the porch he could no longer see the rise and fall of Jeff's chest and could only feel a whisper of air when he put his hand near Jeff's mouth. His pulse was very weak. *Should I awaken Agnes? But what would that serve?*

Franco was not sure when Jeff took has last breath, or when his heart beat the last time. He just slipped away. Franco pulled the sheet up over his head and sat at his side until Agnes came to the door.

"He's gone then?"

"Yes, very quietly, about an hour ago."

"Pastor, thanks for being with him. It means so much to me. What do we do now?"

"Here's the plan, if you agree. I'll make a coffin with lumber from the barn—it'll take only about an hour. Meanwhile, if Iris continues to sleep, will you get a pan of water and wash him? Then we will line the coffin with a quilt or blanket if you have one, and place Jeff's body in it."

Agnes nodded her agreement.

"And Agnes, be sure to wash your hands very carefully before touching Iris. Even though Jeff is dead, all the linens are contaminated with drainage. We will bury it all with the coffin."

"Pastor, we can't do that—I have no more."

"Safety first, Agnes. I've already talked it over with Mira and she agrees. She has linens to spare and wants to give them to you. It would mean a lot to her to help in this way. She insists."

"As you say."

"And Agnes, one more thing. We must have the burial *here* tomorrow morning. Some men will come early to dig the grave. The coffin can remain on the porch until that time."

The community was beginning to stir again by Tuesday afternoon. Franco noticed several people on horseback on the road leading to Chipps. He himself went to tell The General that the funeral would be Wednesday. John would post a notice in his store and get word to Jake. He hoped for

Agnes' sake that some people would come, but transportation would still be a problem.

Mira spent the afternoon ironing the clothes and linens from Monday's wash and then went to her trunks to select a supply of linens to give to Agnes. But all the while she was brooding over something much different—her lack of productivity in the past several days and their dwindling food supply. For dinner they had finished the stew brought the day before by John and Mable. There were only a few jars of canned food left. Their milk and cheese were gone, and dried beef and sour dough bread, and EGGS were getting tiresome. She had never expected that FOOD would be such a big problem. When she expressed her concerns to Franco, he reminded her that thus far they had eaten three meals a day, there would soon be beans, the cows would soon *come-in*, and it would soon be *payday*. "And Mira-honey, tomorrow afternoon after we are back from the funeral I'll go rabbit hunting."

"That's part of the problem, Franco. I don't have anything important to do. All I've been doing for days is worrying about food and washing and ironing clothes. And you are busy all the time. It's been about a week since I had a new medical case."

"Well, I'll admit, the storm brought some disruption, and I know you didn't like not being more involved with Jeff—but storm or no storm, he wouldn't have let you anywhere near him. Let's just relax while we can and read the rest of this day. Tomorrow morning will not be easy. We should leave home shortly before 9 AM."

The trio rode horseback to Agnes early Wednesday morning. Without disturbing her, they quickly surveyed the area and chose a cottonwood tree a stone's throw from the house. Their first task was to clear away the branches and twigs that had come down in the storm—fortunately no large limbs. Once the grave was dug the hands went back to the ranch. Jake sat on the porch next to the casket, in deep reverie, wondering if years ago he could have done anything more or better to have helped Jeff. Something to have turned him from the downward spiral he was on, and that had ended so senselessly. He consoled himself with thinking *no one man can change the hardened heart of another. Me and Cora did what we could, but finally a man makes his own decision. If drinking is part of that decision, the outcome should not be a surprise.* But Jake knew he still had responsibilities. He and Cora would not let Agnes down.

Franco, Mira, Bessie, and Jimmy arrived at about 9AM and were soon joined by Cora, The General, Mable, and a few neighbors who also were church members. The guests came with food, brought it into the house, and after speaking briefly to Agnes went to the porch, sitting on the steps or on the edge of the rail-less porch. Little Iris provided a wonderful distraction for the somber gathering.

At 10 AM Franco, General John, Jake, and one of Jake's men carried the coffin to the graveside. Jimmy walked alongside Franco. The others followed and then gathered around. Mira stood close to Agnes and offered to hold Iris, but Agnes clung tightly to Iris. After the usual greeting, prayer and Scripture Franco spoke—

Friends, few of us knew Jeff well, but he left us a wonderful gift—Agnes and little Iris. We, the congregation, warmly embrace and receive you, Agnes and Iris, and look forward to getting to know you and having you part of our fellowship.

Then looking at those gathered he went on—

I met Jeff only a few times in these last days of his life. Some of you knew him better than I, and we all wish things had been different in his life.

We wish he had made better choices, but for reasons not known to us, he did not. On Monday I talked to him about Jesus, and during his last hours I sat at his bedside reading Scripture to him, and praying . . .

Franco spoke briefly about the love of Jesus, and how he extends it to all until we have taken our last breath. He spoke of the hope we have in God, our refuge and strength. He again referred to God as the shelter in the time of storm.

They lowered the coffin, tossed in the soiled linens and shoveled in the dirt.

The group sang *What a Friend We Have in Jesus* and *Blest Be the Tie That Binds*. After the closing prayer, Franco invited all to stay to eat. The women went to the house, and carried the food out to the porch, spreading it on tablecloths. (The house still had an unpleasant odor—it would need a good cleaning and airing).

By 11 AM most guests left, but Mira and Franco, Jake and Cora, Bessie and Jimmy stayed longer. Jake had earlier told Franco that he (Jake) and Cora had to speak with Bessie and Agnes. It would be helpful if Franco and Mira would watch Iris and Jimmy briefly.

In typical Jake style he told Agnes that he would send men over to work her fields this summer, and that she should take care of the animals. He told Bessie that he would do whatever necessary to assure the success of the farm so that she would get what was owed her in rent.

Jake then walked away leaving Agnes and Bessie rather speechless. Cora, accustomed to her husband's bluntness assured the women that Jake would do just as he said, and she herself would also do what she could for their well-being. Then to relieve a rather awkward moment she said, "Come, let's see what food was left behind." She called Mira to join them. The leftover "perishables" were divided among the three. There were jars of canned food, a loaf or two of bread, jelly, dried beef, and cheese, clearly intended for Agnes. That, with milk from her own cow, eggs, and produce from the garden, Agnes would be well supplied for the time being.

When Franco and the others left, Mira stayed behind, determined to get better acquainted with Agnes. Giving her the linens made a good starting point. Agnes had never seen, let alone owned anything so beautiful. She was deeply touched. She confided to Mira, "I have never been with so many kind people as came to the funeral. Maybe God is giving me a chance to start over. Me and little Iris. As Pastor said, Iris is a gift."

Agnes also told Mira what Jake and Cora had said, but she had no desire to talk about Jeff, so Mira directed the conversation to child care and nutrition. But Agnes wasn't ready for that, either. Maybe physical activity would be better.

"Agnes, I have been feeling so useless the last couple days—the storm changed all my plans. Would you allow me to . . . ?"

And Mira and Agnes spent the rest of the afternoon cleaning and making the best of a rundown shack. *Perhaps Jake will do something about this, too. But I think I will work through Cora to get it done.* Before Mira left, Agnes went to tend the animals, and returned with a half bucket of milk.

"Doctor, with all the food the people left, I do not need so much milk, would you like to take some home with you? I could fill a couple jars, if you think you can carry them on your horse."

"Thanks, Agnes. I can carry the jars because I have saddlebags. I will return them tomorrow."

By the time Mira got home, Franco had two rabbits skinned, butchered and cooling in the springhouse, and water for their Wednesday evening baths and hair washing warming on the stove. He was working on salting the pelts.

"Franco, when are you going to tell me why you salt and save the rabbit skins? I know it has something to do with what Ike told you."

"You're right. But I will tell you later my plans for them."

That evening they discussed the topic for the Sunday sermon—*Prepare to Meet Your God.*

Franco used Thursday to develop the notes Mira had jotted down from their Wednesday night theological reflection and discussion.

Invigorated by the time spent with Agnes on Wednesday afternoon, Mira set out by 9AM Thursday with real purpose. First stop—Iris and Agnes.

Agnes appeared rested, and had already been out to do her chores while Iris was sleeping. "Doctor, I have plenty of milk. Would you like to learn how to churn butter?" Mira was delighted. She had set out to provide emotional support to Agnes, and possibly do some teaching on nutrition. What could be a better setting than over a butter churn? Agnes sent a large *pat* of butter and a jar of buttermilk home with Mira. Mira promised a return visit the following week, and made a point of asking Agnes to come to church on Sunday.

Her next stop found Bessie and Jimmy busy cleaning house and making cheese and cottage cheese. It was still too wet for outdoor work, other than chores. Jimmy told her that as soon as the roads were dry enough they would go to the General Store and barter their cheese for other supplies. "And Doctor-dear, can you guess what my mother is going to buy—not tomorrow, but after she pays General John enough money?"

"I have no idea, Jimmy. Please tell me, if it is not a secret."

"No, it is not a secret. She is going to get a sewing machine! Every week she gives the General a little money. She thinks she will be able to get it by Christmas. Then she will do a lot of sewing and make more money."

Mira glanced at Bessie. "That's right, Doctor-dear. Have you heard of treadle machines? The General showed me one in his catalogue. It is expensive, but he is willing to order it for me when I have paid him half the price. Jimmy is right, I will be able to do a lot of sewing. It will be a good source of income. Here in Dakota, where crops often fail, there has to be a backup plan."

Mira left both Agnes and Bessie, feeling she had learned more than what she had taught. And that uncomfortable feeling of uselessness began nagging at her heart again. She brought it up with Franco over lunch. His only comments, "Before long Mira-honey, you will wonder how and why you ever felt useless. You have so much to offer and give, but the time has to be right."

Mira nodded, but felt less than reassured.

Mira found Jennie up and about the house, feeling much stronger. As Mira bent over the cradle to see the baby she noticed a soft, cuddly little blanket draped over the side. She picked it up and held it to her face.

Suddenly she knew what Ike did with rabbit pelts, and what Franco had in mind. "Oh, Jennie, it is so soft!"

"So soft, and very warm in our cold winters. As you can see if you look at the reverse side, it takes the skins of several rabbits to make a large enough blanket for even a child. But rabbit skins have kept all my children warm. Ike has a real knack for tanning and cutting them into strips which I stitch together."

"Jennie, would you to teach me?—not that I need them yet," she said with a blush, "but Franco has begun salting pelts. He won't tell me why, but now I know."

"I'd love to teach you when the time is right. Meanwhile, just begin by saving them."

Mira, Jennie, and Jennie's oldest daughter spent a couple hours enjoying tea and conversation, much of their talk centering on child care, and especially child care on the prairie where often even necessary supplies were limited. That evening as Franco worked on his sermon notes Mira began jotting down notes in yet a third journal—notes that she would later that summer organize into lessons for the school children, and lessons for women as she and Cora would make their teaching rounds. Maybe she would even be able to hold evening classes for women in the school/church for a couple months in the Fall and Spring.

Mira's sense of purpose was once again renewed. She was grateful to have women like Cora, Bessie, and Jennie to learn from. And even Agnes who had taught her how to churn!

Jimmy came on Friday to play with Mouser and Benny, and brought milk and cottage cheese. But his exciting news was that he and Bessie had seen one of Jake's men go by to help Agnes.

Mira and Franco began observing Sabbath on Friday evening with soup made from left over rabbit, and sourdough bread with butter, and the remaining of Agnes' buttermilk to drink.

To their joy, the beans were ready for picking on Saturday. Fresh green beans, dried beef, eggs, bread, milk, cheese. To someone like Mira who was used to variety in her diet, it seemed sparse, yet she agreed that what they had was nutritious and enough to meet their needs.

The Sunday service was somber as Franco, with Agnes' permission, told the gathering about what had happened to Jeff. This led to his moving sermon on the need for each person to be ready to meet God anytime, anyplace, and in any circumstance. He used *Amos* chapter 4 where God calls

Israel back from rebellion, with the warning that if they do not return, they must be prepared to meet their God, and expect dire consequences.

Anyone one of us can be here today, but gone tomorrow. This is true for people everywhere, and especially so as we live life on the prairie.

He thanked the people for supporting each other in the time of need, and encouraged them to continue to do so. He concluded with,

Few of us knew Jeff well. But most of us know that he had a problem with alcohol which usually leads to other problems, including social problems—how we relate to each other, etc.

We cannot change any of that now for Jeff, but we all have choices to make in life's journey. And let's be blessed by the wonderful gifts Jeff left for us . . .

Looks of surprise showed on many faces as Franco said this.

. . . Yes, Jeff left two gifts for us. A few years ago he brought Agnes to our community, and now we have little baby Iris as well. Which reminds me that I have a couple announcements to make before our closing prayer, song and benediction . . .

One week from today I will be on circuit. At the request of the Board, Mira will be leading the service, and she will welcome anyone with musical talent to assist in the singing. Please see her at the picnic today if you wish to use your musical gifts in next week's service. And two weeks from today when I am back from circuit we will have the baptism of two, possibly three babies.

The service ended on a happier note than which it began.

At the picnic a rancher who often played the harmonica around campfires and a fiddler who played at square dances offered their talents for singing the following week. And the General distributed mail which his rider had brought back from Yankton.

But there was no mail for Franco and Mira. Mira had a hard time hiding her disappointment.

Early Monday morning Franco heard Benny stirring and attempting a little *puppy bark* which was followed by a knock on the door. *Guess we have a little watchdog on our hands.* "Good dog," he praised Benny as he went to the door. It was Axle Rodman, a farmer from south of Chipps who Mira and Franco had met on their first Sunday at Chipps. He greeted Franco with, "My wife is in labor with our third child. Can the doctor come? Labor started about midnight."

Franco turned to call Mira, but she was already up reaching for her clothes. Axle went with Franco to the barn to saddle the horses. Mira would ride out to the Rodmans with Axle while Franco went to notify Cora. Mira was ready, delivery bag in hand, when the men and horses came to the door. With a quick *goodbye* to Franco Axle and Mira headed south, while

Franco went north. Mira used the travel time to get a bit of a history. Fortunately Axle had no problem talking. His wife Mary was in good health, and had already given birth to two healthy, average-sized babies. Her first several hours of labor, were usually slow and easy, but when stronger contractions began the babies had come quickly. As he said this, he picked up the pace of his horse.

He went on, "In this past week Mary's energy level was great. The house is well cleaned; plenty of food on hand, and everything ready for the new baby."

"Has Cora been to see her recently?"

"No, but Mary will welcome Cora's help with the baby the first few hours. Glad Pastor was willing to go out to call her. We heard about the working arrangement that you and Cora have made. Sounds like a good plan to us."

"Thanks. I am blessed to have Cora to work with."

"No finer people in the Chipps area than Cora and Jake."

Day was breaking, making it easier to see the way. Axle quickened the pace again and before long they pulled up to a small, but charming prairie house. They could hear Mary crying out in distress. Axle jumped off his horse, neglecting to help Mira, or tie the horses. Mira took a moment to do so, and then entered the house.

As she walked through the kitchen to the bedroom she noted a cookstove with a well stoked fire and water warming. A couple empty pans, and towels and bed linens stacked neatly on the table. She greeted Mary as she relaxed between contractions. But soon another contraction was heavy on her. When it passed Mira explained that she would like to do an examination and assessment. But Axle was right—when Mary's contractions became strong there was little rest time between. Just as Cora entered the house, Mary was delivered of a baby boy. Cora took over the baby while Mira worked with Mary. She soon had her comfortable, washed, with a change of linens, and Cora placed the baby in her arms. Meanwhile Axle fried eggs and ham for breakfast. The other children slept through it all.

After breakfast Axle said, "Pastor, Doctor, food on the prairie in the winter can be challenging. But I have the reputation for being a good hunter. How's this for a deal—in exchange for coming out early and helping my wife, I'll supply you with venison next winter?"

Mira glanced at Cora who quietly nodded her head. "Sounds good to me," said Mira. Franco agreed, and asked, "Any chance you might be willing to teach me a little about hunting? I've bagged a few rabbits, but I have to do more than that."

"Let's plan on it." With that the men went outside and Mira and Cora cleaned up the breakfast dishes. Cora would stay a little longer to help with the other children when they got up.

Mira went home with a prayer on her lips, "Thank you, God, that it went so well, and thank you for a healthy baby." But a few coins in her pocket would have met her immediate needs better than the hope for venison in the winter. She didn't know if she would even like venison.

Franco helped Mira set up for washing before going out for chores. Franco delighted in caring for the animals, while Mira looked forward to the day when she would be able to hire Bessie to do the washing and ironing.

On Tuesday Mira and Franco went together to see Agnes and Iris and the Rodman family. Agnes, carrying Iris in a sling, was just returning from the field. She had just brought lunch to Sam, one of Jake's hands. "Pastor, Doctor-dear, Sam will be working the fields all summer. You know, with Jeff, I always felt like I was on the outside looking in, but since the funeral and the church service on Sunday I feel like I belong. Could I have Iris baptized when the other babies are baptized?" They spent the next hour talking about what it means when a parent has a child baptized—the parent must be committed and baptized. At the end of the hour, Agnes accepted Christ as her Savior, and agreed to have a couple additional sessions with Mira before the service in which she and her baby would be baptized.

They backtracked a bit, and went on to the Rodmans. Mary and baby were resting, a young neighbor woman was looking after the other two children and preparing meals. Seeing the arrival of Mira and Franco, Axle came in from the fields. After greeting them he went in and told the young woman to fix enough dinner for their guests.

Mary awakened as soon as she heard voices and joined her husband and Franco and Mira on the porch, bringing the baby out with her. Mira and Franco told them of the plans for baptisms on the first Sunday of July, and immediately Axle and Mary said they would like to have little baby Andy baptized also. Both parents were already members of the church.

. On the way home Franco commented, "Mira-honey, that will be five baptisms on one Sunday. How blessed this church is."

"I feel the blessings and thank God for how well our ministry is received. Oh, I know, we are likely to encounter difficult times as well.

When we do, please remind me of this moment when life feels full and complete. Not just the spiritual blessings, but once again we had a nourishing meal that we did not have to prepare ourselves."

They cantered home drinking in the beauty of the prairie.

Wednesday morning Franco spent an hour or two at the General Store meeting and greeting The General's customers, and enjoying coffee and cookies that Mable offered to all.

That afternoon Franco went rabbit hunting, but returned with two grouse. A welcome change for Mira who did not much care for rabbit. However, she was excited about acquiring rabbit pelts. If rabbits were harbingers for starting their own family she would gladly eat rabbit every day. But, she placed little faith in harbingers.

The grouse was delicious.

That evening after baths and hair washing they settled down at their table. "Mira-honey, as you know, I'm planning to use our *foothold* sermon for circuit. Have you decided? Do you want to use it, or do you want us to discuss a new topic for you to use?"

"I'm also planning to use the *foothold* sermon. But I've also been thinking about the sermon for the first Sunday of July. How about *when God speaks* or *how God speaks*? I have heard him in these past several weeks in many ways and circumstances that I have never experienced before."

"Great idea, Mira-honey. It's the Sunday we will have the baptisms. That could be one example of God speaking to his people. What Scripture passages have you thought of, and what personal examples do you have of God speaking to you?"

"My personal examples may not be appropriate to mention—such as my worry about not having enough food or money. More appropriate might be God speaking through the first cry of a newborn; safety for all our people in the storm, etc. Scripture that comes to mind is I Kings 19 and Hebrews 1:1-3."

They spent the evening in conversation and prayer; prayer especially for the time they would be separated while Franco was on circuit.

Franco left after chores and breakfast on Thursday, with the promise to be home late Friday afternoon, likely not having to leave again until early Sunday morning. If all went well, they would be able to observe their *Sabbath-Saturday*, knowing that Sunday would be busy.

Chapter 8 *Separate Ways, Mutual Concerns*

The house felt empty when Franco started off down the road riding Grey. It was Thursday morning. Even Benny whimpered and Mira stooped to comfort him. *Jimmy will soon come. He'll bring in Mouser to do mouse-patrol and you can play with Jimmy outside.* Then, to herself she added *I can't believe I'm talking to Dawg.*

Jimmy came at 10 AM, and announced that he had to be home by noon, and that *Doctor-dear* was invited to go home with him for dinner.

"That's great, Jimmy. I'll do that. But until then we have lots of work."

"What shall I do first?"

"First tie Benny outside, and then get Mouser and let him run loose in the house while you play with Benny. I'm going to work in the garden. You can help me there when you think the animals have had enough play time." Jimmy smiled broadly, eager to get started.

Mira delighted in their garden, thankful that she had some horticultural skills gained from working with her parents' gardener. The tomatoes were blossoming; the potatoes growing well. *I think we'll be able to dig some up early July. Never thought I would be hungry for potatoes!* The second planting of beans was thriving, and the first showed promise of several more pickings. *I'll bring some to Bessie!* Mira hoed and then picked the beans and brought them to the house.

"*Cat!*" she scolded Mouser as he rubbed against her legs, but said no more. Jimmy was too near. But she sneezed several times. Suddenly she realized that this was not the first time she had sneezed when near the cat. *Is there a connection?*

"Jimmy, please bring Mouser back to Pastor Franco's office now. He's done his work in the house for today. He'll be happy there if you take a little bread and milk with you."

Back home from her visits with Bessie and Agnes by 3 PM, Mira was dreading the long lonely evening and night that stretched out ahead of her. But it was a good time to rehearse her sermon for Sunday. The hours passed quickly as she focused on God's message. At 6 PM she fed the animals and fixed herself a huge bowl of beans. That, and a sandwich with dried beef. She chuckled as a feeling of contentment settled over her. This was the life God had called her to. Yes, Franco was gone for the night, and she missed him, but both of them would manage these temporary separations, so long as they kept their feet firmly in the holds God provided. She made sure she had her medical bag and pistol at her bedside before retiring.

Jimmy was at the door by 8 AM the following morning ready to help with the animals. "Mother said I could stay until 10, but not to bother you because she knows you want to have a quiet day preparing for Sunday. She said I must ask *how can I help you today, Doctor-dear?*"

Mira smiled at him. *Was there ever such a precious little boy?* "You will be a big help, Jimmy. While I get dressed for the day, please tie Benny outside, and get Mouser, so he can do mouse-patrol while we are feeding the other animals and gathering eggs." To herself she said *I will honor Franco's wish to have the cat in the house every day, but when he is gone the actual hours he is in will be limited. And I will take note if I sneeze again when he is in.*

When Jimmy left at 10 AM Mira was eager to get to her sermon notes again, and also to her Journals—it was time to make more entries. But first of all, what could she serve her husband for supper? She had nothing in the house to prepare a welcome home meal except green beans. Then she remembered the left over grouse being kept cool in the springhouse. Using the last of the dried vegetables, and a few new onions from the garden Mira concocted a surprisingly good soup.

She heard Franco and his horse about 6PM and went to the barn to greet him. "Oh, Mira-honey, it is so good to see you. How was your time? I missed you so much, but I had a lot of interesting experiences to tell you about. How about if I quickly feed the animals, and then we have the whole evening to ourselves?"

"Sounds good, I'll go in and set the table."

When Franco took longer than expected she went back to the barn, "Oh, Mira-honey, look, Daisy is in labor, about to give birth."

"Franco, I know nothing about cows giving birth!"

"Well, I know a little, and usually they do not need human help. Let's go in and eat, and come out a little later to check."

While Franco and Mira were eating, Daisy gave birth. When they checked on her after supper they were greeted by a gentle low from the cow, her calf well licked and nursing.

"We'll leave them together tonight, and tomorrow morning I will attempt to milk Daisy. I think she will produce more than what her baby will need. But the first few milkings we will not want to drink. Benny and Mouser will love what the calf doesn't want." Mira knew enough about lactation from the human world to understand what Franco was saying. "This is a fine little female, Mira-honey. When she is old enough to wean, we will give her to Bessie to raise as part of the agreement we made with her. We will be depending on Bessie more now. I have a feeling that in another day or two Buttercup will *come-in* too."

"Just think, Franco! I know how to churn now. Agnes taught me. She even showed me how to skim cream off milk! We will have all the milk we need, cream, butter and buttermilk. Thank God for cows. Perhaps eventually I can learn to make cheese and cottage cheese."

"Perhaps. But it is important that we allow Bessie to keep her part of the deal. Anyway, when our lives really start getting busy we will probably have to depend on Bessie and others for some of the home-keeping tasks."

"Like washing and ironing?"

"That too."

Friday night passed quietly. Bessie and Jimmy were at the Welkens' door by 8 AM Saturday morning. They all went to the barn to admire the new calf, and further discuss their work agreement. Bessie would come again on Sunday evening to milk Daisy and every morning and evening after that while Franco was gone, and she would be available to help with Buttercup when and if needed.

The rest of their Saturday-Sabbath they spent quietly in each other's company and in preparation for worship on Sunday.

Sunday morning Franco arose at daybreak to take care of the animals, eat a quick breakfast, and was on the road by 7 AM. His 10 AM service was about 15 miles from Chipps. It was difficult to leave, but they reminded each other that it would be only *three* nights.

Jimmy arrived at 8 AM to for the first ringing of the bell, then again at 9 AM, 9:30, and 10. Between ringings he played with Mouser and Benny, sure to have Mouser in the house, and Benny tied outside by 9:30. Mira spent the hour between 9 and 10 in Franco's office in prayer and meditation. She heard people begin to arrive at about 9:30 and set up for the picnic. Shortly before 10 a couple elders came in to pray with her.

It was a beautiful day on the prairie and Mira greeted the worshipers with the calmness that comes from the Spirit of the Lord at work in one's heart.

The congregation sang with the accompaniment of harmonica and fiddle. Mira spoke of *footholds*, the firm and secure base that God provides for dealing with the twist and turns encountered while living the Christian life and the slippery, insecure, enticing, deceptive *false footings* the devil offers as Christians wrestle with the difficulties of life.

She felt the power of the Holy Spirit speaking through her, and noticed that many in the congregation were paying close attention. She concluded the service with singing and prayer, and invited everyone to stay to eat.

But that afternoon, while mentally reliving the experience of the morning she felt a nagging dis-ease. As she examined it, she carefully reviewed the morning. There *were* fewer people than when Franco preached, some people seemed to ignore her, avoiding shaking hands afterwards, and/or ignoring her at the picnic. And the offering (which was her stipend for preaching) was smaller than what she had expected. Furthermore, it did not *feel* right to not greet and bless the congregation in Jesus' Name, with raised arms—a function reserved only for the ordained.

When Bessie came to milk she immediately noticed Mira's mood. "Doctor-dear, whatever is the matter? It was such a beautiful morning. I expected to find you elated."

There was no use denying it, so she told Bessie, who listened compassionately. "Doctor-dear, don't you see what you are doing?"

Mira shook her head, *no*.

"You are doing just exactly what you told us all not to do—*you are giving the devil a foothold, allowing him to undermine the strong footholds God has given you.* Everything you did and said this morning was done well. And for those who can't accept it—well, just give them time, and prove them wrong. As for not being able to greet and bless in the Name of Jesus—give that time, too. Who knows what God has in mind for you for the future? Meanwhile, work within the calling you now have, and trust the future to God, and keep your feet in *his footholds.*"

Mira knew that Bessie was right and thanked her for her reassuring words. But it was a struggle that would continue to trouble Mira.

Monday at noon, after doing their washing, Mira was just settling down to her lunch (that is what it would be when Franco was gone) of picnic leftovers when she heard General John call as he galloped to a stop at her door. "Doctor, we have a problem. A big one. I know because I have seen it before. A young couple with a child with scarlet fever, arrived at my store a few moments ago. They are new people, on their way to settle on farmland a few miles to your west. I told them how to find you, but I rode ahead to alert you."

Mira felt her heart sink. Scarlet fever! This could affect the whole community, and fast, unless utmost precautions were taken. "Did they expose anyone while in town?"

"Only the father came into the store, no customers were in the store at the time. I told him to get back into the wagon. I've had scarlet fever, so I'm not at risk. But one look at the child told me that we have a very sick little one on our hands. The parents do not know if they've had the fever. There are no other children."

"Both Franco and I have had it. I as a child, and Franco as a young man when they had soldiers at their place."

As they were speaking the wagon pulled up. Mira thanked The General for his information, and calmly walked to greet the family, grateful that Jimmy was not present. She explained to them that she had had the illness and could safely examine the child. The rash was obvious, and the child's skin felt very warm to the touch. He was about two, but looked small for his age.

"Is he eating or drinking anything?"

"Nothing today, except a few sips of water. I try to nurse him, but he's not interested."

"I'm glad you brought him to me, and I will try to help, but you have a very sick little boy. Here is what we will do." She turned to The General. "General, would you go to the cistern for a cool bucket of water, while I get some supplies from the house?"

When she returned to the wagon, The General was talking with the parents. From what she could hear, he was addressing their concern that the *doctor* was a woman.

Don't let this undermine you, Mira she told herself as she approached the wagon.

"First we will try to get him to drink some of this willow bark tea. It sometimes helps to bring down fever, then we will apply some cool cloths to his arms and legs to also reduce his fever."

Mira worked with the baby for about a half hour, sad to notice that he was too weak to put up a protest.

After instructions from Mira to continue the cool compresses every half hour and sips of the tea as tolerated, The General rode out with them to their homestead. Mira promised to stop in the following morning. She also gave them strict instructions to not interact with anyone, unless the person had had scarlet fever. Mira refilled her 5-gallon bucket for them to take along.

The General stopped back to see Mira on his return. "It was as I expected. There isn't even so much as a shack on that land. They will have to live in their wagon. It's not the time of the year to begin farming the land, and they have no animals."

"I wonder what their story is, and what kind of plans they have for life on the prairie."

"I think they are the kind of people who live without a plan—perhaps they heard of this land that was abandoned by someone who previously attempted to homestead it, and thought they had a right to it."

"My heart goes out to that poor child."

"What do you think . . ?"

"I don't think he stands a chance. At best the willow bark and compresses will ease his discomfort a little."

The General nodded. "I'll stop by for you about 9 AM."

Mira felt sick to her stomach; helpless. There was nothing she could do to save the child's life. *And even if I could save it, what kind of life would a child in such a hopeless situation have?*

She spent the rest of the day writing in her Journals and working in her garden. And had a *heart-to-heart* with Bessie when she came to do the milking. Bessie assured her that she and Jimmy would look after all the animals the following day. "Not to worry, Doctor-dear."

But Mira spent the night worried and restless.

General John came at 9 AM, saddled her horse, and they rode out together. Nearing the wagon they heard the baby's weak cry. They also heard angry voices coming from the untilled field. Mira went to the wagon; The General followed the voices.

The baby, wrapped in soiled rags, was burning with fever. Mira doubted that the parents had made any attempt to follow her instructions. The new bucket that Mira lent them was nowhere in sight. She could do nothing without water. She retrieved a small blanket from her saddle bag and wrapped him in it, not wanting to hold him without something to protect herself from the filth. The baby quieted in her arms, but she did not necessarily interpret that as a good sign. In about 10 minutes The General and the baby's parents came into view and stepped up to the wagon, no one saying a word, but The General clearly angry.

After a moment or two the father said, "How is he?"

"Not well. Where is my bucket? I need water."

"We used it all last night. There ain't a well here."

Mira looked at The General. "That's right, Doctor. The well is dry. The horses have had no water. The two adults used the water for themselves last night. I'll ride out to Jake and we'll bring out a couple barrels, and then decide what has to be done."

"Thanks. I'll stay here."

"No, you will come with me."

"But . . ."

"Doctor, did you hear me? You will come with me."

Mira looked at the baby. Except for an occasional whimper, he lay quietly. Mira handed him to the mother and got up on her horse.

"We'll be back in about two hours," General John said. But other than that, remained quiet until they got to Jake's place.

Once there he said, "Let me handle this with Jake. And I know I don't have to tell you this, but be extra cautious, wash up really good at the cistern, and do not go inside."

Mira nodded.

Cora came out and Mira told her the story. "Cora, the baby is going to die."

"As hard as it sounds, Doctor-dear, it probably is the greater mercy."

Jake and The General loaded a wagon with a couple of barrels of water. Mira heard Jake comment, "How much you bet they'll still be there?"

"I know, but we have to try."

Cora did not go along.

It was as Jake expected. The wagon was nowhere in sight. But along the roadside was the bucket and a little white bundle. The baby had died.

Jake got the shovel from his wagon. Mira refrained from asking how he had known to bring it.

It was Mira's first funeral to conduct, and she wondered if she would ever be the same. To place a two year old shrouded in a borrowed blanket in the ground and cover him with dirt and stones—*how cruel could life be on the prairie*? Jake and the general knelt reverently at the grave as Mira recited Jesus' words,

Suffer the children to come to me . . . forbid them not . . . of such is the Kingdom of heaven.

And together they said the *Lord's Prayer*.

As The General took leave of Mira at her door, he asked, "Okay if Mable comes out this afternoon?"

Mira nodded.

Feeling a terrible need to scrub herself—of *what* she was not sure, maybe the tragedies of life—she got water *in their other* bucket and set it to warming. (For reasons she could not identify, she had left the bucket at the gravesite.) As the water warmed, Mira ate a small lunch, and noticed that she needed to make sourdough bread, so she would have something for Franco when he returned the following evening.

Mable came about 2 PM, and Cora showed up shortly thereafter. Mira allowed herself to be comforted and supported by these two wise and kind veterans of prairie life.

Bessie and Jimmy went directly to the barn when they came for evening chores. Within minutes Jimmy was running to the house, shouting, "Doctor-dear"! You have a new baby! Buttercup had her calf. Mama is taking care of him right now. Come and see."

A new baby, indeed. A beautiful, strong little male, already looking for his first meal.

Mira and Jimmy checked for eggs and took care of her horse while Bessie tended the cattle. Then as Jimmy spent time with the cat and dog, Mira told Bessie about the baby and his parents. Bessie listened quietly and then said, "You did what you could, Doctor-dear. The parents are responsible for their own behavior, and the baby's time was in God's hands. Leave it there."

That evening, Mira jotted a few ideas in her Journal for the Sunday sermon, asking herself, *where was God's voice in what happened yesterday and today with that baby? What were you saying, God, that I didn't hear?*

Mira fell into bed exhausted, thinking of Franco's return the next day. She awakened hours later to Jimmy's knocking. It was a new day.

Other than brief interactions with Bessie and Jimmy, Mira spent the day quietly, working in her garden, thinking, reading, writing, checking her medical supplies—*I hope the supplies I requested of my father will soon come; even though it seems like I've done little medical work I sure could use more wraps and drapes—even more linens and towels.* Her stock of medicine was still adequate.

She was hoping Franco would be home by 5 PM, and had the water for baths warming by that time. Five o'clock came, as did Jimmy and Bessie, but Franco did not make it back until 6 PM. Noting that he looked very tired, she helped with his horse before they sat down to supper.

"Oh, Mira-honey, I have so much to tell you—but first, let me ask, how did things go for you?"

"I have a lot to tell you, too—you go first."

Franco told her of the Sunday service, and then the tragedy that struck the community early Monday morning. A young husband, and father of three, was thrown by his horse—his horse apparently had been galloping and had stumbled in a prairie dog hole. He hit his head. Franco wasn't sure if he died of a broken neck or severe head injury. He had been found several hours after the accident by a neighbor. The funeral was held on Tuesday, the community rallying well around the widow.

"And then, Mira, on my way back this afternoon I came upon the most awful thing—that's why I was late, I had intended to surprise you by being home early, and bringing you fresh rabbit. But that's not how it turned out."

"Franco, what happened? You look like you saw a ghost."

"Worse! Several miles from here I noticed a wagon near the side of the road. Two dead horses, both shot, still in harness. When I got closer, I saw the worst, awful scene I've ever seen—two dead adults, both shot. And it looked to me like the male had shot the female and then himself . . ."

"Franco . . ."

"Let me finish, Mira, please. Fortunately, I had seen a farm about a mile to the west, so I retraced my steps, and got the help of the farmer and his wife. We buried the two people. We couldn't even mark their graves with their names as there was no way to identify them. We looked through the wagon—it was filthy; there were even a few baby clothes, but no baby anywhere to be seen . . ."

"Franco . . ."

"Please let me finish, Mira. I asked the farmer if we should bury the horses—he said *no, the wild animals would eat them.* And he would come back later to get the harnesses and wagon—he would burn the contents of the wagon, and then let it stand in the sun for several days."

"Franco . . ."

"But Mira-honey, that's not the worst of it. About 3 miles west of here, just along the roadside, I saw what looked like a new grave of a child. Just a marker without a name; next to it a bucket. I wonder . . ."

"Franco, I can tell you the rest of the story."

"You can?"

"Yes, because I was involved in that part."

Mira told him in detail what had happened, and of the help and support she had received from The General and Mable, Jake and Cora, and Bessie.

"Oh, Franco, this is five burials since we have been here, none the way I anticipated. We must place a marker with a name for the baby. We can give him a name."

Franco nodded in agreement and then said, "Mira-honey, I think the topic for this week's sermon is very timely—*when God speaks, how God speaks.* Are you up to working on that this evening?"

"Yes, but not until after a good, long soak in the tub, and hair wash. You first, while I clean up our dishes. The water for bathing should be hot by now."

Franco prepared his bath and submerged himself in the water.

"Oh, Franco. One more thing—Buttercup had her baby, and all is well. Bessie and Jimmy have been so helpful. And we will soon have more milk than we can handle. I'm glad that Bessie will be using what we don't need for cheese making. By the way, did you get anything for preaching Sunday?"

"Less than a dollar."

"Me too. What are we going to do, Franco? Even with our garden starting to produce, we need more variety in our diet."

"I have some jerky in my saddle bag—someone gave it to me on Sunday. Yesterday was payday. If a deacon doesn't stop by tonight or early tomorrow, I'll track someone down. It wouldn't be begging. I would be just stating a fact: the money is due us, and we need it for food."

The deacon did arrive the following morning with Franco's pay, and Franco and Mira went to the *General Store* for food supplies. Franco also asked The General to order boards for a ceiling. The rest of the day they spent on sermon preparation, and on Friday paid visits to those who would be baptized on Sunday. They fell into bed Friday night exhausted, hoping to keep Saturday-Sabbath the next day.

Sunday dawned with storm clouds but the Dakotans knew their skies well—the church was packed, and the storm held off. In fact, many folks asked Franco to pray for rain. In the sermon Franco spoke of the many ways God spoke to his people in the Bible and then moved on to recent examples in the community where God had been speaking—including through the unfortunate deaths of adults, and even a child. Then he moved on to how God was speaking to them all through the baptism of four children and one adult. In their baptism they would receive the outward sign and seal of cleansing by the blood of the Lamb, and "officially" become part of the family of God.

The General distributed mail at the picnic. To Franco and Mira's great disappointment there was none for them.

That night a dry storm hit the area—thunder, lightning, strong wind, but little rain. Drought was becoming a big concern for the farmers. Throughout the week there were several small showers, but they were only "teasers" and not enough to make a real difference for the crops.

Tuesday at breakfast Franco and Mira commented to each other that they were now in their fifth week of life on the prairie. And how they longed for news from home.

"But Mira-honey, The General assures me that by late August, or early September Chipps will have its own telegraph line. So when mother has her baby, they will be able to telegraph us! Not only that, soon a spur railroad heading north from Yankton will come near, or through Chipps. And The General also told me that he is hoping to build a lumberyard near his store. He says the demand for lumber is increasing as more and more people come west. He asked me if we knew of an enterprising young man in the East who might be interested in coming out here to go into the lumber business. I told him I would write my father, and ask him to keep his eye open for just such a person."

"I admire your energy and enthusiasm, Franco. I'm finding that the hard times—the deaths, and now people fearing drought, really get me down. Yet I see people like you, The General, Bessie, Jake and Cora, and others just take it in stride. Everybody seems to believe that better days—better times—will come. I worry about my faith, Franco. Perhaps our next sermon should be on *Hebrews* 11:1."

And thus another sermon was born, using the story of Thomas who said he would not believe until he could see and touch. And *Hebrews* 11:1—real faith is believing without seeing or having.

At the Sunday picnic they prayed for rain. And a marvelous rain fell that night.

Chapter 9 *Chipps Celebrates*

By the end of their second month Franco and Mira began to feel a routine about their work. Franco made pastoral calls on parishioners and non-churched in the area. Spending a couple hours a week at the *General Store* proved to be an effective way of getting to know people, and getting word out of his and Mira's availability to provide various services to the community and passers-through. At the recommendation of General John both Franco and Mira placed on his bulletin board "advertisement" of their work. People who came to the store, whether locals or travelers, welcomed the opportunity to receive medical attention. And some sought prayer and spiritual guidance.

Caring for their animals and garden—with Jimmy's help—was for Franco mental respite from the weighty concerns of the prairie folk he was growing to love. Mira saw a definite increase in medical cases as word of her work spread—mostly cuts, infections, sprains, fevers, burns, digestive disorders, and expectant mothers. Mira spent long hours developing lesson plans in Hygiene and Bible that she and Franco would both use with children; and on baby and child care for mothers that she and Cora would use. Mira also conscientiously made Journal entries.

And always there was the joy of working together on new sermons and Sunday worship.

Mid July The General's rider came back with letters from their parents. Mira and Franco were delighted to read that the Phillips would be going to eastern Pennsylvania, possibly as early as late October and staying perhaps until the New Year. Dr. Phillips had been able to arrange coverage for himself and he couldn't wait for a respite that was many-a-year due him.

Mira's mother wrote with uncharacteristic enthusiasm about the sewing she was doing. *Mira, I haven't had this much fun since making baby clothes for you—I even got out a few of your old outfits to use for patterns. Fortunately for newborns we don't have to worry about the clothes being "male" or "female." This is going to be the best dressed baby in Pennsylvania! Any chance you might be needing baby clothes too?*

"Franco, I never knew my mother enjoyed anything about me as a baby let alone making my baby clothes! Listen to what she writes." Mira read aloud from the letter.

"Mira-honey, I think this is her way of telling you—in a rather oblique way, to be sure—how much she really loves you."

"Perhaps."

Franco's parents' letter assured them that Nina was doing fine and busily engaging her school children in gardening. They were looking forward to the arrival of the Phillips, glad they were coming early.

One evening at supper Mira asked Franco what they would be doing with Buttercup's calf.

"I'll be talking to Jake about that—the calf will have to be castrated later, and we will raise him for beef. Just don't get attached. Don't even name him. And by the way, I expect that sometime soon Jake will be breeding our horses."

"I remember our agreement with him, but how will we manage without horses?"

"Knowing Jake, he has a plan. I'm sure he realizes that we need two horses at all times, so he will probably lend us two others during the breeding and birthing time. For most of the eleven month pregnancies we will be able to ride them."

The Wednesday morning before Franco's July circuit The General had great news for Franco and all who came to the store. Actually, good news for the entire community. "I have received word that on August 15 the telegraph will be fully installed and a telegraph operator will be moving to town. And by the way, the telegraph operator will also become postmaster for Chipps and surrounding area."

The community had less than three weeks to construct a free standing building, or as The General suggested, a lean-to to his store, large enough for the operator to reside in as he was not married. The General offered to be in charge of the building project and asked Franco to do what he could to get word out into the community as he did pastoral visitation. Neighbors could spread the word to neighbors. Chipps would have a day of celebration as it connected with areas of the country that otherwise took days to access. Since August 15 fell on Saturday and the company and operator needed to have a day to be sure that all was working well, it was decided to have the celebration on the 16th following a 10 AM outdoor worship service.

Mira, at The General's request, was appointed chairperson of the committee that would plan the celebration. Mable would assist her, and they could choose a couple other people to assist. As word of the event spread Mira soon had more than enough volunteers. She had little to do other than keep track of who would do what, and the sequence of events on the day of celebration—

The trio—set up food tables for the picnic.

Cora—supervise serving the meal.

Following the picnic all go to the Telegraph Office for sending and receiving telegrams.

Draw names to decide who would send the first telegram.

Prize for the first person or family to *receive* a telegram—a chance to send one free telegram at a time of their choosing within a year!

Games while people wait their turn to send a telegram.

Bessie and Jimmy in charge of games.

Cleanup—everybody. (The General assured Mira, *That's just how people on the prairie are—we take responsibility without being told or asked. We see work and do it.*)

When Jimmy came to play with the pets the day after he learned that he and Bessie would be in charge of the games, Mira noticed that he was upset about something, and asked him about it. "My mother don't think we should play one of the games I want—she said to ask you."

"What games do you want to play?"

"Well, the games we always play—sack races, footraces, wheel barrel races, kick-the-shoe, horseshoe."

"Those all sound good to me."

"Really?"

"Yes, those are great games—which one doesn't your mother like?"

"The one I haven't told you yet. But me and my friends really like it, and I think the men who chew tobacco would be good at it, too."

"What game is that?" Mira asked with some misgiving.

"Spitting the far-est."

"Ohhh, I see. Well . . . I think your mother is right. I agree with her."

"You do?" he asked with disappointment in his voice. "I was sure you would think that it was a good game."

"Well, I can see that boys your age would enjoy it. But Jimmy, spitting really is not a polite thing to do. I find it very disgusting."

"You do?"

"Yes, I do, and Pastor Franco does too."

"Really?"

"Yes, really. But Jimmy, I know Pastor Franco will like all your other games.

"Well, if Pastor Franco . . ."

"Why don't you go and find him right now? He is in the barn."

As Jimmy skipped off, Mira smiled. She and Bessie would share a good chuckle.

That evening Mira and Franco had a serious talk about the sermon topic for what would become known in the community as *Telegraph Sunday*—the third Sunday of August.

"Mira-honey, as I am out on circuit, and even visiting locally and invite folks to come to church the positive response I get often seems to be because of the social attraction—an opportunity to get together with neighbors. But there is a dearth of understanding regarding THE GOSPEL. What do you think of preparing a sermon on the basic *Good News of Jesus?*"

"I'm all for that. A sermon like that could lead into a series of sermons on Christian living including *Fruit of the Spirit* (Gal. 5:16-26) and putting on the *Armor of God* (Eph. 6:10-20).

"Great ideas. I think we have just opened the door for countless sermons. I'm sure we will think of many more topics to fit under the greater topics of *Gospel and Christian Living*. How about we both give some thought to *Gospel* and then in a day or two explore our ideas."

"What wonderful opportunities we have, Franco, working as a Frontier Team."

After careful thought, prayer, and discussion they chose two passages for the sermon—

Romans 1:16-17—*the Good News of Jesus is the power of God for the salvation of everyone who believes.*

I Corinthians 15:1-3— *we are saved by the Gospel.*

Christ died for our sins;
He was buried;
and was raised again on the 3rd day.

***

The sermon was used year after year on Telegraph Sunday, and referenced in many sermons and discussions throughout the years as Franco and Mira encouraged people to live out their faith.

***

August 16 dawned bright and clear. Jimmy was on Mira and Franco's doorstep at 7 AM wanting to start ringing the bell. Franco said to wait until 8 o'clock, because if the people heard it at 7 they would be confused about the time, or think there was a fire somewhere.

Horse drawn wagons and saddle horses began arriving by 9:30. Fortunately, Jake had the foresight to put up a temporary wire-coral with a load of hay and a stock tank. He was present to direct the parking of the wagons—all details that Mira, to her chagrin, had not thought of. But then she remembered the General words—*prairie people see work and do it without being asked or told.* Jake was the personification of this. *So why does he get under my skin?*

The various committee members milled through the crowd, welcoming and chatting with folks as they arrived. At 10 AM Jimmy did the final ringing of the bell, and General John's booming voice welcomed everyone and asked them to sit.

Franco called them to worship reminding everyone that *this is the day that the Lord has made—a day to rejoice and be glad.* He followed the call with a greeting from God.

People with a variety of musical instruments came forward, and the singing began and continued for at least 15 minutes. Franco observed a young man that he had not seen before spontaneously cue the musicians and keep them together. *Perhaps this will be the beginning of a musical group that can assist in future worship services and other special occasions.* Franco made a mental note to talk to him later.

The singing was followed by prayer led by Mira—a prayer filled with thanksgiving and praise for the blessings that the people of Chipps and surrounding community had received throughout the summer, for rain, the hope of a bountiful harvest in the fall, and for the telegraph. She also prayed for those who had suffered losses through sickness and death, and finally she asked God's blessing on the school year that would be starting before long.

As Franco reached for his Bible the congregation settled comfortably on their blankets. Franco began—

General John's announcement three weeks ago that the telegraph really was coming to Chipps was <u>good news</u> for us. If you are anything like Mira and me you can hardly wait to send your first telegram, and even better than that, receiving word from loved ones far away. You probably have been saving your pennies the last three weeks just for this occasion.

Maybe you've done without something else, just to be able to send a telegram. Heads nodded in agreement.

But folks, there is much better news than even a telegram, and that's what I have for you this morning.

Franco had his audience **hooked.**

The Word for the **good news** *that I am talking about is* **Gospel; the Good News of Jesus Christ** *that we read in the Bible.*

As great as we will find the telegraph to keep us connected to family and loved ones elsewhere, and perhaps even using it for business communications—and as much fun as our celebration will be today, and even sending and hopefully receiving our first telegrams—all that pales in comparison to what God really wants us to hear this morning.

Franco opened his Bible, read selected passages, and laid out before them everyone's need for the **Good News**—
1st Timothy 1:15—*Jesus came to save sinners.*
Romans 3:23-24—*All people are sinners, and need to be freed from their sins. Christ met that need in his death, burial, and resurrection.*

He spoke this in reference to Christ's unconditional, sacrificial love, which is available to all who will take the step of faith and receive the gift of salvation that God offers.

Mira noted smiles of agreement. But she also saw expressions of bewilderment—as though they never heard anything like this before. Franco closed the sermon with a promise to be available for discussion *anytime, day or night.* And also said that he was open to holding evening classes in Chipps, and on circuit.

But Mira wondered: *Will we be able to answer questions that are sure to be asked?*

After a final song of praise, and a blessing given by Franco the people were dismissed for the picnic. With efficiency that amazed Mira, the food was laid out on the tables and serving lines were formed with the children first, then the men, and finally the women. Mira expected that everyone would sit by family groups, but children soon found their friends, men their neighbors, while the women milled around keeping their eyes on everything. Many helped themselves to seconds and as soon as the dessert table was uncovered Cora had to exercise some control to be sure everyone got something.

When General John's watchful eye noted the men stretching out on the grass and the children getting restless he asked everyone to pack up their utensils and walk the quarter mile to the telegraph office.

Once there, he formally introduced the telegraph operator—a congenial fellow who told the group that he was glad to be in Chipps and that as postmaster and telegraph operator he was sure that they would soon get to know each other. He was there to serve the community.

Everyone cheered and clapped a warm welcome and Kjell bowed, recognizing the welcome.

Franco asked God's blessing on the use of the telegraph, and that it would have a positive impact on the community. With that, the telegraph was ready for use. Mira gave instructions to the group.

"I think we have this well-organized. Here is how it will go . . . many of you have already seen the posting that gives the price for sending a telegram. That is in effect already today—every new convenience comes with a price. But Kjell reminded me that when you consider the distance you can send a brief message, and the speed, *a telegram is a good bargain*. It's much faster than a letter and cheaper than traveling yourself!

"So if you want to send a telegram today, choose someone from your family to come to the platform to pick up a small piece of paper and pencil that General John has supplied. Once you have your paper and pencil go back to your family and observe the following steps:
Clearly print the full name of one of *your* family members;
Clearly print the name and full address of the family *you wish to send the telegram to*.
Very clearly print the *brief message* you wish to send.
After about 15 minutes we will send around a 'hat.' Put your message and pencil in the hat. After the hat comes back to me, we will have a drawing. The name we pull out first will send the first telegram. That's a lot of instruction, and you probably have questions, so I will now defer to Kjell—he will tell how to write your message and take your questions. Kjell, please take over."

Kjell gave the instructions, fielded a few questions, and then Mira sent the hat around. When it returned to her she said, "I feel excitement in the air that says, *let's get these messages sent*. We will, but I have one more thing to tell you. The first person to *receive* a telegram will get to send one telegram *free of charge* anytime within the year starting today."

Applause broke out again. "Folks, the time has come. Jimmy, come on up. You can draw the first name." Jimmy excitedly came up on the platform. But as Mira extended the hat towards him, he quieted himself as though this were a very solemn occasion. He carefully pulled out a paper and handed it to Mira.

Mira looked at it, smiled, and said, "Would Jed and Maggie come forward?"

The crowd made way for them. When they reached the platform Kjell said, "Telegrams are always treated with great privacy. But because of this special occasion would you like to tell everyone what your message is and to whom you are sending it. If you wish, it will become part of Chipps history."

"Oh there is nothing private about this—everyone here knows Maggie and I had our first baby, but we are not sure if our letter has yet reached our parents, so we are going to send a message to Maggie's parents in Minnesota."

"Thanks Jed. Let's get the message going, and while we do, I believe The General has another announcement."

"That's right, I do. From the number of papers in the hat, it looks like we will be sending at least seven messages today. That will take some time, so how about we begin the games. As you are playing Dr. Mira will draw a name when Kjell is ready to send another telegram. I will call out your name loudly enough for everybody to hear. When you hear your name, send at least one member of the family to the platform—and don't forget your money! So keep listening, but also enjoy the games. Bessie and Jimmy have worked hard, and it looks like the sacks for the sack race are laid out. If you are ready to compete, report to Bessie near the pile of sacks. Oh, and by the way, there are prizes for the winners."

The children didn't have to be told twice. They got into their sacks and lined up at the start line.

Mira waited for the cheering after the sack race to die down before drawing again. It was Cora and Jake. Although they were long-time residents of Dakota Territory and had no close relatives far away, they did have family in Yankton. So theirs went to Yankton, the closest telegraph station.

The games continued while adults visited, except for the men who played horseshoe.

Mira and Franco were the fifth to be drawn. They'd had a hard time deciding who to send their message to—her parents or his, and had talked it over a couple days earlier. They decided that by keeping their message very brief they could make their money stretch far enough to send to both. *Our community celebrates the telegraph today. Wonderful worship service this morning. We love Chipps, but miss you.*

Shortly after the last message was sent and the community was enjoying ice cream provided by The General and Jake (how they pulled this off remained a mystery), the telegraph began clicking and Kjell took down a message.

Everyone was quiet, holding a collective breath. *Who would it be for?*

Kjell stood tall on the platform. "Pastor Franco and Doctor Mira please step forward." They did, and Kjell gave Mira a small paper with

Kjell's neat script. "Would you like to tell us who it is from? As I said before, telegrams are private, but we are making history and we can record the first message received as part of Chipps' history."

"Oh there is nothing private about this. It is from my parents, Dr. and Mrs. Phillips. They send us their personal greetings, and say they are well. They also congratulate Chipps on this history making day. And they go on to say, *with this blessing, you can expect to hear from us often.*"

Mira was so excited that she got tears in her eyes and leaned against Franco for support. Franco seized the moment to affirm the blessing of the telegraph. "Just think, less than an hour ago we sent a message to Philadelphia. It was received by an operator there, who had it hand delivered to Mira's parents. Her father immediately wrote a message, had it delivered by the same delivery man to the operator. He immediately sent the message to Chipps. Just think folks—all the way to the East and back to us in less than an hour. Many of us remember the days and months it took to get here, and even the days and months it takes for letters to go back and forth. Of course, it isn't likely that it will always go this quickly. There will be unavoidable delays. But this feels like a miracle. God has truly blessed Chipps today. Let's give thanks."

The prayer was followed by a round of applause, and many people stepping forward to thank The General, Kjell, and everyone who helped make this wonderful day possible. There was no doubt—they would do this again next year, and meanwhile the telegraph would keep them connected to a world that many folks had thought they would have little to do with anymore.

The families began to walk back to their wagons—it was time to go home to do chores. Some had more than twelve miles to go. Mira mentioned to Franco on how neat they left everything—no garbage anywhere. Again she thought of The General's words *Prairie folks see what needs to be done and do it.*

But that evening, even though everything had gone so well, Mira told Franco of her frustration about having forgotten to arrange for the care of horses and parking of wagons.

"Mira, *let it go.* You have lived on the prairie less than three months, and are doing an amazing job. Jake has lived here all his life. One thing you might as well get used to—he isn't likely to ever ask you for help or advice, at least not in things that he considers to be *a man's responsibility*. That's just how he is."

"But he makes me feel so inadequate and dumb. If he would just talk to me."

"He won't, but not because he thinks you are inadequate or dumb. But maybe because he feels a bit intimidated by you."

"Jake *intimidated?* Never."

"You might be surprised. I think he is intimidated by Cora. But she knows how to work around him, and build him up."

"Well, I'll never do that."

"Mira, never say *never.* And don't let the blessing of this day and your role in it, be spoiled by something that no one else even gave a thought to. For all they know, you asked Jake to do what he did."

"But I didn't."

"Mira-honey, let it go. Let's thank the Lord for the wonderful success of the day."

The arrival of the telegraph was long remembered and celebrated, but that wasn't all that Chipps had to celebrate that year. By late summer crops were looking good. Rain had been adequate, no hail severe enough to do crop damage and no grasshoppers in numbers that would destroy the crops. Women filled their canning jars and a few asked Mira to come to help and learn. She always returned home with 3 or 4 jars to add to her store.

Mira and Franco's garden gave them a variety of fresh vegetables to enjoy in July and August, but not enough to can. True to his word, Jake saw to it that their animals had adequate hay, even for winter. He took both horses for breeding the day after Telegraph Sunday, but left them with two serviceable replacements. By mid-September both horses were back home. "Franco, how can we tell if a horse is really pregnant?"

"We'll know in eleven months. But frankly, I've heard of horses giving birth when their owners didn't know that a foal was on the way. I think we can expect to see them increase in girth in the last few months. And some mares get a little moody when the time gets close."

Daisy and Buttercup produced more than they and their pets could use. The arrangement with Bessie was beneficial to both families. Fresh milk, cottage cheese, yellow cheese, butter and buttermilk. Bessie was counting the days until The General would order her treadle machine. With the additional milk from Mira and Franco she was able to bring more dairy products to The General, who in turn sold them, and applied the income to her sewing machine account. "Maybe by Christmas," she told Jimmy.

School started the first full week in September. A young woman from one of the pioneer families was hired as teacher, and as previously agreed, Mira and Franco were responsible for daily religious instruction, and one Hygiene class per week. They were disappointed that only five small children came to school the first day—there were at least a dozen desks in the school room. But they were assured that once the crops were harvested older children would come, filling up the room.

All of Chipps and surrounding area were counting their blessings and none more so than Agnes and Sam. The second Saturday in September, just before chore time Mira and Franco heard a wagon drive up. Mira opened the door and saw Agnes hand Iris to Sam. Mira's first thought was *please Lord, don't let baby Iris be sick*. But on second glance she saw that all were smiling, and quickly invited them in.

Mira got out coffee cups while Franco seated them at the table. Benny was particularly interested in Iris. "Pastor, Doctor-dear, we want you to be the first to know—Sam and I want to get married."

Before Mira or Franco could respond Sam was asking, "How soon can you do it pastor?"

"*Do it?* Oh, I see. *Perform the ceremony.*"

"Yes, that's it."

Franco looked at Mira, who was smiling broadly. "Well, this will be my first wedding to perform, but if I remember correctly, tradition requires that your intentions and date be announced in church at least three times, so . . ."

Mira picked up the thought. "We could announce it tomorrow, also next week, and then again the following week as the church service begins—which makes three Sundays, but only two weeks from tomorrow!—and then have the marriage ceremony at the end of the service. And we could have an all church celebration during our usual picnic time. That will be the last Sunday of September. Do you think the weather will hold?"

Sam, who had lived on the prairie all his life responded, "We have some of our best weather in the fall. But if it snows, everybody will wear coats, and we'll have a picnic in the snow."

"I like your spirit," Franco said. I think this calls for a celebration tonight. Mira-honey, is there enough soup for two guests?"

Mira said *yes* but seriously doubted that there was.

While Franco was talking with Agnes and Sam, Mira covertly added more water to the soup. And she was quite sure that she could stretch her sourdough bread to feed all four. Thanks to Bessie, there was more than enough butter, buttermilk, and cheese.

As the simple meal was drawing to a close, and the excited conversation was waning, Mira was struck with an idea, "Agnes, you are about my size. I have many dresses stored in my trunk that my mother insisted I bring with me. Would you like to come next week, and have a look? I would be very honored if you wore one."

"You mean you would let me wear one of your dresses?" Agnes asked in complete surprise.

"Oh, better than that. Not only wear it, but keep it forever and ever!"

"Oh, I couldn't. I don't have enough m. . . ."

"Don't even say the word. It is our gift to you. And in honor of the special occasion, I'll wear my wedding dress, too. Franco and I have been married only a little more than three months, you know. I can't wait to wear it once again." *But I will not wear my veil. That was a one-time event.*

In the next few years several of Mira's lovely dresses would be given to the brides of Chipps. Mira always insisted that she was honored when a bride wore one of her dresses and kept it for her very own. If the dress of choice did not fit well, Bessie did the alteration free of charge as her contribution to a new home and family. And Mira was glad to get rid of dresses that she had no use for. Mira always wore her wedding dress to the weddings that she and Franco hosted in Chipps. Weddings were also a time for Franco and Mira to share their story of the Welken family cross that Mira wore daily.

Wedding Sunday dawned with a chill in the air, but the sky was clear. Jimmy arrived early, eager to ring the bell for the wedding. Franco set him to playing with Benny and Mouser, with the promise that he could do more than his usual bell ringing later.

General John had posted the wedding notice in his store, and Franco had gotten word out on circuit, bringing in more people than usual to the worship service. True to their usual assumption of responsibility, Jake had several tables set up for food, and one side table for gifts. Cora would oversee the serving of the picnic.

When Agnes and Sam arrived Franco took them to his office, and as Jimmy rang the 10AM bell Mira ushered them to the front seats and sat with them.

The area musicians had brought their instruments and the service began with singing. Feeling quite experienced, having been married for almost four months, Franco and Mira prepared a sermon on God's intent for marriage. Franco began the sermon,

Perhaps you have noticed the cross that Mira always wears . . . (heads nodded)

. . . I'm going to tell you the story of that cross, and then move into what both Mira and I have been taught and continue to believe about marriage—that God's intent for marriage is that it be Christ-centered.

The cross that Mira wears has been in the Welken family for centuries and is always given by the oldest son to his bride the night before their wedding . . .

After the sermon, Franco called Agnes and Sam and Mira and Jake forward. Agnes had asked Mira to be her witness, and Sam asked Jake, his employer. That is, his employer until recently when Jake had helped Sam renegotiate with Bessie the rent agreement that Agnes and Jeff had had with Bessie.

After the vows were said, and on cue from Franco, Jimmy went out and began ringing the bell with abandon. Mira noted many smiles as Franco pronounced the blessing on the entire congregation. *The chill in the air certainly has not penetrated the hearts of the people of Chipps,* she thought. The gifts placed on the gift table were from the supportive community. Word had spread of the hard life that Agnes had with Jeff. And the community also knew that Sam was a good, kind man.

At the picnic, women congregated around both Mira and Agnes, commenting on their lovely dresses. Agnes gave credit to Mira, who in turn gave credit to her mother.

As people were leaving Jake took Franco aside. "Pastor, winter is in the air. Your storm cellar must be dug before frost sets in. Believe me, when spring comes with tornadoes and severe storms you are going to need it."

Franco shuddered, "Yeah, I know. That, and the ceiling for our house. There just are not enough hours in a day."

Jake walked away saying no more, but the message of his squared shoulders was *tell me about it.* And Franco felt reproved. *Perhaps this is how Mira feels every time she encounters Jake. I need to be more sensitive to her. And express more appreciation to Jake for all he does.*

The next day when Franco returned from General John's store with a load of lumber in John's wagon *the trio was* digging a cellar just steps from their front door. Franco wanted to help but Jake told him that he might better start the ceiling. He set aside his pastoral responsibilities for the day and with the skill he had learned from his father and grandfather made a good start, even earning a word of approval from Jake.

As Mira was doing her Monday wash, a thought took shape in her mind. *The Brides of Chipps. I will begin yet another Journal and call it* <u>The Brides of Chipps</u>*, telling their stories (Agnes definitely has a story!) describing their dresses, and as time goes by I will record various anecdotes, maybe even the birth of their children.*

Mira was eager to tell the General and Mable her plan. Knowing that she liked to write, they had told her of their desire to leave a legacy for the people of Chipps. Both kept extensive journals of their life on the prairie and the people who came to their store—the settlers and those who passed through on their way farther West.

They told Mira that their long term plan was to begin a lending library in the town. A library that would have a section for archives, to be read in the library only.

At the end of the day Mira commented to Franco, "There just are not enough hours in my day."

"Tell it to Jake."

"What?"

"Actually, I was just kidding. That's what I said to Jake yesterday when he told me I must get the storm shelter dug."

"You said that to *Jake*? What did he say in return?"

"He said nothing. Just squared his shoulders and walked away. But the cellar was dug today—-thanks to him."

"Oh, Franco . . ."

"I think Jake understands very well how busy we are, and only to get busier. Can you believe only weeks ago you were wondering how you would spend your time?"

"I know—and now spending several hours a week with the school children, it is all the busier. But I love teaching them—both the Bible classes and Hygiene. I'm glad though that you will be available when the older children come—especially the boys.

"You are very good at what you do and the children love you. I can see it on their faces."

"They love you as well . . ."

"And I love you . . ."

They drifted off into exhausted sleep.

Chapter 10 *October—Christmas*

General John stopped by early October, wanting to see the ceiling that Franco had put up. "That is some of the finest carpentry work I have seen in this area."

"Thank you, General. And I know where you are going with that comment—the need for a lumberyard and good builders. Mira and I have contacted both sets of parents—both have agreed to keep their ears and eyes open, and get the word out—but so far no one has expressed an interest. Seems like most people who come west either want to homestead or prospect."

"Yes, and probably with less and less success. For those who do have success we need to give support and encouragement. You and Mira are already doing that, but we need additional ways of making life a bit easier and more pleasant. If we don't, people will continue to pack up and return east—defeated."

"And that is sad, because this seems like a land of limitless opportunity."

"I can see why you say that, and I agree. We had a good year. You have seen Dakota Territory at its best—but wait until we have a year or two with almost no rain. By the way, how old is your father?"

"Mid to late forties."

"He still is a young man."

"General, my parents headed west once, but got only as far as eastern Pennsylvania and were stopped short by a tragic accident. After many, many years of hardship they are doing well now and I think I told you that there is a baby on the way—hard as that is to believe. I can't imagine that they would have the remotest interest in continuing their journey west."

"Yes, I suppose you're right. But still . . ."

"General."

"I concede for now. Just don't dismiss it as an eventual possibility. I want you to see my vision for the future. You are an up and coming man here—a community leader. Owning and managing a lumberyard—even a construction company— could be a thriving business for anyone who is willing to work hard. Once the train tracks come as far as Chipps it will be much easier to bring in supplies of wood from Minnesota. Bringing large supplies will keep the price down. Horse and wagon trips to Yankton will almost become a thing of the past.

True to his word, Axle took Franco hunting a couple times that fall, and Franco brought home two deer. With assistance from Bessie, Mira canned and smoked most of the meat, and gave enough to Bessie for several meals.

Franco tanned the hides and promised Mira some warm covers for their bed for what was sure to be a cold winter. He occasionally brought home rabbits for fresh meat, and dried their pelts, still secretive about what he planned to do with them. Mira just smiled to herself, hoping that they would soon have reason to talk about it openly.

"Mira-honey, we are in our fifth month now of frontier living. We have cows, chickens, horses, pets, plenty of milk and cheese, meat, friends and neighbors, each other, a little cash coming in each month. Even the ability to send a message to our parents . . ."

"Speaking of parents—soon mine will be heading to Pennsylvania. And soon you will have a little brother or sister. Don't you wish . . .?"

"Yes, Mira, I do wish. But you know as well as I that the first likely time for us to go East will be for your *graduation*. Unfortunately, as we know from your father's last letter there is no woman in seminary this year. *If* there should be one or more enrolled next year, then it would still be two years before a graduation that included women. Two years, plus this year, totaling three years."

"I know, Franco. I already figured that all out."

"Mira-honey, you are a true pioneer—not just in what you are doing here on the prairie, but in what you did by going to an all-male seminary."

"But why does it have to be so hard?"

"Because it's worthwhile. And I am confident that before too many years pass we will see our families again."

As the days, and especially the nights grew colder Mira pulled out two down comforters from her trunks, and again thanked God that her mother had insisted she bring so many supplies.

Franco always carried a sack with him to pick up chips, but with the diminished buffalo herds, chips were getting scarce. And cobs and wood almost equally scarce. The General had many loads of coal brought in from Yankton, but even that had to be sold judiciously. He felt that it was his responsibility to help *everyone* stay warm—not just those who could most easily purchase large supplies. And so every Wednesday Franco brought home several buckets of coal to stretch their use of cobs and chips. Coal for the school/church was purchased from a community fund overseen by The General.

Cold, but snow was late in coming. However, the winds from the northwest penetrated the walls of their house chilling Mira and Franco to the bone. They had never felt anything like it. There were days when it was not safe to go out even by horse. Jake cautioned that only the most seasoned should be out on such days. In November the church board told Franco to cancel all circuit trips until March or April. Mira was relieved, but Franco was frustrated. There were many days when no children showed up for school. It was unsafe for the little ones, and even the older ones to walk the distance from their homes.

But on most days Franco did venture out locally—certainly as far as Bessie and Jimmy, to bring them milk, and pick up cheese for themselves, and to deliver to the store for sale.

Franco and Mira, each wrapped in a comforter, devoted many hours to study, sermon writing, and developing lesson plans for when school and circuit would resume on a regular schedule.

Mira fretted over medical needs that were going unmet and expressed her concern to Franco.

"Mira, remember, the people here *did get along* before we came."

She did not answer, but felt very hurt. What he said was true, but wasn't their life here meant to *make things better than just getting along?* She supposed they could get along, too, without his preaching.

She soon had answer on both accounts . . .

Families with enclosed buggies or wagons almost never missed a Sunday service, even bringing food to share inside, rather than an outdoor picnic. And Franco's office became a place for Mira to hold "Sunday clinic" for those with medical needs.

After observing this for several weeks Franco had a moment of reckoning, and realized he owed Mira an apology. It was a Sunday evening, the morning service and meal had gone well, and Mira had seen to the needs of at least a half dozen people, several of them children. Over their light supper of boiled eggs, bread and cheese, Franco said, "Mira-honey, I see how wrong I was. The prairie folk need you, maybe even more than they need me. Yes, *they got* along. But they *get* along much better with you. And I don't doubt that some of them even come to the service just because they know that medical help will be available afterwards. And I also acknowledge that the gifts of food, and occasionally a little money goes a long ways towards keeping us comfortable and fed."

Mira nodded her head but said nothing, tears welling up in her eyes.

"Mira-honey, in the future, when I say something inappropriate, wrong, or unkind *please* call me on it when it happens, rather than brood over it for weeks until I finally wake up."

Mira nodded her head again, and said, "But Franco, you don't know how hard that is for me. As you know, my mother is a very proper lady, and she would never *correct* my father, or he her, for that matter."

"Never?"

"Not that I was aware of."

"Well, as you know, my parents, too were proper, *but wow! Could they go at it.*"

"Really? I never would have thought!"

"I know, and now that I think back to those days, I remember my grandparents, too—those dear, gentle people—they didn't always agree with each other, even in my presence or the presence of my parents. But they always insisted *fight fair, get it out in the open, and then get over it and move on. So please,* Mira-honey, please hear me as I say again—*when and if I hurt you by words or something I do, say something,* because it sometimes takes me awhile to guess what you are thinking. Or, I have to see something—like people coming to you with needs after the church service—to wake me up."

"I'll try Franco. "

"Try hard. It will be worth it."

Occasionally there were days when the wind died down and the temperature was mild. Those days brought out people—usually congregating at the *General Store*, and because the farmers had had a good year, The General did a lively business—even long standing bills were paid.

One such day Bessie came to town—she had saved enough money for The General to order her treadle machine. "Bessie, you are an amazing woman! The order will be in the mail as soon as Kjell goes to Yankton—tomorrow, if the weather holds. You will have your machine by Christmas time."

"Thank you General, but I'm not sure that I will have enough money for the balance that soon. Milk production is down a bit, so I don't have as much cheese to sell."

"Bessie, your credit is always good with me. And I can already see all those dresses you are going to make, hanging from racks here in my store, to say nothing of the curtains, aprons . . ."

"General, how you dream!"

"I mean it, Bessie. We could use a community seamstress! Think about it!"

Bessie went home, her head spinning with ideas. *Community seamstress! I like that. In a few years Jimmy will be old enough to do the milking and cheese making, and I can sew to my heart's content.*

One mild day in the third week of November when Franco was spending his usual Wednesday morning at the *General Store* Kjell rushed in with a telegram. "Pastor Franco, look what just came in. I think you will want to read it right away. Then again, you might want to read it with your wife."

Franco could tell from Kjell's expression and excitement that it was good news, so he resisted the temptation to read it on the spot, and hurried home to share it with Mira.

"Mira-honey, a telegram," he shouted as his horse stopped abruptly at the door. Mira bounded to the door, and together they read their parents' great news.

"Oh, Franco! It is better, and more exciting than we could have possibly imagined. We must telegraph them a word of congratulations right away! We haven't used our free telegram yet!"

They sat at the table, first offering a prayer of thanksgiving for new life and that all was well, and then crafted a telegram that expressed their joy and thanksgiving at the great news coming out of the woods of Pennsylvania!

Franco saddled Mira's horse. Their first stop, the telegraph office, and then the *General Store*. John and Mable greeted them. "The two of you are absolutely glowing. Kjell told us the good news—he was sure you wouldn't mind. How does it feel to be big brother and big sister? If we remember correctly you told us before that you both are from single child families!"

"We are ecstatic. And to know that mother Welken did so well at her age."

"*At her age?*" asked Mable.

"Well, yes. Think of it. Franco is 25, so she must be at least 45!"

"It happens! And yes, what a blessing!"

"I can imagine how relieved your father must be, Franco," said The General.

"Indeed. And Mira's father, too, as he was the attending physician. Perhaps you remember me telling you that Mira's parents have been spending several months this fall and winter in Pennsylvania, just for the big event."

"What a wonderful and generous thing for your parents to do, Mira. Wouldn't it be great if both sets of parents would come to Chipps?" said Mable.

"Oh, I live for the day, but it won't happen soon, I'm sure. And my mother, never. Although I didn't expect her to go to Pennsylvania, either." Franco gave her a stern look at the word *never*, and Mable made a mental note to discuss this with Mira at a later date, and privately.

The store was bustling with customers, but the General and Mable were completely relaxed, trusting those they knew to put the money for their purchases on the counter. Mable served fresh coffee to all, and in a spirit of generosity several folks left a small coin or two.

"We're so glad both of you came in, because in addition to rejoicing with you in your good news Mable and I need to talk to you about Thanksgiving Day. Even though we aren't a state yet we celebrate it as a national holiday ever since President Lincoln's proclamation some years ago."

"That's wonderful to hear. Mira and I were hesitant to bring it up since Chipps already has had two big celebrations in recent months—Telegraph Sunday and the wedding. And now with most days being so cold and windy, we didn't know if another community celebration would be likely. Where would we congregate? Even if the weather is pleasant enough for people to come, it's too cold for outdoor activities and the school/church is too small."

Returning from setting a fresh pot of coffee Mable jumped into the conversation, "Oh not to worry! Apparently no one has told you how Chipps celebrates Thanksgiving."

"No, no one has, not even the church board."

"That's probably because the church does not organize it. Cora and Jake and Mable and I do, but many others help and we certainly are counting on the two of you."

"Great—just tell us what to do."

"We alternate between Jake's ranch and our store. This year it's our turn. Everyone knows to come here. I see you looking around. Like *how is that possible?* Well, what you don't know and can't see—I had all the counters and display cabinets built with little hidden wheels. All we have to do is push them to the walls and set up tables and chairs in the center. Everyone will bring cooked food, Jake and Cora will bring the meat—roasted ox. If anyone has a chicken, or maybe has shot a wild turkey, grouse or rabbit . . ."

When General John had finished his list of what everyone would do or bring, Mable simply said, "And the two or you, will you please lead the worship? We can have the service right here."

Mira and Franco agreed.

"And one more thing."

"Of course, you name it."

"Please pray for safe weather."

Franco and Mira worked on their sermon—Mira would deliver it, and Franco would be responsible for the Thanksgiving liturgy, prayer, and leading singing with the musicians who now regularly brought their instruments to services.

And pray they did, every day, but every day brought more wind. "Just wait, Mira-honey, Thanksgiving Day will blow in on the wind."

"I hope it doesn't blow over with the wind."

When Franco awakened early on the morning of Thanksgiving Day he heard nothing but stillness. And a distant coyote. The wind had stopped. The house felt warmer, and when he stepped outdoors the temperature was in the thirties—the ice on the stock tank was beginning to thaw. It was a picture perfect day. He did his chores and then awakened Mira to share the good news with her.

Jimmy was at their door by 8 AM to ring the bell, even though the service would be held in the store.

Wagons began pulling up to the store by 9:30 and horses were corralled in a temporary wire enclosure—the work of Jake. There was also a smoldering "bonfire" over which hung a huge caldron. From the smell, everyone knew that this was the beef for the day, already cooked the day before and now just keeping warm. Women swarmed into Mable's *summer kitchen* adjacent to the store. The fire in the cook stove was well banked. Food could be kept warm in the oven, warming oven and stove top. Her house kitchen served as back up if more stove room or storage place for the food was needed. Everyone seemed to know exactly what to do, except Mira. Mable had told her to not bring anything—she and Franco would be doing their fair share by leading worship. *But still, what is it about life on the prairie that I don't get? What kind of communication is going on that I'm not observing.*

Cora approached her. "Doctor-dear, you look puzzled. What is troubling you?"

"Is it that obvious? Sometimes I feel *so* out of place. Everybody knows what to do. I don't."

"Doctor-dear, do you think anyone, other than Pastor Franco, could stand up and preach a sermon? Do you think anyone other than yourself could attend to all the medical conditions that you do?"

"Probably not."

"Then what is your problem?"

"It's hard to say. I just don't feel like I am one of the people."

"Mira, I'm going to speak a bit boldly, if I may."

Mira nodded her head.

"From what I have observed, you are a good leader, but *following* is difficult for you. You feel embarrassed if you do not know something, and are hesitant to ask. None of us expects you to know it all—we do expect you to *ask*. I see Mable looking in our direction right now. I think she needs help. Let's go and ask what we can do to help her. It really is as simple as that."

Mable was indeed looking for a few free hands—there were seven pies that needed cutting, and several loaves of bread waiting to be sliced.

"You see, Doctor-dear. Watch for clues. Look for what needs to be done and do it. Had I not seen Mable looking for help, I would have suggested that you and I begin cutting and slicing *without being told*. I saw the pies. I saw the bread. Like The General says, *on the prairie, when there is work to be done people see it and do it.*"

The sounds of the 10 o'clock bell carried clearly to the store. Everyone stopped what they were doing and found places to sit—benches and floor. Even on steps leading up to the second floor. The worship began, followed by feasting.

After the feast, cleanup ensued, again everyone seeming to know just exactly what to do. The Trio went out to the coal wagons, making sure that everyone who needed coal got a fair deal. The General and Mable did a lively business. Franco stayed to help with the cleanup. Mira tended to several medical needs. As people left many said to Franco, "We have something in the wagon for you and your wife. The weather between now and Christmas can be brutal, so we don't know if we will make it to Sunday services."

Mira and Franco received so many gifts of canned and dried food, and fresh meat—to say nothing of leftovers—they had to store much of it with The General and come back later to get it.

The wind began again in earnest that night. As Mira and Franco lay listening to it Mira asked, "Why did the people ask us to pray for snow? I would think that would be the last thing anybody would want."

"I wondered the same thing so I asked, and learned about needs here that differ from the well-forested area where my parents live. Here snow is needed for at least three reasons. Moisture. A covering for top soil, to keep it from blowing away. And insulation. Banks of snow against buildings keep out cold wind, and hold in warmth."

"Interesting. Who would have thought?" Mira was quiet for several moments and then said, "And you know what, Franco? I can think of a fourth reason for snow."

"What is that, Mira-honey?'

"Beauty."

"Beauty, for sure." Franco paused, and then chuckled, "Do you remember our snowball fight?"

"Indeed I do. When I was trying to get you to lighten up enough to propose to me."

"Well, we don't need snow for what I want to do now."

"Franco! Maybe being snowed in would . . ."

But no snow came that night, nor in the days and weeks that followed.

Two weeks following Thanksgiving Bessie's treadle arrived—the first treadle sewing machine in the area. At the General's suggestion she put up a posting just above his bolts of fabric:

SEWING
Buy your fabric here
See Bessie for your sewing needs.

Bessie nearly became a celebrity as word got out. And The General benefitted by selling more fabric. He and Mable soon had their catalogue out, ordering more and a greater variety of cloth.

Mira had planned to ask Bessie to alter her dresses to make them more serviceable for prairie life but changed her mind on that, saving most of them for the *Brides of Chipps*. Instead, she purchased fabric with a Christmas gift from her parents, and had Bessie design gently flared slit skirts with hem lines just above the ankles. Perhaps not entirely proper, but she detested hems dragging through the mud, or worse. (She had read about French women wearing culottes that came only to the knee!) The slit would make riding easier, and she wouldn't have to pull her leathers on in the middle of the night.

Bessie refused payment, insisting that the milk she received and the profit from selling cheese exceeded the cost of sewing. (While Franco was not doing circuit Bessie did not help with chores.)

With colder temperatures setting in, fewer people came to church, but Mira and Franco continued their Wednesday night routines of bathing, hair washing, and sermon preparation focusing on the *fruits of the Spirit*. When only a few people came on Sunday they filed their sermon, and had a discussion-Bible study.

Despite the cold, the General Store continued to be a place for socializing, and Franco spent more and more time there. The General offered him a small table and a couple of chairs in a semi-private corner to use for conversation. If someone complained of a medical concern Franco encouraged them to go the short distance to see Mira.

Christmas would fall on Friday this year. Knowing the love the people of Chipps had for celebrations, Franco conferred with his Church Board about what to do. He and Mira had already informally talked with the school teacher about having a combined worship service/school program.

The Board agreed, with one caveat—be prepared to cancel. One of these days snow would come, or else the temperature might drop too low for anyone to be safely out in it.

Franco and Mira fondly remembered Christmas trees and celebrations from Christmases past. It would be different for them this year, but they entered into the enthusiasm of the children as they excitedly prepared for the program and made colorful paper chains to string from window to window. Bessie sewed colorful decorations that Jimmy would bring to school the day before the program. And on the Wednesday before Christmas Mira bundled up and went to Cora to bake Christmas goodies—the food at the program would be limited to sweets and hot drinks.

At the final rehearsal on Thursday the children were wondering aloud what they might receive from The General this year—a candy cane, orange, apple, peanuts?

As the rehearsal concluded The General pulled up to the school, a large sack slung over his shoulder. "A day early this year, children. Hope you don't mind. I got a bag for each of you. Can I count on you to share with your families? Do I have your word?"

The children solemnly nodded their heads.

The General handed out the bags with a reminder *no peekin'*.

But peeking they did. Reflecting the prosperous year that he had, the General was more than generous—a candy cane for each child, along with a handful of roasted peanuts in the shell, and a couple of apples and oranges to share with family.

The General left, wishing them all a blessed Christmas. But fact of the matter—he did not trust the feel of the weather and had his eye trained to the sky.

Franco and Mira enjoyed a quiet Christmas Eve in their house sharing Christmas memories with each other. But with concern Franco noticed that it took more than the usual amount of coal to stay warm, even wearing their coats. For added warmth, Mira allowed Benny to sleep at their feet, on top of the comforters. The deerskins were not yet ready for use.

Early Christmas morning Franco opened the door to a wall of snow. He also noted that the house didn't seem quite as cold. It must be true—snow served as natural insulator. Hopefully this would be true for the other buildings, too, for the protection of the animals. But how to get to them with the door blocked?

He awakened Mira, "Mira-honey, wake up. I don't think you have ever seen anything like this."

As she put her feet over the side of the bed Franco helped her with her slippers and put a comforter over her shoulders. Not comprehending his meaning, Mira thought perhaps he had an unusual present for her. But she saw nothing.

"Stay where you are—I'm going to open the door."

Even in the dim candle light Mira saw the wall of snow.

"Franco! How did that all fall in just the hours we were sleeping?"

"I doubt that there is that much snow on the level. It just banks against anything it comes up against. Now I have to try to figure out how to get to the barn."

"Did you try the door of the lean-to?"

"No, but that's a good idea."

They went into the lean-to and opened the door. It was clear of snow, but the air was filled with whirling, swirling snow. A true blizzard had hit during the night.

"I have to go to the barn. The animals . . ."

"But Franco, we can't even *see* the barn. "

"I know. This is dangerous. But once again Jake has come through for us. Perhaps you haven't noticed, but Jake made a deal with me—a long length of rope, long enough to reach the barn and other buildings, in exchange for helping him put up hay *next* summer. I, of course, got the better end of the deal. For lack of storage space, I put it under our bed, coiled. It's time to use it."

Franco got the rope and tied it firmly to the shelving in the lean-to. Then dressed to go out, but Mira insisted on serving a hot cup of coffee first. Over coffee their conversation went to the day—what would happen to all their plans?

"Franco, I don't see how anybody could possibly get here."

"You're right, Mira-honey. I doubt that anyone will try. Safety for themselves and their animals will be their first priority. It may be days before we see anyone, other than ourselves."

"I feel bad for the children. This program means so much to them."

"Don't forget Mira-honey, they're all Dakotans. They'll make the best of it and learn from it. I think The General suspected this storm. Else why would he have given the children their gifts yesterday?"

"You're probably right, Franco. But why didn't he at least say something to us?"

"He did. It was non-verbal. We have to learn to read behaviors. I dare say some of the older children understood very well."

"You know, Franco, our emphasis on preaching THE GOSPEL—how about after school and church resumes we have the children give their presentation of the Joseph and Mary story, and the birth of Jesus? His birth is a basic story of THE GOSPEL."

"Great suggestion. The children will be pleased. But now I must get bundled up and go outside."

The storm raged for another 24 hours. Franco was able to tend his animals, but attempted no shoveling. The wind would fill a path with snow in short order. While Franco was out, Mira busied herself by opening the front door and began to chip away at the snow bank. She filled her copper boiler and placed it on the stove. Melting the snow did not produce much water, but every bucketful she collected this way saved Franco a trip to the well. It was soft like rainwater—wonderful for washing. The heat radiating from the boiler made the room more comfortable, lasting into the night.

By Saturday afternoon the sky cleared, but the wind continued to howl and snow whipped around making visibility difficult. Using caution and the rope, Franco brought buckets of water to the house to warm and then let the cows and horses drink directly from the bucket—easier than trying to thaw the water in the stock tank.

The chicken coop was almost completely dark, with the snow banked up against the only window. The chickens huddled together trying to stay warm. Egg production went way down.

Franco kept a close eye on their coal supply, using only enough to keep the house modestly warm, cook with, and warm water. He checked on and fed Mouser daily, who seemed no worse for the cold. Mira had clearly established a connection between her sneezing and the presence of the cat—so no more cat in the house. Fortunately the mouse population was well in check. Only an occasional catch in the traps.

Franco wondered how Bessie and Jimmy were doing, but knew that it was unwise for him to go out by horseback. Hopefully someone with draft horses and a sleigh, if the roads were impassable by wagon, would soon make rounds to the neighbors. Or perhaps Sam, if he had snowshoes, would check on Bessie.

By Monday the wind had calmed and Franco got out his shovel. He had hoped to shovel out the front door but when he saw how wide, high and deep the bank was he decided to let nature take care of it, even if it took until spring. (Meanwhile Mira picked away at it from the inside and beneath.) As Franco surveyed the area he saw completely open places, but up against the buildings snow had blown and stayed. He found the door to the springhouse and got some much needed meat, and from the cellar, vegetables.

On Wednesday Franco saddled Grey and went to the store. Several other men had done the same, each having tales to tell.

At Mira's request Franco sent a telegraph to her father asking him for advice on treating frostbite. She had heard women talk about it. Now she was quite sure—at least if the winter continued to be this cold—that she would be asked to treat it.

There was a telegram from their parents, stating that all was well in Pennsylvania; heavy snowfall; the Phillips not yet returning home.

Franco stayed at the store only briefly, as it did not seem fair to leave Mira alone. Not only that—he couldn't wait to share her joy in receiving a telegram from their parents.

Chapter 11 *Meanwhile Back East*

Priscilla lost no time. The day after she and Charles discussed Nina's pregnancy and their trip to Pennsylvania, she shopped for fabric and enlisted the help of her dressmaker and her treadle machine. Hemming diapers and receiving blankets by machine would save hours of painstaking handwork. But Priscilla would hand stitch to perfection all the little garments for the baby. Many evenings she sat knitting booties and hats. She debated with herself, *should I give some of Miranda's baby clothes, too?* But decided against it, hoping that she and Franklin would have children.

For his part, Charles began to train three young doctors who were eager for the experience. Priscilla volunteered the use of their house for whoever would be taking night call. Having young people living in on a rotating basis would give their cook and gardener something to do in the absence of the Phillips. But more importantly, Charles' patients would know where to find help at nighttime. Charles had the doctors begin night rotations almost immediately, first going with them, but before long letting them go on their own, while he served as backup. For the first time in many years Charles got enough rest.

With extra time on his hands Charles had several discussions with the Seminary officials, encouraging the development of the diploma program they had committed themselves to. He regretted to inform Mira and Franklin that no women had applied for entry for the 1873-74 school year. Perhaps it was too soon. More time and effort had to be put into promotion. Charles took it upon himself to contact clergy asking them to inform their congregations of this new opportunity for women—especially those who had an interest in teaching the Bible, and missions.

By the end of September Priscilla was finished sewing and was ready to pack trunks. Her own wardrobe was disarmingly simple. None of her usual layers of lace and ruffles, or hoops and petticoats. Just simple, serviceable frocks, with a few extra for Nina, all sewn by her dressmaker. Her dressmaker remembering, the elegant, *pregnant* country lady also made—free of charge—one fancy dress she was sure Nina would want to wear *for the christening.*

Several letters, even a telegram or two went back and forth between the Phillips and Welkens, and middle October Hiram and Nina welcomed Charles and Priscilla at their nearest depot.

The women chatted like sisters in the buggy ride to the homestead, Priscilla very concerned to hear from Nina how she was doing with her pregnancy. Hiram and Charles kept up a conversation of their own, but Charles listened with one ear to the conversation of the women.

"Priscilla, it's hard to believe, but I feel great; so much better than the other pregnancies I've had. It's wonderful to be at a time and place in life where I can take good care of myself. And Hiram, well, he has always treated me well, but now you'd think I'm a queen. He constantly reminds me to eat well, get enough rest. I have to remind him that getting enough exercise—largely in the form of work—is as necessary as rest, if I am to have enough strength for the hard job of labor and delivery."

"Nina, I am so excited. I can't wait to show you all the sewing I have done. I even had my dressmaker—you remember her—?

"Oh, I do. She was the first to guess that I was pregnant, and encouraged me to talk with Charles!"

"Well, she used her treadle machine to hem diapers and receiving blankets."

"Just think Priscilla, using a machine for sewing—we will have a thoroughly modern baby!"

"Let's open the trunks tonight. I can't wait to show you everything."

"And I can't wait to see. And by the way Priscilla, I see the dressmaker has done some sewing for you also—a different style from your usual," Nina said with a smile.

"I remembered what you said about how to dress for your *style of life*. And I must say *the change is very comfortable. I may never go back to the fancy life style.*"

'Don't give it up completely. It felt so elegant to dress up that week we spent at your house. I told the ladies in my church about the clothes, and they have been insisting—when I could still fit into my dresses—that I wear them to church. The clothes were a feast for their eyes. I actually have seen a few of the women wearing fancier clothes themselves for church. It's been great fun."

The chatter went on until Hiram stopped the team in front of the log cabin and said, "This is it. Our house, joined with the one we first lived in, and then later used for the soldiers. You can have your choice—living in the old, which we have fixed up now for travelers who often need a night's lodging—or you can use Franklin's loft. Don't decide until you have seen both."

They entered. Priscilla immediately noticed how neat and clean it was, but so sparse.

Nina, catching Priscilla's expression gently addressed it. "I know, Priscilla, but soon you will see how practical it is—just like how I dress—it will seem natural."

"I'll be fine! But it will take getting used to. I'm going to have to learn, for the first time in my life, how to do physical work. I hope I won't be more work than I am worth."

Hiram jumped in, "Not a chance! Remember we once lived a very different life, too, but it didn't take us long to learn. Charles, how about coming outdoors with me? I'll go easy on you, at least until you get your *work clothes* unpacked. You are going to love what I have planned for you. As for you, Priscilla, there is no better teacher than Nina."

And with that, Hiram introduced Charles to the chores routine, and Nina introduced Priscilla to the kitchen, setting their first tea.

A few hours later when Nina and Hiram were outside Charles asked, "What do you think, Priss, where do you want us to spend our nights?"

"Believe it or not, the loft looks really good to me. I can manage the ladder, if you can."

"I was hoping the loft would be your choice. Hiram and I already put the trunks in the other house, as space here is limited. But we can move clothes that we need immediately to the loft."

"Imagine Charles! This cabin would nearly fit in our parlor! And before long there has to be room for baby things, too. But I know they'll not be putting the baby in the loft!"

So it was decided—sleeping in the loft, at least in the beginning, and spilling over into the other house as required by space and privacy.

That evening they showed Hiram and Nina the baby supplies. Except for tears in their eyes, and a heartfelt *thank you*, they were speechless. This would be the best dressed baby in the vicinity.

There was already a chill in the air, but the cook stove kept a comfortable temperature inside, even at night, with proper banking.

Soon after their arrival Charles brought up the topic of the delivery. Nina was beginning to move slowly and felt and looked cumbersome. He suggested a four-part conversation, since everyone would have a role in the coming event. Charles led off with a question.

"Previously you mentioned a local midwife. Have you consulted her, and do you want her present?"

"There is a midwife. When she heard that I was pregnant, she approached me and offered her service. She seemed a little hurt when I told her that I would be having *a doctor* for the delivery, but when I explained that the doctor was a relative from the east, she was alright with it."

"I wouldn't be opposed to having her present, especially to help with the baby after delivery. Priscilla, of course, is very good with babies, but you might want Priscilla at your side, too—just in case Hiram is out cold on the floor."

That brought a good laugh from everyone, Hiram most of all.

"What do you think, Nina-honey, do you want Maud?"

"Let's ask Priscilla. Priscilla, what do you see as your role?"

"I think having the midwife to take care of the baby immediately is a very good idea. I love taking care of babies. But the first hours of a newborn—well, I don't know if I would know exactly what to do."

"That settles it. I'll talk to the midwife in a day or two. Would you like to meet her, Charles?"

"Excellent idea. And now I would like to examine the mother."

For a few moments Charles became totally professional, and then broke the suspense by saying, "Nina, you and baby are doing well. I hear a strong heartbeat. Be prepared for a good sized baby. The only thing that I would suggest is that several times a day you sit with your feet elevated. That should help with the swollen ankles—and avoid salted food. How about in the next several weeks you and Priscilla cook without added salt? That would be good for all of us."

"What do you think, Priscilla? Can you manage with me sitting with feet elevated? I don't think I've ever had that luxury!"

"So long as you supervise me, I'll manage. And coming from Charles, *that's an order, not a luxury.*"

Another round of chuckles.

The following day Charles and Hiram went to town. Supplies were needed, and Hiram wanted to introduce Charles to the midwife. En route Charles asked if there was also a local doctor.

"A doctor? You don't think . . . ?"

"No, no, nothing of the sort. I wish all my *young* patients were in as good a shape as Nina. I want to see him just for a collegial visit. I will be in his territory, you know."

"Good point. Of course, we will stop by and see him, too."

They pulled up to the midwife's house first. Hiram went to the door alone. "Good morning, Maud," he called through the screen door. Maud came to the door, drying her hands on her apron.

"Hiram, what brings you? Don't tell me . . ."

"No, everything is fine with Nina. I did bring someone for you to meet, if you will. Our relative from the east, Dr. Phillips."

Maud peered through the screen trying to see the doctor in the buggy.

"Can I bring him in?"

"Yes. Yes, of course, bring him in. I'll fix tea."

Hiram and Charles seated themselves in the parlor, and were soon joined by Maud bearing steaming tea and a plate of crumpets.

"Pleased to meet you, Maud. Hiram and Nina have told me about your good work in the community. I must admit, I feel like I am in your territory, but I trust you understand my family connection with the Welkens."

Disarmed by the gracious comments, Maud nodded her head.

Charles continued, "As you know, the first moments after birth can be *tricky*—both mother and baby needing help. I will do the delivery—are you willing to tend to the newborn's needs? Having you there for the baby would be a big comfort to Nina and Hiram, and would take a load off my shoulders."

"But what about your wife? I figured she would want to help."

"She does. But just yesterday she was saying how much she would appreciate *someone skilled in newborn care* to be there for the immediate needs."

Maud liked those words and replied, "That really is my biggest concern—proper care for the newborn. Just let me know when, and I'll be there if at all possible."

Both Hiram and Charles thanked her heartily for being willing to help, and for the tea and crumpets.

Back in the buggy Charles said, "Whew! That one went well, may the next be as successful."

"Not to worry, Charles. You could charm a fly off a manure pile!" At which Charles laughed heartedly. This was the first he heard proper Hiram being the least bit earthy!

Hiram joined in the laughter and said, "I learned it from Mr. Pierson. For use only when the ladies are not present!"

At the doctor's house-office Hiram again went ahead to smooth the way. He knocked and called through the screen, "Doc, hope you're not too busy to meet a colleague from the East."

"Come in, Hiram. It's a quiet morning. Nina's not in trouble is she?"

"No, she is fine. But our relatives have come—you know the doctor I mentioned to you, and he wants to meet you."

"Bring him in—you never did tell me his name."

Hiram called back to the carriage, "Come on in, Charles. Doc here is free for the moment."

As Charles walked to the door, Dr. McCloud stepped out. "*Charles Phillips, is that you*?! I don't believe my eyes!"

"Daniel, I've never been more surprised."

The two men shook hands. Hiram stepped back, as surprised as the others.

Charles turned to Hiram. "You must not have mentioned our names to either one of us. Daniel and I worked together during the war. He is the finest surgeon I know, even though the work that had to be done was gruesome."

Daniel, nodded his head, but clearly did not want to talk about that part of his career at the moment.

Charles went on, "You know what brings me here, Daniel. Or at least a little of the story. But what about you? How did you come to settle here in western Pennsylvania?"

While Charles and Daniel caught up on old times Hiram did his shopping and then stopped back for Charles.

"We could have talked for hours more. Daniel wants me to stop in again. He has a couple cases he would like to consult with me on."

"We can easily arrange that."

The days passed uneventfully, the Welkens and Phillips thoroughly enjoying each other's company, talking about Miranda and Franklin, and Nina and Hiram telling entertaining stories about the early days of living in Pennsylvania, and later opening the house to care for soldiers. The soldier stories Charles could relate to. He told many of his own.

Priscilla adapted well, showing only occasional irritation at the lack of the conveniences. This was the first time in her life she ever did more than put a small piece of wood in a fireplace, or boil water for tea.

The Sunday night which began the third week of November Nina went to bed with a backache—of enough concern to Charles to suggest that they do last minute preparations. If the baby came this early, he would be small, despite Nina's size, and would have to have assistance in maintaining body heat. They had jars ready to be filled with warm water; then to be carefully wrapped and placed in the cradle which was standing near the cook stove. Hiram carefully banked the fire and set the kettle and a couple pans of water on the cooking surface. Charles set his bag of instruments ready, and Priscilla laid out the layette. Hiram harnessed the horses, ready to get the midwife as soon as Charles gave the word.

As usual, they joined in group prayer, but this night there was added emphasis that God would put his special hand of protection on Nina and the baby.

Nina fell asleep immediately. Hiram could be heard pacing the floor, and Charles and Priscilla only dozed. At four o'clock Nina awakened with a contraction, and knew it was the real thing.

"Hiram, get Charles."

Charles was down the steps before Hiram could call.

"I'll go for the midwife."

"No. Let's wait and see how quickly the contractions come."

At five o'clock Charles gave word to Hiram to get the midwife. As far as he could tell everything was proceeding well, but he wished that a few more weeks had passed. Premature births had a high mortality rate. However, there was nothing anybody could do but their best in a less than desirable situation. This was one of the reasons he and Priscilla had come early.

Priscilla sat calmly at Nina's side, wiping her brow, speaking words of encouragement, and telling her how Nina was the sister she never had, but always wanted. But Nina's focus was on herself and her baby.

Hiram was back with Maud by six o'clock. Maud carefully stayed out of Charles' way, and bristled a bit when he explained the use of jars for warm water. Between spending moments at Nina's side Hiram made coffee and toast. After it was all over he would make a more substantial breakfast, but for now, in deference to Nina, he would avoid the smell of cooking bacon.

Seven o'clock. "Hiram, if you want to do chores, now is a good time. It still is going to be a couple hours. Her contractions are regular and well-spaced."

When Hiram stepped into the house an hour later, he noticed a change. Nina who had stoically endured each contraction thus far was crying out in pain. He went to her side, tears streaming down his face. "Nina, I am so sorry. I wish I could take some . . . "

"Don't say it, Hiram. You don't know what you are talking about. This is a *woman's* pain."

If Hiram felt hurt, he said nothing more. His gentle Nina would not deliberately hurt anybody, by word or deed, least of all, him.

At nine o'clock Charles told Priscilla to fill the jars, screw on the lids very tightly, wrap them and place them along the sides of the cradle. He nodded at the midwife who got the receiving blanket ready and pushed the table with instruments near Charles. "Nina, when you feel like pushing, *push*, working with the contraction." A contraction came on heavy, and Nina pushed, and then relaxed for a few seconds. Then again and again. With one final mighty push Charles had a tiny girl in his hands. He cleared her airway, and with only a gentle tap, the baby took her first breath and cried a good strong cry. He placed the baby in the receiving blanket and cut the cord. The midwife knew her role well. She immediately placed the baby on Nina's chest.

But then the midwife and Charles almost had *words*. She wanted to bathe the baby but Charles insisted that she must wait. The baby must be kept warm, in the cradle. Priscilla took the baby from Nina and put her in the cradle, the hot water radiating a gentle warmth. Priscilla put a little knit hat on her head.

"OHHHHH, another contraction, Charles."

"Not to worry, Nina. That would be the placenta."

It was. But what followed, took Charles completely by surprise. Nina had another strong contraction, and Charles saw another head crown. Keeping his cool, the only thing he said was, "This is going to take another big push—when you feel another contraction." Under his breath he added, "Get me another blanket and scissors."

Maud left off clucking over the newborn and went to help Charles. Hiram stepped to the foot of the bed.

"Back to your wife's side, Hiram."

Another contraction. "*Push, Nina!*"

Nina pushed and then relaxed. She said breathlessly, "I didn't remember that delivering the afterbirth was so painful. Did you get it?"

"Just follow my orders, Nina. Push with the next contraction."

In another moment a contraction was heavy on her, and she pushed, delivering a baby boy, slightly bigger than his sister.

The joy in the room was great. Two healthy, tiny babies, using their lungs freely.

"Good thing you made that cradle large, Hiram. You might want to start working on a second. This one will soon be too small for two babies!"

Two days later, when they were absolutely sure that all was well, Hiram sent a telegram to Mira and Franco. The telegram that Kjell gave to Franco on Wednesday, the week before Thanksgiving Day.

As for the Welkens and Phillips—Nina regained her strength slowly; nursing two hungry babies took everything she had. But Priscilla never was more energetic. No babies every had more tender loving care than these two. And no mother ever had more love, help, and support than Nina. Not only from Priscilla, but also from the men.

Charles asked Hiram if he knew anyone in the vicinity that raised donkeys. He had read that donkey's milk agreed with newborns better than cow's milk. They also asked Charles' colleague, Dr. McCloud, and put up a request in the general store. All without results. It was up to Nina, and eventually their cow.

Charles and Hiram got along well, Charles taking to outdoor work, even wood chopping and milking. He also made many trips to town to visit and assist Dr. McCloud. As for his own practice—he heard regularly from the doctors who were covering for him. They assured him that although his patients missed him, the practice was going well—even getting larger.

The Welkens invited the Phillips to stay for Christmas, only a few weeks away.

And then a blizzard struck. The Phillips stayed in Pennsylvania until spring, after the christening. Nina, wearing the new dress made for the occasion by Priscilla's seamstress, never looked more lovely. And Priscilla beamed with pleasure.

The names of the children? Priscilla and Charles. Or Prissy and Chuckie, for short.

PART 2

ONE YEAR FOLLOWS ANOTHER
1874—1880

Chapter 12 *Mira Sees the Sky*

Mira literally dug a snow cave leading out from her front door, picking away at the snow bank the entire month of January. And then one day she poked through and saw a patch of blue. She excitedly told Franco when he came in.

"Franco, I saw the sky through a hole. I feel hopeful that life will return to normal."

"Life will return to normal, and you have dug enough—let nature do the rest."

But for Mira digging was a necessity. It gave her something physical to do and it helped Franco by reducing the amount of water he had to haul in. Every day she brought in boilers full of snow for melting. She loved the soft water for bathing and washing. Plus, digging helped keep her sanity.

But one day Mira dug too much and a mountain of snow crashed down on her. It did not totally cover her, but she could not extricate herself. Franco came running from the barn, hearing her call. He dug her out, a shaking and embarrassed Miranda. Franco wrapped her in blankets and sat her near the stove with a cup of warm tea. Then he finished the digging, clearing the front door and the path leading to it. It eventually became a joke in the community, and a time marker—*the winter Dr. Mira saw the sky*. She took it in good grace. But she never again dug through a snowbank.

It *was* a winter to remember. The blizzard of Christmas Eve, followed by extreme cold, and wind.

As Franco expected, Sunday services in January and February usually were a Bible study for the few who came when they could—Mable and John, Cora and Jake, Bessie and Jimmy, Sam and Agnes, and a few others who could enclose their wagons, and had horses that could endure the wind.

The school board cancelled school for these two months, or *until further notice*.

Mira dreaded the day when she would get her first case of frostbite, but she knew it was inevitable—the farmers had to get out to care for their stock.

She received an answer to the telegram Franco had sent to her father: *Warm affected area gently, slowly. Then treat as burn. Prepare to amputate.*

Mira pored over a surgical text on amputation, and reviewed the use of her instruments. How she wished her father had allowed her to help in the hospital when he was treating the soldiers. She discussed the procedure with Franco, telling him that she would need his help, should the situation arise. Particularly she would need him to administer chloroform, and possibly saw the bone if she did not have the physical strength. Franco did not flinch. He had seen what his father and grandfather had done for soldiers with gangrene. He just wished he could spare Mira.

Mira and Franco prepared themselves just in time, for an urgent request came from Cora via one of the cowhands. Jake had been out searching for missing cattle and did not come home one night. Cora hoped and prayed that he would find shelter in an abandoned hut where he could make a fire. But he found none. To keep his hands and face from freezing he thrust his hands deep into his coat pockets, and leaned forward in his saddle, burying his face in the horse's mane. He gave his horse full rein, trusting him to find the way home. About eight the next morning the horse stopped in front of the house and Jake fell off. The horse—Jake's favorite and most trustworthy—had to be shot. Its lungs were ruined from having faced below zero wind for hours.

Jake was nearly stiff. Cora and their sons pulled him in, and put him in front of the fire on a sheepskin, stripping off his frozen clothes and covering him with blankets.

One of the ranch hands went with an enclosed wagon and got Mira and Franco. *Warm affected area gently, slowly, and then treat as burn. Prepare to amputate.* These words went through Mira's mind as they made their way to the ranch. It would be much too soon to know if amputation would be needed. First they had to save his life, and then work to prevent gangrene.

Mira was glad to see that Cora and her sons had him well wrapped and were attempting to spoon warm tea into him. He could swallow. That was encouraging. Mira carefully felt for pulses—carotid and wrist. She could feel a heartbeat. Then she uncovered his legs. From knees down they were cold to the touch and she could feel no pulse, nor could he feel her touch him.

Franco and Cora watched Mira's face carefully, understanding what she was doing and thinking.

Mira stood and looked at Cora. "My father recently sent instructions on treating frostbite. He says to *warm affected area gently, slowly, and then treat as a burn.*" She avoided the word *amputation.*

"You and your sons have done exactly the right things this far." Cora's shoulders visibly relaxed. "Now we'll switch to warm moist cloths and see if we can get the blood flowing to his lower legs, feet, and toes again. As the affected area begins to *wake up* it is likely to be painful. Actually, as strange as it may sound, pain would be a good sign, because it means *life*. As I'm sure you noticed, right now he feels nothing when I touch his lower legs."

"We'll do anything you say. We are not drinking people, but we do have a flask of whiskey . . ."

"No, Cora, no alcohol. That would do more harm than good. But I did bring laudanum. I would like to give him some right now, while you prepare some warm—not hot—moist cloths. And we will switch from your tea to willow bark tea—that should help keep fever and inflammation down. I brought some with me."

Cora nodded her agreement. Mira went to Jake's head. "Jake, it's Mira. With your permission, I'm going to give you some strong pain medication. I know you don't have pain now, but as feeling begins to return (she wished she was as confident as she was trying to sound) you'll have pain. We want to spare you as much discomfort as possible, so you can put your energy into healing, rather than into fighting pain."

In a weak voice Jake said "Do whatever needs to be done. You have my permission, and if I'm not able to speak, Cora will speak for me."

Before giving the laudanum Mira checked his breathing—regular, but shallow. *We'll have to work to prevent pneumonia, frequent turning while on bed rest; sit up when possible.* Carotid pulse—fast, but regular and strong. She gave him a recommended dose of laudanum, enough to keep him from being restless, but not to totally sedate him or depress his respirations, and then began the slow process of gently warming. She monitored him closely for change in vital signs, and the beginning of pain.

When word reached The General—one of the ranch hands had gone to tell him—he dropped everything, arriving on the scene about a half an hour after Mira and Franco. By this time Mira had begun the treatment, with Franco and Cora assisting and the sons carefully letting small amounts of warm willow bark tea trickle into Jake's mouth.

The General was known for use of his voice. Low and gentle, or loud and booming, as the situation required. He entered the room carrying a bucket of snow, nearly pushing Mira aside, voice booming, demanding to treat his friend.

"*Everybody knows you treat frostbite with snow. That's how we did it in the war. You rub snow onto the frozen area. And give plenty of whiskey.*"

Mira looked at Franco. Franco looked at Cora. They all looked at The General. This was the first that Mira and Franco experienced any tension with The General, although they had heard stories from others. Franco spoke first, "General, no disrespect intended, but Mira is following treatment protocol that she just recently received from her doctor-father—what are the words Mira?" (He wanted to give Mira a voice.)

"*Warm affected area gently, slowly. Then treat as burn.*" Mira continued the warm moist cloths.

The General opened his mouth, but Franco cut him off. "General, how often did you see loss of limb following frostbite?" Franco asked in a quiet voice so that Jake would not hear.

The General lowered his voice accordingly. "Well, most of the time, in severe frostbite."

"This *is severe frostbite*, so what have we to lose by trying Mira's method?"

The General was not an unreasonable man, but it was hard for him to concede ground, so he turned towards Cora for support. But before he said a word Cora said, "We will use Mira's method."

As he turned to leave he said, "Just be sure that someday Jake knows what my recommendation was." He took his bucket of snow, but left his flask of whiskey.

They applied the warm moist cloths intermittently for the next several hours, and did their best to keep the rest of Jake's body warm. The sons faithfully kept the fire burning brightly, the radiating heat filling the room. And they slowly gave him as much warm fluid as he would take.

After several hours Mira halted the warm applications temporarily so she could check for natural body warmth delivered by the blood supply returning to the tissue. To her joy, from the knee to several inches below there seemed to be some natural warmth, but she could feel no pedal pulses. She advised that they now begin using warm <u>dry</u> cloths, which would be less heavy on the skin. Cora warmed cloths in the oven while Franco and Mira gently applied them. Cora worked tirelessly, glad for something helpful to do, and spoke words of encouragement to Jake. When Jake began to mumble nonsense Mira hoped it was from the laudanum and not delirium related to fever.

They continued to apply warm cloths with Mira checking periodically for natural warmth and pulses. By 3 PM she was relatively sure that she could feel natural warmth almost down to his ankles, but she still could not feel pedal pulses, and his feet still felt cold, *but maybe not **as** cold* she noted to herself. But she had no way of measuring skin temperature except with her own hands.

About this time Jake's mumbling increased. The sons thought he said *pain*. Mira checked vitals, which were still in satisfactory range. So she gave another dose of laudanum.

Cora took a break from what she was doing and fixed sandwiches. At 5 PM Franco went home to do chores. The temperature had come up considerably during the day, and the wind had died down, so he borrowed one of Jake's horses. Before leaving, they all gathered around Jake and prayed for healing. Franco would come back in the morning and bring whatever supplies Mira might need, personal or medical.

The evening and night were uneventful, with Mira and Cora taking turns at Jake's side, offering fluids and laudanum. One of the sons stayed in the room also to keep the fire burning.

When Jake began to stir the next morning he had to be oriented to the events of the previous day. The laudanum left him rather foggy mentally.

"Why are my lower legs hurting but not my feet or toes?" he asked Cora. "I can't feel my toes."

Mira was present to hear the question, so she told him as gently as possible, "Jake, as far as I can tell, your lower legs are going to be just fine, although I am starting to see some blisters on them which we will have to dress carefully so they'll not get infected. I'm hoping that we'll be able to save your feet. But several of your toes will be a problem. I still cannot feel any warmth in them."

"So what does that mean—will I lose my toes?"

"It's too soon for me to know."

"But my legs and feet will recover?"

"I'm hopeful about them—the pain is a sign of life. Believe me, we will all try our very best to get you through this as intact as possible."

He reached for her hand, "I trust you Dr. Mira. And I am sorry for what The General put you through yesterday. I heard it all, and remember it, but I was too drugged to say anything. By the way, what did you give me? I think I could use some more about now."

"Laudanum, and yes, you can have some now. Could you eat some breakfast also? You've done well with fluids. Both fluids and protein foods are going to be very important for healing."

"I'm tired of this hard floor." He turned to Cora, "have the boys move a bed in here and get me in it. Then I think I could eat a little."

While the boys were working on the bed, Jake asked the question he hated to ask, and they dreaded hearing. Taking a deep breath he said, "My horse? I think I heard a gunshot."

Cora went to him, and in a sacred moment they wept together.

When he heard the boys return to the room, Jake turned to Franco, "I'll be claiming those babies your mares are carrying. Old Samson was the father."

"You got it, Jake. They are all yours."

But Cora wished their sons had seen him cry. Boys *need* to see their father cry, she believed. It helps develop the compassionate aspect of their character. She *would* tell them later.

Franco had returned about 9 AM. He suggested that one of the ranch hands drive Mira home in a wagon so she could rest. A suggestion she took him up on—but not until they had Jake in bed, and wounds and all blistered areas dressed and protected. She might not be able to prevent gangrene of the toes, but she was determined not to let the blistered area become infected. She also suggested that he remain on the sheepskin even in bed, since that was excellent for the prevention of pressure sores.

After a couple of days Mira was quite certain that lower legs, feet, and big toes would be saved, but she saw no evidence of blood supply to the other toes. She carefully instructed Cora and her sons on dressing the lower legs and feet, again thankful for the medical supplies her father had insisted he ship.

Her goal now was to prevent infection and watch for gangrene in the toes—a sure sign that she would have to amputate. A thick handwritten letter from her father arrived by mail. It was information from his experience, as well as that of Dr. McCloud, on treating frostbite, and the care following amputation. *Your nose can tell you much about what is going on with the human body. Your nose will tell you when the tissue has become gangrenous.*

The day came when Mira was absolutely certain that she would have to amputate. Her nose was indeed her guide. Cora had noted the smell, too, while changing dressings. Franco, Cora, and their sons were present when she told Jake.

Jake took the information stoically—really not surprised at all. Just grateful that it would be *only toes* that would be amputated. *A cowboy, so long as he has a horse, can get by without toes.*

What Mira did not tell him immediately was that they would have to continue to monitor and treat the health of his feet and lower legs. The amputation was to get rid of the dead tissue, and hopefully prevent infection from setting in the healthier, but still healing, tissue. *One step at a time; don't tell the patient more than he is ready to hear if you can avoid it.* More words of wisdom from her father.

Jake asked to have The General present. He was, after all Jake's best friend. A few days earlier The General had a conversation with Jake and Cora about his earlier conduct. Being the fine man that he was, he then stopped to see Mira and Franco and apologized to Mira, conceding that she and her father were right.

Removing the dead tissue was not difficult (except for the smell). The harder and more sensitive work was to know how far back to cut away tissue. What tissue would heal and remain healthy, and what would die? Her father's advice was to watch the blood supply closely—*if the **raw** area bleeds freely, the tissue might survive, so do not cut away too much initially. Observe closely every day for color, temperature, and fresh bleeding. If tissue looks and smells necrotic cut it away.* **This is likely to be a lengthy process, requiring expertise and patience.** *Keep the patient comfortable with laudanum and no weight bearing until the wounds are healed.*

Franco gave the chloroform. The general assured adequate lighting throughout the procedure, tirelessly holding and adjusting lanterns. Having seen frequent surgeries, especially amputations, he knew how essential good lighting was.

Mira worked until she was satisfied that she had reached good blood supply and then rinsed the wound with copious amounts of clean warm water. Next she gently packed the area, leaving the wounds open. If all went well, the wound would heal with granulation tissue from the deepest area, outward, and eventually the skin edges would unite.

While Franco lightened the anesthesia, The General and Mira bandaged the surgical site, attempting to apply enough pressure to curtail bleeding, but to not impede the blood supply. It would take frequent monitoring for the first 24 hours, and then redressing and observation for many days to follow. If infection, local or systemic, did not set in, Jake stood a good chance of recovery.

Jake was a cooperative patient, and after a couple weeks, Cora and sons did most of the care, with Mira and Franco checking in several times a week. Cora suggested that Franco and Mira use her buggy. It was much more comfortable in the cold weather than horseback. They could rest their feet on warms stones.

Dressing changes were painful, requiring a dose of laudanum each day. But between the dressing changes, willow bark tea was soon sufficient. Jake never did use the General's whiskey flask.

Following Mira's advice, Cora frequently propped Jake up with pillows. Franco showed the sons how to cross their arms between them, making a "chair" which they could use to carry their father the short distance to sit on a chair near the window. Jake's lungs remained clear and he developed neither infection nor pressure sores.

Chapter 13 *One Season Follows Another*

The weather remained very cold and windy through February and into early March. But there was almost no additional snow to that of the blizzard of Christmas, 1873. The farmers were concerned about drought and loss of topsoil.

Mira's medical work, other than Jake's needs and a few people who stopped by on Sunday or Wednesday, nearly came to a standstill, as did Franco's work. They spent most of their time studying, discussing new sermon topics, and writing.

In mid-March when the temperature came up to twenty or above and stayed there, the Board reopened school, and people returned to church.

About this time Mira was confident that Jake was no longer in danger of infection setting in and that he would lose no more tissue of his feet. She had chronicled everything she had done and sent the report to her father. He wrote back congratulating her. *Let this be a lesson to all of us—prevention of infection when dealing with wounds is key to healing.* **If only we knew more** *about the prevention and treatment of infection. What you have done, you have done well. No father could be prouder.* **Always keep extensive records of your work, and learn from your records—what works and doesn't work. Look for cause and effect.**

Word of Mira's treatment of Jake traveled far and wide. But Mira dreaded the day when she would get a child with a badly infected wound.

In April Mira received another lengthy communication from her father. He would be shipping a supply of *carbolic acid (phenol)*. Dr. Phillips had received information from Dr. McCloud about a doctor in England (Lister) who discovered the connection between dirty wounds, unclean techniques, and infections. He also discovered that using carbolic acid for cleaning dramatically reduced the occurrence and spread of infection. *Mira, this sounds like the key to prevention. Clean all your instruments and the areas that you use to treat patients with phenol, especially the areas that come into contact with pus. After cleaning your instruments with phenol rinse them in clean water (phenol is caustic) and let them air dry on clean cloth; then wrap them in clean cloth. I wish we knew more about the "science of infection" and how to treat it. But if we can prevent it, we have done a good and helpful thing.*

Cleanliness! Not easy on the prairie, especially when water is in short supply. But she would renew her focus on teaching it in her hygiene classes.

A couple weeks later another letter came. *Mira, Dr. McCloud has made an amazing offer. He would like you to work with him for several weeks. He is willing to teach you everything he knows about wound treatment, and even some surgery!*

And hear this: a tremendous answer to prayer. Two women will be entering seminary the fall of this year, 1874. That means they will be graduating in the spring 1876. A perfect time for you and Franco to come so you can receive your diploma and visit us; then you could go to Pennsylvania and work and study with Dr. McCloud and visit Franco's parents.

But for those two letters and the good success she had in treating Jake, Mira would have despaired. Winter on the prairie can leave one hopeless and vulnerable, physically and emotionally.

April and May were warm, with only one small rainfall. By June, it was so dry that the farmers knew that except for the first cutting of hay and what they could harvest of the hardy prairie grass, there would be no harvest. In hope of conserving well water the farmers who had access to a river or stream watered their cattle and horses from these sources. Others sold most of their animals, or slaughtered them to dry or can the meat. General John and Jake bought up much for this purpose. The tallow was used for making candles and soap. Two tasks that Mable taught Mira.

Mira and Franco did not bother with a garden, not even planting the flower seeds Mira had set her heart on. But of even greater concern was what they, and their neighbors, would eat without fresh produce and large enough supplies to can for the winter.

Franco and Mira's first wedding anniversary came and went with little ado. But Mira remembered the fine china, silverware and candlesticks that her mother had insisted she have. She sorted through trunks that she had not yet, in a year, unpacked.

They celebrated privately, eating rabbit on fine china. Mira used this opportunity to bring up the subject with Franco that she had already figured out the answer to. But she needed to hear Franco say it, both for her sake and his.

"Franco—the rabbit skins that you carefully save and preserve—you must have at least 20 of them by now. What are you going to do with them?"

"Mira-honey. I am saving them, to make blankets to wrap our children in."

"*Our children?* Franco. Are you disappointed, and particularly are you disappointed in me, that we have no child?"

"*Disappointed in you, Mira?* No, never. I could never be disappointed in you. You have already given me more happiness than any man deserves to have. But yes, I do hope that we will have children someday."

"Me, too, Franco. Me too. Keep shooting rabbits and someday I will put the skins to use!" She had no idea how dire her hope and prediction were.

Following chore time one evening in mid-July Franco came in grinning. "Mira-honey, I think tonight will be the night for Dapple. She is beginning to . . ."

"Oh Franco, I've never delivered a foal!"

"And you won't have to! Even though she's never had a baby, she will know exactly what to do."

"But can we . . . ?"

"Let's eat first, and then we can check on her, hourly, if we want, but there is no need for us to stay with her. In fact, my father always said that *horses want privacy*. Checking on her periodically is enough. Most likely she will deliver when we are not there."

And so it was. Hourly checks until midnight. But no baby. But when Franco went to check at 4 AM a beautiful little filly was standing on unsure legs getting her first meal. Franco gave Dapple many words of praise, a sugar cube or two, and replenished her water and hay.

Then he called Mira. Her feet barely touched the ground between her house and barn. She first praised and petted Dapple and then when she felt she had Dapple's permission, began stroking the baby.

"Mira-honey, don't get too attached. This is Jake's foal. We'll have her only until she is weaned."

"I know, but why not enjoy her while we can?"

"Jake does put great store in his horses getting used to people as early as possible. What do you think? Shall we ride out to Jake, using the horses he lent us for the summer, while Dapple spends time with her baby? We should check on Jake anyway to see how he is doing on his crutches." (Franco had previously constructed a set of crutches for Jake to use until his healing was complete and he was ready to start walking on his own again.) "Perhaps he and Cora would like to come out by wagon to see the baby."

"Great idea. But I must get dressed and fix breakfast. And we should wait until at least 8 AM."

It had been several weeks since Mira and Franco had been out to the ranch. As they drew up to the house they heard voices coming from behind and followed the sound. There they saw Cora and Jake (on his crutches) working in a huge flourishing vegetable garden.

Seeing their surprise, Jake said with a grin, "Well, what do you think of our efforts to make *the desert bloom?* Irrigation works wonders on this land. For years I have been mentally designing a system that I wanted to try, first on a garden. This was the year. The boys and I—they doing the physical work—found a way to channel water from the river to the garden. It is working so well, that if it is dry again next year, which likely it will be, we might even try it on a small field!"

"Jake, this is amazing!"

"Wait until you taste the fresh beans—we'll send some back with you."

"Can you come in for coffee?" Cora invited.

"We can, however, we have a different idea. We want you to come to our place. Thought maybe you could come out by wagon, unless of course, you have already been on horseback."

"Not quite yet. Need first to get the *go ahead* from Dr. Mira. But we can take the wagon, can't we, Cora? But wait a minute. What are you telling me?"

""Yep, we are telling you, Jake, Dapple had her baby last night. A filly."

"We'll be right out, won't we Cora?"

"We will. I'll get the wagon and the team."

Franco went to help her.

"What do you think, Doc? Can I get up on a horse soon?"

"How about I have a look at your feet at my house? But if you are walking as much as you appear to be without opening the wounds, I don't see why not."

Jake and Cora praised Dapple, admired the filly, and encouraged Mira and Franco to gently handle her as often as possible.

Over coffee they discussed a name, but did not settle on one. Mira pronounced Jake's feet well enough healed to do some weight bearing without crutches, and to get up on horseback.

That night, in private, Grey had her baby—a robust little colt.

When Jake saw the two together, he immediately named them *Joy and Pride*.

The summer plodded on. An occasional small shower. Frequent dark clouds, wind, but no real rain.

Franco did his monthly circuit work, coming back with depressing stories of hardship among the pioneers. A few had planted small plots of land, but as the summer progressed no one held out hope for crops. There were frequent conversations of packing up and heading further west. And those who felt really defeated talked of going home—east. The General generously carried many people on his books, knowing that it would be a long time before he would see payment.

Mira's medical work that summer was not much more than a couple deliveries, a few cuts to suture, and sprains to wrap. Income from her work was zero, not even food. Only promises.

As before, Mira led the worship when Franco was gone, but found it hard to speak words of encouragement to people who were losing so much. Yet there were many who had gone through years like this before and showed a determination to keep on. Somehow they would survive, and they did.

The community made an effort to celebrate the first anniversary of Telegraph Sunday, but only with a picnic following the church service, and games for the children. The General used the opportunity to update everyone on the progress of the train tracks coming from Yankton. "Work on the track went faster than expected because many farmers are looking for employment this summer. Should be completed by late October. The train will be coming twice a week, bringing coal, food, supplies, lumber and mail. I will no longer be sending a weekly rider to Yankton."

"Sounds good, General," came a cynical voice from the audience, "but where are we going to get the money to buy all those goods you are talking about? The only thing we can do is ship out the few remaining cattle that we have."

"Your point is well taken. But we know that these hard times don't last. For a few years probably, but the rain will return. I will be praying for a lot of snow this winter—not just one blizzard like we had last winter. And folks, you know that Mable and I are committed to helping you all we can. Last year with the good crops, you conscientiously paid your bills to the best of your ability. Your credit is good with us."

And so the people felt some renewed hope, even as they tightened their belts. But summer on the prairie can leave one as hopeless and vulnerable as winter.

Winter came with a storm late October, and Franco did no more circuit work until April 1875.

At Thanksgiving time there were no crops to give thanks for, yet chickens continued to lay a few eggs, old hens were stewed, cows gave milk, cheese was made, steers and pigs were butchered, deer, rabbits, grouse, and wild turkey were hunted, and people drew from their canned and dried supplies they had put up in good years. So, true to their religious faith, the people of Chipps gave thanks together at a worship service and communal meal, assembling this year at Jake and Cora. Thanks to the preserved produce from Cora and Jake's garden, roasted beef from their herd, and smaller contributions from others they enjoyed a hearty Thanksgiving dinner.

Mira and Franco expected few people for the Christmas service. As the previous year, they planned a program with the school children, but on Christmas it was too cold for anyone other than those who lived closest to the church to come.

The General and Mable came, bringing two crates.

"These came on the train yesterday, with your names on them."

Franco and General John brought the crates in while Mira welcomed Mable. A couple other enclosed buggies pulled up. Franco had not lit the stove in the church/school as he did not expect many to come.

It was a cozy time that the few worshippers spent together, singing and reading the Christmas passages. But Mira had a hard time keeping her thoughts from the crates. She wanted so badly to open them.

However, she made an attempt to be a good hostess. Following their worship they shared a meal. Everyone had brought something. To the delight of all, Mira served the food on her fine china.

When their guests left, Franco opened the crates. He unpacked one, Mira other. Both were amazed at their parents' perception of their needs, for they had written nothing about the scarcity of food—just that it had been a bad year for crops because of the drought. Both crates were ladened with dried fruit and vegetables, beans, barley, and other non-perishables that would not be affected by the cold in the railroad car.

"Franco! How did they know?"

In each crate was a newsy letter. From the Phillips mainly about medical work and happenings in the church. Oh! And the women at seminary were doing well. The Phillips frequently had them over for Sunday dinner, as a way of encouraging them. The Phillips also included a generous money gift. "You have told us that The General keeps his store well stocked. Rather than send flour, we thought you might use this money to buy flour and potatoes (if he has any). Eat well. But knowing the two of you, we are sure you will feel compelled to share. Perhaps a good way to do that would be to provide Sunday dinner for those who can make it to the service. Use your own judgment, but take good care of yourselves."

The Welkens' letter was full of news about the twins—now one year old. Healthy, happy and active children. What joy they were bringing to their parents. Franco and Mira, despite their joy for Franco's parents, felt a twinge of envy.

That evening Mira wrote letters of thanks and updated her journal, carefully identifying how she felt about the good times, and the difficult ones. Standing out clearly was God's faithfulness through it all.

Jake and Cora and their boys stopped by often that winter to spend time with their foals, always reminding Mira and Franco that come May or June they would be taking them to the ranch. Mira dreaded the day they would leave, as she loved the little animals. But a deal was a deal. More than anything, she felt sorry for the loss that all four horses would feel when separated.

The ground remained white until the middle of March, with many snowfalls adding to what had come early. The General's prayers were answered!

Church attendance was small, but as word got out of Mira's weekly fresh bread and stewed dry fruit, (served on fine china with real silverware) attendance picked up. Franco particularly liked the concoction Mira made with dried apricots, prunes and raisins, thickened with a handful of barley. "Really sticks to the ribs," he observed, and promptly dubbed it *Mira's Good Health Porridge*.

In March Franco fired up the school/church stove once again and children started back to school, and regular church services were held. Mira always supplied a large amount of freshly baked bread, but her dried fruit was running low. Others now brought dishes to share. Mouser enjoyed the increased attention, although Franco had brought him food every day. Benny loved to romp in the snow with Jimmy.

The General's prayer for abundant snow may have been answered, but spring and summer brought little rain. Other than a good first cutting of hay and abundant prairie grass, there were no crops. Except for Jake, who with his sons managed to devise an irrigation system for not only his garden, but this year also for a small field of corn.

Because of the abundance of water from melting snow that soaked into the ground, people used well water for watering gardens. So despite the drought many people had fresh produce that summer, even enough for drying and canning.

Mira and Franco planted a large garden including flowers— marigolds, fox glove, cosmos, zinnias, and coneflowers. And dandelions grew wild. The marigolds she would use on skin wounds, sprains, stings— even boiled in water they could be used for stomach ulcers and to induce sweating in a fever. A brew from coneflowers could be used to treat catarrh, even in children. Foxglove was used to treat heart disease, but her father advised to use with caution, because correct dosing was difficult.

Mira and Franco spent hours lugging buckets of water to their garden, and their efforts paid well. Mira was able to exchange produce with Bessie for assistance in canning and drying. Sometimes Mira felt she spent more time just finding a way to exist than what she spent in ministry. Yet on Telegraph Sunday in August 1875 many people came for the worship service and there was a greater sense of optimism than the previous year. Many expressed their appreciation to Franco and Mira "for sticking it out." They knew that Franco and Mira could leave and have a home and work to go to back east, but they were choosing to stay.

So Chipps and surrounding area went into the fall of 1875 with more hope than the previous year. But few were able to pay off what they owed The General. Just a few coins made it into his coffer. Yet he was as generous as ever. It was rumored that he had financial holdings in the east that kept him afloat.

Their third winter, that of 1875-76, was milder than before. Still much snow, making it necessary to cancel church and school, but the temperatures and wind were less severe. Franco was usually able to keep up his Wednesday morning time at the General Store, meeting with the few people who came. Mira would pack her medical bag and go with him and often dispensed medicine to farmers to take home to their family. All gratuitous, but with a promise for payment in the future. Mira did not bother *to keep books*.

Along with a wonderful crate of food supplies sent at Christmas, Mira's father resupplied medicines that Mira could not concoct herself, and bandages and other wraps put together by their church.

Franco's parents sent food similar to that of the year before, along with an update on the twins.

But what kept their spirits up more than anything else, was their plan for going "home" in May for Mira's graduation, and the six weeks Mira would spend working with Dr. McCloud and learning from him. Early in March they had a conversation with Bessie asking that she and Jimmy work their garden and care for their animals. Dapple and Grey would go to the ranch, to be bred once again.

Franco would return the middle of June, whereas Mira would be gone through the middle of July.

Chapter 14 *Graduation*

Early May 1876 Mira sorted through her clothes. She would have to bring several of the good dresses her mother had insisted on three years earlier—ones that she was saving for the *brides of Chipps*. But there had been few weddings, although she expected several more in coming years. Daughters of their friends and neighbors who seemed so young when she and Franco had come were now blossoming into teenagers. But by being careful, she could wear the dresses, and still give them to brides later. Bessie was always ready with her sewing machine to repair, alter, and add lace or a ribbon or two. Mira would take along her own wedding dress, minus the veil, train, and bustle. Her mother would have several social occasions for them to attend. And of course, the graduation.

"Franco, do you think the frocks that Bessie made for work would be suitable for the weeks I stay with your parents, and work with Dr. McCloud?"

"They'll be perfect. But don't forget your fancy things for Philadelphia."

"Oh, I won't. I've already selected the ones to pack. Plus my wedding dress." She paused then added with a giggle, "I wonder what mother will say when she sees me arrive with no flouncing petticoats? Especially when I tell her that we ripped them up to use for drapes and bandages."

"She'll likely outfit you with a new supply."

"I think so—and we can put them to good use when I get back here. Franco, it will be our first lengthy separation. I wish you could stay with me the whole time."

He held her close for a couple moments. "I wish that, too, but we both know that isn't possible."

"I know."

"I do have a major concern though."

"What's that?" Mira asked with alarm in her voice.

"Your hair. Who will help you wash your hair?"

"Oh, Franco. You scared me for a moment. I thought you were serious."

"I am."

"The answer is simple—I'll just have it cut."

"Over my dead body!"

She raised a restraining finger to his lips. "Please, don't say that!" she said with a shudder.

They boarded the spur train that passed through the Chipps station on Tuesday, made their connection in Yankton, on to Chicago, and finally got off at the depot only a few miles from the Welken's farm in western Pennsylvania. Mira's trunk would go straight through. Their stay here would be brief, not more than a night or two, and then the Welkens would join them for the rest of their journey to attend Mira's graduation and see the Phillips.

Mira and Franco were keenly disappointed when no one was at the depot to greet them.

"It's not far, Mira-honey, they'll be here soon. Maybe they had shopping to do in town."

"Do you suppose they got the day wrong?"

"I don't think so. But the twins could have delayed their best intentions."

"True." Mira paused and then said, "We have only our carpetbag—why don't we walk into town? I'm eager to meet Dr. McCloud. Maybe we can find his office."

"I know exactly where it is. Let's go."

As they approached the office Franco saw a familiar buggy and horse. "Mira-honey, I think they are seeing the doctor."

They were greeted at the door by Mrs. McCloud, "Come in! Come in! This isn't quite the greeting your parents were planning to give you, but Chuckie fell this morning, splitting open his chin. Dr. McCloud is stitching him up."

As she was speaking, Hiram holding Prissy, came through the door.

"Welcome! But this isn't how we had it planned."

A voice came from the treatment room, "Come on back, we could use a couple more hands to hold this little wiggler."

But in fact, Dr. McCloud was putting in the last stitch, and Chuckie had been holding very still, since being promised a candy cane.

After a round of greetings Mrs. McCloud invited them for tea and cookies, giving Mira and Dr. McCloud a brief time to get acquainted and make plans for her stay on her return from Philadelphia.

The twins, now two and a half years old, warmed up quickly to Franco and Mira. They sensed the family bond. Looks and overheard comments from passengers, as they headed towards Philadelphia, suggested that many thought that Mira and Franco were the parents of the twins and Hiram and Nina the grandparents.

The Phillips warmly welcomed them all. Mira had never seen her father so relaxed. He had kept on the three assistants he hired three years ago. They now had a large shared practice, and Charles greatly cut back on his patient care hours, spending much time reading every article he could get his hands on about the use of clean technique. Also, he was intrigued by naturopathic and homeopathic remedies, knowing that Mira had to often rely on these methods for her medical work.

At dinner that first evening Charles and Priscilla laid out plans for the next several days. "There is so much to do, and so little time to do it—graduation is Friday. Do you have your speech ready, Mira?"

She nodded her head.

"The two young women who are graduating would like to meet you ahead of time..."

"So we invited them and their families here for dinner on Thursday evening," Priscilla contributed. "And we can have a party here celebrating your graduation on Saturday."

"Mother, who would come to celebrate? I never really had any girlfriends, and I have been gone three years. Who even remembers me?"

"Nonsense!" It was her father. "The whole church is excited and can't wait to see you and Franco again. We'll just make it an open house, and whoever wants to come is welcome."

"I think it is a great idea, Mira-honey. I'm looking forward to seeing the church-folk again. Remember, they have done much to support us in the past."

Again Mira nodded, but said nothing. She had not expected this kind of welcome and support.

Thursday evening, following dinner Mira spent a couple hours in lively conversation with the two women graduates. Few comments were made about their actual seminary experience. Mira understood that the experience was still too raw to discuss. *How would I have done it without Franco and father?*

But tomorrow they would have their day. So the two excited young women spent their evening listening to Mira's experiences of life on the prairie, and Mira listening to their hopes and goals.

"Have either of you thought about getting some medical training? No matter where you decide to go, you, the educated person will be expected to be the medical expert in addition to everything else you will do!"

Neither woman had thought of this, so they ended their time together that evening with a plan. On Saturday morning, after the excitement of graduation the night before had cooled a bit, the three of them would approach Dr. Phillips and ask him about some *basic training*.

Miranda was asked to lead the procession, followed by the other two young women and then the larger group of males. Her parents, Franco, and the Welkens with their twins sat near the front. The graduates took their seats on the stage.

During the commencement address Mira noticed the twins getting restless and Hiram took them out. The voice droned on, but finally the part in the program that everyone was waiting for came—the handing out of the diplomas.

But this year there was one more speech—Mira's!

The President introduced her as the recipient of the first diploma to be given for the *religious education/missions* course of study, and the first female graduate. There was a sprinkling of applause.

Mira spoke briefly of having finished the course three years earlier and their—hers and Franco's—move to Dakota Territory and their work there. She also referred to this graduation ceremony as an honor for her and the other two women who were graduating. She congratulated the young men and thanked the faculty, board, and parents. She said nothing of the obstacles and attitudes she and the other women had encountered, or how her father had worked tirelessly to make it happen. She ended by saying, *May God bless us all, men and women, as we work together to serve our Lord by serving others, in many ways and many places.* She did not mention that she preached once a month, and that she and Franco always prepared sermons together.

The applause at the end of her speech was more enthusiastic than when she was introduced.

By 9 AM Saturday morning Mira's two new friends (and ardent admirers) were on the Phillips' doorstep. Mira had alerted her parents to their coming.

Charles enthusiastically embraced the idea of giving them basic medical training, and Priscilla opened their home for the women to live with them while they trained. Neither of them had yet made definite plans for where they would do their ministry, so after a short break with family they would spend six weeks learning from Dr. Phillips. This medical training would greatly enhance the options of where they might serve.

Dr. Phillips was mentally planning the course of study before the young women left the room.

Almost as many people came to Mira's graduation party as had come to her and Franco's wedding. And about as many gifts were given. Books, personal and household items—doilies, towels, sachets, canned and dried fruit, and nonperishable food. There would be crates to pack and ship once again.

Mira and Franco used this gathering to thank the people for their generosity—not only now, but for their ongoing support in the past three years.

But through it all, something in Mira longed for the people of Chipps.

That evening Mira commented to Franco on the change in her mother. So different from how she had seen her mother interact with others most of her life. "But Franco, why is she still so cool towards me?"

"Mira-honey, you are a grown woman now. You have a responsibility . . ."

"But she's my *mother* . . ."

"And you're her *grown* daughter."

It was a troubling conversation for Mira—Franco heaping responsibility on her that she did not feel was hers. Even her father never approached her on it. Maybe Nina would have some insight. *But I'm not about to let this bother me now. I just received my seminary diploma, and am going for some intensive medical training with Dr. McCloud. Mother will just have to wait, unless she makes the first move.*

Despite the early hour they would have to get up Monday morning, Franco and Mira talked long into the night, wondering how they would get along without each other, so close they had become over three years functioning as a team.

But Mira's final comment before drifting off to sleep was about petticoats. "Franco, can you believe that mother hasn't yet said anything about getting me more petticoats?"

"Yeah, and not only that! It looks to me that she is wearing fewer herself!"

"Franco! But now that you say it, I think you are right. Those months she lived with your parents did bring about some good change in her."

Mira curled safely into Franco's embrace and slept soundly for the next several hours.

Franco, his parents and the twins left early Monday morning. As before, Priscilla had a hard time telling them good-bye. How she loved those twins. And Hiram and Nina definitely had become the brother and sister she never had.

The noisy train ride and active twins gave Franco little time to talk with his parents. He was glad he had decided to stay with them a couple of days on the way back. He needed to talk to them about relocating to Dakota Territory, as he had promised The General he would. Not that he expected anything other than a genuine *no thank you. Moving would be impossible with the two little ones.*

So the first night, after the twins were settled in bed, Franco took a deep breath, but before he said a word, his father spoke. "Franco, there is something your mother and I urgently need to talk to you about. There just hasn't been a quiet moment until now to bring it up."

He had Franco's full attention. This sounded serious.

"We have done a lot of talking. With these two little ones that we have been blessed with we feel a big need to be near family—you and Mira. We are wondering if what you wrote us about some time ago—General John's interest in setting up a lumber business—is something he still hopes to do. And if he still is interested in having me join him in the venture?"

"Still interested! He hounds me whenever he sees me, and had me promise to discuss it with you."

"Franco, I can't tell you how proud you make me. If he has that much confidence in me, without meeting me, he must see me in you, or at least assume I have the qualities you practice every day."

"Thanks. Hearing you say that means a lot."

They were all silent a moment and then Franco continued, "You know, I'm completely surprised that you are willing to take The General up on his offer without talking to him or seeing Chipps."

"Don't forget, we have taken risks before! Not only that, you and Mira have written such honest and thorough letters, I think we have a pretty good insight into life there."

Franco turned to his mother, "But Mother, can you see yourself on the prairie? It is very different from life here in the woods of Pennsylvania. Just think of this one example. In our area there are no woods, just a few trees here and there. You would love our big cottonwoods, though. There is nothing like the sound of their rustling leaves, even on the quietest of days." Franco paused. It wasn't really the trees he had been thinking of.

"Franco, as much as I love living here, my home is where my husband and children are. Your father and I have talked about this extensively, and we see it as a continuation of the journey west we started about 30 years ago, and were forced to abandon. We, of course, will leave much behind . . ." (Franco knew she was referring to the graves in the nearby plot) ". . . but are young enough to give our little ones a good home in Dakota Territory. And you and Mira will be there."

Franco nodded. "And we will be happy to have you all come. The people of Chipps will welcome you." Franco paused, and then added, "I'm surprised you did not mention your intentions when we were with the Phillips."

"Actually, I did tell Charles privately. But we both thought it best not to talk about it then. It would have detracted from the well-deserved attention that Mira was receiving. And frankly, we are really torn about telling Priscilla. She truly looks at us as family. Our move will put more distance between us. That will be hard for her. Charles suggests that we write them a letter, saying that The General has been talking to you about this often in the past couple years, you have passed the word on to us, and after much thought, prayer and discussion have decided to make the move. The letter will also include how we truly see this as the completion of the journey west we started so long ago."

"But no matter how we do it, Priscilla will feel the pain. How she loves these little ones! The clothes she sent along will keep them dressed for the next three years! Charles says Priscilla is never happier than when sewing little outfits, and her seamstress is equally as excited when sewing for the twins. Which reminds me, I'm going to write the seamstress and ask her to make me several new frocks for Dakota!"

"You could, but we have a seamstress also, with a treadle machine."

"Well, I'll be sure to use her, too. But I feel a special bond to Priscilla's seamstress. She guessed I was pregnant when we were there for your wedding."

"This changes the subject, but we will need a place to live. Our main income will be from the lumber business, but it would be nice if we could have a place in the country, with buildings for animals, and a garden. I expect to get a good price for our land here.

"I'll keep my ears and eyes open. Between The General and Jake, the problem of where to live is likely to be solved easily. They know everybody, and can make things happen. But don't expect a log cabin like you have here. There are not enough trees. But once you get the lumber business going, you might be able to build yourself a house of your own design."

"One more thing, Franco. I already know two men who are looking for land. We'll have no trouble selling, once the crops are harvested. We could be in Dakota by late fall."

"You folks mean business! So even though I will be back in Chipps in a few days, I'm going to send The General a telegram tomorrow. Then you can't back out!"

They talked until midnight—there was a lot of planning to do. Franco left two days later. Hiram and Nina would tell Mira when she came, and then they would write the news to the Phillips.

The days Mira spent with her family were uneventful. They crated and sent the gifts she and Franco received and the medical supplies her father insisted she have.

On Thursday Mira was on her way to stay with Franco's parents, even as Franco was heading for Chipps. She would begin her six-week training with Dr. McCloud on Monday. This gave her opportunity to spend time with the twins, and to dream of the day she and Franco would have their own children.

The first evening with the Welkens they told her about their plans for moving to Chipps. Mira could hardly contain her joy. As much as she loved the people of Chipps, to have actual family right there was more than she had ever thought would happen.

But then a troubling thought came to her mind, "How do you think my mother will accept this?"

"That's a question we've thought and prayed about long and hard. I talked to your father about it."

"So he knows?"

"He does, and we told Franco when he was here. As you can imagine he is overjoyed . . ."

"And as for your mother's feelings, Mira-honey, as much as we care for her, we cannot let what she thinks or feels govern our lives. We have to do what is best for our children. We believe that having the twins grow up near their brother and sister is what is best for them." Nina paused, and then added, "And we are excited about continuing our journey west. A thirty year delay is a long time."

Mira smiled, sensing a hint of humor in Nina's voice. "What did my father say?"

"Very much what we have just said to you. He thinks that we should write her a letter telling her of the thought and prayer that has gone into our decision making. He says he's confident that on a rational level she will accept it. It's not like we are next door neighbors. Even by train, it's a long trip to Philadelphia."

Mira nodded, but in her thoughts she was asking, *why is life so full of challenges?*

In the next couple days Mira had several good heart-to-heart talks with Nina. When Mira asked Nina why she could not talk about the important things of life with her own mother Nina only sadly shook her head, and said, "Mira-honey, your mother is carrying a heavy burden that she is not willing or able to share, not yet, anyway. Hiram and I are puzzled by it, as you are, but neither of us has sensed a readiness in her to discuss it. And it is not for us to ask. But we often pray about it. The closest we are to an answer comes from observing how she has taken to our twins. We think there might have been a loss of a child. But why she can't tell us, we don't know."

"*A loss of a child.* I've never thought of such a thing. Surely my father would have told me. It just doesn't make sense to me. *If* she lost one child, why treat the one she *does have* so coldly?"

"Mira-honey, what you say makes sense rationally. But we are dealing with feelings and emotions, heart matters, which usually do not make sense to the rational mind. We have to accept her as she is, and most of all, for her sake, pray that someday she will be relieved of this heavy burden."

"But it is not fair to my father."

"Mira-honey, did your father say that?"

"No."

"It is obvious to me that he loves her very much, just the way she is. He might wish she would change, but not to make his life different or better, but to make hers more enjoyable. And that's where we have to leave it—except to pray that she will be relieved of her burden, whatever it is."

Mira said no more to Nina about the topic at this time. But she would try to discuss it once again with Franco. Her good relationship with Nina only accentuated the coolness of her relationship with her own flesh and blood mother.

And then another troubling thought entered her mind. *What if I'm not really a flesh and blood child of Charles and Priscilla? Where did my auburn hair come from? Now that I think about it, it is the same color as Distant Cousin Pete's hair. But no, that could not be. Not my proper mother.* She dismissed her own thought as scandalous.

Her time with Dr. McCloud was exciting and helpful. But he did not overwork her, sensing a weariness that could only have come from years of stressful living. His primary goal was to teach her what he was learning about clean techniques, how to treat wound infections once they had set in, and how to prevent all kinds of infections—especially infections that followed surgery, or the suturing of wounds that were not necessarily dirty wounds. Such as the chin wound he had sutured for Chuckie.

"Think about it, Miss Miranda. Chuckie fell against a chair in the house and split open the skin. Nina immediately applied pressure with a washed and ironed cloth. I poured clean water over the wound and then used instruments that had been cleaned with phenol, and clean suture material. Nina and Hiram brought him here as soon as they returned from Philadelphia. It has healed beautifully—hardly even a scar for him to brag about when he gets bigger!"

"I know. I saw it."

"So what I am saying, Miss Miranda—cleanliness is the key. I wash my hands with soap and water between patients—I would use phenol if my skin could handle it! Your father has become a believer, now, too, and he is doing his best to enforce clean techniques with the doctors he works with. His big challenge is to get changes in practice in hospitals. But knowing your father, he will take it on, undaunted."

Mira smiled her agreement. She could see it already.

Mira spent clinic hours with Dr. McCloud every morning, and made occasional house calls in the afternoon. But Thursdays were the big days—wound clinic days. Word had gotten out far and wide of the work Dr. McCloud was doing. Civil War vets, with draining leg wounds dating back some 10 years came.

"Miss Miranda, sometimes I just do my best, not understanding even what I am doing. It seems that when infection gets into the bone it just stays there and festers and drains. There's not much I can do. As long as a man's leg is somewhat functional and the pain not too bad, I don't amputate. But, of course, should the infection move into his system, he most likely will die." Mira nodded her head, thinking of the burn patient, Agnes' first husband, when they had just come to Chipps.

Dr. McCloud continued. "In these cases, where there is no cure, I try to make life more livable for the patient and family. As you know, the smell of an infected, draining wound is awful. But by teaching the person and his family, how to **daily** remove the soiled dressing, burn it, or wash and boil it, and rewrap with a clean dressing can do much to increase the comfort of the whole household. By coming here once a month, or sooner if necessary, I can examine the wound, and debride it if necessary."

"The debridement—can you teach me about it?"

"We will have many debridements in the next few weeks—we always do. This will give you a chance to learn some surgical techniques, as well as the use of ether and more about the use of chloroform. I hear Franklin has already administered that a time or two for you. And remind me, we must talk about the post-surgical complications of both anesthetics, and how to manage the problems.

Chapter 15 *Relocation Times Two*

After six weeks of work/study with Dr. McCloud Mira returned to Chipps, feeling more qualified for medical work, her scope of practice now broadened. Her father would be pleased! Yet she would not attempt abdominal surgery—not without a better knowledge of anatomy, especially of nerves and blood vessels. *Maybe someday.* Mira seemed to think that if she could satisfy her quest for learning, maybe an emptiness in her life would be filled. And there was still the matter of ordination for her. *How will I be able to do in a lifetime all that I would like to do? Especially if Franco and I have our own children?*

Franco and many friends were waiting at the depot to welcome her back. But once the greetings were received and she got back to her house, she hardly knew what to do first. Franco said to expect many medical cases in the next several days. And sermon preparation. And the garden! Friends and neighbors had planted their garden. Franco tried to keep up with the weeding, but finally hired Jimmy to do that, along with helping with the animals. Bessie did what Jimmy could not do and Franco could not find the time for doing.

Crops looked exceptionally good, ensuring that even Franco and Mira would also have a better cash flow this year.

But most of all, Franco and Mira were glad to be back together so they could face life and ministry as a team once again.

Although word had gotten out in the community that Franco's parents would be moving to Chipps and joining The General in starting up a lumber business, Franco used Telegraph Sunday to make the formal announcement. The community excitement was great. A new and much needed business in town, a new family related to the pastor, and even a set of little twins!

Jimmy was the only one who was concerned. He didn't want anyone taking his place in the life of Pastor Franco and Dr. Mira. Once Bessie confided this to Franco and Mira, they had an affirming talk with Jimmy. *The twins were much too small to take his place. He could be a big brother to them. There was much to teach them about life on the prairie. They were even too small to take care of Mouser and Benny, and to ring the church bell.* Jimmy was convinced. His role would be enlarged rather than diminished.

Franco, Jake, and the General had several conversations as the fall season of 1876 came on, discussing the move of the Welkens and where they would live. Bessie was soon included in their talks. *Would she be willing to sell her house and farm buildings to the Welkens and make the short move to the town of Chipps?*

The suggestion took Bessie completely off guard. "Where would Jimmy and I live? What about my animals and cheese business? And Jimmy. I wonder if he would adjust to living in town, especially since he sees himself as indispensable to Pastor Franco and Dr. Mira?"

"Bessie, we do not put this to you lightly," Franco responded. "If you do not agree, we have other options. But we want to give you first choice. You see, The General is willing to build you a fabric shop and small living quarters adjacent to his store. In other words—help set you up in business as *Chipps' seamstress.*"

She took a moment to process the generous offer, and then asked, "But what about my animals, cows, chickens, and my cheese business? And the land I now rent to Sam and Agnes?"

"We don't have all the answers to those questions yet, Bessie," Jake answered, less brusque than he used to be. He had softened considerably since the loss of his toes, and the help Mira and Franco had given him. "But there are a few things for you to think about. We know you put Jimmy's needs first in your decision making."

The General had a hard time keeping quiet, and now entered the conversation. "The easy part first, Bessie. You can keep on renting the land to Sam and Agnes, or you might wish to sell it. As you know, Sam is a good farmer. He might want to buy the land. As for your animals and cheese business—perhaps you can work out something with the Welkens—they're farmers at heart, you know."

Franco, nodded his agreement. "I can't imagine my father without animals to care for—all the more now with the twins. He'll be wanting them to learn."

"But Jimmy . . ."

"There will always be something for Jimmy to do. I assured him of that when he first heard about my parents coming *with children*. I told him that he would never be replaced."

Bessie looked relieved and overwhelmed, "It's just so much to think about. I need some time."

"Nothing has to be decided right now," Jake said. "However, if you are not interested, we will have to know soon, so we could make other plans. If you decide to go along with what we propose, well, The General has some building to do! And we would have a little remodeling to do on your farm place to make it ready for the Welkens."

"It's not that I don't want to do it. I see advantages for Jimmy and me, and I can see how it would be helpful for your parents, Pastor Franco. It's just that it is so much so fast. Just a few minutes ago I had no idea of any of this. And now suddenly many unexpected doors are opening to me. I don't know how I can go through them all!"

"Don't forget, you and Jimmy have the whole community that will help you. But to help you think it all through step by step, why not you and Jimmy come over for supper with Mira and me tonight? As you have already mentioned, this affects Jimmy maybe most of all. We want to be sure that he feels part of this."

"Thanks, Pastor. That's a good plan for now. And General and Jake, I think that Jimmy and I will have an answer for you in a day or two."

"You know where to find us."

Jimmy was excited to go to Pastor and doctor-dear, as he still insisted on calling her—even though many others were now saying *Dr. Mira*. Bessie told him nothing of the pending changes. She would let Pastor Franco do that.

Franco began their discussion over a bread-pudding dessert. "Jimmy, Jake, The General, and I had an important talk today with your mother. We have some plans which include you. As you know, my parents and their little twins will be moving here soon and they need a place to live. The General wants to build a little sewing shop with living rooms for you and your mother, connected to his store."

Jimmy turned to look at his mother. She smiled at him and said, "Just hear him out, Jimmy. I think you will like the plan."

"Your mother would have her sewing business right in town. You would have a nice place to live, and you will still be close enough to us to work for us, and come to school, and ring the church bell."

Mira, Franco, and Bessie remained silent while he took a moment to think about what Franco had just said. And then true to Jimmy, he asked, "but what about *our* animals? They need me to look after them. And I don't think The General has room for them."

"We talked about that, but haven't decided on anything yet because we want to hear your thoughts."

Jimmy went quiet again, thinking deeply, and then said gravely, "Well, I suppose our cows and chickens could stay, if your father knows how to take care of them."

With all seriousness Franco assured Jimmy that his father knew how to take care of animals very well. And that he would be expected to help, and to teach the twins as they grew older.

"Mother, what do you think we should do?" Jimmy asked, beginning to feel the weight of decision making that he thought was being placed on him.

"These ideas are all very new to me. I'd miss our old place very much. But the place that The General would build for us sounds good, too. And just think, Jimmy, we'd be helping Pastor Franco's family. And we'd be helping all of Chipps. I think it is a good deal."

Jimmy remained silent.

"Jimmy, you and your mother don't have to decide tonight. Let's all pray about it now, and then you and your mother can talk more at home. By tomorrow morning you might have your answer."

They agreed to Mira's suggestion, and spent the next ten minutes placing their concerns and questions in God's hands.

Jimmy and Bessie continued their conversation at home until bed time. As she tucked him in, she was relatively sure what her answer would be the next morning.

Jimmy did his morning chores at home and for Pastor Franco and then went to school. He had commented to Bessie over breakfast, "Moving to town won't be so bad if I can help Pastor Franco's father with *our* animals." That was all Bessie needed to hear. She harnessed her horse to the buggy, stopped at Mira and Franco, and suggested they all go to see The General.

"But what about Jake? He'll want to know as soon as possible."

"Let's talk to The General first. He has the most work and planning to do. Then, if you don't mind, could you go to tell Jake? I'd go, except you on horseback can do it so much faster than I by buggy."

"Agreed. Do we have to wait, or can you tell us now?"

"As if you can't tell from my expression! Anyway, I'm sure Jimmy has already told you. He has probably told the whole school by now."

The General showed no surprise that Bessie agreed to his plan, but was surprised that Jimmy didn't need more convincing.

"Can you all stay for coffee?" Mable asked. She always knew when to keep herself scarce, and when to show up with her coffee pot. Franco excused himself to go to Jake, but first stopped at the telegraph office to wire his parents that by the end of October there would be a vacant farm with house for them to purchase.

Mira and Bessie sat at the round table. The General had momentarily disappeared, but soon joined them, papers in hand. "Bessie, I had a little time to do some sketching. What do you think of this plan?" He showed her plans for a fabric shop that would open onto the street, and also into his store. He would move his bolts of cloth into it, plus at Bessie's discretion order additional. There was a little sewing nook with a large window and an area that could be curtained off for a fitting room. Behind the shop, but with doors opening into it were two bedrooms, a small kitchen, and small living room.

"General, did you think of all of this?" asked Bessie. Mable cleared her throat.

"Well, I had a little help."

"It's lovely. And so convenient. I thought I detected a woman's touch."

"That you did," replied The General, always gracious to his wife.

Since Bessie's husband's disappearance she had become an astute business woman, what with renting out her land, raising animals, her cheese business, and in recent years sewing for profit. She could not let The General's plan for her to go further without discussing and coming to an agreement on the financial aspects.

The General was not surprised that she insisted on "no charity," but he was surprised that she insisted on owning the inventory of the shop, and that she rent, with the option to buy, the shop and her living quarters. And that there be contracts to that effect.

"But Bessie . . ."

"General, you know I can. Maybe not all up front. But let's work out an agreement."

He agreed, and at a meeting still to be arranged they would make a financial plan and contract that Jake and Franco would witness.

In the buggy ride back to her house Mira commended Bessie for her forthrightness with John.

"You know, *doctor-dear*, he's a good man, but he has to be held in check occasionally. The way he controls is by his generosity. As time goes by, he is going to have to realize that he cannot run the town and entire community by himself. I strongly recommend that Pastor Franco's parents get all their business transactions on paper, as signed and witnessed contracts. Something tells me that Chipps is entering a new era! Before long we are going to need a bank, a lawyer, and a sheriff."

Mira nodded. She and Franco would have a long conversation this evening. For now she gratefully remembered that Hiram had business experience, even if as a young man his family had lost a huge fortune.

But another thought troubled Mira also. As she was observing the plans for Bessie's new home and shop she had felt a twinge of covetousness. What she and Franco had for living quarters was adequate, but not homey or comfortable. They didn't even have a bedroom. Just a small curtained off area.

The General lost no time in marking off the area for Bessie's shop and living quarters. He was already receiving train cars of lumber. Some of it would be used for this new structure. He hired a few farmers who had their crops in, to begin building.

The following week a letter arrived from Franco's parents:

Thanks for your telegram. Things are moving swiftly here. Our farm is sold! The only regret we have is that we feel like a tie has been severed that has connected us to the Piersons. But we have many good memories, and their legacy lives on in us and you, Franco . . .

Tell Bessie that we will have payment for her upon arrival. We are trusting that the buildings, etc. will be suitable for us. And who knows? As time goes by, we might build a bigger house. These twins take up a lot of room . . .

We are having many discussions on what to ship by rail, and have decided to bring our wagon and buggy, most of our household items. And our 4 horses, and dog. We've already talked to the railroad, and while it will be expensive we will have enough cash for the move and paying Bessie.

There have been a few letters back and forth with General John. He sounds like a strong character with many plans, most of which sound good to us, but there will have to been some negotiation to make it workable for him and us . . .

"Mira-honey, fortunately my father is a business man at heart. I think he already has insight into The General's character, even as Bessie has."

"I expect that you are right. But I wonder about shipping the wagon and buggy, and all their household goods. Didn't we tell them that supplies are available in Yankton?"

"We did. I think their desire to hang onto these things comes out of their memory of once having lost almost everything except the clothes on their back. They don't want to go through that again if it can be avoided. These are the things that connect them to the Piersons. And the horses and dog—well, they are almost family."

"I hope they will find Bessie's house suitable. To me a house with a separate bedroom sounds wonderful—and Bessie's house has *two* bedrooms."

"Mira-honey, are you saying . . .?"

"Don't worry, Franco. I am not dissatisfied. Just feel a little cramped, especially with my medical practice getting busier. Even from a health perspective, it is not a good idea to be seeing sick people in our kitchen-bedroom, especially with all we are learning about the transmission of certain illnesses."

"As usual you bring up a very good point, Mira-honey. I think it is something that the church board should consider."

"Maybe better still would be to have a *town council*. The town where Dr. McCloud lives and works has a council and he finds them to be helpful when decisions have to be made for the well-being of the town and surrounding area. It relieves him of the burden of decision making, at least as regards the physical health of the community. He would not be able to have his large wound clinic without the support of the council."

"Mira-honey, I can see it happening here! It's a great idea for many reasons, not the least of which is your work. But also for the growing town."

"And it might help keep The General in check," Mira said with a giggle.

"I think he might chafe a bit. My father might have ideas on forming a council."

"I hope from the bottom of my heart that his working with The General will go well."

"Me too. Actually, I think it will. My father can be diplomatic and respectful at the same time. And he is not a pushover. I know he will insist on a contract for his work-relationship with The General. I suspect a contract where he will at first work as an employee, and if that goes well, a future part ownership in the business. Anyway, that's how I envision it."

"Exciting days are sure to come. In fact, I think they are already here!"

The work on Bessie's new quarters and fabric shop progressed quickly, and she and Jimmy moved in by the end of October. Then The

General sent a crew to make improvements on the buildings of Bessie's farmyard and house.

The Welkens had sent word to expect them the Monday before Thanksgiving Day. Most of Chipps was at the depot to greet them, and the train made a longer than usual stop to unload their goods, including buggy, wagon, and horses.

As Mira, Franco, Hiram, Nina, and the twins reunited the community men and women, with the leadership of Jake and Cora quickly and efficiently took charge of all the goods, and soon a procession was making its way to the Welken's new home. Brightly colored curtains, sewn and hung by Bessie were fluttering a welcome from the windows.

Nina looked on in astonishment as her household items and various supplies were put on shelves and in drawers, and beds were made up. She expected to spend days settling in. Now others did it for her in only hours! Hiram toured the barnyard with several of the men, and soon the horses had a new home with the cows he would purchase from Bessie. There was even storage space for his wagon and buggy.

By noon dinner was spread out on tables made of sawhorses and boards. While Hiram and Nina had many friends in Pennsylvania, they had never seen a community come together like this to welcome newcomers. And the twins got more than their fair share of attention.

After the meal and cleanup the neighbors left, many before Hiram and Nina could properly thank them. "Don't worry about it," Franco advised. "You will see most of them on Thanksgiving Day, and if not then, in church on Sundays."

Mira chimed in, "and in this community there is always opportunity to serve others, before long you will be doing as you have been done to."

Before leaving The General caught Hiram, "Stop by the store soon—we have business to discuss. This afternoon, would be fine."

"Lookin' forward to it, General. But we've had a tiring journey and need the rest of this day to get used to being here, and to see Mira and Franco."

Franco nodded in agreement, glad to hear his father assert himself right from the beginning.

Nina and Mira settled down to a cup of coffee while the twins explored the house and found their box of toys that had been put in their bedroom. Franco and Hiram looked over the property in more detail, and then finding a comfortable spot in the hayloft, settled in for a father/son conversation.

Franco and Mira invited the Welkens for supper, but they declined. Everyone was exhausted and the twins needed to go to bed early.

That evening, in their separate houses both Welken families thanked the Lord that they were now living close together.

Franco would go with Hiram early the next morning to pay Bessie, and then work on plans for the lumber business with The General.

Chapter 16 *Holidays, New Year and an Unexpected Arrival*

The weather was unusually cooperative the week the Welkens arrived. They settled into their living accommodations easily. Bessie was elated with the money received from Hiram, and immediately paid General John what she owed him, with some left over. Hiram, with Franco's support got business agreements made with The General, contract and all. The sale of lumber, at least initially would be transacted in the store, and Hiram would be responsible for running what would come to be called *J&H Lumber*.

Jimmy spent most of his early morning and after school hours with both Welken families, endearing himself to Hiram and Nina and the twins. But Bessie always insisted that he be home by suppertime.

This year the community Thanksgiving service was held in the school/church. During the worship service the warm food was stored in Mira's kitchen space and the other food in Franco's office. As usual, Jake and Cora brought barbecued beef. Others, a variety of game.

After the service the men quickly assembled sawhorse tables and put the benches in place around them while the women brought in the food.

There was one heavy snowfall between Thanksgiving Day and Christmas—enough to shut school for a week.

"Franco, for several years we have helped the children prepare a Christmas program, only to cancel it. Do you think it is worth the effort?"

"I know, Mira-honey, but think of how they enjoy the planning and practice, and how much they learn about the meaning of Christmas. They are prairie children and handle disappointment well. I think my mother would thoroughly enjoy being involved, given all her years of teaching. And can't you just see little Chuckie and Prissy taking part?"

"They would be adorable. Shall I talk to your mother?"

"As soon as possible. But don't forget to involve our school teacher."

"Good point. I'll talk to her first. Somehow, I think she will be relieved. She seems tired lately. I think she might be expecting, although she hasn't said so to me."

The following morning Mira did as she said she would. She invited the teacher, Jenny Seweyn, for tea while Franco conducted the early morning devotions and Bible Class. Jenny was greatly relieved to learn that Nina might take an active role in the program. She went on, "Dr. Mira, I have been exhausted lately, along with nausea in the morning—so glad you and Pastor Franco take the early classes. Do you suppose I might be expecting? If so, Chipps is going to need a new teacher before this school year is over. Given how I feel now, maybe as early as January."

After further discussion and examination Mira confirmed the pregnancy. *Given Nina's many years of teaching, I wonder if she would . . .? But there are the twins to think about.*

Mira always respected a person's privacy so she could tell no one—except Jenny said she could tell Franco. Jenny herself would tell the school board.

Nina immediately warmed up to planning a school Christmas program, all the more so when Mira suggested that the twins take part, too.

Christmas Day was cold and bright. Just enough snow on the ground from the earlier storm for a festive feeling. Many people came in horse drawn sleds, bells jingling. The children sang and performed with enthusiasm. Franco told the story of Jesus' birth, followed with congregational singing accompanied by instrumentalists, always willing to play impromptu.

General John concluded the service by distributing bags of candy and peanuts to every child, and fruit for each family.

It was the last time there would be a church service or school for a couple months—a severe storm struck the following day. When the school board met in early January it decided to cancel school for January and February. Jenny had told them of her pregnancy, and given the weather, cancelling seemed the only reasonable thing to do. Having heard of Nina's teaching experience the board approached her about taking the job when school resumed.

Sunday service, as in other years was held in Franco and Mira's home—a time for Bible based discussion and prayer for those who could come. Mira always had a pot of soup or stew warming on the back of the stove, along with sourdough bread.

"Franco, isn't it great to have enough food on hand and not worry about the next meal?"

"It is. But we never went without."

"True. But there were days when I was very hungry, trying to stretch the little we had."

"Mira-honey, I didn't know."

"That's because I always made sure that you had enough."

"Mira-honey, what are you telling me, and why are you telling me now?"

"I'm sorry, Franco. I shouldn't have told you, even now. It's not only that there wasn't enough food. I had a hard time learning to eat things like rabbit, venison, and some of the food that people brought."

"Mira-honey, I had no idea."

"It was part of the sacrifice I had to make for prairie living. I'm over it now."

Mira, Franco, Hiram, and Nina talked long and seriously about Nina teaching, and how to care for the twins should she do so. It was Mable and John who came up with a solution. Since Nina's teaching time would not begin until 10:00 AM either Mira or Franco could bring the twins to Mable to care for from 10-3. Hiram would be in the store, available to help Mable if needed, especially until the weather warmed, and business would get busier. Fortunately they both still took long afternoon naps. Mable could hardly contain her joy, as she had no children or grandchildren.

School resumed in early March and ran through the middle of May. The twins thrived with having for the first time a "grandma."

Both Nina and Mira threw themselves in to gardening—rain in May got things off to an early and good start. Mira made special effort to grow medicinal plants, ordering seeds for marigolds, coneflowers and foxglove, and rose plants from Yankton. Some grew in the wild, but with the exception of dandelions, it was far simpler to harvest cultivated plants. Both Hiram and Nina were amazed at the wide stretches of land, almost barren of trees, except those that grew along rivers, or were deliberately planted and cared for by farmers. They cherished every cottonwood they saw.

One morning late in May while eating breakfast, Franco answered a knock on their front door. They we greeted by a rough and ruddy looking man, with a shock of auburn hair. His smell kept Franco from inviting him in. Franco would recognize that smell anywhere—a wound, long time a-festering. Before Franco could say anything, the man said, "Word on the prairie and as far west as Oregon has it that Chipps has a doctor who treats old war wounds. Are you the doctor?"

"My wife . . ."

Mira stepped forward and stifled a gasp. She would recognize that hair anywhere. It was the same color as hers. The man was distant cousin Pete, only a few years older than herself, but looking worn and weary from hard living and illness.

"I'm the doctor, and I do treat wounds, but not in the house. Franco, would you set a chair outside for him?" Then to soften what might have come across as rude, she added, "And while I prepare to treat you, could we offer you coffee and breakfast?"

Pete readily agreed, but did not recognize her from days gone by. He had not seen her for many years, and Mira had grown and matured considerably in that time. Not having kept contact with the family, he had no idea of the changes in Mira's life.

While Pete ate, Mira bundled up her own hair and told Franco that she recognized him as her cousin who had gone west to prospect. As far as she knew, her family had never heard from him again. Given his leg wound they assumed that he was no longer living.

"Franco, what must we do? What can we do?"

"Mira-honey, we must treat him just like we would anybody else."

"I know that, Franco, but all the other patients come to be treated and then return home until I hold the next clinic." (Mira held wound clinic under the cottonwood, and when the weather got cold, in their lean-to; not ideal, but she did not want to bring infected wounds into their living area. Wound clinic almost came to a standstill in the winter, but Pete's arrival was a sure sign that others would soon come. Franco planned to ask Hiram to build a small structure for wound cases.)

"We can't take him in; I wouldn't want to take him in, even if we could. My father—who always gives everyone the benefit of the doubt—never trusted him."

"I'll get him around back while you prepare to treat him."

"And Franco—don't say a word to him or *anybody* else about the family connection."

As Franco often did with these cases, he assisted Mira, removing the dressings, and burned them in an outdoor fire. Meanwhile Mira irrigated the draining wound with copious amounts of warm water.

"How have you been taking care of this?"

"Just keep it wrapped—don't know what else to do. I don't want an amputation. I've been able to live like this. But when I heard about a doctor in Chipps, I thought it worth a try."

"And what are your plans?"

"I'm hoping to find a little work around here, and come for treatments. You can help me, can't you?"

Franco re-entered the conversation, "Everybody who we treat lives within traveling distance from here and comes only weekly. If that often. When they and their families learn how to take care of themselves, they are pretty much on their own."

"But I have no one—that's why I'm hoping to find a place to live here, and some work."

The compassionate side of Mira wanted to help, but *professional distancing* that she had learned from her father was overruling her heart. Fortunately Franco also knew how to set boundaries.

"There is nothing more that we can do, other than irrigate it and pack and wrap it. For the rest you are on your own."

"I see a church here. Could the pastor help me? I'm a god-fearing man, and I served my country in the war."

"I am the pastor. But the church does not provide room and board for passers-through, or even for people who stay and become part of our community. Do you have family?" Franco asked feigning ignorance.

Mira took a few steps back so Pete could not see her face.

"I grew up with relatives in Philadelphia. But I left home, lying about my age, and went to war for the north. This is what I got to show for my patriotism," his voice betraying bitterness.

"What have you done since?" Franco asked, hoping to get more history.

"I returned to Philadelphia and was treated by an *old quack*."

Mira felt her dander rise but said nothing.

"But I heard the call of the west, and if it weren't for this bum leg I'd spend my life in the mountains prospecting for gold."

"Do you still have family in Philadelphia?"

"Last I heard, the people who brought me up—you see, I was an orphan—were still living, and I might have a cousin or two. But my family wants nothing to do with me. Why they ever took me in, I don't know. The only good memory I have is of one beautiful young woman who would come and play with me."

This was all Mira could hear; she hurried back to the house to calm herself. She trusted Franco to know what to do and say. In fact, Franco was fascinated and continued to draw out more of Pete's story, thinking *there might be a place in Chipps for Pete, after all. The General will help; he has a special place in his heart for vets.*

After packing and wrapping the wound Franco gave Pete a bucket of warm water and soap and took him to the barn to clean up. While Pete was washing, Franco went to consult with Mira.

"Mira-honey, out of Christian compassion—if not family ties—we must do something to help him. I'm going to take him to General John and see if we can come up with a plan."

"Whatever you think best, Franco. Just be careful not to mention the family connection. I'm afraid that if he stays people are going to note how exactly our hair matches. Or *he* might make the connection, especially if he learns that I am from Philadelphia. Did you ever see anyone else with hair the color of ours?"

"Mira-honey, that's it! His hair! It's his hair that I like about him! Perhaps we can invite him to our Wednesday night hair-wash-operation!"

"Franco! You wouldn't!"

"You're right Mira-honey! I won't. Just teasing."

After feeding and watering Pete's horse Franco and Pete went to the store, Pete looking greatly improved wearing a set of Franco's clothes. Franco burned the old smelly ones.

The General, always fascinated by people who came into town with stories from the west, to say nothing of someone who had been in the Civil War, took to Pete immediately.

Before long The General offered him work as a "baggage man" for the train, and checked with an elderly couple who had an unused lean-to and might need help with odd jobs around the house. Thus Pete, who had knocked on Mira and Franco's door by 8 AM, a vagabond, by 12 noon was employed, had a place to stay and looked quite respectable.

When Franco told Mira, she just shook her head, and marveled at how some people can just land on their feet, whereas she had to work so hard, just to do what she did.

"Mira-honey, are you going to write your parents about Pete?"

"No."

Her swift, abrupt answer took Franco by surprise. "Mira-honey, what are you not telling me?"

"I'm not sure what I'm not telling you. About my only memory of Pete is that I was jealous when my mother played with him and she never played with me. And also, I remember that my father never had anything to do with him, except treat him for illness. The *old quack* he referred to was my father."

"Mira-honey, I will honor your wishes, but I do think sooner or later your connection with him will be *uncovered*. The hair color is a dead give-away. That, plus if word gets out that he has roots in Philadelphia, even as you do, people are going to make the connection."

But Mira was not convinced. She would avoid distant cousin Pete if possible, except to treat his wound. And she would keep her hair up in a snood.

The gardens flourished in June; the twins thrived on the prairie, delighting in all the attention that people showered on them, and especially enjoyed *big brother, Jimmy*.

As so often happened, July turned much drier. Storms brewed, but with little rain. Mira and Nina got backaches from watering their plants, but the effort paid off in abundance of food. Jake and his sons expanded their irrigation project, and got good return from the irrigated areas. Other farmers fared less well.

Hiram built Mira a small wound clinic—big enough for a stove, treatment area, and dry supplies. The General wanted it in town, but when Franco insisted that he and Mira had enough money to pay for the lumber, and Hiram would build it gratuitously, it was built on the school/church property near their garden. By moving her wound supplies to the clinic Mira now had more space in the lean-to to store her newly dried herbs and medicinals. And she could now see non-infectious cases in the lean-to rather than in their kitchen.

Mira's wound practice and general practice grew as word of successful treatments spread. She and Cora enjoyed their joint work on maternity cases, teaching expectant mothers and delivering their babies.

Mira and Franco continued their Wednesday evening sermon preparation, and Mira preached in Chipps on the Sundays Franco was gone. Despite her love for all things medical, nothing thrilled her quite so much as leading God's people in worship. Even conducting funerals brought satisfaction as she ministered to people in their times of deepest need. She longed for the day when she could administer the sacraments and perform marriages. Franco supported her in her wishes, but urged her to give it time. *Look at what progress has been made in just a few short years.*

Pete *cleaned up well*—so well in fact, that he made himself indispensable to The General and people of Chipps as baggage man and *handy-man-about-town*. His limp, that he knew how to use to his advantage, and auburn hair and beard (which he got neatly cut and trimmed) made him stand out in a crowd.

But Mira kept her distance, even asking Franco to do his weekly wound care. When Pete commented on this Franco assured him that he was very capable, having experience working with his parents caring for wounded soldiers. Plus he had learned from Mira.

Franco and Mira told Hiram and Nina of the family connection. They urged her to make her identity known to him. *He seems a likely enough fellow. Yes, he lived a rough and ready life for many years, but underneath we sense good early childhood training.*

But Mira stood firm, remembering her father's reticence in dealing with Pete.

As Telegraph Sunday approached the usual committee got together to plan the festivities. But this year the people who came would have a new challenge to consider.

It came out of an earlier meeting called by Jake and Cora and attended by members of the school and church boards and included Mira and Franco, Hiram and Nina and The General and Mable.

Jake called the meeting to order with the words: *Chipps is changing, Chipps is growing; we must deal with the present and be ready for the future. In short Chipps needs a town council.*

A lively discussion followed, Hiram contributing many insights from having served on a town council in Pennsylvania, even though he lived on a farm. The argument for that was that the area farmers do much to support the livelihood of the town, and vice versa. The General was not so sure that a council was necessary. *Weren't things going well as they now existed?* Implication, *under his leadership.*

Everyone affirmed what he had done over the years to take the town forward. But with the influx of people, there was now need for *a boarding house, restaurant, bank, perhaps even a larger medical clinic, infirmary, library, etc.* It would take a council made of a variety of people to begin and supervise these enterprises.

Fortunately, The General had great respect for Hiram's wisdom and ability and was willing to have the idea of a Council put to the people on Telegraph Sunday.

The worship on Telegraph Sunday was held outdoors under the cottonwoods and was followed by the usual potluck. But before the games a business meeting was called and a town council was proposed and agreed upon. Council members were selected with Hiram being voted in as President. And best of all, in Mira's opinion, several women including herself became members of the council.

Then the games began and it was a day of celebration that went down in Chipps' history. Mira had much to add to her *Journals*.

The General's health declined that winter, and he willingly turned over much of his activity to Hiram. Hiram and Nina and their family developed a relationship with Mable and the General much like they had with the Piersons, only now Hiram and Nina were the *mature son and daughter* and the twins, instead of Franco, the *grandchildren*.

The winter passed rather uneventfully with the usual blizzards and cold temperatures; the closing of school and limited church services. No circuit riding for Franco.

Mira and Cora attended a couple births. There were the usual respiratory infections and fevers, and stomach ailments. Mira freely used the medicinals she had dried and stored in the summer and fall. (Her father continued to send supplies as well.) Wound clinic came to an almost standstill, although Pete showed up every Tuesday morning and was dressed by Franco.

Chapter 17 *Unexpected Changes*

Early November 1877 The General asked Hiram to go with him to Yankton—there was business to transact that would require lawyers.

Wanting to be prepared, Hiram asked about the nature of the business.

"Hiram, I had confidence in you before I ever met you. For two reasons—a man like Franco surely has trustworthy parents. But more than that. I knew, or at least *knew of* your family in Boston long ago. They suffered awful financial ruin—some of it due to your father's lack of skill in management, but largely because your father was not willing to ruin others who were out to do him harm. As sometimes happens, a person suffers negative consequences for doing right. I believe your father was an honest business man who was taken advantage of, and he did not retaliate."

"Thanks for telling me, John. There are so many details that I do not know or understand. It's good to hear that you believe my father was honest and upright. But I often wonder *how it is that an honest and upright man can fall to such ruin, and the deceitful prosper?* Nina and I left destitute. We almost felt driven out. Now I suspect that it was shame that caused my parents to totally retreat and die in bitterness. Nina and I never returned. Everything about the last year or two we lived there suggested that we were not wanted."

"Don't take upon yourself guilt and shame that is not yours, Hiram. You can't change the past. Despite his losses, your father still had *responsibility to you as a father*. So if he has any fault at all, it is that he did not live up to that responsibility. You were fortunate to find *new parents* in the old couple in Pennsylvania."

"You're right, General. You've given me good insights. Thank you for the confidence you place in me and Franco. Now what can I do for you?"

"Our business in Yankton might take several days. We will be meeting with lawyers. I have felt my health failing for about a year now. Just don't have the old stamina and will anymore. It's time for *changing of the guard*. And you are the man, Hiram."

"I'm not quite sure what you mean by that, but I am willing to listen to what you have to say."

The General told Hiram that he was still invested in lumber in the East—what he was doing in Chipps was his *hobby*, not his income. It was now time to sell the business in the East.

"Mable and I have talked this over, and by the time it is all finalized it will take months; up to a year. But here is the plan—half of the profit will be set aside for the people of Chipps, to be administered by you, Hiram. I know you are dreaming of a *boarding house, restaurant, separate church and school buildings, library, clinic, bank, local law enforcement*. One quarter of the profit will be in my and Mable's name, with Franco and Mira as our beneficiaries. And the final quarter, Hiram, is for you, the new *General* of Chipps."

"You can't mean it, General. I mean the part of giving me and Nina so much."

" I do mean it, Hiram. And Mable is in complete agreement. You and Nina have become the son and daughter we never had. And little Chuckie and Prissy (The General's eyes filled with tears), why, they are our grandchildren." He cleared his throat, and then went back to his *General* voice, "and I won't take any argument on this."

When Hiram did not respond, The General stood up and extended his hand to shake Hiram's. "Well, then it's off to Yankton tomorrow."

The General said he would put Pete in charge of the store. To Hiram's skeptical look, he responded, "It's kind of a test; so far he has proven himself to be trustworthy. I sense good upbringing in him, and as we said before *he cleaned up well*. He can't do much damage in a couple of days, and Mable will be here. If he does well I just might hire him for more than *handy-man* and baggage man. Remember, Hiram, I believe in giving a man a chance. That's what we do in the west."

Hiram nodded.

"One more thing, Hiram. You have observed Mable and me living very modestly, by our own choice. We have always felt that this was the best way for the unofficial leader of the area to stay close to the people. But we want to see you and Nina live in a beautiful home, suited for Nina and appropriate for the official leader of our town. If Mable is still living when the house is built, perhaps you could prepare a small living space for her, too."

Hiram again nodded, too overcome with emotion to speak, and eager to go home to tell Nina. They slept little that night, but Hiram met The General at the train station at 8 AM.

They were gone several days as predicted, and Pete did a flawless job of running the store.

The General prayed daily that his health would hold until the final papers were signed, and he had Hiram convinced to build the fine house *worthy of the ladies who would live in it*. During this time of legal work, no one in

Chipps, except Nina and Hiram, Mable and John, knew of what was discussed behind closed doors. Hiram and The General made many business trips to Yankton that year.

As Hiram led the Council into planning for the future it was with caution, because until the money was available, only small steps could be taken, such as getting community support for building a much needed boarding house.

Mira consulted with her father frequently on The General's health, both suspecting heart failure. There was little to do, and it became difficult for the community to see such a fine and generous gentleman fade away. But neither he nor Mable made any complaints.

Hiram consented to the house because it was his heart's desire to give Nina something that would come close to what she had growing up in Boston, only with a taste of the prairie, including several cottonwood trees on the property. He also insisted that there be a cornerstone that said *The House That General John Built* and a welcoming sign at the driveway that read *This home was built in honor of Chipps' first General.* The building project began in the spring 1878. A contractor from Minneapolis was hired, and many farmers and young boys earned extra cash and learned new skills as day laborers. All of Chipps assumed that at long last Mable and the General were building a home in which they would retire.

That same spring Franco confronted Mira one evening during their hair washing. "Mira-honey, this has gone on long enough . . ."

"What? Helping me with my hair? I thought you enjoyed it."

"No, not washing your hair—you know these Wednesday evenings are my favorite part of the week. It is a sacred time for both of us. But yes, it is about your hair, and much more."

Mira stopped her sudsing, and reached for a towel before the soap was rinsed out. "What do you mean, Franco? I think you better explain yourself."

"I will, but first finish rinsing, and dry yourself. We'll talk as I brush out your hair."

There was a brief pause in the conversation as Mira wrapped her head in a towel, dried herself, and put on her night clothes.

Then as they always did, she sat at the table, and Franco began brushing out her hair.

"Mira-honey, ever since Pete has been here—and that is going on a year now—you have been bundling your hair in your snoods and won't let so much as a curl escape."

"I take it down every night."

"Mira-honey, listen to me. People are beginning to talk; they notice that you avoid Pete; some wonder if you are sick and losing your hair; I've even heard it suggested that you stuff your snoods with cotton, just to make it look like you still have lots of hair."

"Franco! That's terrible! I can hardly believe that people would say that."

"Believe it. People say and think lots of things when they observe uncharacteristic behavior, like yours has been for quite some time now."

Mira did not respond, trying to comprehend what Franco was saying.

"I think The General and Mable suspect a biological connection. Surely one of these days Pete is going to ask questions, especially if he finds out that you are from Philadelphia. Mira-honey, I can even see characteristics beyond the hair color. Like the way you both tilt your head when listening. How you use your hands when speaking. I feel like we are living a lie and it must stop. If you do not tell Pete, I will."

"Alright, Franco, you win. I'll tell him. But I must write to my parents first to let them know that Pete is here."

"Fair enough."

"And I must say *you do not seem to know how I feel about this.*"

"I think I know how you feel. I just don't know why you feel this way."

"*You don't know why I feel like I do??!!* I've been JEALOUS—J-E-A-L-O-U-S of *distant cousin Pete* all my life. He had my mother's affection. Affection that she never gave me. He, a little orphan from Europe, and I, her daughter. And now he shows up here."

Franco wrapped his arms around Mira, and said, "Mira-honey, I think that this will require more than a letter. You must go home and sort this all out with your parents. There is more to this story than what they have ever honestly discussed with you."

Mira nodded, her head against his chest. "You are right, Franco, I'll write them tomorrow to let them know I am coming. And please Franco, just *cover* for me a little longer."

But Mira never got that letter written. The following morning, Franco came galloping home with a letter marked *Urgent*. It was from her father.

They sat at the table and Mira opened it with trembling hands.
Dear Miranda,

This is the hardest letter I have ever had to write. Your mother has been sickly all winter. Nothing I gave her has strengthened her. Several days ago she showed me how her usual very slim abdomen is increasing in girth. It appears to be filling with fluid. I brought in several of my colleagues for consultation, and we all agree that it is ovarian cancer, *well advanced . . .*

Mira handed the letter to Franco, "Please finish reading."

. . . Your mother is taking this with her usual grace, and fortunately is almost pain free, but has a general malaise, and weakness. I have hired a nurse to spend several hours each day to help with her care.

Miranda, she says that her dying wish is <u>that you come home</u>.

Is it too much to ask? Could you come? And the sooner the better. Time is running out. I wish I had told you earlier, but really until just the last few days I did not know how ill she is.

Franco paused. Mira thought he had finished reading.

"Let's wire them immediately. I can be on the train Saturday.

"Wait Mira-honey, she has another dying wish as well."

Mira felt a sense of foreboding. "Read on, Franco."

Her second dying wish is—well, how can I say this?—she keeps saying, <u>oh to see Pete one more time, to tell him that I love him, and forgive him for all the pain that he has brought to the family</u>.

Mira bit her bottom lip to keep from crying out, letting Franco continue.

As you know, Mira, I never much cared for him, but I would move mountains if I could, just to honor her wish . . .

There were just a few more words of closing and Franco put the letter down.

No longer able to contain her hurt, Mira jumped up. "Now do you get it, Franco? For my mother it was and is always Pete, Pete, Pete. Even on her deathbed, who is it that she really wants? P-E-T-E—PETE."

Mira collapsed on the floor, spent. Franco sat by her but did not touch her until finally she reached out a hand. He helped her up and once again they sat at the table.

Now composed, but with a tear-stained face, she said, "This is what we will do. You will help me, won't you Franco?"

"Of course."

"Give me a moment, and I will write a brief telegram to my father, to tell him that I hope to be on the train Saturday, and will send another wire Friday with more details."

Franco nodded, and waited for her to say more.

"And Franco, please invite Pete for supper tonight. Apologize for the short notice. Just tell him that something has come up that we must discuss with him. I have chicken soup and sourdough bread and canned fruit to serve."

"I'll get right on it, Mira-honey. After completing those two errands, I'll come back home and help you with whatever you need help with."

"Thanks Franco—I will need one of my steamer trunks. I don't know how long I will be gone. There could be many legal things to contend with, considering the wealth my mother inherited from her parents. While you are in town, I'll ride out to see Cora. She and I have several maternity cases that we are working on. I want to be sure that she has all the information she needs for the classes, and that she will get word out to the expectant mothers to call her, not me. And Franco, you will see the wound clinic patients, won't you?"

Mira spent the rest of the day sorting clothes—she would do laundry on Friday, and finish packing her trunk late Friday evening. Thankfully she would not have to worry about meals for Franco. He was always welcome at his parents. And the twins adored their big brother.

As she worked, her mind was occupied with what the meeting with Pete might be like. She decided that for the first time in a long time she would wear her hair down, in a braid. Other than that, she would just . . . well, she didn't know.

Franco answered the knock on the front door promptly at 6 PM. It was Pete.

Mira took a step forward as he entered, saying "Welcome . . ."

Pete was dumbfounded for a moment, his jaw dropping, and eyes huge. "Miranda! Little Cousin, Miranda. You have changed and grown, but I would recognize your hair anywhere. It's just like mine."

Franco was not about to let him do the talking. "Have a seat, Pete. Miranda and I have a lot to tell you. As you can see, her life has changed dramatically in the past 10 years."

"Franco, will you pour us all some coffee? We'll eat later."

Franco got the pot from the stove and poured three strong cups.

"Pete, I recognized you that very first day about a year ago when you knocked on our door. You, too, had changed, I'm sure you remember. But I would have recognized your hair as a match to my own anywhere, anyplace. I have chosen at great inconvenience to myself to keep my identity concealed from you and our *distant relationship* concealed from the community. Maybe not for good reasons, but they were my reasons, nevertheless, and Franco helped me. I was planning to tell you soon, but not until I first communicated with my father—who you have referred to *as an old quack in Philadelphia*."

Pete cringed, but said nothing.

"Something has happened that has made this conversation necessary *now*. This morning I received an urgent letter from my father, telling me that my mother is dying from ovarian cancer and has asked for me to come home . . ."

"You mean . . ." Pete interrupted.

"Hear her out, Pete."

Mira took a deep breath and tried to steady her voice, "She has also said repeatedly that she wishes she could see Pete one more time."

"You mean, the beautiful cousin that used to come and play with me when I was a little boy wants to see me again?"

"That's what she says."

"Oh, you won't believe this, but I'm actually making plans to go to see her sometime in the next several months. I have such good memories of her."

"Not so fast, Pete. This is not first of all about you."

"But Miranda just said . . . "

"I know what Miranda just said. She and I have talked this over and have come up with a plan. Miranda is leaving for Philadelphia on Saturday. You can travel with her *as her cousin*. I will get word out in the community to that affect. I know that there are already people who suspect a family connection."

Pete nodded, wondering why they seemed, well, *almost hostile*. As far as he knew, he had never done anything to harm them.

"Tomorrow I will wire my father to let him know what day I arrive. I will tell him that I am bringing a *surprise* with me. The details will have to wait. And now let's have our soup."

Pete left soon after supper saying that he would get his ticket the following day. Franco gave him a final word of caution, "Despite what Dr.

Phillips said about *moving mountains* to find you, don't expect a warm welcome from him. He is doing this only for his beloved wife's sake."

The next day Miranda again wore her hair in a braid. It would be a longtime before she bundled it away in a snood again. Jimmy stopped by after school to say *good-bye*, and she reminded him that should Pastor Franco get called away to be sure to check on all the animals, etc. Fortunately it was a warm, sunny, windy day and she got all her laundry done and her trunk packed.

Nina and Hiram and the twins brought over supper. Hiram and Nina were deeply grieved over Priscilla's illness, knowing they would never see her again. They spent a lengthy time in prayer, committing it all to God. They also promised Mira to support her daily as she had to deal not only with her mother's coming death, but also her feelings regarding Pete.

That night Franco held her close, and said, "Mira-honey, there is more to this story than meets the eye. Be prepared."

Pete was waiting for the train when Mira and Franco arrived. Hiram and Nina and the twins were there with a huge basket of food for their travels.

"Mira-honey, the only thing you should have to buy along the way is something to drink."

Mira nodded her thanks.

"And here is a letter for your parents."

Pete and Miranda boarded a few moments later. No one en route would question the propriety of their traveling together. Their hair said it all.

Mira said little on the journey. She brought her journals up to date, jerky train notwithstanding. Pete respected her reserve, uncharacteristically saying little.

At the Philadelphia depot Mira insisted that Pete stay in the train car until she had a chance to greet her father and tell him that she brought him.

After a heartfelt greeting Mira said, "Father I did bring the surprise. I'm not sure how you will receive it, but you did say that *you would move mountains to find him*."

"You don't mean . . . ?"

"Yes, Cousin Pete is with me. It's a long story. Let me call him off the train before it moves on."

Mira beckoned Pete to come. It was an awkward meeting, but Charles did his best to welcome him and assured him that Priscilla would be pleased. "But the meeting will probably not take place today. She is very weak, and first of all, I want her to spend time with Miranda."

"Of course, I understand."

"And you can stay with us while you're here."

"Thank you. I appreciate it."

If Pete was anything, he was full of surprises. Sometimes he seemed self-centered. Other times, such as now, he seemed mature, and demonstrated good upbringing, no matter the strange path he had chosen as a young adult. For Priscilla's sake Charles was determined to give him the benefit of the doubt.

Pete was shown to his room. Miranda went to her old room to freshen up before seeing her mother. When Charles walked her to Priscilla's room her stomach felt tied in knots.

Priscilla extended her hand as Mira approached her bed. She looked a mere shell of the beauty she once was. Mira could hardly stifle a gut-wrenching response. "Miranda, thank you for coming so soon. Come, sit by me." Charles quietly slipped out of the room.

"Mother, I am so sorry for what you are going through—I had no idea until I received Father's letter, hardly a week ago."

"No one knew. Even I didn't, other than I had little energy this past winter. But when my abdomen started to swell I knew I was in trouble and told your father."

"He told me. And I am here for you now and want to take care of you the best I can."

"How is Franco, and Hiram and Nina and the twins?"

"They're all well, but deeply saddened by your illness. They wish they could have come. Nina and Hiram sent a letter, and I think even the twins made pictures for you. Perhaps Father and you can read the letter together. It is for both of you."

"Miranda, you said you were bringing a surprise. I could imagine only one thing—that you are expecting. But you are as slender as ever—even without a corset—so that can't be it."

"No, Mother, I'm not expecting. And you bring up a sore subject. Franco and I have been married going on five years, and still no baby. You didn't have that problem, did you, Mother?"

"No, I suppose I didn't. As a young woman, I had babies quite easily."

"*Babies,* mother?"

"Forgive me. My tongue slipped. I don't seem to be thinking or talking clearly anymore."

Mira remained silent as Priscilla drifted into light sleep. But it was only momentary. "Oh, I'm so glad you are still here."

"I'll stay as long as necessary. But Father and I are both concerned that you do not tax yourself with too much talking."

"But I have so much to say."

Miranda said nothing, thinking the time had finally come when her mother would express some words of love, but instead, Priscilla said, "Seeing you was one of my wishes. My other wish is that I could see little Pete once again. I know he is not little anymore, but I keep thinking of him as he was way back then. So cute, so much fun to play with. And everybody commented on his hair." Then as an afterthought, "As they did yours."

Perhaps it wasn't appropriate, but in the moment Miranda really did not care. "Mother, I have always been puzzled about our hair. You do not have auburn hair. I do not know anyone in your family who does. Was there some distant relative *in Europe* with auburn hair, and somehow . . .?"

"Actually, you never knew her, but your great grandmother had hair just like yours and Pete's."

"But . . ." Miranda looked at her mother, and then cut herself short.

"If only I could see little Pete again."

"Mother, I'm going to step out and call Father. You need to rest, and I think it would be comforting to you to have him sit with you and read the letter from Hiram and Nina."

Mira stepped out. It was all she could do to keep from shouting *Pete.* Not to call him, but in frustration. Franco was right. There was much more to this story. *Babies, indeed!*

Charles went to sit with his wife, and when she awakened he read her Nina and Hiram's letter and they looked at the pictures the children sent. Her nurse came in with some broth and then prepared her for the night. Pete would have to wait until tomorrow. He made no complaint.

But Mira had words for her father that evening. "This has gone on long enough. I am a grown woman. When are you going to tell me the truth about Pete?"

"Tomorrow."

Charles sat at his wife's side that night, an emotionally drained man. Keeping vigil with his beloved wife has hard. Living with deceit even harder. And now to have his precious daughter angry at him. But she was right. It had gone on long enough. Tomorrow they would set it straight.

Priscilla rallied a little after a night of rest and informed Miranda that she was looking forward to the surprise that she brought.

"All right, Mother, if you are ready, I will tell Father. He will do the 'presentation'." *And I will be nowhere in sight.*

"But you will be here, too? A surprise that you brought would not be complete without you."

"This one will be, believe me. I'll inform Father that you are ready."

Charles went in and gently told Priscilla that Mira's surprise was Pete, who was waiting outside the door.

"Oh Charles, you don't mean it."

"I do mean it, and believe me I am as surprised as you. I knew nothing of this."

Priscilla said nothing, letting it sink in. Charles paused, and then went on, "I think you should tell him that you are his mother. Tell him you love him. But above everything else you might wish to say to him, *do not say that you forgive him for the hurt he has caused our family*. He is not guilty—I see that now. There is enough guilt to go around, but it is not Pete's guilt, nor Miranda's. *We and your parents could have made better choices.*"

Priscilla looked as though she had been hit across the face. Charles had *never* talked to her like this before. He took her hand. "Priss, dearest, my intent is not to hurt you. No man ever loved you more than I, but I did wrong to both of us, and to Miranda and Pete, by allowing us to be deceptive about his birth. Withholding truth is never right."

Priscilla lay motionless, her eyes closed.

"Priss."

Her eyes fluttered and she said, "You are right, Charles. And I am even more guilty than you. And in saying that I feel like the heavy burden I have carried all my adult life has been lifted. Just to admit guilt! I know God forgives me, and you forgive me, but will Miranda and Pete?"

"They will Priss, they will. All in good time."

Again a pause. Then Charles remembered that Pete was waiting to come in, probably wondering at the delay. "Pete doesn't have to know the details now. Tell him that I will fill him in later. Just enjoy some mother-son time together. And while you are talking to Pete, I will tell Miranda. She deserves to know. She is hurting greatly."

Priscilla nodded. "I'm ready, Charles."

Charles went to the door and let Pete in. Then he went to find Miranda.

Miranda was in the garden where she had played as a child, and learned from their gardener.

"The moment for truth has come, Father. I have been deceived far too long. And the deception has made my life miserable."

"I see that now, but that was never our intent. Listen with your ears and heart as I tell you the story."

Mira nodded. There was no way she could remain angry with her father. She owed him everything.

"Mira, I have adored your mother from the moment I set eyes on her. I would do anything for her—even withhold truth from you. And for that I am deeply sorry. But let me start at the beginning . . .

"One day many years ago when I was a young doctor becoming recognized in this area as a promising physician—and remember, doctors *were not men of high social standing,* but out of necessity we were often called to the homes of wealthy families.

"Well, one day as I was in my small office that also served as my home, waiting for patients, a prominent local businessman came—John Underwood. You will recognize *Underwood* as your mother's maiden name."

Mira nodded but said nothing.

"I assumed I was being summoned for a house call. But it was nothing of the sort. *He wanted me to court his daughter.* I had heard that she was a real beauty and a social belle. I had also heard—news travels in a community—that she and her mother had taken an extended trip abroad, but was now home.

"I think I remember his words to me and mine to him almost verbatim—they have gone through my mind so often since then."

Mr. Underwood, you want me, a physician, to court your daughter, when there are so many eligible young men of her social standing? I am not a naïve man. I know why wealthy women and their daughters take extended trips to Europe and sometimes come back with an orphan child, who they wish to raise as their own. Is that what happened here?

You certainly cut to the chase, Dr. Phillips. Yes, that is what happened.

"There was a long pause in our conversation, but finally I spoke again."

And what of the child? Especially, should I agree to court your daughter, what of the child?

Priscilla, that's my daughter's name, has really taken to him. But my wife and I do not think it is a wise relationship. My wife and I have decided to raise him as our distant orphaned cousin from Europe. No doubt, many people have, or will guess, but no one dares to cast the first stone. Too many have found themselves in a similar predicament. Only most do not bring the baby home.

Mira listened intently. Her father paused, trying to read her expression. She said nothing.

How would this courtship take place? And should we decide to marry how will we live? Your daughter is used to a life far above what I could provide on the meager income of a physician.

First of all, I will arrange for you to casually meet at social gatherings. And a lawyer will be involved to draw up financial papers. Believe me, Dr. Phillips, you will live well.

Living well is not what I am after for myself. If we should decide to marry, it will be because we love each other. And if we marry I would want her *well cared for—better than what I could provide. And one other thing.*

Name it.

The child will not live with us. He will continue to be her cousin, living with you.

Understood—on both accounts.

We both stood up and shook hands.

Expect an invitation to a dinner and dance at our house soon. There will be other young people your age; perhaps even some that you know, so it should not be awkward.

"Oh Miranda, how life can change with the shake of a hand!"

"Indeed. And the changes had ripple effects."

"There is more to tell, but the rest of the story is just details that can wait a bit. I think we should go inside and see how Pete and your Mother are doing.

"I'll go in, but not to mother's room just now."

As they entered the house, Pete stepped out of Priscilla's room with an expression on his face that could be described as dumbfounded joy.

"I had no idea."

"I didn't know, either, Pete. Father just told me. Why—we're *half brother and sister*! No wonder Franco could see similarities that went beyond auburn hair and *distant cousin*.

"You two have much to talk about, and I'd like to be part of the conversations, too. But could we all agree that for now, we put that on hold, and do what we can to support your mother, my wife in her remaining days. Or maybe only hours.

"Agreed," they said simultaneously, and for the first time ever, smiled at each other.

They spent that day taking turns at Priscilla's bedside. She seemed to be aware of their presence, but made little effort to speak. But Miranda noticed a look of tranquility that she had never before seen on her mother's face. The nurse was in constant attendance. Charles kept vigil all night, and at daylight summoned Miranda and Pete.

"It won't be long now. Join me at your mother's bedside as she passes from time to eternity."

Charles laid a hand on her brow, while Pete and Miranda held her hands. But Miranda could not bring herself to say *Mother, I love you.* All she could murmur was, *Mother, we'll miss you.*

And for that she grieved deeply for a long time.

Within a few hours Mira sent a telegram to Franco. *Mother died peacefully this morning. Father, Pete, and I were at her bedside. Details by letter.*

The first of many letters were written that evening.

Dearest Franco,

How I wish you were here. *You were right in saying,* there is more to this story than meets the eye.

Franco, expect many letters. I plan to write every evening. Please save every word, for I want the letters to be part of my journal, and I do not want to write it more than once. It's too raw. Too painful.

Franco, when I left, I left with a distant cousin. *I will return with a* half-brother. *And that, I'm sure you have already figured out.*

While I am very bitter about the deception, I realize that Pete and I are not the guilty ones. And thus I am resolved to accept Pete for who he is—my brother.

Oh Franco, I know your heart is big enough to accept him also. It will take some explaining in Chipps. We will have to carefully consider how to do this. It is a delicate subject, to be sure. I'm already thinking that a series of sermons on honesty, forgiveness, and family relationships might be a good idea.

Tomorrow we'll make funeral arrangements. I expect the funeral itself will be a small private service. I'm going to try to convince Father to have her dressed in the gown that she wore to our wedding. Remember how beautiful she looked that evening when we modeled our wedding gowns? Even in death she is beautiful and looks peaceful. Father expects that many of his associates and patients will stop by the house to pay their regards.

The day after the funeral we will be meeting with a lawyer. Father said that our grandparents left detailed instructions in their will about dispersing their wealth, should mother die before father. I had no idea they were so wealthy . . .

More to follow tomorrow . . .

Dearest Franco,

Father and I had a long conversation this morning. The weather is beautiful, so once again we sat in the garden. The place itself is peaceful, but our topic unsettling. However, we are working it through. Franco, although Father knew the truth, the truth has hurt him deeply, too.

This is what he said:

Miranda, I adored your mother from the moment I saw her. Coming down the steps in an elegant gown. But despite her beauty there was sadness about her. I could see it, because I knew. I knew of her baby, and I knew that she knew that this was the evening she would meet the man that her father asked to court her.

Our eyes met briefly, and then she was lost in the crowd, but later was seated at the dining table next to me. Much later she told me that the moment our eyes met she knew I was the one, and she determined that she would get to know me, and give me a chance.

She did give me a chance, and within a year we were married. No man could have been happier than I. A poor doctor with no social standing. Fortunately I learn quickly, and fit in quite well, although we had few social engagements. Fine with me. And she didn't seem to mind. The beautiful house we live in was built for us by her parents. She would receive royalties throughout our marriage and at their death a sizable inheritance, but not the total estate.

Miranda, here is the painful thing, and I want you as a grown woman to know this, to help you understand her better—

Miranda, I was not her first love, any more than you were her first child. She has held them both in her heart above us, all these years, and there is nothing we could have done to change that. You must never feel that you are to blame for any of this. Nor is Pete. You are both victims.

But to my shame, I wrongly held it against Pete, until you brought him. In these last few days I have begun to see him through new eyes. I saw how his presence comforted his mother.

I should have never insisted that she continue to call him her distant cousin *who she could visit only occasionally.*

I never learned who the man was that fathered her child. She never told me, but I suspect he was killed during the war. There was a period of time during the war when she became very withdrawn, but would not tell me what was on her mind.

Franco, I mourn her death, but even more than that I mourn her life. I mourn what could have been, but never was. And that, too, I can't change. Only with the grace of God, and your love and support I trust I will come to accept it.

How I wish you were here. But I'm sure you understand when I say that Father and I (and even Pete) have much to attend to before coming back. Pete truly feels that Chipps is his home, and he has plans for settling there permanently. . .

Many folks stopped by, bringing food and other tokens of appreciation in honor of their beloved doctor's wife. Her gravestone read
1878
*This is the final earthly resting place of Priscilla Underwood Phillips,
beloved wife of Charles Phillips,
and mother of Miranda and Pete.*

Dearest Franco,
Father is trying to say and do all the right things *but I know he harbors resentment towards Pete.*

We met with the lawyer today in his office. First it was just Father and me, but the lawyer asked if we knew anyone by the name of Pete Underwood, *and if so, he should also be present.*

Father asked:
Are you sure? John Underwood told me shortly before he died—about 5 years ago—that he had drawn up a will to be read at the time of his death. At that time Priscilla would receive half of his holdings—which she did, and the other half would be dispersed at the time of her death.

The lawyer replied:
Well, there is one thing that John didn't tell you—half of the remaining half is to go to Miranda, that is, one quarter, and the second quarter is to be held in trust for ten years after Priscilla's death for Peter Underwood. If ten years pass, and he still is unaccounted for, the money is to go to various charities.

Fortunately, Father is a man of great self-control, principle, and a real gentleman. He sent for Pete.

Both Pete and I are left with a sizable inheritance, and father is comfortably provided for with mother's inheritance.

What will we do, Franco? I want nothing more than to live simply in Chipps. Oh, a warmer house someday might be nice, and a clinic, perhaps even an infirmary for our patients. But I am in no hurry to make changes . . . .

I would like to stay at least another week to help Father decide what to do with the house and all household items. I can hardly imagine him living here by himself. He is already looking for comfortable bungalows for our faithful gardener and cook. I'm sure he will continue to provide for them financially as well. They too are grieving. They loved Mother.

Miranda chose to ship the furnishings of her bedroom, including the mirror that helped her realize she had to loosen up a bit in her relationship to Franco. Finally, after 5 years she and Franco would have a comfortable bed, and chests of drawers to store their clothes, rather than steamer trunks. And she would ship a small dining table, four chairs, and rocker.

Dr. Phillips sorted through his wonderful library and offered to give the books to Miranda. She suggested instead that they donate them to the *still to be built* library in Chipps.

Dearest Franco,
  I can't wait to get home, but I feel I must stay with Father a little longer. And Pete and I have to look into how best to invest our money.
  For us, Franco, at least initially, I'm going to invest some of it, and have an account set up so that there is money available, should we decide to use it for building, or whatever. (Franco, after things settle down let's take a trip, just you and I, and see something of the beautiful west. Wouldn't horseback be fun?)
  The lawyer is advising Pete on investing, also. He dearly wants to return to Chipps, work for The General, and court Sally Jenkins, the recently widowed woman with four children.
  Father has promised that after about a year he will come and pay us a lengthy visit.
  On the way back I want to stop a night or two in Pennsylvania to see Dr. McCloud. There is always something to learn from him. And I would like his opinion on Pete's wound, even though it is almost healed—thanks to your good work!
  Franco, I have written almost everything that needs to be written—I'll wire you before we leave, and then again from Pennsylvania.
  Oh, before I forget! I told Father about the mansion that the General is building and that your parents will be living in it. Father wants to pack up all of Mother's beautiful furniture (since I do not want it) and ship it to your parents for their

new house. It would mean so much to him if they would receive it as a gift from him and Mother.

Father doesn't need their answer now, but it is something that we should discuss with your parents soon after I am home. Finding suitable living for our gardener and cook is a priority. Once that's done, he wants to sell the house and live simply.

And one more thing, Franco. A bit frivolous, to be sure, but Pete and I are going to get berths, and eat in the diner!

Oh, and for the first time since he was discharged from the army Pete is using a last name—Underwood.

Can't wait to get back to the frontier—home! . . .

Chapter 18 *Confessions*

Miranda and Pete arrived in Chipps on a Thursday. It seemed the whole town was out to greet them. Pete and Miranda had agreed for the immediate to not comment on their new found relationship. But that night Franco and Mira had a long discussion.

When Franco expressed reserve and distrust about Pete, Mira came to his defense.

"Franco, I understand how you feel, and why you feel as you do. My own feelings about Pete, and how I treated him all the months after he showed up in Chipps are still fresh in my mind. But my father helped me understand—even though he still harbors negative feelings which will take him a long time to overcome—that for all Pete's quirks, and many foolish choices in his young adult life, he is not to blame for the sins of his parents and grandparents. He has been victimized, and so have I. *You, Franco, have sensed it in my very being,* and it has influenced everything I've done, and how I've done it. *I want to grow and change, Franco, and become the person God knows I can be. But I cannot become this person without forgiving the wrongdoers. And frankly, I don't think I have yet fully forgiven my mother.*

"But back to Pete, he has forgiven all those who have hurt him."

"And well he might. He has gained a lot."

"No, Franco, don't you see? He has been the biggest loser. No father, no mother, no siblings—all of that went into his choosing the life of a vagabond. But even before knowing his real identity, we have seen him this year in Chipps, trying to get his life together. Let's support him, and love and help him as family does. *Please Franco. Please."*

Franco paced the floor. He eyed the bed that Mira had shipped and had arrived several days earlier. He wanted nothing more than to spend the night in her sweet company. But now he had to deal with *this*.

But he knew she was right. "What *must*, and *can* we do, Mira-honey?"

Mira had already spent days thinking about this.

"Pray, seeking God's direction. Talk with Pete. Talk with your parents, who are wise and fair. And then do as I suggested in one of my letters—come up with a plan to tell Chipps in the most sensitive way we can, but also in an honest way.

"I would like pre-sermon time on Sunday to tell the congregation, but I want you and Pete and your parents to help plan *what* to say, and *how* to say it. I would like to use these comments, as I suggested in my letter, to introduce what I believe to be important— a series of sermons on *truthfulness and honesty* in family relationships. If my family has been wracked in this way, I only wonder how many other families, right here in our community, have also been affected by deceit and dishonesty. Deceit and dishonesty keeps us from being the persons—and families—that God would have us be."

Franco nodded his head, but remained silent.

"Franco, I have truly missed you. Right now, I want nothing more, than to spend the night with you. Thanks for setting up our *new* bed."

They awakened Friday morning, refreshed, and ready to begin the new day. Franco left early to invite Pete and the Welkens for supper.

Hiram and Nina, ever gracious, listened with head and heart as Mira and Pete told in detail of their final days and hours with their mother. It was hard for them to think of Pete as Priscilla's son, yet they didn't doubt the truth of it. It shed light on the heavy burden they had seen Priscilla carry.

"What we really need to talk about tonight is how to tell the people of Chipps the truth about our relationship. How do we say that Pete and I are half brother and sister without casting my mother in a negative light?"

"Mira-honey, what your mother did she did at a very young age. No one can hold that against her forever. Your father certainly did not, and we do not." That was from Nina.

Hiram added, "And Pete, we do not hold it against you. What happened wasn't your fault. And we applaud you for the efforts you have made, even before you knew the truth, to begin to turn your life around. And yes, the people of Chipps must be told of your brother-sister relationship. It won't be long before most of them guess, anyway. Truth is best."

"But *how* do we tell them?" asked Franco. "Mira already suggested to me that she use pre-sermon time to give, at least briefly, the story and use it as a lead-in to a series of sermons that we would develop on honesty and truthfulness within the family . . ."

"May I suggest" it was the first time Pete spoke "that Miranda tell the congregation that she recently learned that her mother, Priscilla now deceased, had a child—me—before meeting Miranda's father? It was at Priscilla's parents' insistence that they—my grandparents— raise me as their own. I left home at a young age to join the Union Army, and returned only briefly for medical treatment. After which I left for the West, and finally ended up here about a year ago because I had heard of a clinic that was treating wounds. I didn't know that *Dr. Mira* was anyone from my past.

In fact, the truth about my relationship to the Phillips family was deliberately withheld from *both* Miranda and me. It is hard to forgive, because so much unnecessary pain has been inflicted on innocent people. But I say, before God, and by his grace, that I forgive everyone who has done me wrong—most of all my own mother and grandparents."

The others were silent for so long that Pete began to wonder if he had said something inappropriate. He cleared his throat and started to apologize, but Mira interrupted.

"You say it very well, Pete. Perhaps you should be the one to speak."

"No, Miranda, I am not a public speaker. And it is your story, perhaps even more than mine. But if you wish, I'll come tomorrow, and we can write it out together." Miranda nodded her agreement.

Pete turned to Franco. "And Franco—may I call you that now...?

Franco nodded.

"Franco, will you also be present as we write it? This has to come from the three of us."

"I'll be there. What time can you come?"

They enjoyed a rabbit stew dinner with a sense of relief—despite their grief over Priscilla—that none of them had experienced for a long time.

The people of Chipps were gracious, rejoicing in Pete and Dr. Mira having found each other, and the sense of family that they were establishing. As time went on, even Franco relaxed in Pete's presence and accepted him as a brother-in-law. In fact, developing the sermons on *God's plan for families* with Mira, and even asking Pete for insight, especially on forgiveness, had a maturing effect on Franco's faith.

Late in the fall of 1878 the mansion was complete, and Hiram, Nina, and the twins moved in. They gladly received Priscilla's fine furniture, and even Mira conceded that the classic pieces had an elegance matching the house.

Everyone expected The General and Mable to move in. But he convinced them that the *new general* of Chipps must live there, and that it was built with plenty of room for him and Mable to move to when they desired. No one except Hiram and Nina, Franco and Mira, and John and Mable knew that the house actually belonged to Hiram and Nina.

Most intriguing to everyone—especially the women—was the *Tea Room for the Ladies of Chipps*. That same fall Mable and Nina began sending *preliminary invitations*, each with a complimentary coupon to Bessie's fabric shop for a new dress to be made by Bessie. The Teas would begin in late spring, giving Bessie plenty of time to make fancy dresses.

Hiram continued his lumberyard work, and as president of the City Council, he oversaw the building of the boarding house—*Chipps Boarding*—built with money raised by the people of the town and community. It was finished that fall and provided part time and full time work for several women—cleaning, laundry, cooking. Pete took a room there and became manager, and continued his work for The General, but gave up his baggage job. With people coming in by train, and some still passing through in covered wagon, there was rarely an empty room at *Chipps Boarding*. It was a steady source of revenue for the town.

In early 1879 General John's legal work was finished—his eastern holdings sold, and the money dispersed according to his wishes. It now fell to Hiram to put The General's well thought out and financed plans for Chipps into action. Hiram entrenched himself in his role as *the new general* (president-for-life) of the City Council.

At the first council meeting in the new year Hiram told the council of The General's generous gift to the city and that it was to be used wisely to build up the city and resources in the city so that the most people would benefit in many ways and that eventually these projects would become self-sustaining, or sustained by taxes.

The most ambitious project would be to build a *Town Hall*—a large structure that would house, if not all immediately, certainly in the future: *bank, small offices to transact town business, lending library (with books supplied by Dr. Phillips, Dr. Mira's father), large community room for socials and available to the church and school for special events.*

They would advertise in Yankton, Sioux Falls, Sioux City, even Minneapolis for an architect and builder. They would also advertise the need for a blacksmith and livery stable.

Not all on the Council readily endorsed all of the plan. What did they need a bank for, and offices? Too much and too many new things would bring unwanted changes, and who knew what kind of people would respond to the advertisements?

Hiram wisely delayed saying anything at this time about changes to the church/school; the need for law enforcement, the need for a restaurant, the need for a medical clinic.

It took three council meetings to bring them all into agreement, but by the end of March they were ready to place their advertisements, and by June construction on the Town Hall began. As with building the mansion, so with the Town Hall, many farmers supplemented their income by day work. As rain was scarce again this year farmers who otherwise might have "gone under" were able to at least maintain. Jake and Cora breathed a sigh of relief that fewer people now depended on them for assistance. Jake and his sons increased their efforts to irrigate their land.

That spring, 1879, almost a year to date of Priscilla's death, Dr. Phillips came to visit. It was a bitter-sweet time, reliving with Mira and Franco and Nina and Hiram good and difficult times. The first evening, in a pre-supper conversation he told them that he felt he had aged ten years in the past year.

"Father, I had no idea. Why didn't you . . .?" Franco shot her a warning look.

Charles paused briefly, giving Mira an understanding smile. She was so much like him, always wanting to solve something. Sometimes even before knowing the true nature of the problem.

"I felt I owed it to my patients and associates to continue to do as much as possible. And there were still things to be hammered out with the lawyers. Also, finding suitable living for our cook and gardener and setting up funds so they can live comfortably. They served us well for many years. I felt I owed it to them. But the worst, *the very worst,* was to come home every evening to an empty house, and to spend the next twelve or so hours without my lifelong companion. Even in her worst days of melancholia and illness, she was always *there*. Packing up the house, and selling it was hard— but the alternative, *staying,* would have been harder. He paused, and the others respected his silence, although Mira with difficulty.

"You can't imagine. *You just can't imagine the emptiness.* I had to move to something smaller, where I would have less reminders of *what was.*"

Then in answer to their unasked questions he said, "I have a cot in my office and eat in a local hotel."

"But Father!"

"It's temporary, Mira. Until I can sort out what I want to do with the rest of my life."

"You mean you are thinking of a change. Maybe . . ."

"Mira, I'm planning a several week visit with you all, and we'll have plenty of time to talk. I've already talked long enough." Glancing at the table he added, "I haven't seen such a lovely table set in a long time. Thank you, Nina."

"Charles, we are so glad to have you here, despite the circumstances, and even staying with us. Just let me say that we appreciate the lovely furniture you sent. I admired it when we stayed with you, and it's even more lovely than I had remembered."

"You have quite a mansion here, Hiram! It sets off Priscilla's furniture beautifully."

"It does indeed. And in case you are wondering how this all came about—remembering our log cabin in Pennsylvania—well, not many people other than Mira and Franco and Mable and John, know, but we will tell you. But enough talk for now. Let's eat. As you say, there will be plenty of time for talking. And I can't wait for you to meet *General John*."

"I'm eager to meet him, too. I've already heard about him."

"He is expecting a thorough physical exam from you, Father. I know he trusts me, but I can tell that he is hoping that you will have something to suggest that will revive him a bit."

They sat down to eat, the twins begging to sit on either side of Dr. Charles.

The following morning Charles spent several hours with The General, most of it just talking, but as to his physical health, Charles had to tell him that his heart was wearing out. Perhaps some adjustment of medication, especially foxglove, would help for the time being. And so they tried, but with little improvement. The General continued to weaken and became increasingly short of breath.

In their evening discussions around Hiram and Nina's dining table, Charles hinted that he would like to move west in a few years—when he felt ready to completely turn his practice over to his associates.

"Father, do you mean it? You would actually move here? We could be in practice together!"

"We could indeed! We've done it before, you know."

"Do you have a target date?" Franco asked. "Anytime would be good for us!"

Nina and Hiram readily agreed.

"I'm thinking that in 1883 I will begin to transition all my patients to my associates, and then early 1884 I'll be ready to head west."

Mira looked disappointed. "Four or five years into the future—that's a long time!"

"It is! But remember, just a few moments ago you didn't even know my intentions."

"That's true, but your coming makes the plans that Franco and I are discussing more exciting."

All eyes now turned to Franco and Mira. *Was Mira . . .?*

"It has to do with the money we inherited from mother. Franco, why don't you tell them?"

"We've been talking about building a clinic with rooms that could be used for patient treatment, and eventually function as an infirmary/hospital. Adjacent to these rooms we'd have our own living quarters. Our little shack, furnished by the town to the pastor is livable, but winter is very difficult."

"I would hold regular clinic hours, not only for the wound clinic, but for all other medical problems as well. With the influx of people to town and the area, and even passing through, whether by train or wagon, my practice is getting busy, and treating people in our living space is not wise. It could also help eliminate house calls except for deliveries."

Charles and Hiram and Nina quickly endorsed their suggestions, and many nights were spent in developing the plans that Mira and Franco already had in mind.

Charles stayed a month and then returned to Philadelphia. Mira felt a great loss at his leaving, but at the same time was caught up in the excitement as Chipps continued to grow—especially as the Town Hall took shape.

Pete and Sally announced their plan to marry. Simultaneous to the construction of the Town Hall, Pete hired locals to build a house that would be large enough for Sally's four children, and hopefully more of their own. No one even questioned where Pete got the money to build such a house. Anything seemed possible in Chipps these days.

Mira went to her steamer trunks to check on her supply of fancy dresses which her mother had insisted she bring to Chipps. One remained. If Sally were willing she could wear a dress connected to Pete's mother. Both Pete and Sally were delighted. With Bessie's alterations to the dress Sally was a beautiful bride.

But Mira felt an unexpected sadness—her trunks, so well stocked by her mother were almost empty now—except for the household goods that she eventually would use in her new house. Tears welled up in her eyes, thinking of a relationship that might have been, but never was.

Another sad thought entered her mind. *I wonder how soon I should begin a journal on "Widows of Chipps?" Bessie is a widow. Agnes was a widow, though just briefly. And Sally is a widow, also briefly. I wonder who will be next?* She shut down that thought. For now.

The General's health continued to decline. But with Hiram taking a public role, few people noticed that he was keeping a low profile. Rain and crops were marginal, but enough to get by. Farmers welcomed a little extra income from working by the day on the building projects.

Everyone approached Telegraph Sunday with festive spirits. But General John enjoyed it only from the sidelines, and as the day progressed he became more and more lethargic. Mable stayed at his side and Mira kept a close eye on him. About 3 PM he told Mable that he must go home and wanted her, Nina and Hiram, and Franco and Mira to come also.

They gathered around his bed. He was turning blue around his lips. Mable held one hand, and he reached out the other to Hiram.

In a weak voice he said, "Oh God, why does an old fool like me have to be brought to his death bed before making confession?"

He paused and looked at Hiram, and then with a voice that strengthened just momentarily he went on, "Hiram, I spent years of my life doing good for many people, but I regret *why* I did it. I was trying to *atone for my sins*. Hiram, I along with several other men brought your father down. Please forgive me . . ." and with that he lapsed into unconsciousness.

Franco moved in closer, and in prayer commended him to God for all eternity. At the end of the prayer Mira listened for breath sounds and heartbeat, but there were none. The General had departed this life.

Mable remained composed, knowing she had to say something. "Hiram, Nina, Franco, Mira, there are details I will tell you later. How I wish he would have heeded my advice and told you himself. I urged him to. But for now, can we set this aside, and give a great man, though not a perfect man, an honorable burial?"

"Of course."

"Thank you. Franco, Mira, how soon do you think we can hold the funeral?"

Franco and Mira looked at each other, remembering how quickly a body decomposes in warm weather. Mira spoke first, "No later than Tuesday morning." Franco nodded in agreement.

"Then Tuesday morning it will be. Hiram, will you please go out and inform the people, and invite them to the Tuesday morning service, to be followed by a community dinner in John's honor? And please ask Jake and Cora to come to see me immediately. They will have to make preparations for the dinner."

Hiram went out feeling stunned but did as Mable asked.

After he left, and as they were waiting for Jake and Cora, Mable broke just a little as she asked, "Will you all ever forgive us?"

Nina was first to reply, "We will. We do. It may take Hiram a little while to take this all in, but I assure you, there is already forgiveness in his heart. And don't worry—none of us will ever breathe a word of any of this to the people of Chipps. It would serve nothing to speak of it now. Let's remember him for the good he has done."

Mable's eyes filled with tears of gratitude and sorrow as she clung to Nina. In a matter of minutes Jake and Cora entered and the others left, Hiram requesting that Jake contact them as soon as they were needed to help with plans and preparations.

A large community funeral was held with many people testifying to how The General had helped them. Mira, Franco, Hiram, and Nina carried out their part with grace, but inwardly reeling from the deception. They were ready to listen, as soon as Mable was ready to talk. But her knowledge of what happened was sketchy as it happened before she met John. He admitted to her that

he and several others built their successful businesses by ruining Hiram's and Nina's parents' joint business. Not only was the business ruined—the parents were completely devastated.

Some years later John had a spiritual conversion while on the battlefield. He became very burdened by what he had done but there was no way to undo it. The parents had already died, and Hiram and Nina, the only heirs, were assumed dead. So he did what he could—doing good for others, hoping that this might make right the wrong he could never make right with the people he had wronged.

And then one day the people of Chipps hired a young pastor with the name of Welken. But he was from Pennsylvania and educated in Philadelphia. It just didn't add up. But John did his research, talked with Pastor Welken, and made the connection.

The rest of the story needed no further telling—they had lived it.

All were silent a long while. So long that Mable went to make tea, realizing that the four Welkens needed time to think and talk.

When Mable came back with the steaming teapot Hiram spoke, "Mable, we do not hold you responsible for what John did—not even his silence. In fact, we hurt deeply for him at having carried a burden of guilt to his deathbed, having tried to expunge it all his life by doing good. Yet we firmly believe that he was a man of God, and had the gift of faith and grace that Mira and Franco spoke of this morning. John truly knew that he was saved by grace through faith. We honor him for all the good he did for others."

Nina nodded and added, "We are deeply grateful for the provisions he has made for us and our children. Our prayer is that we will live up to his high example of doing good to others."

They all agreed that the people of Chipps should be told that The General and the parents of Nina and Hiram, now deceased, had a previous business connection, and because of that Hiram and Nina inherited some of The General's wealth. The town was also was beneficiary of The General's generosity.

"It seems to me that this is a situation where God has worked great good out of what was originally an evil situation," was Mira's observation.

Everyone agreed. But later that evening Franco commented to Mira that the people most deserving of justice—his biological grandparents—never received it. Money was one thing, but their names had never been cleared. Furthermore, even today neither Franco nor his parents would be honored in Boston.

"But that's life," was Mira's comment. "*Unfair.*"

Mable moved in with Nina and Hiram soon after John's funeral, and Pete and Sally opened a restaurant in the quarters where Mable and John had lived for many years. As before, Mable spent much of her days in the store, and now also in the restaurant.

Bessie was so swamped with work making *tea dresses* that she had to hire an assistant.

Chapter 19 *Chipps Booms*

Chipps was booming as 1880 began, and continued to boom because of the construction and money brought in by The General and Mable's generosity. And also from the inheritance from Priscilla that Franco and Mira used for building the medical clinic. But most of all because of the high morale of people. Hiram was a leader everybody looked up to. He led by encouraging and helping people believe in their abilities.

Mable fit in comfortably with Hiram and Nina. The Teas were a great success. A frequent comment was, especially from those who had come from comforts in the east, *I never thought I would enjoy such loveliness again, or wear such a beautiful dress again.*

Nina, because of increasing social responsibilities and with the twins now school age, gave up her teaching position. It was filled by a young woman from the community who spent a year in Minneapolis getting teachers' training. But Nina did not give up her gardening classes. The children came to her garden. Franco and Mira continued their religious education and hygiene classes in the school.

Western migration continued, and some people, seeing the prosperity of Chipps settled there or in surrounding areas. As Franco observed his circuit congregations growing he began discussions on what would take a few years to accomplish—each parish hiring their own pastors.

Jimmy was now an almost teenager. He still considered himself indispensable to Mira and Franco, and was a huge help with the animals, garden, and any odd job that Franco had for him.

He no longer wanted to be called *Jimmy. That was for little boys.*

"How about James?" Franco asked.

He shook his head. "I don't know anybody in the *west* with **that** name. That's for storybooks, and maybe important people. I want to be called *Jems.*"

And so the name was resolved but it took time to catch on. Franco, however, had a greater concern to discuss with Bessie.

"Bessie, as the years go by Jems has become very attached to me, and copying what I do and how I do it. More than a big brother; more than a pastor; almost like a father. How do you feel about that? Is it good? Is it harmful?"

"We talk about his father. I tell him the good things. I also tell him that his father's disappearance remains a mystery, perhaps never to be solved, but most likely he got *lost on the prairie* during a storm. The prairie can be very unforgiving, Pastor Franco. (Franco shuddered.) Even a small boy must learn that. As for his relationship with you, yes it is close, but he knows that you are his pastor and good friend. In fact, he looks at you as a role model. Don't be surprised when one day, perhaps soon, he tells you *what he wants to be when he grows up*. But I will say no more now. I promised him I wouldn't."

"Thanks Bessie. I am honored, and I won't say a word. He can tell me when he is ready."

But Franco told Mira, who was equally thrilled, for she had been concerned, too. He also told her what Bessie said about the prairie. "We must be very careful, Mira-honey. In our few short years here we have seen tragic things."

Mira nodded her agreement.

Chipps may have been booming because of the building projects and the support jobs that resulted from the construction, but Dakota Territory in 1880 had problems. There was economic hardship from drought, hail, and ceaseless wind and dust. Some ranchers with hopeful determination packed up and continued the journey they had begun years before—farther west. Others called it quits and went east. Some hoped that Minnesota or Wisconsin would have something for them. If not, there were other states, even in the far south.

Franco and Mira spent evenings discussing the clinic and their living quarters. After many discussions with Hiram and Nina, and remembering advice given them by Mira's father they decided on *a squared off C structure*. Admittedly, not aesthetically the most appealing, but functionally very sound.

Also, at Charles' recommendation and Mira's insistence, all infectious diseases and infected wounds would continue to be treated apart from other medical care, in separate buildings.

The city sold them the land adjacent to the school/church. The purchase included the shack where they lived, the barn, the chicken coop, several acres of land, and one of the two beautiful cottonwood trees.

"Franco, I think I have a solution for separate wound care and other infections. We already have our small wound clinic; we can continue to use that. But let's remodel our shack and use it for infectious diseases. But we would need a place to live until our new quarters are built."

"Great ideas! And living space will be no problem. My parents would love to have us live with them—always—but even a short time will please them. Even with Mable there, they still feel like they rattle around in that big house. I'll talk to them tomorrow. I can see the excitement of the twins already."

Mira and Franco moved in with Hiram and Nina the last week of May. They left the medical supplies in the lean-to and steamer trunks in the barn. The stove stayed to warm *The Shack* and to heat water. Jems took Benny to live with him and Bessie. Mouser continued to keep residence in the church/school.

Franco, with the assistance of two others renovated *The Shack* in 5 days. Mira preached that Sunday, and the service included an outdoor picnic and dedication of *The Shack*. Mira felt energy and enthusiasm surge through her. She knew that what they were doing and how they were doing it was right and good.

Ground preparation for "*The C*," as the Clinic would be called, began the second week of June. Franco, though capable of doing much of the work himself, had to attend to pastoral needs, and since money was no problem for them now, they hired builders.

The target date for completion was Telegraph Sunday in August. Mira began early to plan the dedication. It would be a community event celebrating a place where *General Medicine* would be practiced. *If only Father could come soon. He knows so much more than I.* But Charles' delay in coming wasn't only what he had mentioned—transitioning his practice—but also wanting to give Mira more time to establish herself. He felt that if he came too soon his presence would overshadow her.

Seeing plans on paper was one thing. Watching it all take shape was another. Even small things meant a lot. "Franco, won't it be wonderful to have both sides warm at the same time?"

Franco gave her a quizzical look, and then burst out laughing. "I know what you mean. That's a luxury I've never had. One winter when I was 7 or 8 I stood so close to the stove that I burned myself. Grandma Pierson kidded me for years for having *scorchies* on my butt. But really, it wasn't funny. They were serious blisters. But I learned my lesson."

Mira kept her father apprised of the progress. *How I wish you were here to see it all. The town sold us a sizeable piece of land, so 'The C' stands at a northwest to southeast orientation. The northwest 'arm' will be the clinic, pharmacy, and laboratory. The southeast 'arm' will be a laundry/bathing room with an adjacent kitchen that will open directly into the dining area .The two 'arms' will be connected by a 'spine'—the first room of the spine (opening into the dining area) will be our living/reading room. The next three rooms are bedrooms*—*the two closest to the clinic will be available for patients who must stay one night or more.*

Does this sound like the beginning of a hospital? I think it is! Before we know it we will have to hire medical staff!

Franco and Hiram think that the space between our place and the town will be filled with buildings before long. That's progress, I guess. But I do love the wide open spaces.

Dr. Phillips wrote back with encouragement and advice—most of which Franco and Mira had already thought of, but accepted with appreciation and good grace. *Be sure that your clinic has many windows. Good light is essential for examining a patient and giving treatment. And patient rooms need windows for light and fresh air.*

Have you considered that you might need a surgery theater and delivery room some day?

Mira responded, *Thanks for your suggestions for the clinic. Franco will talk to the builders and order more windows. We will put one or two windows on all outside walls so every room will have good lighting. And get this*—every room *will have a small coal stove, except the living room. We will have a fireplace in that. Oh, the laundry and kitchen will each have a cook stove.*

The two arms of 'The C' will be connected by an enclosed hallway that runs the length of the spine. Each room along the spine will have a door that opens into the hall. And each room will have a door that opens into the adjacent room. At least for now the hall will not be heated, so it could become rather cold in the winter. Using the inner doors will be a way of getting around that. But in warm weather the hall will be very convenient.

As for a surgery theater and delivery room—we haven't discussed that. Perhaps a bedroom/patient room could be converted. I think we will put that on hold until you come to stay. As you know, I am not qualified to do internal surgery. And I don't expect that women will come to the clinic for delivery unless they have complications . . .

And so the letters went back and forth in June and July.

In the first week of July, Mira and Franco took the train to Yankton to order the stoves, furniture, cupboards, a desk for each of them, and bookshelves. Bessie was already making curtains for the windows. Mira breathed a prayer of thanks when she remembered the trunks of kitchen supplies and linens her mother had insisted she bring with her—some of it untouched for more than seven years. They would still be like new—unless mice had gnawed their way into them. Mouser notwithstanding, mice continued to be a problem. Mira wondered if her mother had intuitively known that the day would come when Mira would need and appreciate it all. Mira stifled a sob at not being able to say *thank you*.

The train trip to Yankton was brief and they couldn't help but chuckle over the memory of the three-wagon-ox-train that brought them the 20 miles from Yankton to Chipps seven years earlier, taking close to 12 hours. And how their impression of *the trio* had changed since then.

"Franco, why do you suppose *the trio* seemed so unfriendly when we first met them? Jake rarely said a civil word to me until I saved his feet from amputation."

"I don't know, Mira-honey. But I suspect they were testing us. Did we have what it takes to live on the prairie?"

"Well, I guess we showed them."

"That we did."

"Do you have any regrets, Mira-honey?"

"About living in Chipps, you mean?"

Franco nodded.

"Not one."

"Not one?"

"Well, I often wonder if I had been with my mother during her illness, if things might have been different. But my Father told me that I should not live with the *what ifs* and the *maybe I should haves*. So I try not to, and it's getting easier."

They both fell silent until suddenly Mira had another thought. "Just think, Franco, by having a separate laundry room with a stove, we no longer will have to take our baths and wash our hair in front of the kitchen stove!"

"I'll miss that. That's how I've done it all my life."

"Tough! No sympathy from me. I predict you will adjust well."

By the end of July Franco told Mira that the clinic would be ready for dedication on Telegraph Sunday and she would be able to see her first patients in it the next day.

On the Friday before Telegraph Sunday they set up office, moving in the supplies and furniture. Bessie hung brightly colored draw curtains in the windows and around the examination table. With deep emotion Mira ran her hands over the examination table and cupboards for medical instruments and reference books and magazines that Dr. Phillips had sent. Mira couldn't help but think that it was the finest medical office in Dakota Territory.

From its inception Mira had begun yet another journal, this one chronicling the progress of the construction of the clinic. This journal would become an essential part of the development of her medical records, and an important part of the history of Chipps.

At the church service Franco preached on the compassion of Jesus as he healed many who had come to hear him. It was a sermon he and Mira had carefully discussed in the weeks leading up to this special day.

At the dedication Franco presented Mira with a sign, handmade by himself, for the door of the clinic: *General Medicine Practiced Here*. It was a fitting tribute to The General who had done so much to make Chipps the town that it was and was becoming.

The day was a great success with people coming from distances of 10 and 15 miles.

Despite her plans to open the clinic on Monday morning, when Mira saw the needs of many people who approached her during the potluck, she opened the clinic doors and treated 20 patients that afternoon.

As she was doing this, games and activities filled the air with sounds of celebration.

But none who came from a distance were able to pay except with promises. The times outside of Chipps were too hard.

Their living quarters were ready for occupancy by September. Mira kept the décor simple—colorful muslin curtains made by Bessie and heavy drapery to help keep out cold in the winter. Nina insisted that she have one of her mother's china cabinets to display the fine china her mother and others had given her when she got married.

Meanwhile the Town Hall was completed, and another dedication was held the last Sunday of September. An indoor church potluck was the first activity held in the Hall.

After school hours the school teacher, Mira and Franco organized the public lending library. Most of the books had come from Charles' library and held special memories for Mira.

Hiram set up a modest office for himself in one of the rooms reserved for office space. He held several council meetings that fall in which they discussed a new school building to be built in the town. They also discussed remodeling and enlarging the church to accommodate the growing congregation. Both the school board and church council would be consulted before anything was decided. Franco felt strongly that anything which involved the church should also have the approval and financial support of the congregation and anything that involved the school needed input from parents.

Most urgently, Chipps needed a bank. A room in the Town Hall was already designated for this purpose. It even had a safe. Presently all the transactions involving The General's money were done through the bank in Yankton. With more businesses having opened, or soon to open, a bank and professional banker were essential. Once again they advertised in places as far away as Sioux Falls, Sioux City, and Minneapolis. The new bank opened for business in December. Jems was one of the first to open an account! He proudly told Franco that he was beginning to save money to go to school in *the East*.

Wanting input from the community on the construction of a new school, the Council kept that conversation for the community Thanksgiving celebration. With the assurance that the money was coming from what The General had given, the proposal passed easily. Franco assured his congregation that by spring time 1881 the church would begin conversations about remodeling and enlarging.

The only hard sell was the need for a sheriff and a jail. That was tabled until the following year. Hiram commented to Nina, "No doubt there will have to be an incident before there is agreement on this. I just hope that whatever happens won't be too serious."

PART 3

ONE DECADE FOLLOWS ANOTHER
1881-1890

Chapter 20 *Life and Death Move Chipps Forward.*

Hiram was right. It took an incident. And except for Pete's observation and quick acting it might have been worse. But it was of enough concern to get the Council's approval and support of the town and community for a sheriff and jail. And it gave Mira and Franco a topic for a series of sermons: *Living Together in Community.*

The Boarding House continued to thrive, some patrons staying on indefinitely; others only a night or two. Though Pete did much less *hands on* there than before his marriage when he had lived there, he made it his responsibility to stop in at least once a day. He commented to Hiram, "There's a need to keep an eye on the clientele. I've lived around enough myself to know that these kinds of places can attract non-trustworthy people. I'm pretty good at spotting trouble before it happens, or being there when it happens. And I do carry a gun."

Hiram nodded and said with a chuckle, "So does your sister."

"I know. She told me. I'm glad she does."

Early in January Pete began noticing someone who might mean trouble. Nothing specific, but he seemed to have no real purpose in Chipps. When Pete tried to engage him in conversation he became evasive and defensive. Pete noticed that his presence at the supper table was sporadic. This was unusual because patrons rarely missed a meal, as the price was figured in with the length of time they held a room. Pete also noticed him casing out the bank, seeing him near the bank often *during the supper hour.* But he would rarely go in. The banker told Pete that he had no transactions with the man. Pete suggested that the banker *beware, and keep a gun handy.*

After a couple weeks of this behavior Pete figured the man would strike soon, or move on. Pete was right. He struck during supper hour, just as the bank was closing. Pete *just happened* to walk in as the man was demanding money at gun point. He whirled around as soon as he heard the door, and faced Pete who also had his gun pulled *and aimed.* The robber fired off the first shot, but totally missed Pete, hitting the door frame. Pete's aim was right on target, and the man dropped dead with Pete's first and only shot.

The town soon gathered. This was the first anyone could remember hearing a gunshot in town, even though the ranchers always carried guns. It was the way of the west.

It took only this incident to convince the community and town that a sheriff and jail were needed and they thought Pete was their man. But he declined. He liked what he was doing, and valued his family life.

In early spring construction began on a house for a sheriff with adjacent jail cells. Simultaneously advertisements for a sheriff were placed.

The growing season of 1881 looked as bleak, if not worse than the previous year. Once again the farmers supplemented their income by working in construction—the house/jail, a new school, and remodeling and enlarging the church. By this time Hiram was sufficiently skilled in building and supervision that they did not have to hire anyone from out of the area to oversee.

Once again Telegraph Sunday marked the day for dedication of new buildings. Much had been accomplished since The General's death. But there was also a sense of sadness—no more new projects would come directly out of The General's legacy. The remaining money would be spent on maintaining what he had built, until everything would be self-sustaining, or subsidized by tax-money.

If farming did not *pick up* in the next few years many farmers would *pack up* and that would mean hard economic times for Chipps.

The success of Mira's medical practice continued to spread in the greater community. People coming for treatment brought business to the Boarding House, restaurant, and General Store. But there was a prevailing attitude that health care should be free, coming out of Christian compassion, and all the more since *the doctor* was the pastor's wife, and an able pastor herself.

It's true that some did pay a token of the cost in coins; and not infrequently with a jar of jam or meat left in the examining room. But not nearly enough to cover the cost of running a clinic and putting food on their own table. Charles continued to send supplies—much of it coming from donations of his church and medical practice. Dr. McCloud in Pennsylvania was also generous.

But Mira felt taken advantage of by the very people she had come to serve. Except for some investments, Priscilla's money had been nearly all spent on the clinic and their residence.

Pete had a suggestion. *Post charges for a clinic visit and basic procedures near the front door, and run the payment of bills through The General Store. As a patient leaves give him a paper stating the charge, and say that settlement can be made at the store.*

Mira and Franco looked at each other, each hoping the other would speak first. Franco did, "It seems to fly in the face of ministry. Yet given my modest salary, to say nothing of your work for the church, I don't think we are asking too much from the community if we expect payment for medical expenses."

Mira nodded, and then added, "But we wouldn't turn an emergency away for not being able to pay."

"Agreed. Let's give Pete's suggestion a try."

And so they worked out a plan for fair charges, along with a system for payment. It added to Pete's work at the store, but he didn't mind. The story of how he handled the bank robbery was becoming part of the folklore of Chipps and while Pete never threatened anyone, people much more readily turned money over to him than to Franco or Mira. A holstered pistol helped.

Over the years paying for medical care became an accepted practice. But even then, it was not unusual for a jar of jam or meat, or a few eggs to be left in the office. Mira knew it was in lieu of cash payment. And frankly, Mira quite appreciated these gifts.

Every church service in the winter of 1882 and 1883 included prayer time in which the congregation prayed for adequate snow cover and early spring rain.

While the snow was enough to keep soil from blowing away during the winter, spring rain was very little. In 1883, until June there was not so much as a flash of lightning or clap of thunder. Only wind, ceaseless wind. Drying wind. Depressing wind. Wind that worked away at the human spirit. Mira felt it keenly. She was becoming depressed and physically rundown. Her patient load was small. Farmers rarely came to town now that construction was done and they had no cash to spend. Mira and Cora had an occasional delivery, and went out together at least once a week to check on pregnant women, but the whole community had a listless feel to it.

Franco's circuit work was now down to two parishes, because in the "good years" a couple new pastors had come to the area and taken over some of the outlying work.

Mira bade Franco goodbye the third Thursday in June. It had been months since he had been out, so he planned to be gone until the following

Wednesday rather than come home on Friday evening and stay until early Sunday morning, as he had done in earlier years.

With only a few patients to see, Mira devoted most of Thursday, Friday and Saturday to prayer and sermon preparation. Jems came to help water the garden and take care of Mouser, bringing Benny with him. Both animals were showing their age. Wryly, thought Mira, *so am I. And Franco. And Hiram and Nina and the twins, now almost 10 years old.*

Mira and Franco had given up on cows and chickens some years earlier, but Dapple and Grey still served them faithfully. And Jake continued to breed them and furnish hay. He promised them the next two foals. Dapple would soon deliver. Franco was out with Grey, not bred this year.

And Jems was now almost 16. It seemed like only yesterday when she and Franco had treated a frightened little boy. It truly was the beginning of a special relationship. And just recently Jems had told Franco his plans. He had almost enough money saved to go to college in the East. By East he meant Minneapolis and St. Paul. He was planning to become a pastor *just like Pastor Franco.*

Mira awakened to storm clouds on Wednesday morning. The first time in months. She rejoiced. Maybe the drought would soon be over. But then she remembered Franco and his fear of storms. *Oh God, delay the storm, or direct him to follow his own advice:* **Find shelter.**

By noon the thunder and lightning began and the wind whipped up. But the rain delayed. Would it be a rainless storm? But by 4PM the rain began. Torrents of rain. Mira had spent the afternoon writing in her journals, preparing bath water, and fixing a favorite supper for Franco. By 6 PM he still had not arrived. She tried to believe he had found shelter. By 8 PM the storm had subsided. At 9 PM she heard the laundry room door open—the door Franco used at the end of a day.

She went to greet him. But it was Hiram. "Just checking to see how Franco fared in the storm—he is home, isn't he?"

Mira shook her head. "I was hoping you were he."

"Well, not to worry. Surely he followed his own advice. He never would stay out in a storm. The moon is already breaking out. I think I'll ride down the road towards Jake, and meet him. That is the direction he would be coming from, right?"

Mira nodded her head. She did not miss the look of concern on Hiram's face, but tried to mask her own feelings. "I'll make a fresh pot of coffee. Tell him I'm keeping his supper warm on the stove."

Two hours passed and she heard the door again. Hiram. Alone. "Mira, the storm was even worse out Jake's way. He and his men are organizing a search party. They're on the road by now."

"You are really worried, aren't you?"

"I can't deny that. I must go and tell Nina, but I'll be back soon."

He was back in a half hour, Nina with him. Mable stayed with the twins.

They talked. They prayed. They were quiet. At 4AM they heard a wagon pull up to the door. It was Jake. One look at his face told the story. They had found Franco. Dead.

Jake came in, but for now he told the story only briefly. *About 10 miles beyond his homestead, far from any shelter, Jake's men found Franco's body and that of his horse. It was lightning.*

"Where is he now? I have to see him."

"I brought his body in the wagon."

Mira started to the door but Hiram put a restraining hand on her arm. "Wait. Jake and I will carry him in. Where . . .?"

"On the cot in the clinic for now. Will you . . ."

"As soon as it is daylight, I will start working on a coffin."

As the men stepped out Nina and Mira clasped each other in an embrace of sorrow. There would be so many plans to make, but all of that could wait until daylight. For now they gave expression to their feeling. A son! A husband! A brother. A friend. A pastor.

Taken in death, by a storm that brought life to the community. Oh, the irony!

Before leaving Jake assured her of his and Cora's availability to help with anything. Hiram and Nina offered to stay, but Mira declined. There were things to do that only she could do. The first was to go to her trunk of clothing that stored her wedding dress. She gently withdrew her train. The elegant, beautiful train. This she would use to line the coffin. Then she cut about an inch off one of her braids and tied it with a ribbon. She would put the little bundle of hair that Franco loved so much in the suit coat pocket— his wedding suit—that he would be buried in.

Next she did what she dreaded doing—removed his clothes and examined his body, and pronounced him dead. Seeing the damage the lightning had done she said, *Thank you God that his face and head are not marred—the rest is bad enough.* She then took a basin of the still warm bath water and gently bathed his burned and mud encrusted body.

She put a *Closed* sign on the clinic and tried to get some sleep.

Nina knocked on the door by 7 AM, and Pete shortly thereafter. Nina had stopped by Pete's house to tell him. Hiram was already working on the coffin.

Pete stayed only briefly, stating that he would ask Bessie to keep an eye on the store for the day. And he would post a sign informing the community of Pastor Franco's death, and that funeral services were pending. He would return soon to be with Mira.

Hiram came to the house at 10 AM, followed shortly by Jake and Cora. Mira was composed. *Too composed*, Nina thought. But she knew that Mira had a way of going into *clinical mode* to get through a crisis, and then later the true feelings would emerge. *Perhaps that's the best way to handle something like this where her leadership is needed.* But Nina's heart was breaking. Her oldest son was dead, and her daughter-in-law was a young widow. *That's how it goes on the frontier of Dakota Territory.*

"Mira, what can Jake and I do for you right now?"

"Father! I must tell my Father!"

"Can you write out a brief telegram? Jake and I will take it right over to the office."

"Yes. Thank you. And as soon as you come back, we must start to plan the funeral. Word must be sent out into the community."

Hiram, Nina, Pete and Mira sat quietly all thinking the same thing. *The funeral must be soon.*

"I will have the coffin ready by tonight."

"I will check with Bessie for a lining for the coffin."

"Please get something soft and satiny if you can, to use against the wood. And I will cover that with the train of my wedding dress."

"The t—"

"Yes the train of my wedding dress. And I have already washed him, and have him dressed in his wedding suit." She did not tell them about the little bundle of her hair tucked away in his pocket.

Jake and Cora returned in a few minutes. They all agreed, given the hot, and now humid weather, the funeral should be the next day—Friday. Jake and Cora would send out riders to inform the community. And they would have their cooking staff prepare and serve the meal. It went without saying that most guests would bring food also. As Jake and The General had often told Mira and Franco, *When there is a need people on the frontier know what to do. And they do it.*

Nina went home to check on the twins and Mable. She dreaded telling the children what had happened to their big, dearly loved brother. As

Hiram worked on the coffin, he said over and over *No father should ever have to do this for his son. Why?*

And Hiram was not one to question God.

Pete stayed with Mira, insisting that she eat something and rest.

"I will, but not long. I have to work on the farewell message for tomorrow."

Pete nodded, and then kept watch. People stopped by, but he did not let them in. There would be time for condolences later.

Mira awakened at 4 PM—she had slept much longer than she had intended. Pete had a sandwich and coffee ready for her.

"People stopped by. Several brought food. I told everybody who came that between now and the funeral you need time by yourself. Hiram and Nina will stop in a little later tonight."

Mira nodded her head, "Thanks Pete. Thanks for understanding."

"I'll be back early in the morning. Oh . . . I hope this is all right—I told Jems that he can stop by tomorrow morning, early. I think he really needs to see you."

"He and Franco were so close. This is going to be difficult for him. And now if you will excuse me, I must pull together some thoughts for the service tomorrow."

After Pete left, Mira secluded herself in the reading room with pen and paper. *What to say? What can be said at a time like this? It's not that I haven't done funerals. I certainly have when Franco has been on circuit. But this is different. It's Franco that we are saying farewell to. My husband. Nina and Hiram's son, and the community's pastor. Lord give me words.*

She put her pen down and listened. *Speak from the heart Mira-honey. There is no need for a sermon. Just make it a farewell. And let the Holy Spirit be your guide.*

She sat quietly for about an hour, and at least for that time, peace flooded her heart. Then she got up and fanned the coals into flame. She had not found time to bathe the night before. In fact, she had used the water to wash Franco's body. Now, while the water warmed, Hiram and Nina stopped by. The coffin was finished. Mira and Nina lined it while Hiram got Pete. Together they placed Franco's body in the coffin.

After they left Mira allowed herself to soak in the bathwater and then washed and rinsed her hair. It wasn't until she began brushing it—what Franco had done for her the past 10 years—that she noticed unevenness where she had cut her braid. Finally the tears came in earnest. *Lord, that's how my life is going to be now—uneven, unbalanced. I can't even do a simple thing like care for my hair. Where is my scissors?* Franco's comment from several years earlier popped into her mind. *Over my dead body.*

"Well, Franco," she said as she went for her scissors. But before doing what she might regret, there was a knock on the door. It was Kjell from the telegraph office. Her father had responded.

She fell asleep that night grasping the telegram in one hand, and her cross in the other.

She awakened to a rap on the door the next morning. It was Jems, red-eyed and grieving deeply. "Doctor-dear *(no one had called her that in years!)* When I ring the bell this morning, can it be one gong for each year of Pastor Franco's life?"

"Jems, you are so thoughtful. That would be a fitting honor to the life of Pastor Franco. Thank you for thinking of that."

The bell began tolling at 10 AM. As Miranda walked the short distance to the graveyard an old thought entered her mind. *But **I** am not ordained. Chipps needs an ordained pastor.*

It seemed that the whole community had gathered. The earth had been washed clean by the storm and rain. The same storm that now brought them to this graveside. The air had a pristine quality to it. Clean; fresh. The hole had been dug earlier in the day and the soil piled nearby. She was grateful for the thin veil which shaded her red, swollen eyes. She drew a deep breath.

"Friends, thank you for coming. You know how much Franco enjoyed gatherings, the bigger the better. So I say on his behalf *Thank you for coming. It is good to see each of you.* And after saying that, he would tell us of the abundance of food that we would enjoy as part of our gathering. And then he would give thanks.
'Let's do that right now—

Heavenly Father, we have gathered for a final farewell, as we have done so often in the past. This time it is for our beloved Pastor, friend and husband. (Her voice cracked slightly).
As we speak and remember, we acknowledge that everything that Franco did flowed out of a heart of love—love for you and his fellow humans.
We know that lightning was the cause of his death. It seems so strange Lord, that of all the things on the frontier that might have scared Franco, nothing really did, except lightning. He often cautioned us not to be out in lightning storms, and he himself tried to avoid them.

Yet Lord, for reasons known to only you, Franco was out in a severe storm. Lightning struck him, and you used it as a dazzling occasion to welcome him into glory.
We respect and accept your choices.
But our hearts will long remember and miss this servant of yours who humbly and gently led, and wisely guided.
In Jesus Name, AMEN"

At the *AMEN* the crowd began singing, giving her a few moments to collect herself.

She read from John 14, reminding them that Jesus is preparing a place and would come again, and that meanwhile he would not leave them comfortless.

And she spoke of The Resurrection. Her voice was strong and clear and full of conviction.

She paused briefly and then continued,

"Friends, Franco would want us to remember God's faithfulness, goodness, and love. How he is always a shelter in the time of storm—that was the topic of Franco's first sermon in Chipps—and that we have a responsibility to seek that shelter. Yet ironically, God took Franco in a storm. We might want to ask, *Franco, why didn't you seek shelter?* But he would help us see that God has taken him to the greatest shelter of all—heaven. And he would remind us of countless times when we have been sheltered by God as we have experienced life and death in our community.

"He would also encourage us to express our grief. I can't tell you how often he said to me *Have a good cry, Mira. Allow yourself to feel; you need to feel before you can heal.*

"I could tell you many stories of our life and work together—but you know them because you have been a part of them for ten years. Rather let's share stories."

And so they did for the next hour. But before anyone spoke up she continued:

"I have one story to tell that I think you have never heard—the story of our names—*Franco and Mira*. Those are not our actual names."

Heads nodded. Folks wanted to know, but had been too polite to ask. They knew him as *Pastor* or *Rev. Franco*; few knew if it was first or last.

"Franco's name is *Franklin Welken*. Somehow, as I got to know him in our courting days *Franklin* just didn't fit! It was okay in a seminary, but for the rest of life? NO! It was too formal for a man with such a sensitive and caring nature.

"*Frank*? No, that was too abrupt. It needed a second syllable to complete it."

"*Frankie*? Oh no, he would not hear of it; he had been called that as a child."

"One day without realizing what I said, I called him *Franco* and it stuck."

"It sounded regal to me. Franco seemed regal. Franco was a king; a very down to earth king, but he had quality about him that many of you saw too (*heads nodded in agreement*) that invited people to follow him and work alongside of him. But most of all, as was apparent to us all, he lived his life as a child of the King, here on the frontier that has few trappings of royalty."

"My name, *Mira*, is a shortened form of *Miranda*, thanks to my father and the people I served with him back East. I'll save that story for another occasion. I'll just say here that Franco loved it, and knew the real reason for it, though he often kidded me that it was short for *mirage*—now you see me, but look again and I'm gone."

When she finished speaking there were smiles on many faces, and the stories began.

Finally a song broke out again, a closing prayer, and the lowering of the casket.

She took a handful of dirt and gently sprinkled it over the casket, believing with all her heart that death had already been conquered for her beloved Franco. It was the portal to heaven for him, where he would spend eternity with his King, and Lord and Savior. Still, one must say the words *Dust . . . to dust . . .* Her voice broke. Someone gently led her away and the crowd broke, heading towards the rustling cottonwood trees . . .

The first Sunday after Franco's burial the congregation gathered for prayer, singing, reading of the Word, and fellowship. But nothing was expected of Mira. During the week, however, members of the church Board stopped by to see her. They apologized for coming so soon with a request, but asked her to hear them out—

"Doctor-Mira, you have often served as our pastor when Pastor Franco was on circuit. And we know that all the sermons preached here in the last 10 years were as much yours as his. Would you consider being our pastor?"

"But I am not ordained. I cannot do baptisms, weddings . . ."

"But you preach and give pastoral care. We would not expect you to do circuit work. This was Pastor Franco's last summer for that anyway."

Mira paused and then said, "I need time to think and pray about it."

"Of course. And while you think and pray, will you be willing to prepare to lead worship this coming Sunday?"

Mira smiled. That request told her that what she needed to know. *She truly was wanted. There was a place and work for her in Chipps. And not just medical. They were counting on her to move* all *the work forward seamlessly.*

"And Doctor Mira, it's time to tell you, as Pastor Franco obviously did not..."

"Tell me *what?*"

"The Board has discussed several times in the past year the possibility of ordaining you. We know that you have done most of the *schooling* and what you did not learn in seminary you have learned here in Chipps working alongside your husband. Your father is in on this too. He has talked with your sending church and they agree. They are even willing to send representatives for the occasion!"

Now Mira *was* shocked. "That my father has been working on this, I'm not surprised to hear. But are you are telling me that Franco and you-all have been working on this *behind my back?*"

"That's one way of putting it. Pastor Franco would have told you soon, but he wanted to spare you disappointment if we could not get agreement from your sending church. They readily agreed, thanks to your father, no doubt. They did say that there will be an oral *exam*. But it'll be a *mere formality.*"

"This is too much, too fast. My husband just..."

"And we are not rushing you. But no doubt you are already thinking about how to go forward from here. We just want you to know that this possibility exists, and ask you to take it into consideration. There will always be a place for you here. Just what that place looks like is for you to decide."

Mira thanked them for coming, and said that at the very least they could count on her to lead worship on Sunday.

Before doing anything else that day she sat down with pen and paper and wrote her father a lengthy letter. First about the funeral, and then her excitement about ordination. She felt her heart about to burst—with simultaneous sorrow and joy.

After posting her letter she settled herself in her reading room and spent the rest of the day writing in her journals.

At the end of the day she suddenly realized that no patients had come for two days. And then she remembered that she had not yet taken the "Closed" sign off the clinic door. When she went to retrieve it she found Jems and Benny sitting on the step.

"Jems, what are you doing here? How long have you been sitting on the step?"

"Most of yesterday and today. Doing what Pastor Franco would want me to do—watch out for you."

"Watch out for me?"

"Yes, you need time to grieve. I'm keeping patients away."

"Keeping patients away?"

"Yes. Anyway, only a few came. They didn't seem to be very sick. I told them that I thought by tomorrow you would take the sign down. And you just did."

"Thank you, Jems. And talking of grief—we can grieve together."

And they sat for an hour talking about Franco, laughing, crying. Bessie found them at about 6 PM and said *supper is ready. Would Doctor-dear join them?*

She would, indeed.

The heat and humidity continued oppressively, although there was no additional rain. On Wednesday morning Mira could hardly drag herself out of bed, but she knew she had to. Jems said that he would be on the clinic step by 8 AM to let people know that she would be seeing patients.

Perhaps a cup of tea and a piece of sourdough toast would help.

But it didn't. She couldn't keep it down.

However, as the day progressed she focused on her patients and felt somewhat better by noon. Nina and the twins surprised her and Jems by bringing over dinner. It was the first noon meal Mira had eaten in a week. Not because there was no food. There had been mountains of it, but her appetite had waned, accompanied by bouts of nausea.

By 3 PM she had seen the last patient. She thanked Jems for his help and told him that she definitely wanted him to continue to care for Mouser (Mouser still served as *mouse patrol* in the church, wound clinic and The Shack) and to keep Benny for his own. She would continue to hire him for yard and garden work, but did not expect him to help at the clinic. He had other jobs and was saving money for college.

"But Jems, you are always welcome here. Just as you were when Pastor Franco was with us. If I need you for something special, which no doubt I will, I know where to find you."

Jems seemed content with that. Maybe even a little relieved.

"Doctor-Mira, have you thought about getting another cat for *mouse patrol* in your new house and clinic?"

"Jimmy! Excuse me, *Jems*, you haven't seen a mouse here, have you?"

"No, not yet, but . . ."

"Yes, I know, what with bringing in firewood, chips, etc. I'll keep watch and let you know."

Jems left, and Mira went to the laundry room. It was time to bring in water for her bath and start it to heating. But on the stove was the copper boiler three-quarters full with a small fire beneath it.

When had Jems done that?!

As the water warmed she sat at her kitchen table. *Lord, give me ideas for my Sunday sermon. Franco and I never ran out of ideas. But now my head is blank and my heart empty. And speaking of my head, I cannot face washing my hair without Franco. I just can't. He did say* over my dead body. *If that was his condition for me cutting my hair, well he is dead now, and I'm getting my scissors. I just about did it last week. I'm doing it now.*

She got up and took her scissors from her sewing box, and with two big snips, she cut her lovely braids off at their base. Returning to her chair, she let out one long and loud wail. Just one, but it was the most honest expression of pain she had ever made in her life. It was primal. And it felt good. It felt right.

Just then she heard the laundry room door open. It was Nina. "Mira-honey, I heard your cry as I opened the door."

Mira did not answer or look at her.

In the next moment Nina saw what Mira had done. She said nothing, but just held her for the next hour. They cried together.

After they were cried out Nina said, "Mira-honey, this is the night for your bath and hair wash. I'll draw the water, and once you have bathed and washed your hair, I'll help you with it. I think there is still enough to catch up the back in a snood. Perhaps we can come up with a new hair style for the ladies of Chipps."

Nina was so kind, so gentle. While Nina prepared the bath water Mira took her braids to her bedroom, to be dealt with later.

As she bathed an idea for her Sunday sermon came to her. *Moving forward; finishing the race.* Franco's race was over. He had kept the faith, finished the course and received his crown. But the rest of them were still in the race. She challenged the congregation and herself to the same level of faithfulness and endurance that Franco had shown them. Her sermon was based on Philippians 3:12-21.

Chapter 21 *The Big Picture vs. The Big Puzzle*

A letter from her father reached Mira on Friday—his first communication since Franco's burial exactly a week earlier. Dr. Phillips told Mira that he was hopeful that by early October he could come to visit and stay several weeks. *At least I have this to look forward to and plan for. And perhaps one more thing. Morning nausea and other symptoms make me think that I might be pregnant!*

Summer plodded on for Mira. One more rain came two weeks after the storm that took Franco, and then the humidity left and it became hot and dry again. By middle July, still not feeling any better, Mira was sure of pregnancy. She kept her clinic closed until 10 AM. But somehow she managed to pull herself together for Sunday morning worship. Jems, despite his other jobs, was invaluable to Mira. And she noticed that Chuckie was beginning to shadow Jems, much as Jems had shadowed Franco.

Pete and Hiram stopped by daily, offering to help around the property in any way they could. Nina stopped by frequently, giving help and support. "Mira-honey, we're very concerned about you. You've become entirely rundown, almost listless."

"Are people talking? Do they think I'm not doing my work responsibly?"

"No one is speaking negatively. But people do ask how you are, noticing that the clinic does not open until 10 AM. Cora stopped to see me a couple days ago. She and I are both wondering . . ."

"Cora visited you, and you talked about me? What right . . .?"

"Yes, and I'm going to be forthright here, Mira-honey. We think that what we are seeing in you is more than grief." (Mira took a deep breath as Nina continued.) "We think you might be pregnant. If so . . ."

"You are right, Mother. It *is* more than grief. But I didn't know for sure that I'm pregnant until just recently. I would have soon told you and Cora."

"Did Franco know?"

"No. And now he never will. I hesitated to tell him *maybe* lest he be disappointed were it not true. But now I wonder if he would have gone on circuit had he known that I *might be pregnant*. If he hadn't gone on circuit, he would still be alive today." Mira broke down and sobbed.

Nina took her hand. "Mira-honey, that kind of thinking and blaming yourself is not helpful. *If only-s* accomplish nothing and are actually harmful."

"I know. Franco had a way of reminding me to look for God's big picture. I'm sure he would do that right now, *if only* that were possible."

"Mira-honey, you're right. In fact, I think I remember a sermon on that topic."

"True. Perhaps I should pull it out of the files. Maybe it is time for all of us to hear it again."

By the beginning of August Mira was feeling considerably better and wrote her father about her pregnancy. She eagerly watched the mail for his response. And she resumed 8 AM clinic hours.

One of those days Cora stopped by to talk.

"Doctor-Mira, for the time being I do not want you on horseback going to deliveries or house calls. I'll do the deliveries, as before. Jake is always willing to go with me at night. If the deliveries are complicated we'll try to get the patient to the clinic."

Mira protested, "Even if I do not go out for deliveries, the church is expecting me to do pastoral visits. So I have to ride."

Cora nodded and was silent for a moment and then smiled, "Listen, Doctor-Mira, what do you think of this? Why not use some of the inheritance from your mother and buy a buggy. An enclosed buggy! You'll be riding in style, and will use it for years and years for visitation and house calls, and even carry your baby in it! The congregation will love it!"

"I like that idea!" Mira said with a smile. "When Pete stops by today, I'll ask him to order one. Oh Cora! What an idea. Will Dapple be able to pull it?"

"Absolutely! Jake or one of his men will jump at the chance to train her."

Pete put in the order that afternoon, but told Mira that it would be at least two months before it would arrive.

Mira looked forward to Telegraph Sunday, and dreaded it. The General and Franco would be greatly missed. At least the community was not expecting anything more from her this year than the Sunday sermon. She spent hours updating *The Big Picture* sermon that she and Franco had written a couple years earlier.

It was a beautiful day. People came from far and wide. To accommodate the large congregation they met under the cottonwood trees. The musicians brought their instruments and started the service on a joyful note. Several people offered prayers of thanksgiving. Others prayed for God's blessing on the crops, and the other means of livelihood that continued to develop in Chipps. Some prayed specifically for Pastor-Doctor-Mira.

Mira stood behind the makeshift pulpit, hoping her voice would carry over the crowd.

"Friends, thank you for understanding that life and work is complicated for me right now. And thank you also for giving me continued opportunity to serve you. You have noticed, I know, how rundown I have become recently, and probably believe that it is because of loss and grief, and it is. But there is more to it than that."

Mira took a deep breath and continued,

"There's more to it than just the grief, although that is reason enough. Before I tell you what else is going on, I want you to know that in the recent weeks I have reviewed the sermons that Pastor Franco and I wrote and delivered in the past 10 years.

"Then I spent time reflecting on Chipps—the people who have come and gone, and how we have grown and changed. And how we have stayed the same. Thinking about all of this, I realized that the words Pastor Franco and I spoke in these 10 years continue to have meaning. And because there are so many people here now that were not here when we first came, it seems to me that with some reworking, our sermons will continue to have powerful messages for us as we move into the future. I discussed this with the Board and they endorse reusing the sermons, revising them as necessary for our present situation.

"Today's sermon is The Big Picture."

She saw some heads nod.

"Looks like some of you remember it. Pastor Franco preached it a couple years ago when we experiencing severe drought. Yet the people of Chipps and the community continued to experience God's blessing as there were opportunities to earn money by working on construction.

"What about now as we face the future without our beloved pastor? Can we see the big picture in this—or do we only see a puzzle with a missing piece? That's a question I must face, maybe more than any of you.

"I'm going to tell you something this morning. It's a topic not normally spoken of in church. But the circumstances are very unusual, and I think in fairness to myself and to you it must be publicly spoken of . . ."

She had everyone's attention now.

". . . but let's first hear the sermon . . ."

Mira spoke of the God of the big things and the God of small things, and how he takes *paint brushes*, sometimes using broad strokes and other times fine lines, sometimes smudges, sometimes clearly defined colors, but all coming together in one big picture called *Life in God's Plan*. But even in the grandest *painting or plan,* some things are missing or smudged over. Or perhaps there is something there that seems completely out of keeping with the rest of the picture. Like drought. Like sickness. Like death. Etc. Etc.

> *"Friends, without Pastor Franco here, it feels like there is something missing in the picture. I have been searching to understand how God's Big Picture can be complete without Franco in it. And maybe that is just the point. Even God's Big Picture is not yet complete.*
>
> *"And now, I'm beginning to see something emerge in the picture that has taken me totally by surprise.*
>
> *"Franco and I dearly wanted to have children. But it didn't seem to be part of the picture. Until now."*

She heard a few gasps in the congregation. She paused, and then went on.

> *"Yes, you heard me right. Franco and I are going to have a baby . . ."*

Her voice broke.

> *. . . and now I am struggling to see where Franco is in* The Big Picture. *He would have been so happy. It seems like God painted him out, or smudged him over by taking him to heaven.*
>
> *"It's not that I have lost my faith. I haven't. But for the time being, I have lost some of my understanding. Understanding these kinds of things was much easier when I was not personally affected. Frankly, sometimes* The Big Picture *seems more like* a big puzzle.
>
> *"I am so grateful that all of you are part of God's wonderful art work, and that I will be able to count on you . . ."*

At the conclusion of the service Mira was surrounded with words of encouragement, promises of support, and enough advice to last a life time. The rest of Telegraph Sunday proceeded much as previous years— potluck, games, and a drawing for sending a free telegram, to be used anytime during the year.

The next two weeks were uneventful. Mira missed not going out to make calls, but Cora's advice was wise. She asked Jems and Chuckie to move her writing desk to an empty corner in the examination room. Now she could read and write between patients. Because Jems did so much work for her this summer, she gave most of her garden produce to Bessie. Mira would buy food for the winter from the General Store. But Bessie, being Bessie, gave at least half of it back, canned.

Mira thought back to the days of the first year or two in Chipps. So hungry, without enough money to buy from the store. Yet they always had at least a little to eat. Now she was blessed with plenty.

The last day of August was unusually hot. Mira felt draggy all day. By noon she had abdominal cramping, but when she checked she was not losing blood. She saw her last patient of the day about 3 PM. Jems and Chuckie stopped by as they usually did to help her close.

"Chuckie, when you go home, will you please ask your mother to come? I need to talk to her."

Chuckie was off in a flash, but the always sensitive Jems asked, "Are you feeling poorly, Doctor-Mira? You look pale."

"Just tired I think, Jems, and a little pain."

"I'm getting my mother, too."

"No Jems. I'll be fine. Just need to talk to Mrs. Welken."

Jems did not look convinced, "I'll go now, but send someone for us if you need us. We are here to help, anytime, day or night."

While Chuckie was getting Nina, Mira checked again. Bleeding had begun. Nina found her a few minutes later, head buried in her arms, sitting at the kitchen table.

"Mira-honey . . ."

"I'm losing the baby," Mira said with a sob.

"You don't know that."

"Oh, but I do."

"Let's get you to bed. Then I'll send Hiram for Cora. Do you want to go to your bedroom, or to the clinic?"

"Let's go to the first room adjacent to the clinic. We seldom have overnight patients."

Nina got her situated and then told her not to get up.

"I'll tell Hiram now, and then stop by to tell Pete as well."

Mira nodded her head.

Hiram was on the road within minutes. And Pete came immediately, Bessie with him. She was in the store when Nina told Pete.

They both wanted to *do* something, but there was nothing to do at this point, except pray. And they did. Then Bessie went to heat water. This would not be a viable baby, but if Mira miscarried she and Cora would insist on cleanliness, nevertheless.

Cora, Jake, and Hiram were there within the hour. The men discreetly left the room. "Doctor-dear (the old affectionate name came so easily) I'm going to wash my hands, and then examine you. Nina, will you please light several lanterns and place them near the foot of the bed?"

Bessie met her at the door with a basin of warm water.

Cora smiled her thanks.

There is plenty more in the kitchen. Bessie mouthed the words.

"Doctor-dear, you are bleeding to be sure, but not heavily. How is the cramping?"

Mira was about to answer but before she could, another cramp, the strongest yet, gripped her,

After the cramp had passed she said, "That was your answer."

Nina wiped Mira's sweaty brow. "Don't give up hope, Mira-honey."

"I can't give up what I don't have. I don't think God ever wanted me to have a baby. Why did I have to get pregnant, only to have Franco die, and now I'm losing my baby, too? There definitely is something missing in God's Big Picture. God's Big Puzzle. It'll have two pieces missing."

Nina, Cora, Bessie could have said many things but wisely chose to say nothing. Mira would go through a hard time, but she would rebound. They would support and love her in every way possible. The whole community would.

Mira dosed off following light sedation that she allowed herself, but her sleep was restless. After a couple hours she was awakened by a very strong contraction—more than just a cramp.

"Cora—now!"

Bessie ran to get the water. Minutes later Mira delivered her baby—a 3 ½ month fetus. It was just beginning to show recognizable human features.

Mira was quiet for several moments while Cora attended her.

Her first words were, "We will bury my baby next to *its* father."

"I'll call Hiram."

Mira nodded and then asked Cora to let her hold the baby, now gently shrouded in a white towel. Mira did not try to examine it or touch it. She had seen enough aborted babies in her career to know what she would see. She just held it without showing any obvious emotion.

Hiram took her hand. "We must have the funeral tomorrow. Will you please make a little coffin, and once you have it made please line it with rabbit skins."

"I will make the coffin tonight. But rabbit skins? I don't think I can get rabbit skins by tomorrow."

"You can. In *The Shack* lean-to. You will find a box with many cured rabbit skins. Franco was saving them for our first baby—to make a blanket for the crib."

Hiram was speechless. He just nodded his agreement.

She turned to Nina. "Please go to my bedroom where I have a trunk. My wedding dress is in it. Take the veil. I want to wrap it around this towel. My braids are also in the trunk. I want to bury them as well."

By morning active bleeding had nearly stopped and Cora let Mira get up and prepare herself for the burial. Only immediate family, Mable, Jems and Bessie attended. Jems asked if he could lead the prayer and read Scripture. He chose the passage of Jesus blessing the children. And as he read Mira could visualize her baby, formed and beautiful, safe in the arms of Jesus.

Healing had begun, and Mira would rebound.

In the afternoon she telegraphed her father, and followed it with a lengthy letter.

That evening she had supper with Nina and Hiram. After the twins went to bed Mira knew the time had come for her to do yet another difficult thing. While pregnant she thought maybe she would never have to do it. But now all hope of passing the cross on to Franco's heir was gone.

Clutching her cross in her hand, still on the chain around her neck, she turned to Hiram and Nina. "The time has come to give the cross back to its rightful owners—now that Franco will never have an heir. I know you will want Chuckie to give it to his bride someday. It is only right that he does."

She caught them completely off guard. Getting the cross back from Mira had not entered their mind.

"Oh, no, Mira-honey. That cross is for you to wear until the night before Chuckie gets married—hopefully not for a long time."

"Do you mean it? I can continue to wear it until Chuckie marries?"

Hiram responded, "Of course. We want to you wear it. The cross belongs to no *one person*. It is a family heirloom, meant to be passed on to, and worn by the right person at the right time. That person is you for the time being."

"Oh, thank you. You can't imagine how difficult it would be to give it up now. But I felt I had to offer."

"There is something we would like you to do." Nina was speaking.

"Yes?"

"Sometime in the next year when the time feels right, we would like you to tell Chuckie about the cross—how you received it from Franco; how it was supposed to go to Franco's oldest son, if he had one. And that now, he, Chuckie, is next in line to give it to his bride the night before his marriage. After you do that, we ourselves will tell Chuckie more of the history."

They sat in silence for several minutes. Finally Mira rose to go back to her lonely house. Fortunately she had not yet begun to make and collect baby clothes. The first thing she had planned to do was to give the rabbit skins to Bessie to make blankets and hoods.

At Cora's insistence Mira closed the clinic for the rest of the week. Jems and Chuckie watched for patients, and explained that she was ill and needed to rest. She spent most of her days reading, writing, and in sermon revision. But Sunday found her back on the pulpit again. Word of her most recent loss had already made its way through the community. Mira needed the congregation as much as they needed her.

Chapter 22 *A Dream Come True*

Charles replied to Mira's telegram. He would do his best to rearrange his work and arrive in Chipps the second week in September— two or three weeks earlier than first planned. And he would stay through October, hoping to head back to Philadelphia before winter hit the prairie.

Mira prepared the second room from the clinic for him. She checked with Pete in hopes of getting the buggy sooner. She was uncomfortable with her father going on calls by horseback on the prairie. But there was nothing Pete could do to hasten the order. The first week of October would be the earliest for the arrival of the buggy and then Dapple would have to be harness trained.

Father and daughter spent hours and hours talking of things past, present, and future. Though rushed, Charles had found time to pack medical supplies and his most recent medical journals. During the weeks of his visit Mira resumed making combined medical-pastoral calls by horseback while Charles tended the clinic.

One night they were awakened by a banging on the door. It was Jake. He and Cora brought a patient in their buggy. She had been in labor for 24 hours. Cora shook her head as she looked at Mira, and whispered, *I think it is too late for the baby. I can't hear a heartbeat. And she is making no progress with the delivery.*

Dr. Phillips and Mira both listened for a heartbeat but heard none, and then did a more complete exam. While Cora stayed with the young woman (Jake was in the kitchen with the husband) Mira and Dr. Phillips stepped out of the room to confer.

"I suspect that the baby died hours ago. The mother is so young, hardly yet mature herself. Her pelvis is too small. There is no way she can deliver this baby. I'll have to take it."

"From below?"

"Yes, *and I don't want you there.* Cora can help."

"No, I must learn. This is the first time in 10 years that this has been necessary but it will happen again. If I do not learn the procedure from you, in the future it will not be only the baby that dies. I know it will be gruesome, but at least we can use chloroform for the mother. Cora can administer it."

Charles did not argue, but went to talk to the father while Mira and Cora prepared the patient. Jake took the father to the lumberyard and together they made a small coffin. Even though it was the middle of the night Jake stopped by Bessie and asked for a couple rabbit skins.

The patient survived, and was able to return home after about a week of bed rest.

But Mira was shaken. Not that she hadn't had patients die—even babies and children. But her own experience of having been pregnant and then miscarrying now made losing a baby *personal*.

The buggy arrived by train on schedule, the first week of October. Jake was able to train Dapple to safely pull it in just a few days. Then Mira began making her first calls by buggy, delighting in the feeling of luxury. But then she would remember Cora's words to her before her miscarriage—*you will be able to carry your baby in it*—and sadness would steal over her again.

Dr. Phillips was a hit at the clinic. He joked with Mira one evening, "I think all the men in Chipps and surrounding area have saved up their illnesses and problems for years. I have treated more back, knee, and shoulder problems, and prostate, than you can imagine. But frankly, most men here are in basic good health. Hard work and outdoors are good for the constitution."

"I'm glad they are coming to you. Many used to confide in Franco, and he would consult with me. But I'm sure they will benefit from hands-on-care with an older man. And I have noticed that even in the few weeks you have been here our income has almost doubled. How do you do it?"

"I not only charge for a procedure, I also charge for giving advice! And some of the things they ask me they probably would not ask you."

"Father, as you can see, I really do need you here. Chipps needs you. There are many doctors in Philadelphia. I'm the only one here—and I am not really a doctor."

"Don't sell yourself short, Mira. I hear nothing but good about you. And you are carrying a double load. *But when can I come to stay?* As you know, our house is already disposed of, and our cook and gardener well taken care of."

Mira nodded, "So . . ."

"And as you point out, there are many doctors in Philadelphia. Still, I have lived there all my life, and it will take a while to disassociate myself from all my responsibilities. I'm on several boards and committees, and involved in church work. Speaking of which, in my last conversation with the church board, they suggest ordination for you next summer."

"Next summer!"

"Yes. I was thinking maybe on that special day you Chipps people call *Telegraph Sunday* . . ."

Their conversation went late into the evening, tentatively deciding on *Telegraph Sunday* as the day for Mira's ordination. Charles would leave Philadelphia the end of March, and spend about a month working with Dr. McCloud en route to Chipps. He wanted to arrive in Chipps early May to begin gardening with hopes of growing plants that he could use for pharmaceuticals. Especially he wanted to grow poppies, hoping to make his own Laudanum. Mira was skeptical of this, not sure that the poppies he would grow were the right kind, but for now, she kept it to herself.

By the end of Dr. Phillips' six week visit Mira felt ready to assume all the work again, and sharing the prenatal work and deliveries with Cora as they had done for many years. The medical work tapered off as it usually did when the colder months set in. But Mira attributed some of the decline to the many men who had consulted with her father. She was sure they would wait with whatever they could until he returned!

Before leaving they reviewed patient records together—particularly those who would need ongoing care. Mable was one of them.

"Mira, I'm really concerned about her. Her blood pressure is high, but there is so little we can do. I told her to limit salt and stress. And she should not be working everyday all day at the store—I told Pete this also. She can spend some time there each day. Mainly serving coffee and visiting."

"What can I do?"

"Just reinforce what I have told her. I did tell Hiram and Nina, too. They will do what they can to get her to take it easy. But you know, Mira—*coming home to pasture, or keep on working and die in the saddle. I know what I plan to do.*"

Mira sighed. "I'll keep an eye on her, for all the good it will do."

"A couple more things. Have you noticed that Prissy has been stopping at the clinic after school? I put her to work cleaning instruments, etc. She has asked for *medical things* to read. I'm aware of her age, but some of the medical books are appropriate for her to page through—there are some excellent anatomical drawings."

"But . . ."

"Before you protest, you were only 10 when you started looking at my books. Not much later you were seeing patients with me. Not much later you were assisting with deliveries. And then before long you were doing deliveries on your own."

Mira smiled. "How did mother allow it?"

"We almost never argued. I know she did not like it, but she left it alone. I'm glad she did."

"I think you should tell Hiram and Nina."

"I did, and they are alright with it. They said they trusted my judgment. After all, look how you turned out! And they trust your judgment, too. I think you should encourage her to work with you after school. She'll catch on quickly to everything. Who knows? It might be the making of a great surgeon."

Chuck also became a great help to Mira as he learned from Jems. In fact, little by little Jems turned his responsibilities over to Chuck, first the care of Mouser, then ringing the church bell, then drawing water daily for the clinic, and by the spring of 1884 care of Dapple and the buggy.

"And most of all, Chuck, when I leave for school in the East you must keep an eye on Dr. Mira and the clinic and do any *odd job* she might want you to do. That's what I do, because that's what Pastor Franco would want me to do. And because I love her. I know you do too. Neither of us can take Pastor Franco's place—not even you, his brother—but we can do our best."

Chuck solemnly agreed to this grave responsibility. He would do anything Jems asked him to do. And he would do it for Mira and Franco's sake.

Mira frequently had supper with the Welkens. It was a good opportunity to check on Mable. Mable thought all the fuss unnecessary. *Sure, I'm slowing down a little, but who doesn't at my age?*

But early one morning in December Mira awakened to a knock on her door.

Not a delivery, I hope.

It wasn't. It was Hiram. "Mira, we awakened to a thud. Mable fell. We got to her within seconds, but we could detect no sign of life. Can you come?"

"I'll be ready in a minute."

From what they could piece together, looking at the rumpled sheets and blankets, Mable had a restless night, and when she tried to get up she fell, hitting her head. There was no sign of movement once she went down.

"Probably heart attack or stroke, but we will never know."

Mable's funeral was held on the following Sunday as part of the morning worship service. Expecting a large community turnout Mira asked to use the Town Hall. Following the burial, the community gathered for a potluck. Many spoke of the huge impact that The General and Mable had on the community and on individuals.

Several days later the town's lawyer called on Mira. The portion of The General and Mable's wealth that Mable had retained after The General's death had been designated for Franco and Mira upon Mable's death. *Even posthumously The General is trying to right an old wrong. And once again I'm a wealthy woman! Not that I ultimately put my trust in money and things, but it's nice to not concern myself with making ends meet. And I can be generous with my patients.*

That winter Bessie and Jems spent many evenings with Mira. Bessie would bring hand sewing and listen as Mira and Jems discussed theology. Bessie often injected insights into the conversation. Jems asked to borrow some of Mira's books, wanting to prepare himself for school the following year. He learned so well, and with such eagerness, Mira was sure that he would finish school in three years instead of four.

She asked the Church Board for permission for him to begin to participate in the liturgical parts of the worship service. Jems welcomed the privilege when permission was granted.

Pete and his family came over at least once a week. One evening they surprised her with hand cranked ice cream made in Pete's new freezer. Mira had forgotten how good homemade ice cream was. "Pete, I think you have hit on something here. Why not sell it by the dish in the restaurant? You could even make it in the summer if there is enough ice in the ice house."

The community readily embraced the ice cream, and there were days when one freezer-full was not enough. Soon Pete ordered more freezers and was making flavored ice cream. Several little boys in the community earned coins and a dish of ice cream for cranking.

Despite several storms, which slowed Mira's work considerably, by March winter seemed to be over, and Mira began counting the weeks, and then days until her father's arrival.

Hiram and Nina offered to have him live with them, but Mira wanted him to live with her, at least initially. Since the second *patient room* was seldom used Charles would stay there. If later he wanted to move, arrangements could be made.

Late April Jems and Chuckie dug up additional garden space, and fertilized the soil. If this plot were not large enough for everything he wanted to plant, Nina offered space as well. Both Jems and Chuckie looked forward to gardening with Dr. Phillips. They had already discussed it with him the previous fall. He had promised to bring seeds of all kinds.

The platform was filled with people anticipating Dr. Phillips' arrival. Mira chuckled to herself, *looks like the men of Chipps saved up their problems all winter!*

Once again, Charles brought crates of supplies, including all his office equipment and instruments. He settled in quickly and soon was seeing patients, giving Mira more time for her maternity work—it was time she and Cora update their teaching protocols. And her hygiene and Bible class curricula needed revising. Then there were weekly sermons. She found that revising sermons was almost as much work as writing new ones. Many days found her out with her buggy by 7:30 AM. When possible she reserved her afternoons for writing, and studying for her "oral exam" which would take place the Friday before Telegraph Sunday—the day for her ordination.

But as the anniversary of Franco's death approached Mira began to withdraw and had to push herself to do her work. The loss of Franco, followed so shortly by her miscarriage was still raw. To her great relief, the Telegraph Sunday Committee freed her from doing any of the planning for the day except the worship/ordination service itself. Charles said that the delegates from the Philadelphia church would arrive on Thursday and wanted to meet with the local Board that same evening. A pastor was one of the delegates and he would preach.

By early August Mira had regained her strength. And she marveled at her father's energy, carrying the bulk of the medical work, gardening, and in the evenings he questioned her on theology, touching on areas he was sure would be part of the exam.

But he did admit to Mira that he was having some arthritic stiffness and pain. *Related to his outdoor work*, he claimed.

"Are you taking anything for it?"

"Well, you may have noticed that I've been soaking in a tub of hot water every evening, even in this terrible heat. And I brew myself willow bark tea. Oh, and occasionally, when it is really bad I use a little Laudanum."

"That we will have to discuss."

Charles smiled. It was the same thing he would have said in a reverse situation.

Charles, Mira, and many of the town's people welcomed the delegates as they stepped off the train. They were shown their rooms in the boarding house, and treated to a wonderful supper, prepared with the best the prairie and local gardens had to offer. They were well impressed when they heard a report from The Church Board on Thursday evening which highlighted the outstanding work of Pastor Franco and Doctor-Mira in the past 11 years.

The oral exam, conducted Friday morning, was open to attendance by all church members. The questioning dealt with theological and Biblical knowledge and pastoral care. Mira did them all proud, and no one beamed brighter than Jems, thinking back to the hours of theological discussion he and Doctor-Mira had engaged in. No doubt, also thinking of the time in the future when he would be the one examined.

Mira opened the Sunday service as she usually did. And as they usually did, many members brought their musical instruments. The guest pastor preached on Isaiah 6, considering what *being sent* meant to Isaiah, what it means to New Testament believers, and how Franco and Mira had been willing *to be sent*. He also spoke of the significance of *laying on* of hands, and invited the Church Board, the delegates, and all who played a role in Pastor Mira's faith formation and ongoing *practical education*. Jems was the first to step forward, as did Bessie, followed by Jake and Cora, Hiram and Nina, and Charles. The delegates and Church Board completed the circle around her.

At the close of the service for the first time Rev. Mira raised her hands in blessing. It was a moment like no other.

As the years went by Mira recognized that the two most significant and sacred events in her life—and she could not put one ahead of the other—were her marriage to Franco, and her ordination as pastor of Word and Sacrament. Even when men came to call, some with the obvious intent of marriage, she dismissed them quickly. No future relationship would come close to what she already had. She was as content as anyone this side of heaven could be.

Chapter *23 The Busy-ness of Being Alive*

After the garden work was done that fall, the fall of 1884, Charles' arthritic pains lessened. However, he continued hot soaks in the tub and drinking willow bark tea, and told Mira that he had stopped taking Laudanum. Nevertheless, she kept an eye on the supply.

Bessie put up all the garden produce that was not eaten fresh, keeping some for herself, giving the rest to Mira and Charles.

When the weather took a major change toward the cold, Bessie closed her shop by 4 PM and came to Mira's spacious kitchen and made supper for them all.

The evenings were spent with chairs pulled up near the pot-bellied stove, Bessie doing her hand sewing, Charles reading medical journals, or discussing theology with Mira and Jems. Jems continued to have an active role in the Sunday service

As the winter progressed Mira noticed that Charles and Bessie were often engaged in their own conversation, and Mira began to think that a romance was developing.

But many evenings they all went to Nina and Hiram who still missed Mable, and of course, Franco. Bessie saw it as a good opportunity for Jems to still be *a boy*, as he played with Chuck and Prissy. She sometimes worried that he spent too much time in the adult world, and not enough time just having fun. Jems told himself that playing with the twins was what Franco would want him to do. He also noticed that Prissy was turning into a lovely young girl—*but still very young.*

As community leaders, they spent the evenings discussing how they could best serve the people, especially how they could help parents prepare their sons and daughters to be outstanding citizens.

Charles and Nina made extensive plans for a community garden in 1885. It would be similar to what Nina was already doing, but much bigger and Charles would include *the science of growing plants and eating right for good nutrition.* The *eating right* would be a reinforcement of what Mira was already teaching in her hygiene classes, but Charles' classes would all be outdoors during the gardening season.

With the increase in the town's population school rarely closed in the winter anymore. Charles easily convinced the school board to approve all the plans that were developed at the Welken's dining room table. After all, the *non-classroom* teaching would all be gratuitous.

Bessie began teaching sewing in her seamstress shop and she and Nina held classes on the basics of food preparation, including canning and drying. They used Nina's large *summer kitchen* which had cook stoves.

During the school year of 1884-1885, under Mira's supervision, Jems taught Bible to the children through 8th grade. They helped children write plays based on Bible stories and held *theatres* for the community. (This lived on long into the future, with the school and community putting on many plays in the Town Hall.)

Hiram offered basics of carpentry for the boys in the lumberyard. City leaders—Pete, the banker, the lawyer, the sheriff, and librarian—held classes on their specific specialty, and the children rotated through the *specialties* (including the Clinic) to get a *feel* for what the work was like.

Everyone donated their time, but it was time well spent, for not only *the children* benefitted. Most saw an increase in business from grateful parents of happy children. Never had there been so much enthusiasm among the school children as there was that winter and the years that followed. The variety of teachers with classes in various settings, using hands-on-learning was the key.

Jems had far exceeded what 8th grade education offered so Charles spent countless hours that winter tutoring him on a variety of academics, ensuring his entrance into advanced formal education in Minneapolis when the time for application came.

Although the medical work tapered off in the winter months as it usually did it was a busy winter for everyone. Enough to elicit a comment from Hiram, "Charles, is life always this busy when you are near?"

Charles just laughed, but Mira nodded her head, remembering the whirlwind that she had often felt as she was growing up. *No one could accomplish more than her father, or get more people engaged in activities.*

The children worked especially hard the summer of 1885 knowing they could take fresh produce home. Also, the girls took home what they canned and the boys sold excess produce in Pete's store, the proceeds going for new books for their school. It was a dry year, but Jake, who for years had been devising ways of irrigation for his ranch helped them with a system of bringing up well water and channeling it to the garden. No one was more excited than Charles when the first water reached the garden.

Jems left for school the fall of 1885. His leaving created a big hole not only in Bessie's heart. Chipps itself seemed different without this young man who had a way of endearing himself to all he met.

The school year 1885-1886 in Chipps went much like the previous year, only now they could *continue* the programs that had been newly started the previous winter. But Mira sorely missed Jems in the school and the evenings they had spent discussing theology and planning worship services. She saw much of Franco's good training and example come alive in Jems.

Without Jems, Chuck was like a lost puppy, moping around for weeks. He did all the work Jems had outlined for him in helping Mira, but he obviously was lonely. Finally Mira wrote Jems and asked him to write Chuck. He did. Chuck did not share the letter with the others, but after receiving it he began to pep up and count the days until Jems would come home for Christmas.

As for Jems, per his frequent letters to Bessie and Mira, he loved school and Minneapolis, but greatly missed Chipps.

Bessie continued to come several evenings a week to fix supper and visit with Mira and Charles. Before long she and Charles were deeply engaged in helping Mira prepare for Sunday worship.

Suspecting that a romance was developing between Charles and Bessie, Mira would, as the evenings wore on, excuse herself, saying she had writing to do.

After several months they confided in Mira. *Yes, they had a romantic interest in each other. But they also had a big problem. Bessie did not know for sure if her husband was dead, or if he had headed West, never to return.* They had talked to the town lawyer who said that he would research to see what the law said about such uncertainties.

"Mira, what do you think? Would you be willing to marry us, *if the law calls it desertion*, or after a search (that I am financing) the *law declares him dead*? More than 10 years has passed."

"If the law declares him dead, I would be willing to perform the marriage ceremony. But I can't help but think of Pete—for all the years he was missing, and then suddenly shows up."

"I know. I've thought of that too."

"How long would the search take?"

"The lawyer says at least a year."

"Which brings us to about Christmas of 1886. Jems would be home!"

"How public are you going to be about the search, and your interest in each other during the year?"

"I'm going to write to Jems tomorrow—we wanted to tell you first."

"And after Jems receives his letter, and responds, we see no reason to keep it private."

"Good ideas. It may surprise you, but I think most people suspect your interest in each other."

"It's been that obvious?"

"I think so. And folks will be delighted to know for sure."

"And you, Mira?"

"The two of you make a wonderful match. I'm happy for you!"

And so was Jems.

Jems had a two week break for Christmas and New Year. He did as he promised Chuck—spent lots of time at the Welken home with Chuck, but to Chuck's chagrin, Jems included Prissy in their activities—sledding, playing games, etc. Finally Chuck told Jems that they needed *man time* together *without* Prissy.

The Welken's home became a festive *open house* those two weeks for Miranda, Charles, Bessie, and Jems. In fact, it seemed all of the town and community stopped by at one time or another. Charles and Mira also noticed an increase in the clinic work as people came to town to shop or have hot chocolate and cookies.

Preparing the soil for gardening began early May, and by middle May peas were planted. Charles and Nina sent word to the parents of all school age children that their children were expected to come and plant the last Saturday of May, and following that there would be a regular schedule of garden work and outdoor classes for the rest of the growing season. Bessie's cooking, canning, and drying classes would continue throughout the summer, as would Hiram's carpentry classes.

When Jems came home for summer vacation the Church Board gave Mira permission to turn over much of Sunday morning responsibilities to him. He was allowed to preach under supervision. And as they had done in the past, they spent many evenings planning Sunday services.

Mira used her days to make pastoral/medical calls. Weather permitting, she saddled Dapple, took her bag, gun, and Bible and went on horseback. By horseback she could go places not easily reached by buggy.

She loved those days and was often gone long hours. But she also noticed something of concern—an unusual number of dead skunks, raccoons, coyotes, even an occasional wolf or fox lying in the fields or path.

Occasionally she spotted one walking about in daylight. They seemed to have no fear of human or horse.

Thinking this rather strange, she stopped by Jake and Cora to consult with them.

"Doctor-Mira, steer clear of these animals, dead or alive. I've ordered my men to shoot any they see, and to bury or burn them, and not to touch any. To use pitchfork and spade. Do you carry your pistol with you?"

Mira nodded her head.

"Do not deliberately go within shooting distance, but if accidently you get up close enough to shoot, shoot it dead. Don't bury it yourself. Let me know. My men will do that."

"So you are thinking . . ."

"*Mad*. We actually shot one of our dogs. It was in a fight with a raccoon. We take no chances with rabid animals, or even ones we suspect might be rabid."

Mira felt herself go weak and pale. Rabies was not something she or Charles were prepared for.

"Thanks for the information. I'll do as you say and also tell my father. I'm sure he will say that we must educate everyone on the dangers of rabies and how to protect ourselves from bites."

"That will help. Meanwhile my men will hunt our whole ranch and shoot anything that looks suspicious. We'll tell our neighbors to do the same."

Charles was very concerned. "In town there is little we can do except to tell people *to not let their* dogs *run free*—but I doubt that many will comply—at least not until there is a case. I'll talk to the sheriff. He can post notices and enforce keeping dogs under supervision."

"Have you ever seen or treated rabies?"

"No. And it's one disease I do not want to see. Ever. I have, however, recently learned of a scientist in France who is working on a vaccine to give to someone who has been bitten. Tomorrow I will wire my colleagues in the east and ask them to get their hands on the latest information and forward it to me. But you know, Mira, *while it is important to be as ready as possible, always, we must not be alarmists, borrowing trouble that has not yet happened. If we do, we will not fully live today.*"

Those were brave words, they both knew. Yet good words to live by.

Mira continued her country-calls, but keeping a lookout for rabid animals took much of the joy from her rides. Even Dapple seemed skittish.

Meanwhile Charles and Bessie began to plan a Christmas-time wedding. The lawyer had told them that now, well into the search, no one resembling Bessie's husband had been found. If he did not surface by December he would have him declared dead and they would be free to marry.

In mid-July Charles heard back from his colleagues. They confirmed that the French scientist, Pasteur, was working on a vaccine to use in the prevention and treatment of rabies, but it was not yet available for use.

Both Mira and Charles felt a pall hanging over Chipps and the community.

What could they do short of preemptively shooting every dog and wild animal? Although the sheriff engaged in *dog patrol*, Charles often saw loose dogs when he walked Bessie home in the evening. He felt it was only a matter of time before he would get his first patient.

When Jems returned to school early September he seemed anxious about leaving, but said nothing other than *he would miss them all.*

One morning about 10 days after Jems left, Mira awakened to Charles yelling, "Mira, get your pistol, there is a mad dog snarling right outside our hall windows."

In seconds Mira was out of bed and in the hall, pistol in hand.

"I'll open the window just enough for you to take aim."

In the early dawn light as she squeezed the trigger, Mira saw that it was Benny, Franco's and Jems' dog. Mira remembered Jems sadness in leaving. *Did he know something he was not telling?*

The dog went down, but did not die with the first shot. Charles went out to finish the job and as he did he saw Bessie coming towards him.

"Stay back, Bessie. No further. Benny has rabies."

Bessie stayed back as Charles fired the second shot. Then she approached and said, "I know, and he just bit me."

"No, Bessie!"

"Yes, on my leg."

"Come to the wound clinic. We'll cleanse it thoroughly."

As Mira, Charles and Bessie went to the clinic the sheriff arrived. He had heard the gunshots. Mira gave him the details. With a pitchfork he carried Benny to the brush, there to burn him. The sheriff quickly began to spread word in Chipps. The General Store, as usual, was the center for communication.

It was a deep, ugly bite.

"Bessie, we do not sew dog bites—just clean them thoroughly, and let them heal from bottom up. You'll have an ugly scar."

"I don't care about the scar. But I *will die*, won't I? Just when I've been finding happiness."

"Yes, Bessie, in all likelihood, you will die. And I will be with you to the end." Charles wrapped his arms around her and held her for a few moments. Charles, too, had been finding happiness.

"Now Bessie, we must get on with this. It is going to be painful, because in order to clean out the saliva, I must cut deeply through all the puncture wounds."

Bessie nodded her head. "I'm ready."

Mira handed Charles the scalpel and he swiftly made deep incisions through each puncture wound. Then while Charles supported Bessie, Mira irrigated each wound with copious amounts of water and then a disinfectant. Finally she applied pressure. When the bleeding stopped she packed and wrapped the wounds.

Nothing in Charles' practice—not even amputating legs without anesthesia in the war—had demanded so much from him as doing what he had just done to the woman he loved. But Bessie did not so much as scream.

When Mira finished the dressing, finally with tears in her eyes, Bessie looked up at Charles and said, "We must notify Jems. He will want to come home, and I want him here."

"I'll wire him after we get you home."

It was not far, but Hiram was waiting outside with his buggy. He lifted her in.

Once home and settled in a chair, Charles at her side, Bessie asked, "Charles, how long do I have?"

"Since your wound is on your lower leg, it is likely that it will be several weeks—perhaps even several months—before the infection reaches your brain. Until that time, you will be feeling normal. When it reaches your brain, you will feel restless, probably get a headache and high fever, and likely also have spasms and pain, especially in your neck. We will do whatever we can to keep you comfortable."

Charles spared her the worst details, and at least for the present she asked no more questions.

Later that day Charles and Mira asked Bessie more about Benny's behavior in recent days. The sheriff was present for the conversation.

"Last night was the first I noticed that Benny did not seem himself. I figured that he was missing Jems. I put him in the porch, as we usually do, but he did not want to eat or drink. During the night I heard him pacing. When I went to feed him in the morning—that would be this morning—he snarled at me. I tried to ease myself around him so I could get out the door and call you. As I opened the door I felt his teeth sink into my leg. I fell against the door and it opened widely. He escaped and went to your place. I followed because now I really needed help. Just that soon I heard the first gunshot, then Charles yelling at me to stay back, and the second gunshot. And you know the rest."

"Well, not all of it." The sheriff was speaking. "Do you have any idea how he got rabies? You and Jems, of anybody in town, have so conscientiously kept your dog inside."

"It's true, we have. Jems would have told me if Benny had been out unsupervised."

"I'm sure he would have," agreed Charles. But Mira was not so sure, though she did not say so.

Jems' school was cooperative, telling him to take as much time as he needed. If he studied under Mira's supervision, he could write his exams when he returned in January.

In all the years that Mira had known Jems she had never seen him anything but joyful. Now, even when Bessie had no symptoms, he was despondent. Charles noted this too, as did Bessie. Even spending time with Chuck and Prissy didn't help.

Charles asked Mira, "What do you suppose is going on? I thought having him home would be helpful to Bessie. I'm not so sure it is."

"I have an idea what it might be, but I'm not going to say anything—yet. But if, after a while he does not open up on his own, I will do some probing."

Charles said no more, trusting Mira.

Several weeks went by and Bessie developed no symptoms. Her leg wound required daily dressing changes. Charles remained vigilant, spending most of his free time with her, but by early November with still no symptoms he allowed himself to hope. *Maybe Benny hadn't had rabies after all. Or maybe Mira had cleaned the wounds so well that all the infected saliva was washed out. But if so, it would be the first time ever,* he admitted to himself.

Jems continued to carry his heavy burden—whatever it was—but gradually, as Bessie developed no symptoms he became more interactive, especially with Chuck and Prissy. And he faithfully prepared his assignments and discussed them with Mira. When he did not show his usual enthusiasm for taking part in the worship service everyone understood. *His mother was dying.*

On Thanksgiving Day Bessie got up with a headache—she had been restless all night. When Charles stopped by to take her to the worship service Jems met Charles at the door and told him.

Charles stepped inside. Bessie was in her usual chair. He went to her side, took her hand—it felt warm—and motioned Jems to come near. "This is what we all knew would likely happen, even though we were hoping and praying it might be otherwise. Now it's time to put into action the plans that we have carefully made. Jems, I'm going to go and talk to Mira and get supplies and my personal effects and be back in about an hour. During that time pack your things, books and everything that you'll need for staying at the clinic. Bessie and Jems, this is your time to say goodbye to each other. Remember, we've already talked about no close contact. We cannot take any chances on transmitting the illness. There is still so much we do not know once the symptoms set in, as they now have."

Charles was back in an hour, having reviewed with Mira what they had mutually decided earlier. "Just pray, Mira, that her time will come quickly. You can tell the people at church that her symptoms set in overnight. You can say *headache and fever*, but no more than that. We must not hold out false hope. Pray with the people that her transition from time to eternity will be peaceful and soon. *And absolutely no visitors."*

Charles was not given to much emotion, but he took his daughter and held her closely for several minutes. She could feel him trembling.

"We must be strong, Mira, for Bessie, Jems, the whole community. And even for ourselves. When you come with supplies, knock and I'll meet you at the door. I will burn all her bedding etc. as it becomes soiled. Be sure to keep delivering a supply of sheets, and if you have old worn ones, I'll use them for cooling rags. I have a good supply of willow bark tea and some pain relievers, but once the spasms set in, she will have no oral intake. Remind Jems to keep a steady supply of water coming."

After Charles left, Mira went to the worship service and Thanksgiving dinner. She hoped that Jems would soon come. She didn't want him to be alone. *Lord, of all days, why Thanksgiving Day? But I will do as instructed—tell the people, and together we'll pray for Bessie's peace. And for father. And Jems.*

Mira knocked on Bessie's door after the dinner, bringing food. Bessie was in bed, severe headache, restless, feverish, but still lucid.

"Father, what are you going to do if you need help during the night? How can you call me?"

"Remember our plan, Mira—the sheriff or his deputy will stop by every couple of hours after dark. They will keep you updated, and if I need something during the night that I have not thought of, you can pack it and they can deliver it. Were they at church this morning?"

"Yes, but I didn't talk to them."

"It might be good to stop by and remind the sheriff. Have you seen Jems?"

"He didn't come to church or the dinner. I saved some food for him and hope to spend time with him this afternoon, if he will allow me. And I'll remind him to bring water. I'll stop by again about 6 PM."

Jems was waiting for Mira when she returned.

"Pastor Mira, I do not understand why Dr. Phillips will not let me help with mother."

"Jems, this is all new territory for us, too. We know so little about this disease. But we know that it is transmitted from saliva to wounds; even to open areas on the skin. *But we do not know for sure if there are other means of transmission.* For example, if the patient sneezes or coughs and droplets fall on someone's hands or face—what then? Could it be transmitted? We don't know."

"But what about your father?"

"As a doctor, and someone who loves your mother, that is the chance he is willing to take."

"But Pastor Mira . . ."

The conversation went on for a long time. But Jems did not open up about what was bothering him in the depth of his soul.

Finally Mira reminded him to bring water. It was time for her to check in, too. Charles met them at the door, but would not let them in. He said that he was unable to keep her fever under control.

About midnight the sheriff rapped on Mira's door with an update. "Dr. Charles says to tell you that Bessie is deteriorating quickly. She is having spasms in her neck, and refuses anything to drink. But he says for you not to come—just stop at the door when it is morning."

Mira slept fitfully, imagining the great distress of Bessie. And of Charles, for that matter. *If only he would let her help.*

But he would not, except to receive breakfast from Mira when she stopped by. "Mira, I expect this to be a difficult day. The spasms became more generalized during the night. The pain is extreme. And there is nothing I can do. I suspect that one of the spasms will actually asphyxiate her if it is prolonged. Oh, Mira, pray that the end will come soon. Gather as many people in the church as you can, and pray."

Jems stopped by with water and firewood, and left them at the door. He did not ask to go in. Nor did he show up at the prayer meeting.

At noon Charles' report to Mira was much the same. But that night there was a change. Bessie became quiet. She did not speak, but her body had relaxed. Saturday morning Charles gently removed all soiled bedding and bedclothes, bathed her, and put on a clean gown. She did not stir. Paralysis of her arms and legs had set in. Once her respiratory muscles were involved she would die. Charles kept vigil all night, dosing for a moment or two, only to be awakened to answer the deputy's knock.

At daylight Sunday morning Mira stopped by with breakfast.

"Our service this morning will be focused on prayer."

"Come back after you are finished. I think God will answer as you pray. Oh, by the way, Jems is here. When he came with water this morning I let him in, since Bessie was no longer thrashing. I did, however, insist he keep his distance."

Charles met Mira at the door about 11 AM. God had answered the people's prayers a few minutes after 10 AM.

The funeral was Tuesday morning—once again a large community event. Bessie had helped many young girls with sewing and cooking. In tribute to her, Nina helped her students prepare a fine dinner. Many women wore dresses, hats, and coats that had been made by Bessie in her seamstress shop. Even babies came wrapped in rabbit skin blankets and wore rabbit skin hats.

Bessie was a humble servant. But the whole community was proud of such an outstanding citizen.

Charles disposed of all effects that Bessie may have been in contact with during her infectious time, including his clothing. Then he scrubbed the room with carbolic acid, and ordered it closed for several months. When Mira questioned this as being rather extreme, he answered *there is still so much we do not know about this awful disease. I am going to write up everything I learned from this experience and submit it to a medical journal—probably even send it to Dr. Pasteur in France.*

Jems' demeanor did not improve. In fact he became more reclusive, to the point where Mira decided something had to be done. After consulting with Charles, she approached Jems.

"Jems, there is no way you can go back to school unless you talk to us about what is on your mind. We know you are grieving. We all are, but life must go on."

He paused so long before answering that Mira thought he would say nothing. But finally he took a deep breath and said, "I killed her. *I killed my mother.*"

"No Jems! She died of rabies. *No one killed her.*"

"What I did was the same as killing her. Benny got out one night, but I didn't tell anybody because he seemed perfectly fine."

Mira felt her legs go weak. "Jems, give me a moment. I have to think this through." Finally she said, "Although what you did was unwise, even careless, you did not break the law and you had no criminal intent. But this is bigger than the two of us. We must talk to the sheriff, the lawyer, and my father."

Jems nodded his head.

"I'll get them right now. There is no point in waiting. Do not go anywhere."

In a matter of minutes Charles, the lawyer, and the sheriff were there. All sat at the table.

"Tell us everything you know, Jems. In all likelihood the story need go no further than these four walls. But for your sake, you must talk. Else you will continue to carry a heavy, unnecessary burden," the lawyer said, opening the conversation.

Jems took a deep breath and began to talk. "Two nights before I left for school Benny was missing for a few hours. I went out to look for him but couldn't find him. When I got back he was on the doorstep. There was no evidence that he had been in a fight with another animal." Jems paused, and then with great effort went on, "Well, actually, he did have dried blood, on his nose. But nothing else."

"That's all it takes, Jems. Just a puncture wound from the teeth of another animal," Dr. Phillips said as gently as possible.

"I know that now. I keep thinking that it was a squirrel. He loved chasing and catching squirrels."

"But it would be strange to be chasing a squirrel at night . . ." the sheriff said.

" . . . unless it were rabid," responded Dr. Phillips.

Seeing Jems' grief-stricken face at these comments Mira's pastoral heart had to say something affirming. "Jems, we aren't accusing you of careless behavior. Everybody was allowing their dogs to run about despite the sheriff's advice and patrol. You and your mother are the only ones who conscientiously kept your dog inside—except for this one accidental escape. I have noticed that since your mother came down with rabies there are fewer dogs running around, so people are keeping them in. Something good has come out of a tragic situation."

"That's not much consolation. My mother is dead. Because of me."

"Jems," it was the lawyer speaking, "none of us is blaming you. Benny's escape was an accident."

"Yes, but I should have told Dr. Phillips. I know he would have said to keep him *isolated* for a period of time to see if he would become mad. But I didn't, *so in effect, I killed my mother.*"

"We can all ask ourselves what we would have or should have done differently, but the fact is, rabies is a terrible disease, that we know so little about. But now the whole community will be safer because of the death of your mother."

Everyone was quiet. The clock never ticked more loudly, nor the minutes stretched out more slowly.

Finally Mira said, "Jems, I can see that we have not convinced you regarding what you believe to be your guilt. I have two questions for you. Don't answer now. I want you to write out the answers. You cannot go back to school until you complete this assignment."

The doctor, the sheriff, the lawyer held their breaths wondering what the pastor would ask her student.

"Jems, here are the questions. You can take as much time as you need, and they can be as long or as short as you feel necessary.

'First of all, *what would Jesus say to the guilt that you believe you have?* And then, *what would your mother say?*"

The next morning Jems brought Mira *three* papers.
On the first he wrote,
    Jesus said, **I forgive you.**
On the second he wrote,

> *Mother said,* ***I forgive you. Now you must forgive yourself.***

On the third he wrote,

> *Pastor Mira, forgiving myself is the hardest of all, but by the grace of God, I do and I will. I believe this will help me become a better pastor than I ever would have been without this awful experience. Thank you for helping me through it. Thanks for understanding. Maybe someday I will use it as an illustration for a sermon on guilt.* ***But not yet.***

PART 4

ONE CENTURY FOLLOWS ANOTHER
1887-1918

Chapter 24 *Jems Grows Up*

Charles was true to his word, spending long hours in reflection and writing. He often visited Jake and asked him about what his men were finding on the prairie during the winter. He was pleased to learn that no more wild animal carcasses were found. Perhaps winter slowed down the transmission and by spring there would be no new cases of rabies. Fortunately no dogs other than Benny came down with the illness. Never had the town's people been so conscientious about following the sheriff's orders.

Charles found that what he was doing was, for him, a constructive way to grieve. His paper was experienced-based rather than a truly scientific paper, and that's what seemed to draw people to it. It spoke not only of the physical care of the victim but also of the emotional and spiritual care to the victim and those who loved her. Once it was published in a medical journal word got out about the *country doctor* in Chipps, and soon newspaper writers came to interview him. And doctors came to discuss patient care for a variety of illnesses with him and Mira. Charles commented to Mira, "Chipps is on the map now. But we do need a surgeon. How soon will Prissy be old enough for formal training?"

"You know, father. You delivered her in 1873; now it is 1887."

"True. She just seems so mature. Not quite fourteen yet. If we continue to have her work with us, and continue her education privately, she should be ready for medical school by the time she is eighteen. That to be followed by a couple years of surgical training."

"Those are all exciting plans, and I hope they work out, but we must remember that Hiram and Nina, and Jems all might have opinions on the matter. And most of all Prissy. It has to be what she wants."

Charles not only found solace in writing. He also found it in memories. He had believed that after the death of his lovely, reclusive and complex wife, Priscilla, he would never find another. However, he had found companionship and love in a simple prairie woman. And it had been good.

But he had to go on serving others as he had done all his adult life. So in addition to the medical practice Charles continued teaching and tutoring and threw himself into gardening once again. He also had a freestanding laboratory built near the garden and spent many hours concocting brews from medicinal plants. He was determined to come up with something that resembled Laudanum in effectiveness, but less addictive.

One evening that spring the sheriff came to Mira and Charles' door. Over a cup of coffee he told them some rather startling news.

"A man named Jesse Samson has been located on a ranch about 200 miles west of here. Has a rather bazaar story of being lost on the prairie about 15 years ago and was taken in by many people, working here and there. For years he did not know his name or where he was from. Finally he did remember, but by then so much time had gone by, he had no interest in returning to Chipps. So now we are faced with a couple questions. *Is he Bessie's husband?* And *do we tell Jems?*"

"Jems is a grown man, and he has a right to know," answered Charles.

"True, but I think we should wait until he comes home this summer. He's had too many distractions this school year," Mira added.

They agreed to wait.

Mira looked forward to having Jems return but wondered how much she would be able to count on him to assist with pastoral responsibilities. *Would his school have a set protocol for the summer before his final year? Would he be emotionally ready to take up life in Chipps again, without Bessie and Benny? Have his goals changed, given the trauma he has gone through?*

Fortunately there were a few things Jems would *not* have to contend with. At his request Pete sold Bessie's inventory to an aspiring young seamstress and leased the shop to her. This gave Jems enough money to pay tuition and other expenses for the rest of his schooling. And he would be able to live in the same rooms he and Bessie had lived in, for Bessie had owned them and they were now his. By the time Jems came home Dr. Phillips said that Bessie's totally stripped and disinfected bedroom could be safely used.

Dr. Phillips, noticing that some mice had taken up residence in Bessie's rooms, suggested that Chuck put Mouser in the rooms for a few days.

He did, but several days later came to Mira and Charles very upset. "Mouser is gone. I haven't seen him in two days. I've looked. I've called. I've set out milk. But he is gone. Jems is really going to be mad at me. Every letter *Prissy* gets from him, he always asks how Mouser is, and says to tell me to take good care of him because he was Pastor Franco's cat, and Franco always let Jems play with him and take care of him, because you didn't like Mouser, Mira."

Well, he got that right. I've never liked Mouser, but with Benny dead and now Mouser gone my ties to Franco are becoming less and less.

As Mira was pondering this Jake and Cora stopped by.

"Pastor Mira, I've been keeping my eye on Dapple. Looks to me that this winter has been hard on her. She is showing lameness in her right foreleg. It's time Dapple comes back to the ranch to live out her days. Her foal from a couple years back is trained now, and she looks just like Dapple. You'll like her."

The same old Jake, making decisions for me. When will he get it?—Life isn't as simple as swapping one animal for another.

Cora saw Mira's expression; read her mind.

"We really think it is best, Mira-honey. You are a very good horsewoman—we saw that the first day you got up on Dapple—many years ago. But this is for your safety, and the well-being of the horse."

"Well, putting it that way, I can't argue. How soon can we make the change?"

"How about coming out to the ranch tomorrow?"

Mira took one last, leisurely ride on Dapple, arriving at the ranch at 8 AM. Cora and Jake were just finishing breakfast. She joined them for a cup of coffee as they reminisced years gone by. *Especially that winter when Mira dug a hole in the snow that had banked up against the front door of the shack where she and Franco lived and saw the sky. And about Jake's frostbite and loss of toes.*

"It all seems like ancient history. What a lot of living we have done," said Cora.

"And how much death we have seen," added Mira.

Jake, not given to sentimentality, suggested they go to the corral. There he showed Mira the horse he had in mind. Dapple all over again. Just more spritely. Mira thought back to her birth. At that time she had hoped that this filly would be the one Jake would eventually let her have. It was.

"Want to get up and try her out?" Jake already had her saddled.

Mira nodded and got up. As she usually did, she was wearing her split skirt.

"Oh, by the way, we have not yet named her—been waiting for the new owner."

"I'll think of one as we ride."

Mira was gone almost an hour—enough to cause Cora concern. "Don't worry! She needs the time."

Mira came back, well-satisfied. "I've named her *Prairie-Runner*. She can go like the wind."

"Great name. You can take her home with you now. I'll stop by later to trade out harnesses."

"And remember, Mira-honey, you can come anytime to spend time with Dapple. Even ride her, so long as you do not *run like the wind*."

"Thanks. I appreciate your watching out for me."

Jems came home early June. Pete's wife prepared Bessie's place—now Jems'—for occupancy. He dreaded going there. No Bessie. No Benny. But perhaps Pastor Mira would allow him to have Mouser.

He was saddened to learn that Mouser was also gone.

Jems spent his first evening with the Welkens. Mira and Charles were there too. Everyone tried to keep the conversation light, but finally Mira could hold back no longer. "Jems, I'm really eager to talk about summer plans . . ."

"Please, not tonight, Pastor Mira. It was a grueling school year, and now to come home to such emptiness, including Mouser being gone. I need some time. Tonight I would just like to play games with Prissy and Chuck."

The twins jumped up with delight. At least tonight would be like old times. But Mira was concerned as she watched them. There was still a gravity to Jems that had not been there before the rabies incident. *Perhaps it's here to stay. Perhaps this is the mature Jems that Chipps will have to get used to.*

The following morning Jems came to talk with Mira *to map out my summer, and the rest of my life.*

"Pastor Mira, as we have discussed in the past, the hope for my life after graduation—one year from now—is to have a joint pastorate with you. Much like you and Pastor Franco had."

Mira nodded her head.

"But my adviser said I should develop a broader scope of ministry before deciding on that for sure."

Mira felt her heart drop. She did not want to lose Jems. She and all of Chipps were counting on him. The Church Board had already given their approval. "What exactly does *broader scope of ministry* mean, Jems?"

"In practical terms, it means spending most of my summer traveling, visiting churches. Helping other pastors. Becoming aware of how things are done in various pastorates."

"Jems, I want to hear all about that, but before you say anymore, something has come up that I must tell you."

Now it was Jems who felt his heart drop. *Please God, not another disappointment. Just as I'm starting to feel some enthusiasm for ministry again.* But he swallowed it, and said, "Go on, Pastor Mira."

"Something came to our attention last spring, but we decided to not tell you during the school year. But now you must know."

Mira took a deep breath.

"Tell me, Pastor Mira."

"Think back to when my father and your mother were courting. At their request, the sheriff and town lawyer launched a search for your father."

"Do you mean to tell me . . . ?"

Mira nodded. "A man with the same name as your father was located on a ranch about 200 miles west of here."

Jems let out a long, low whistle. "I must go to him."

"We figured you would want to. But Jems, it could be that he is not the same man, although some of his story fits—like having been lost on the prairie, and having suffered from memory loss for many years, certainly fits the story."

"Pastor Mira. This changes things, at least for the immediate."

Mira nodded.

Jems continued, "Then again, maybe not. My adviser is allowing me to choose the churches I visit. Maybe . . ."

Together they came up with an 8-week plan in which Jems would head west, visiting and working with pastors along the way—offering to preach and do some pastoral calling.

After making preliminary plans with Mira, Jems headed to the sheriff's office to map the route. He was on the road with one of Jake's horses the next morning.

If Mira had any regrets, it was that she was looking forward to Jems' help this summer. But thinking of Jems' well-being, given his disruptive year, she knew that this trip was needed for his healing, and the experiences along the way would be helpful for his future.

Jems was back just in time for Telegraph Sunday, and took part of the activities much like the Jems that everyone remembered. Only now there was a maturity about him that enhanced his pastoral calling.

Along with Mira, Charles, the sheriff and lawyer were eager to hear about Jems meeting his father. They all got together for coffee Monday morning.

"By the time I reached the ranch where he was working I was four weeks into my journey. Pastor Mira, I'll be writing up my experiences along the way to report to school. I'd like you to read the first draft because there are many things to discuss with you. But for now I'll tell you all what you are waiting to hear—meeting my father . . ."

" . . . after four weeks in the saddle, and sleeping many nights outdoors with nothing but Jake's horse—which by this time felt like a part of me—a ranch with a bunk house sounded inviting. Thanks to you, sheriff, the directions were helpful in finding the ranch, which by the way, is nothing like Jake's spread. It is very rugged, and when I say *bunk house*, well, I'm talking about a few little shacks that give minimal protection from the weather. I never did ask what they do for winter. But I managed to find the owner easily. He and his wife were the only ones in the barnyard. The others were on the range with the cattle. The owner immediately recognized the name, *Jesse Samson*. And when I told him that I thought I might be Jesse's son, he offered to take me to the camp. But not until the next morning. He offered me a meal and a bed for the night, and looked after my horse. We talked that evening, and when I told him that I was in training to be a pastor, he said, *We could use a little religion here. It's been a long time since we've had a Sunday with a preaching service. Could you stay a few days? We'll put you up in exchange.*

'That was too good an offer to refuse. True to his word, he took me out the next morning. Along the way he said, *You'll have no trouble recognizing your father. He looks like you, only much bigger. He lives up to his name—Samson.* Suddenly I had an idea for my sermon!"

Mira smiled. "I'm eager to hear that one—how about next week?"

Jems continued, "When we approached camp the rancher said *Better let me. You stay up on your horse.*"

"That sounded ominous. A few minutes later the rancher appeared with a large, burly man, a little unsteady on his feet . . ."

Jeb here says you are my son.
Might be, we have the same last name, and both come from Chipps, if I got my story straight.
No mights *about it—you just have some growing to do, Boy. Did you bring your Ma, Bessie? Did you come to fetch me? 'Cause if you did, I ain't going, not after all these years. How did you find me anyhow?*
Whoa! Wait a minute, Samson. Give him a chance to answer.
I didn't come to fetch you, but there are some things you should know. The sheriff and the lawyer of Chipps searched months for you, and finally were informed that someone answering to the name Jesse Samson *was working on this ranch.*
Sheriff? Lawyer? Since when? And why were they looking for me?
I'm getting to that. My mother wanted to know for sure if you were dead or alive, because she had plans for marrying a very fine man—the doctor of Chipps. If you could not be found after a reasonable search, and after all these years, she would have had you declared dead, and she would be free to marry.
Well, there ain't no call for that now, Boy, seeing as how I'm alive. Think she would join me here? You, too, Boy.

"I leveled him my most withering look—from the safety of my horse."
Your right, there is no call for that now. Mother died Thanksgiving Day, last year. Died of rabies.

'Suddenly Jesse's knees buckled."
Rabies? What fool dog bit her? And what about the fine doctor? Why couldn't he save her?
There is no saving from rabies. And it was my dog.
Your dog? Why you . . .

"Jesse—I just can't call him father—started to get up, but Jeb pushed him back down."
*Samson, that's enough. Jems here—**Boy**, to you—is my guest on my ranch. He is a preacher man, and will be staying for a preaching service on Sunday. Until then you stay in camp. You do not come up to the main house. And sober up, if you want to keep your job. If Jems wishes to speak to you again, we will ride out to see you. But you <u>will come</u> to the preaching service.*

"I thought that rather brave of Jeb. But he did carry a gun. And he is the boss."

"Other than work on my *Samson Sermon,* the next few days were relaxing, and the food great. The *preaching service,* I'm afraid, fell on rather deaf ears, although Jeb and his wife were pleased. They even sent a huge package of food for me to eat along the way."

"I spoke to Jesse again after the service. I must say, physically, he cleaned up rather well. And apparently he had used the time between first meeting me and the Sunday service for sobering up and thinking. He told me some stories of my childhood and they matched stories my mother had told me.

"But he had no explanation for leaving Chipps, and most of the years are now a blank. He just said that he must have wandered around, working here and there, until finally one day he *just woke up* and knew who he was, and where he had come from. He has no interest in returning to Chipps, and I think that is best. I did not encourage it. But in all honesty, he seemed proud that I had done well. And finally we talked a bit about Mother, and it brought tears to his eyes. I told him that I hold myself responsible for mother's death, since I did not report that Benny got out. He said *to not blame myself.* That means a lot.

"As I said, he apparently did some thinking between meeting me in camp and the preaching service.

"As a pastor I am deeply concerned for him, but honestly, as a son, I'm angry."

"Perhaps in time . . . ." Mira was thinking back to her negative feelings toward her mother.

"Perhaps."

Jems was due back in Minneapolis the middle of the first week in September. That gave him only two weeks to do what hardly seemed possible.

In terms of priority, spending time with Prissy and writing his summer report ranked highest. He was a supper guest at the Welkens every night and spent the evenings playing games—including Chuck out of necessity. Wednesday evenings were the exceptions—he and Mira went back to the tradition of discussing sermon topics.

There was business to attend to also. Pete approached Jems about renting out his rooms for the school year. A single woman was coming to town to teach, and needed a place to say. Jems readily agreed to rent them.

Finding a place to stay for Christmas vacation should be no problem. And the added income would be helpful. Except, given the wages a woman teacher would get, he would not be able to charge her much. He let the details up to Pete.

Jems and Mira spent almost every afternoon in conversation—discussing his summer experiences and plans for the future—his and Mira's and how the plans could best mesh for the benefit of the Lord's work in Chipps.

"Pastor Mira, I know that you could have used me here this summer, but what I learned in my travels will benefit both of us, and the people of Chipps . . .

". . . Every church welcomed me. I preached every Sunday and conducted some midweek services. And when I got back in the saddle on Monday morning it was usually with names of people between *this church* and *the next church* who would benefit from a pastoral visit. What impressed me most about my visits was that in one place the pastor might be Lutheran, in another Methodist, in another Congregational, etc. Occasionally I came across a Catholic priest. But the people in the congregations were diverse denominationally. Chipps, is somewhat larger than these very small towns. Have you heard any talk about other denominations starting up?"

"No, except for a group of Catholics, who are visited about every six weeks by a priest from Yankton. Some of them come to our church between time."

"Chipps is going to keep growing, I'm sure of that. Wouldn't it be great if our church would continue to grow right along with it, rather than ending up with *a different church* on every street corner?"

"Denominations are important to many people."

"True—still, it hasn't happened here yet. As a matter of fact, until I got to Seminary, I hardly knew that there was such a thing as *denominations*. I just thought *church*."

"Sooo, what can we do?"

"Since the Church Board already has plans for ordaining me next summer, and for me to work with you in ministry, I suggest that one of my first responsibilities be to form a team that will go out and meet all the new people who come to the area, tell them about our church, and welcome them. The sooner we can get people to visit us, the more likely there will not be talk of starting new churches. Chipps is a unified community. It would be very sad to see it split along religious views."

"It sounds like a wise plan. Really, the only thing that I see as standing in the way is finances. The bigger a church is, and the more pastors it has—in this case two—the more money it takes to run it. There are many things to be considered. Will the present building be large enough? etc. An influx of people doesn't necessarily mean more money to work with. As you probably know—and if you don't, you should know now—almost everything you see in this town comes from The General's large gifts, and the inheritance from my mother. And of course, from Hiram and Nina's wise management, and the giving spirit of my father. Then there is Jake and Cora, truly the backbone of the larger community. And your mother, Jems—she invested much of herself in teaching the children and women of the community. I don't know how Pastor Franco and I would have made it those first few years without her. And you, too, Jems. Even as a little boy you were Pastor Franco's right hand man. If it were not for these people and their gifts of money, wisdom and helping others get started, there probably would be no Chipps today. It would have dried up like the ghost towns on the prairie."

"Pastor Mira, I knew some of what you told me, but not nearly all of it. Are you telling me that the clinic is really a gift from your mother, and that you can keep your fees so low because of it?"

"It comes from my inheritance, and much of what you see today— including the public library—is because of my father's generosity. The time will come sooner or later, despite the good grounding Chipps has, when Chipps will have to stand on its own. Other leaders will have to rise up."

"So what about church?"

"I think you have an excellent approach, and frankly, occasionally there has been talk about starting a second congregation, but it has always been turned down—really for the very reason you have touched on—we are a unified community. But we need more than the *unity argument*; we need a plan like you have just suggested. My father is on the Church Board and he is very persuasive. I can envision having many meetings with the Board this winter that will work towards the plan—maybe we could call it a *goal*— that you propose."

"Pastor Mira, there's one more thing to talk about before I leave, but it can wait until tomorrow."

"Prissy?"

"Prissy."

To herself Mira said *I think that conversation could wait until next year. Or perhaps 5 years from now.*

"Pastor Mira, I don't know if you know that I'm very attracted to Prissy. Ever since she was a little girl, I've known that she is the girl I want to marry. She's a teenager now. Should I tell her?"

"Jems, do you want my advice?"

"Well . . . yes."

"Keep on playing board games; go sledding when you come home at Christmas. And be sure to include Chuck in all the activities."

"But . . ."

"No *buts, Jems*. Write her *newsy* letters if you must. And talk to Hiram and Nina. They are the ones that should know.

"But do you think . . ."

"If you are wondering, that is all the more reason to talk to Hiram and Nina *now*. Certainly before you leave for school. And don't forget that Prissy is a very bright girl. My father and I are preparing her for medical school—let's see, in another four years she should be ready to go to Chicago for four years of medical training and experience, and then on to Boston for 2-4 years of surgical training. Soo, in another 10 to 12 years she should be ready to come back here—if that is her desire, which we certainly hope it will be."

"I had no idea!"

"Now you do!"

Jems left. Mira noticed him walking towards the Welkens, shoulders slightly drooped. She hoped she hadn't been unkind. But he had to be practical and realistic. And Prissy needed the freedom to make unpressured choices.

Chapter 25 *A Frontier Team All Over Again*

Late May 1888 Mira, Nina and Hiram, Chuck and Prissy boarded the train and headed to Minneapolis. It was the first time Nina had gone beyond Yankton since her arrival in Chipps years earlier. And it was the first for the twins.

To no one's surprise Jems graduated first in his class. As Mira listened to his speech, her mind went back to what she and Franco had experienced together, completing their academics, and then immediately getting married and moving west. Franco would be so proud this day. As would Bessie.

Jems gave a fitting tribute to Pastor Franco and his own mother, and then called Mira up to the platform and said without reservation, "This is the woman—Rev. and Dr. Mira Welken—that I have learned more from, both practically and academically, than you can possibly imagine. I am very pleased to say that she and I will be sharing a joint pastorate. And though I haven't told anyone that I'm going to say this—actually the thought just came to my mind—we will welcome students as interns to work with us."

Mira stepped to the podium. "Jems is right—he didn't tell anyone he would say that. But I second what he says. Let me add—Jems grew up being my late husband, Rev. Franklin Welken's, *right hand man,* from the time he was 5 or 6 years old, doing everything from enthusiastically ringing the church bell to taking care of the church cat. Jems, our little town, Chipps, is pleased that you are coming home. Well done."

The crowd responded with a resounding applause.

Jems returned taking up residence in the rooms he had inherited from Bessie. The teacher who had lived in them during the school year was getting married, leaving the rooms and teaching position vacant.

The Church Board in conjunction with the School Board began planning meetings with Jems and Mira in June. The plans they drew up set the pattern for ministry in Chipps for many years to come—

- Mira and Jems to share preaching responsibilities.
- Jems to form an outreach team that would contact all new families in Chipps and surrounding area, inviting them to church, and informing them about the school and social activities that were integral to the life and faith of Chipps.

- Jems would teach the elementary school, with Charles, Mira, and other community members continuing to teach the children in the areas they were already involved.
- Charles and Mira would expand the tutoring they were doing with Prissy to include other post-elementary students who were interested in education. These efforts set the ground work for a *high school* in Chipps.
- Mira and Jems would continue their literary efforts in community plays, book clubs, etc.
- Charles' medical work would chiefly be in the clinic, freeing Mira to do what she loved most—spending long hours on the prairie with her horse, Bible and medical bag, making medical/pastoral calls.
- These plans would be reviewed yearly, and adjusted throughout the year as needed.

Jems was ordained on Telegraph Sunday, August 1888. At this time the congregation was informed of the ministry plans for Chipps and were invited to discuss them and vote. Following only minimal discussion the congregation voted to endorse the plans.

By early September the plans were underway.

***

Prissy became invaluable to Charles at the clinic and in his gardens. Hiram and Nina continued to put restraints on Jems' interest in her, not allowing serious courting, but in the summer of 1891 when Prissy was preparing to leave for 4 years of medical training in Chicago they allowed him to propose marriage, so long as there was no pressure on her to change her educational goals.

His proposal was no surprise to Prissy. Being aware of her parents' reservation at this time, she and Jems both had to be content with a provisional agreement to marriage, but no formal engagement.

Fortunately for the medical work several other young people, men and women, were asking to work with Charles and Mira. They did not want to discourage anyone who was truly interested in learning, but had to choose wisely. They allowed those who were studying with them in the *high school* to rotate through the clinic and to make calls with Mira. By the end of six weeks it was usually apparent who had aptitude and who did not. Some became nurses. Others went on for medical training or to theological school.

The students who came as interns from the Seminary were primarily Jems' responsibility. In the summers they often had two interns, and usually one who stayed an entire year. Mira and Jems invited them to be part of the Wednesday evening sermon discussion that Mira and Franco had begun so many years earlier. A favorite *ice breaker* for Mira was to tell them how the tradition got started—with a water fight. And then she would tell them of Franco's death, the loss of her baby, and how she had in grief cut off her braids. And how life moved on in fruitful ministry that grew out of what she and Franco had begun 20 years earlier.

Prissy managed to come home for a week each December, and for a couple weeks in the summers.

Though Mira was finding it harder and harder to leave medical responsibilities to Charles because of his decreased mobility related to his arthritis, she did go with Hiram and Nina and Jems to Prissy's graduation in Chicago in May of 1895. By this time there were two reliable nurses. Mira gave strict instructions about keeping an eye on Charles, and without saying why, reminded them to keep the Laudanum in a locked cupboard. The pastoral intern was responsible for the spiritual care and preaching in Chipps during the week of Jems' and Mira's absence.

On their train ride, Nina found a moment for private conversation with Mira. "Mira-honey, I am concerned about Hiram. He is short of breath with only minor exertion."

Mira nodded, "I've noticed. I know my father has examined him a time or two."

"He's slowing down in much the same way The General did. Do you suppose he has heart problems?"

"It's possible. We must do everything possible to limit exertion on this trip—like rapid walking, and step climbing and lifting. And I'd like to talk to him."

By shuffling seats Mira approached the topic of his health with Hiram, and he admitted to slowing down and having seen Charles. "It's my heart, Mira-honey. I don't want to alarm Nina."

"She already knows. She just told me. That's why I'm talking to you right now. And I would like to tell Jems. You must limit your exertion on this trip. If possible, let's try to keep it from Prissy now. But she might guess. She is highly trained medically now—even more than I or my father. She has to be told when we get back."

Reluctantly Hiram agreed.

Mira changed seats again and elicited Jems' support.

The graduation was a solemn event. And by pacing themselves, and with Jems claiming most of Prissy's attention, they were able to keep Prissy free from suspicion regarding Hiram's health until they returned home.

The first week Prissy was home was spent planning a community celebration honoring her graduation. A celebration in which Jems and Prissy would also announce their engagement, even though she would be in Boston for most of the next four years for surgical training and experience.

The summer flew by. Prissy, Mira, and Charles, along with Nina and Hiram, Jems and Chuck all discussed Hiram's health. Prissy was insistent that he cut back on his work. He was as reluctant as The General had been to give up responsibilities. But being an honorable and honest man he had frank discussions with the Town Council. The decision was to put his position up for vote, and make it a paid position. Chuck became the leading candidate, and was almost unanimously voted in at the age of 22. He had already proven himself as a leader and business man in Chipps. The title *General* was more suitably changed to *Mayor*. On Telegraph Sunday, August 1895, Hiram officially retired, and Chuck took over.

Two weeks later Jems and Prissy, Nina and Hiram were on a train heading to Boston with a stopover in Pennsylvania to visit their old home, and friend, Dr. McCloud. Dr. McCloud noticed Hiram's condition immediately and insisted on examining him and started him on a new medicine.

The emotion that Hiram and Nina felt as they approached Boston took them by surprise. Many years had passed, but the changes and modernization were beyond their expectations. *And* they still had fears that the *Welken* name might be recognized and not trusted. Yet, Prissy was registered in the school with that name, and thus far no questions had been raised.

After settling her in school, there were two things Nina and Hiram wished to do. Locate the mansions where they had grown up, and visit the grave sites of their parents.

Several days before they were due back in Chipps, Chuck received a telegram from Jems. *Return trip delayed. At grave site Hiram suffered heart attack. Did not survive. Private burial next to his parents. We will stay several more days with Prissy. Will wire again just before departure.*

Chuck sought out Mira and Charles. All were stunned. With the help of the Sheriff and Pete they got word out to the community. There would be a service honoring Hiram after the return of Nina and Jems.

Later that day Mira looked at Charles and said, "Almost everyone I have known and cared about has died." Charles knew it wasn't exactly true—Mira had many people in her life, but he understood, so he only nodded, and held her close. Together they wept the death of a great man and leader.

Nina returned with her usual dignity and poise, but she had visibly aged and asked to be relieved of teaching the young girls of the community for the current year.

A service was held in Hiram's honor the first Sunday of October. A marker and plaque were placed in the Chipps graveyard beside his son, Franco. And Mira, as she did so often when she grieved, spent many hours that winter writing a tribute that honored Hiram and Nina, and the dedication with which they served the community of Chipps.

Prissy came home in December, but because of the many miles the visit was brief. She had thrown herself into her educational experience and loved it and found coming home without Hiram there difficult. She seemed almost eager to leave when the time was up, but Jems had a hard time letting her go.

As usual, Mira cut back on her pastoral-medical calls in the winter. Cora told her that she was no longer physically able to assist with teaching expectant mothers or go out for deliveries. Fortunately, the nurses, with Mira's assistance, readily agreed to take on the responsibility. Even Mira, though not yet 45, was beginning to feel the aches and pains of aging. Life on the prairie had a way of strengthening a person, and wearing one out.

Even Charles was less enthused about gardening than before. Getting moving in the morning was particularly difficult. Chuck, though deeply grieving his father, felt himself at his prime. His new responsibilities as Mayor, running the lumberyard, and doing everything else that Hiram had done came easily. He offered to assist Charles with the *garden school*—as they now called it—including teaching the children. He also found himself a bride, Sally Johnson, and they made plans to marry when Prissy would be home for a couple of weeks in the summer of 1896.

Mira showed Sally and Prissy her *Brides of Chipps Journal*, including the sketches she had made of the dresses that Bessie had remade from the dresses Mira had brought with her in 1873. They chuckled long and hard at the dated look. But when they saw Mira's dress they both asked if they could wear it, first Sally, and then Prissy. Mira had a hard time saying *yes*.

Her wedding dress was the one and only fancy dress that she had ever liked. But how could she say *no?*

Both girls would have their own veil and train. Mira told them that hers had been buried with Franco and their baby.

The night before the wedding Nina hosted a dinner for Sally's family, Mira, Charles, Prissy and Jems. It was the night that Mira would give up her cross to Chuck, who in turn would give it to Sally.

Nina told the story of the cross, and the tradition of the family. Mira clutched the cross in her hand as Chuck loosened the clasp. She then gave it to Chuck to put it on Sally. As he did, Mira charged Sally to wear it every day, until the day—should God so bless her—*her* son would marry.

Then Mira then went out to Franco's grave and wept 'til she had no tears left. Chuck found her there hours later. For the first time she realized what Nina must have felt when she gave up the cross, only she then still had Hiram. Mira did not have Franco. And Nina now no longer had Hiram.

Chuck and Sally lived in the mansion. Nina gave up her rooms, and moved to the rooms that The General's wife had occupied.

Prissy came home a couple weeks the summers of 1897 and 1898. There were many discussions about setting up an operating room for when Prissy would complete her education. Charles encouraged her to seek out her professor-surgeons on the latest and best instruments and to begin to order them and send them to Chipps. And to learn as much as she could about current drugs used for anesthesia and methods of administering them, and about the latest and best in aseptic technique.

In May of 1899 Nina, Mira, and Jems went to Boston for Prissy's graduation.

Mira left her father with trepidation—his arthritic pain with swollen joints was becoming increasingly intense, to the point of slowing him down greatly, and she feared, he would not admit to it, that he was trying too many home remedies, along with Laudanum.

Although Pete and Charles had never gained a close relationship, Mira asked both Pete and Chuck to keep an eye on him. And the nurses as well.

Jems and Prissy married that summer. As so many events were, this too was a community event and was held the day before Telegraph Sunday in August.

In addition to planning the wedding and doing their daily pastoral and clinical work, many hours were spent on plans for remodeling the clinic and Mira's living quarters, to convert them to *Chipps General Hospital*. Mira donated the property to the town. The administrative work of the hospital would be overseen by a Board of Directors. Mira and Charles looked forward to moving to the Welken mansion, and Jems and Prissy to Jems' rooms.

Mira's kitchen and laundry room would serve the hospital; her sitting room, a lounge for families and patients; the clinic would remain a clinic; the adjacent room was designated for the operating room, and the bedrooms as patient rooms. The old *Wound Shack* would be remodeled, but remain detached.

But before the remodeling took place, one morning in the Fall of 1899 Charles did not show up for breakfast. Mira went to check on him. She found him dead in bed with a bottle of homemade brew at his bedside. It smelled of alcohol. But the label, in Charles' printing said, "poppy juice." It obviously was his attempt at making an effective medication for pain management, and was a combination of a number of things that proved to be lethal.

All Chipps mourned for their doctor. Mira kept the details of his death to herself, but the community knew of his experimentations with home brews, and many swore by his concoctions.

Mira took his death hard, as he was her only living blood relative, except for her half-brother, Pete, and his children. While Charles was living the relationship between Pete and Mira was somewhat strained. This changed quickly, as Mira greatly felt the need for the relationship. And Pete was open to developing a brother/sister tie with Mira, which for the sake of Charles' feelings, he had not pursued.

One of the first things Mira and Prissy did after Charles' death was to dispose of the bottles of *brew* that he had been concocting and xperimenting with. They saved his lab equipment and notes, and eventually the building would be used as a hospital laboratory and pharmacy.

In the spring of 1900 reconstruction of Mira's home and clinic was begun, and by Fall they had an up-and-running hospital with an operating room, running water and telephone. Charles's and Mira's dreams were fulfilled.

Mira and Prissy along with several nurses, and occasional interns served the medical needs of Chipps well into the new century. Simultaneously Jems and Mira, along with interns, served the spiritual needs of Chipps.

Epilogue

Mira spent many hours that winter writing a fitting tribute to Charles. She wrote of his work in Philadelphia, including how he had taught her. She wrote of his work caring for wounded Civil War soldiers, and his work in Chipps. He was always a pioneer and a man ahead of his times. She wrote of his devotion to his wife, her mother, and of the love and devotion he and Bessie had for each other, and especially how he took care of her to the very end.

Mira, Jems, Prissy and Chuck worked tirelessly the first decades of the new century. They lived to see running water, central heating, telephone, electricity, automobiles, and even heard of flying machines. Many of Chipps sons served in WWI, and not a few died.

The influenza epidemic came to Chipps in 1918 and, despite the medical staff's attempts to care for and quarantine patients, many died. Nina, nearly 90, was one of the first of the community to succumb.

Mira, at the age of 66 found her own strength waning, but giving up was not in her nature. However, one morning when she did not come for breakfast Sally and Chuck went to check on her. She was unresponsive and burning up with fever.

Just before her last breath she clutched her chest wall below her neck—the very place where she had worn her cross.

Mira joined her Lord whom she had served so long. Those who were present were quite certain they heard the words *Well done . . . enter . . .*

She entered eternity with a smile on her face.

Miranda Phillips Welken was laid to rest next to her beloved Franco—more years widow than wife. Nearby their baby, Dr. Phillips, Bessie, and Nina reposed as well.

Chipps knew how to celebrate; Chipps also knew how to mourn, and mourn they did.

The community was what it was this day, in part because of the young couple who went West to serve the Lord and later were joined by Hiram and Nina Welken, their twins and Dr. Phillips.

Prissy and Jems carried on the work begun by Mira and Franco into the 1940s.

Mira's many journals chronicling the life of two eastern families having gone west, and the difference they made are kept in the Library of Chipps.

The journals are also a tribute to the people of Chipps and surrounding community, without whom the story never could have been.

But for these journals much of what happened would have been lost forever.

The community was led by deeply religious people, who received their ultimate guidance from their holy book, *The Bible*. Scripture is not directly quoted in the book but is alluded to and paraphrased. The versions of the Bible that the people of Chipps likely used were what was available at that time—in the early years of Franco's and Mira's ministry the *King James Version* and in later years also the *American Standard Version*.